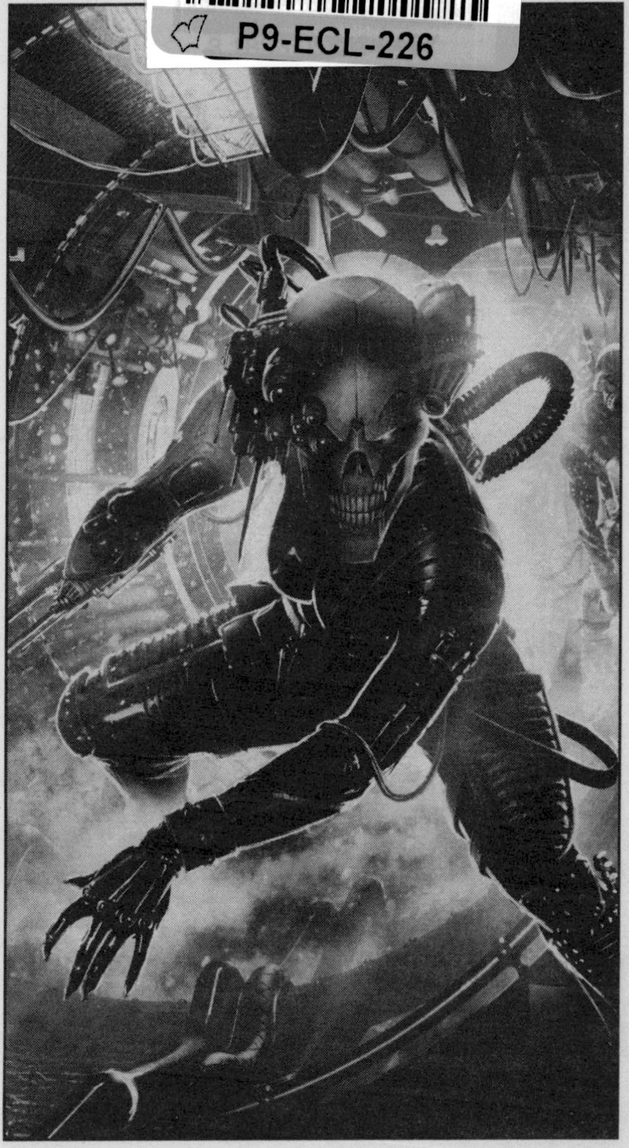

# THE HORUS HERESY

*James Swallow*

# NEMESIS

*War within the shadows*

BLACK LIBRARY

*For Aaron & Katie – Clear Skies and Good Hunting.*

**A BLACK LIBRARY PUBLICATION**

First published in Great Britain in 2010 by
The Black Library,
Games Workshop Ltd.,
Willow Road, Nottingham,
NG7 2WS, UK.

10 9 8 7 6 5 4 3 2 1

Cover and page 1 illustration by Neil Roberts.

A CIP record for this book is available from the British Library.

ISBN13: 978 1 84416 869 9

Distributed in the US by Simon & Schuster
1230 Avenue of the Americas, New York, NY 10020, US.

See the Black Library on the internet at
**www.blacklibrary.com**

Find out more about Games Workshop
and the world of Warhammer 40,000 at
**www.games-workshop.com**

Printed and bound in the US.

# THE HORUS HERESY

*It is a time of legend.*

Mighty heroes battle for the right to rule the galaxy. The vast armies of the Emperor of Earth have conquered the galaxy in a Great Crusade – the myriad alien races have been smashed by the Emperor's elite warriors and wiped from the face of history.

The dawn of a new age of supremacy for humanity beckons.

Gleaming citadels of marble and gold celebrate the many victories of the Emperor. Triumphs are raised on a million worlds to record the epic deeds of his most powerful and deadly warriors.

First and foremost amongst these are the primarchs, superheroic beings who have led the Emperor's armies of Space Marines in victory after victory. They are unstoppable and magnificent, the pinnacle of the Emperor's genetic experimentation. The Space Marines are the mightiest human warriors the galaxy has ever known, each capable of besting a hundred normal men or more in combat.

Organised into vast armies of tens of thousands called Legions, the Space Marines and their primarch leaders conquer the galaxy in the name of the Emperor.

Chief amongst the primarchs is Horus, called the Glorious, the Brightest Star, favourite of the Emperor, and like a son unto him. He is the Warmaster, the commander-in-chief of the Emperor's military might, subjugator of a thousand thousand worlds and conqueror of the galaxy. He is a warrior without peer, a diplomat supreme.

As the flames of war spread through the Imperium, mankind's champions will all be put to the ultimate test.

# ~ DRAMATIS PERSONAE ~

## Execution Force

| | |
|---|---|
| ERISTEDE KELL | Assassin-at-Marque, Clade Vindicare |
| JENNIKER SOALM | Secluse, Clade Venenum |
| 'THE GARANTINE' | Nihilator, Clade Eversor |
| FON TARIEL | Infocyte, Clade Vanus |
| KOYNE | Shade, Clade Callidus |
| IOTA | Protiphage, Clade Culexus |

## Officio Assassinorum

| | |
|---|---|
| MASTER OF ASSASSINS | A High Lord of Terra |
| SIRE VINDICARE | Master and Director Primus, Clade Vindicare |
| SIRESS VENENUM | Mistress and Director Primus, Clade Venenum |
| SIRE EVERSOR | Master and Director Primus, Clade Eversor |
| SIRE VANUS | Master and Director Primus, Clade Vanus |
| SIRESS CALLIDUS | Mistress and Director Primus, Clade Callidus |
| SIRE CULEXUS | Master and Director Primus, Clade Culexus |

## Legio Custodes

| | |
|---|---|
| CONSTANTIN VALDOR | Captain-General and Chief Custodian |

## The Imperial Fists Legion

| | |
|---|---|
| ROGAL DORN | Primarch of the Imperial Fists |
| EFRIED | Third Captain |

### The Sons of Horus

| | |
|---|---|
| HORUS LUPERCAL | Primarch of the Sons of Horus |
| MALOGHURST | Equerry to the Primarch |
| LUC SEDIRAE | Captain of the 13th Company |
| DEVRAM KORDA | Veteran Sergeant, 13th Company |

### The Word Bearers Legion

| | |
|---|---|
| EREBUS | First Chaplain of the Word Bearers |

### Imperial Personae

| | |
|---|---|
| MALCADOR THE SIGILLITE | Regent of Terra |
| YOSEF SABRAT | Reeve of Iesta Veracrux |
| DAIG SEGAN | Reeve of Iesta Veracrux |
| BERTS LAIMNER | Reeve Warden of Iesta Veracrux |
| KATA TELEMACH | High-Reeve of Iesta Veracrux |
| ERNO SIGG | Citizen of the Imperium |
| MERRIKSUN EUROTAS | The Void Baron of Narvaji, Agentia Nuntius (Taebian Sector) |
| HYSSOS | Security Operative, Eurotas Trade Consortium |
| PERRIG | Indentured Psyker, Eurotas Trade Consortium |
| CAPRA | Citizen of Dagonet |
| TERRIK GROHL | Citizen of Dagonet |
| LIYA BEYE | Citizen of Dagonet |
| LADY ASTRID SINOPE | Citizen of Dagonet |

'For those that defy the Imperium, only the Emperor can judge your crimes.

    Only in death can you receive the Emperor's Judgement.'

— maxim of the Officio Assassinorum


'The monster boasted of what he would do once he conquered the home of the god-king, little knowing that Nemesis heard his words and took note of them.'

— excerpted from texts of the ancient
Terran poet Nonnus


'We live in peace and pretend at it. But in truth there are always wars, thundering unseen around us, just beyond the curve of our sight. The greatest foolishness is that no man wishes to know the truth. He is happy to live his life as silent guns cut the sky above his head.'

— attributed to the remembrancer
Ignace Karkasy

# PART ONE

# EXECUTION

# ONE

### Object Lesson
### Tactics of Deceit
### The Star

GYGES PRIME WAS a murdered world, dead now, all but an ashen ember. Around the encampment, porous black rock ranged away under a cowl of low mist, the haze itself the remains of cities pounded into radioactive dust by countless bombardments from orbit. Arsenals of nuclear munitions had been emptied to bring the planet to the executioner's block, and now the cooling corpse of the world lay swaddled in its own death-shroud, a virulent and silent pall of radiation that smothered everything.

Here, in the canyon where the invaders had made their planetfall, high walls of shield rock did their best to cut the fiery winds from the shattered landscape. Men, such as the soldiers that had crisped and burned like paper in the onslaught, would have died for the sake of living an hour outside in this nightmare, had any of them survived this long. The invaders had no such weaknesses, however.

The lethality they laid over Gyges Prime was to them a minor irritant. Once they were done in this place, they would return to their warcraft high above and clean the stink of the dead planet from their robes and armour as one might wash dried mud from a soiled boot. They would do this and think nothing of it. They would not stop to consider that the air now passing into their lungs was laced with the particulate remains of every man, woman and child that had called Gyges Prime home.

The planet was dead, and it had served a purpose in dying. The dozen other colony worlds of the Gyges system, each of them more valuable, more populous than this one, they would look through their mnemoniscopes and watch this ember cool and fade. *Why choose to attack that world and no other?* The question they first asked as the warships passed them by had now been answered: *for the* lesson *of it.*

Tobeld did not dwell on this, as he moved around the lee of the temporary pergolas set up beneath the wings of the tethered Stormbirds, hearing the mutter of conversation among the warriors around him amid the snap of guyropes and wind-pulled fabric. Messages were already coming in from the ships in orbit. The other worlds, the orbital platforms, the system defence fleet, all were surrendering. Twelve planets teeming with people, giving up their freedom without a single word of defiance. *Lesson learned.*

The taking of the Gyges system had been a swift and almost cursory thing. Doubtless, in decades to come, it would be less than a postscript in the annals of the war. No casualties of note had been taken by the warfleet, none that mattered to the architect of the conflict that this small venture was but a fragment of. Gyges was merely a stone in the path, a path that began in the Isstvan system and wound its way across the galaxy towards Terra. Gyges was a passing footstep, beneath which the blood of millions left no mark. By conventional battle logic, there was no reason for any of the invaders to even step on to the surface; yet still they had come, in this small party, for reasons that could only be guessed at.

Tobeld stifled a cough with his hand, pushing the thick robe of his hood to his face to muffle the sound. It came away wet and he tasted copper in his mouth. The radiation had killed him the moment he stepped out from the shuttle, him and the other serfs brought down from the flagship in order to serve the invaders. The serfs would all be dead before sunset. He knew he would share that fate, but it was a price worth paying. In the dimness of his dormitory capsule back on the warship, Tobeld had used a quarter of the elements of his weapons kit to fabricate a strong dosage of counter-radiation drugs; the rest he had turned to the building of the compound that nestled inside the finger-long glass vial strapped to the inside of his wrist. He had done his best to dispose of the remnants of the kit, but he was afraid some trace might still be discovered; and the counter-rads were working poorly. He had little time.

He passed behind the engine bells of a drop-ship and through the black haze he spied the largest of the tents, a low pavilion made of non-reflective cloth. For a second, the wind snapped at the entrance flap and showed him a glimpse of things inside. He saw what might have been firelight jumping and moving off slabs of polished ceramite armour, and wet shapes like animated falls of blood. Then the breeze passed on and the sight was lost to him. Still, the confusion of impressions made him shiver.

Tobeld hesitated. He would need to cross open ground to get from the Stormbird to the pavilion, and he could not afford to be challenged. He was entering the terminal stage of his mission now, after so long. There could be no mistakes. No one had come this close before. He could not risk failure.

Tobeld took a shaky, tainted breath. He had sacrificed a solar year of his life to this mission, breaking out from under a cover he had spent half a decade building as a minor Nobilite clan cook-functionary. He had willingly discarded that carefully-crafted disguise to embrace a new one, such was the gravity of his new mission; and through cautious steps, with doses of poisons both subtle and coarse to smooth his path, Tobeld had made his way into service aboard the battle cruiser *Vengeful Spirit*, the flagship of Horus Lupercal.

Two years had passed since the betrayal at Isstvan, the bloody backstabbing that opened the way to Horus's insurrection against the Imperium and his father, the Emperor of Mankind. In that time, his steady progression across the galaxy had gathered momentum. As this day showed, every system that passed beneath the keel of Horus's warships either swore fealty to him, or else they burned. Worlds and worlds, united in the aftermath of the Great Crusade, were now torn between loyalty to a distant Earth and an absent Emperor, or to a victorious Horus and his army of warlords. The glimpses Tobeld got from his lower-decks vantage point showed an armada of turncoat-kindred consolidating power degree by punishing degree. Horus closed his steel grip on sector after sector. One did not need to be a tactician to know that the Warmaster was marshalling his energies for the advance that had to come – an eventual thrust towards Terra herself, and to the gates of the Imperial Palace.

Horus could not be allowed to take that step.

At first it had seemed an unassailable objective. The Warmaster himself, a primarch, a demigod warrior, and Tobeld just a man. A killer of superlative skill and subtlety, indeed, but still a man. To strike directly at Horus aboard the *Spirit* would have been madness, an impossibility. Tobeld toiled aboard the flagship for almost five months before he even laid eyes upon the Warmaster – and the being he saw that day was one of such magnitude that it set him reeling, the question hard in his thoughts. *How do I kill this one?*

Conventional poisons were worthless ranged against the physiology of an Astartes; they could ingest the harshest of venoms as Tobeld might sip wine. But Tobeld was here precisely *because* poison was his weapon of choice. It could be swift; it could be patient, escaping detection, lying dormant. He was one of Clade Venenum's finest tox-artisans; in his apprenticeship he had manufactured killing philtres from the most base of components, he had terminated dozens of targets and left no trace. And he slowly came to believe that he *was* capable of this, if fate would only grace him with a single opportunity.

The weapon lay in the vial. Tobeld had created a binary agent, a mixture of molecular accelerant gels suspending a live sample of gene-altered Baalite thirst-water – a virulent fluidic life form that could consume all moisture within living tissues in a matter of seconds. When Horus had announced he would be leading a landing party to the surface of Gyges Prime, Tobeld heard the tolling of fate in the words. His chance. His single chance.

There was rumour and supposition aboard the *Vengeful Spirit*, down on the lower decks where the human serfs and servitors toiled. Men spoke of strange things afoot on the levels where the Astartes walked, of changes, of apparitions and peculiarities in parts of the vessel. Tobeld heard whispers of the so-called *lodges* where these changes took place. He listened to stories of rites made on the surfaces of conquered worlds, things that sickened him as much with their nauseating similarity to crude idolatry as with their hints of inhumanity and horror. The men who spoke of these things often vanished soon after, leaving nothing but fear in their wakes.

He concentrated on the weapon, listening for the wind to drop. Horus was there, no more than a dozen steps away, inside the pavilion with his inner circle – Maloghurst, Abaddon and the rest of them – engaging in whatever ritual had brought them to this place. Close now, closer than ever before. Tobeld prepared himself, forcing away the pain in his throat, his joints. Entering the command tent, he would introduce the weapon to the jug of wine at Horus's side, fill the cups of the Warmaster and his senior battle-brothers. One sip would be enough to infect them... and he hoped it would be enough to kill, although Tobeld held no doubt he would not live to see his mission succeed. His faith in his art would have to be enough.

Time, then. He stepped out from underneath the Stormbird's wing; and a voice said 'Is that it?'

A reply, firm and cold, returned from somewhere close at hand in the smoke-haze. 'Aye.'

Tobeld tried to turn on his heel, but he was already leaving the ground, taken off his feet by a shadow that dwarfed him, a towering man-form in steel-grey armour holding a fistful of his robes. Leering out of the gloom came a hard face that was all angles and barely restrained menace. A patchwork of scarification was the setting for eyes that were wide with black mirth, eyes that bored into him. 'Where are you going, little man?' He marvelled at the thought that someone so large had been able to approach him in utter silence.

'Lord, I...' It was hard to talk. Tobeld's throat was as dry as the winds, and the grip the Astartes had on him pulled the material of the robes tight about his neck. He struggled for breath – but he did not struggle too much, for fear the turncoat might think he was making some futile attempt to defend himself and respond in kind.

'Hush, hush', said the other voice. A second figure, if anything larger and more lethal in aspect than the first, stepped from the smoke. Tobeld's eyes instantly fell to the intricate etching and jewelled medallions adorning the other Astartes's chest, symbols of high rank and seals of loyalty among the Sons of Horus Legion. He knew this warrior immediately, the laughing face and the shock-blond hair, without need to survey the rank sigils upon him, though. Luc Sedirae, Captain of the 13th Company.

'Let's not make a song and dance of this,' Sedirae
went on. His right hand flexed absently; he wore no
gauntlet upon it, showing to the world where the limb
had been lost and replaced by an augmetic in polished brass and anodised black steel. The hand had
been taken from him in battle with the Raven Guard
at Isstvan, so it was said, and the captain wore the
wound proudly, as if it were a badge of honour.

Tobeld's gaze flicked back to the warrior holding
him, finding the symbols of the 13th Company on the
other Astartes. Belatedly, he recognised him as
Devram Korda, one of Sedirae's seconds; not that such
knowledge would do him any good. He tried again to
speak. 'Lords, I am only doing my duty as–'

But the words seemed to curdle in his throat and
Tobeld choked on them, emitting a wet gasp instead.

From behind Korda, following the path that Tobeld
had taken around the parked craft, a third Astartes
emerged from beneath the shadows cast by the drop-
ship. The assassin knew this one, too. Armour the
colour of old, dried blood, an aspect like a storm captured in the confines of a man's face, eyes he could not
bring himself to meet. *Erebus*.

'His duty,' said the First Chaplain of the Word Bearers, musing on the thought. 'That is not a lie.' Erebus's
voice was soft and almost gentle, raised only slightly
above the low keen of the Gyges winds.

Tobeld blinked and felt a tide of terror growing to
fill him. He rose on it, caught by the icy certainty of
the moment. Erebus *knew* what he was. Somehow,
Erebus had always known. All his careful subterfuges,
every piece of flawless tradecraft he had employed –
the Word Bearer walked towards him now with a

swagger that told the assassin it had counted for nothing.

'My duty is to serve the Warmaster!' he blurted, desperate to stall for time, for a moment more of life.

'Quietly,' warned Erebus, silencing him before he could say more. The Word Bearer threw a glance towards the command tent. 'Nothing will be gained by disturbing Great Horus. He will be... displeased.'

Korda turned Tobeld in his grip, like a fisherman evaluating a disappointing catch before tossing it back into the ocean. 'So weak,' he offered. 'He's dying even as I watch. The boneseekers in the air are eating him inside.'

Sedirae folded his arms. 'Well?' he demanded of Erebus. 'Is this some game of yours, Word Bearer, or is there real cause for us to torment this helot?' His lips thinned. 'I grow bored.'

'This is a killer,' Erebus explained. 'A weapon, after a fashion.'

Tobeld belatedly understood that they had been waiting for him. 'I... am only a servant...' he gasped. He was losing sensation in his limbs and his vision was starting to fog from the tightness of Korda's hold.

'Lie,' said the Word Bearer, the accusation clicking off his tongue.

Panic broke through what barriers of resolve still remained in Tobeld's mind, and he felt them crumble. He felt himself lose all sense of rationality and give in to the terror with animal reaction. His training, the control that had been bred into him from his childhood in the schola, disintegrated under no more than a look from Erebus's cold, cold gaze.

Tobeld flexed his wrist and the vial came into his hand. He twisted wildly in Korda's grasp, catching the Astartes fractionally off-guard, stabbing downwards with the glassy cylinder. Motion-sensing switches in the crystalline matrix of the vial obeyed and opened a tiny mouth at the blunt end, allowing a ring of monomol needles to emerge. Little thicker than human hairs, the fine rods could penetrate even the hardy epidermis of an Adeptus Astartes. Tobeld tried to kill Devram Korda, swinging at the bare skin of his scarred face, missing, swinging again. He did this mindlessly, in the manner of a mechanism running too fast, unguided.

Korda used the flat of his free hand to swat the assassin, doing it with such force that he broke Tobeld's jaw and caved in much of the side of his skull. Tobeld's right eye was immediately crushed, and the shock resonated through him. After a moment he realised he was on the ground, blood flowing freely from his shattered mouth and nose into a growing puddle.

'Erebus was right, sir,' Korda said, the voice woolly and distant.

Tobeld's hand reached out in a claw, scraping at the black sand and smooth rock. Through the eye that still worked, he could see the vial, the contents unspent, lying where it had fallen from his fingers. He reached for it, inching closer.

'He was.' Tobeld heard Sedirae echo his battle-brother with a sigh. 'Seems to be making a habit of it.'

The assassin looked up, the pain caused by the simple action almost insurmountable, and saw shapes swimming in mist and blood. Cold eyes upon him, judging him unworthy.

'Put an end to this,' said Erebus.

Korda hesitated. 'Lord?'

'As our cousin says, brother-sergeant,' Sedirae replied. 'It's becoming tiresome.'

One of the shapes grew larger, coming closer, and Tobeld saw a steel-plated hand reach for the vial, gather it up. 'What does this do, I wonder?'

Then the vial glittered in the light as the Astartes brought the assassin's weapon down and injected the contents of the tube into the bruised bare flesh of Tobeld's arm.

SEDIRAE WATCHED THE helot perish with the slow, indolent air of one who had seen many manners of death. He watched out of interest to see if this ending would show him something different from all the other kills he had witnessed – and it did, to some small degree.

Korda placed a hand over the man's mouth to muffle his screams as the helot's body twitched and drew into itself. On the Caslon Moon during the Great Crusade, the captain of the 13th had drowned a mutant in a freezing lake, holding the freak-thing down beneath the surface of the murky waters until it had perished. He was reminded of that kill now, watching the helot go to his end from the poison. The hooded servile was drowning dry, if such a thing were possible. Where he could see bare skin, Sedirae saw the pallid and rad-burned meat of the man first turn corpse-grey, then lose all definition and become papery, pulling tight over bones and muscle bunches that atrophied as the moments passed. Even the blood that had spilled onto the dark earth became cloudy and then evaporated, leaving cracked deposits bereft of any moisture. Korda eventually took his hand away and shook it, sending a rain of powder from his fingertips off on the winds.

'A painful death,' remarked the sergeant, examining his fingers. 'See here?' He showed off a tiny scratch on the ceramite of the knuckle joint. 'He bit me in his last agonies, not that it mattered.'

Sedirae threw a look at the command tent. No one had emerged to see what was going on outside. He doubted Horus and the rest of his Mournival were even aware of the killing taking place. They had so much to occupy them, after all. So many plans and great schemes to helm...

'I'll inform the Warmaster,' he heard himself say.

Erebus took a step closer. 'Do you think that is necessary?'

Sedirae glanced at the Chaplain. The Word Bearer had a way of drawing attention directly when he wished it, almost as if he could drag a gaze towards him like a black sun would pull in light and matter in order to consume it; and by turns he could do the opposite, making himself a ghost in a room full of people, allowing sight to slide off him as if he were not there. In his more honest moments, Luc Sedirae would admit that the presence of Erebus left him unsettled. The captain of the 13th could not quite shake the disquiet that clouded his thoughts every time the Word Bearer chose to speak. Not for the first time, despite all the fealty he had sworn to the Luna Wolves – now the Sons of Horus in name and banner – Sedirae asked himself why the Warmaster needed Erebus so close in order to prosecute his just and right insurrection against the Emperor. It was one of many doubts that he carried, these days. The burden of them seemed to grow ever greater with each passing month that the Warmaster's forces dallied out here in the deeps, while the prize of Terra herself remained out of reach.

He gave a low snort and gestured at the corpse. 'Someone just tried to kill him. Yes, cousin, I think Horus Lupercal might consider that of interest.'

'Tell me you are not so naïve as to imagine that this pitiful attempt was the first such act against the Warmaster?'

Sedirae narrowed his eyes at Erebus's light, almost dismissive tone. 'The first to come so close, I would warrant.'

'A few steps more and he would have been inside the tent,' muttered Korda.

'Distance is relative,' Erebus replied. 'Lethality is the key factor.'

Korda stood up. 'I wonder who sent him.'

'The Warmaster's father,' said Erebus immediately. 'Or, if not by the Emperor's direct decree, then by that of his lackeys.'

'You seem very certain,' Sedirae noted. 'But Horus has made many enemies.'

The Word Bearer gave a slight smile and shook his head. 'None of concern on this day.' He took a breath. 'We three ended this threat before it became an issue. It need not become one after the fact.' Erebus nodded towards the tent. 'The Warmaster has a galaxy to conquer. He has more than enough to absorb his attention as it is. Would you wish to distract your primarch with this triviality, Sedirae?' He prodded the corpse with the tip of his boot.

'I believe the Warmaster should make that choice for himself.' Irritation flared in Sedirae's manner and his lip curled. 'Perhaps–' He caught himself and fell silent, arresting the train of thought even as it formed.

'Perhaps?' echoed Erebus, immediately seizing on the word as if he knew what would have followed it. 'Speak your mind, captain. We are all kinsmen here. All brothers of the lodge.'

He deliberated for a long moment on the words pushing at his lips, and then finally gave them leave. 'Perhaps, Word Bearer, if matters such as these were not kept from Horus, then he might wish to move along a swifter path. Perhaps, if he were not kept ignorant of the threats to our campaign, he might–'

'Push on to the Segmentum Solar, and to Earth?' Erebus seemed to close the distance between them without actually moving. 'That is the root of it, am I right? You feel that the measured pace of our advance is too slow. You wish to lay siege to the Imperial Palace tomorrow.'

'My captain is not alone in that regard,' said Korda, with feeling.

'A month would be enough,' retorted Sedirae, showing teeth. 'It could be done. We all know it.'

Erebus's smile lengthened. 'I am sure that from where the warriors of the 13th Company stand, it doubtless seems that simple. But let me assure you, it is not. There's still so much to be done, Luc Sedirae. So many pieces to be placed, so many factors not yet ready.'

The captain gave an angry snort. 'What are you saying? That we must wait for the stars to be right?'

The smile faded and the Word Bearer became grim. 'Exactly that, cousin. Exactly that.'

The sudden coldness in Erebus's words gave Sedirae a moment's pause. 'Clearly I lack your insight, then,' he grated. 'As I fail to see the merit in this leisurely strategy.'

'As long as we follow the Warmaster, all will be as it should,' Erebus told him. 'Victory will come soon enough.' He paused over the corpse, which had begun to disintegrate into dust, pulled away by the winds. 'Perhaps even sooner than any of us might expect.'

'What do you mean?' said Korda.

'A truism of warfare.' Erebus did not look up from his examination of the dead assassin. 'If a tactic can be used *against* us, then it can be used *by* us.'

DAWN BROUGHT WITH it the clouds, and under the mellow amber glow of the rising sun, the bright jewels of the Taebian Stars began to fade away as pure blue washed in to lighten the darkness of lost night. Pressed to one window of the coleopter's cramped cabin, Yosef Sabrat took a moment to pull the collar of his greatcoat a little tighter around his neck. The long summer season of Iesta Veracrux was well and truly over, and the new autuwinter was on the horizon, coming in slow and careful. Up here, in the cold morning sky, he could feel it. In a matter of weeks, the rains would come in earnest; and not before time, either. This year's crop would be one for the record books, so they were saying.

The flyer bumped through a pocket of turbulent air and Yosef bounced in his seat; like most of the craft in service with the Sentine, it was an old thing but well cared for, one of many machines that could date back their lineage to the Second Establishment and the great colonial influx. The ducted rotor vanes behind the passenger compartment thrummed, the engine note changing as the pilot put it into a shallow port-side turn. Yosef let gravity turn his head and he looked past the two jagers who were the only other passengers, and out through the seamless bowl of glassaic at the empty observer's station.

Sparse pennants of thin white cloud drifted away to give him a better view. They were passing over the Breghoot Canyon, where the sheer rock face of red stone fell away into deeps that saw little daylight, even at high sun. The terraces of the vineyards there were just opening up for the day, fans of solar arrays on the tiled roofs turning and unfolding like black sails on some ocean schooner. Beyond, clinging to the vast kilometre-long trellises that extended out off the edges of the cliffs, waves of greenery resembled strange cataracts of emerald frozen in mid-fall. Had they been closer, Yosef imagined he would be able to see the shapes of harvestmen and their ceramic-clad gatherer automatons moving in among the frames, taking the bounty from the web of vines.

The coleopter rumbled again as it forded an updraught and righted itself, giving a wide berth to the hab-towers reaching high from the cliff top and into the lightening sky. Acres of white stucco coated the flanks of the tall, skinny minarets, and across most of them the shutters were still closed over their windows, the new day yet to be greeted. Most of the capital's populace were still slumbering at this dawn hour, and Yosef did in all honesty envy them to great degree. The hasty mug of recaf that had been his breakfast sat poorly in his stomach. He'd slept fitfully last night – something that seemed to be happening more often these days – and so when the vox had pulled him the rest of the way from his dreamless half-slumber, it had almost been a kindness. *Almost*.

The engine note grew shrill as the flyer picked up speed, coming in swift and low now over the tops of the woodlands that bracketed the capital's airdocks. Yosef watched the carpet of green and brown flash past beneath him, trying not to get lost in it.

A word from the low, muttered conversation drifting between the jagers came to him without warning. He frowned and dismissed it, willing himself not to listen, concentrating on the engine sound instead; but he could not. The word, the name, whispered furtively for fear of invocation.

Horus.

Each time he heard it, it was as if it were some sort of curse. Those who uttered it would do so in fear, gripped by some strange belief that to speak the name would incur an instant punishment by unseen authority. Or perhaps it was not that; perhaps it was a sickening that the word brought with it, the sense that this combination of sounds would turn the stomach if said too loudly. The name troubled him. For too long it had been a watchword for nobility and heroism; but now the meaning was in flux, and it defied any attempt at categorisation in Yosef's analytical, careful thoughts.

He considered admonishing the men for a brief moment, then thought better of it. For all the bright sunshine that might fall upon Iesta Veracrux's thriving society, there were shadows cast here and some of them ran far deeper than many would wish to know. Recently, those shadows ran longer and blacker than ever before, and men would know fear and doubt for that. It was to be expected.

The coleopter rose up to clear the last barrier of high Ophelian pines and spun in towards the network of towers, landing pads and blockhouses that were the capital's primary port.

THE SENTINE HAD dispensation and so were not required to land at a prescribed platform like civilian traffic. Instead, the pilot moved smartly between a massive pair of half-inflated cargo ballutes to touch down on a patch of ferrocrete scarcely the width of the flyer. Yosef and the pair of jagers were barely off the drop-ramp before the downwash from the rotor became a brief hurricane and the coleopter spun away, back up into the blue. Yosef shielded his eyes from the dust and scattered leaves the departure kicked up, watching it go.

He reached inside his coat for his warrant rod on its chain, and drew out the slim silver shaft to hang free and visible around his neck. He ran his thumb absently down the length of it, over the etching and the gold contact inlays that indicated his rank of reeve, and surveyed the area. Unlike the jagers, who only wore a brass badge on street duty or patrol, the reeve's rod showed his status as an investigating officer.

The men from the flyer had joined a group of other uniforms who were carefully plotting out a search pattern for the surrounding area. Behind them, Yosef saw an automated barrier mechanical ponderously drawing a thick cable lined with warning flags around the edge of the nearest staging area.

A familiar face caught his eye. 'Sir!' Skelta was tall and thin of aspect, with a bearing to him that some of the other members of the Sentine unkindly equated to a rodent. The jager came quickly over to his side, ducking slightly even though the coleopter was long gone. Skelta blinked, looking serious and pale. 'Sir,' he repeated. The young man had ideas about being promoted beyond street duty to the Sentine's next tier of investigatory operations, and so he was always attempting to present a sober and thoughtful aspect whenever he was in his superior's company; but Yosef didn't have the heart to tell the man he was just a little too dull-witted to make the grade. He wasn't a bad sort, but sometimes he exhibited the kind of ignorance that made Sabrat's palms itch.

'Jager,' he said with a nod. 'What do you have for me?'

A shadow passed over Skelta's face, something that went beyond his usual reticent manner, and Yosef caught it. The reeve had come here expecting to find a crime of usual note, but Skelta's fractional expression gave him pause; and for the first time that morning, he wondered what he had walked into.

'It's, uh…' The jager trailed off and swallowed hard, his gaze losing focus for a moment as he thought about something else. 'You should probably see for yourself, sir.'

'All right. Show me.'

Skelta led him through the ordered ranks of wooden cargo capsules, each one an octagonal block the size of a small groundcar. The smell of matured estufagemi wine was everywhere here, soaked into the massive crates, even bled into the stone flags of the flight apron. The warm, comforting scent seemed cloying and overly strong today, however, almost as if it were struggling to mask the perfume of something far less pleasant.

Close by, he heard the quick barks of dogs, and then a man's angry shout followed by snarls and yelps. 'Dockside strays,' offered the jager. 'Attracted by the stink, sir. Been kicking them away since before sunup.' The thought seemed to disagree with the young man and he changed the subject. 'We think we have an identity for the victim. Documents found near the scene, papers and the like. Name was Jaared Norte. A lighter drivesman.'

'You think,' echoed Yosef. 'You're not sure?'

Skelta held up the barrier line for the reeve to step under, and they walked on, into the crime scene proper. 'Haven't been able to make a positive match yet, sir,' he went on. 'Clinicians are on the way to check for dentition and blood-trace.' The jager coughed, self-consciously. 'He... doesn't have a face, sir. And we found some loose teeth... But we're not sure they were, uh, his.'

Yosef took that in without comment. 'Go on.'

'Norte's foreman has been interviewed. Apparently, Norte clocked off at the usual time last night, heading home to his wife and son. He never arrived.'

'The wife report it, did she?'

Skelta shook his head. 'No, sir. They had some trouble, apparently. Their marriage contract was a few months from expiration, and it was causing friction. She probably thought he was out drinking up his pay.'

'This from the foreman?'

The jager nodded. 'Sent a mobile to their house to confirm his take on things. Waiting on a word.'

'Was Norte drunk when he was killed?'

This time, Skelta couldn't stop himself from shuddering. 'For his sake, I hope so. Would have been a blessing for the poor bastard.'

Yosef sensed the fear in the other man's words. Murder was not an uncommon crime on Iesta Veracrux; they were a relatively prosperous world that was built on the industry of wine, after all, and men who drank – or who coveted money – were often given to mistakes that led to bloodletting. The reeve had seen many deaths, some brutal, many of them sordid, each in their own way tragic; but all of them he had understood. Yosef knew crime for what it was – a weakness of self – and he knew the triggers that would bring that flaw to light. Jealousy, madness, sorrow... But fear was the worst.

And there was much fear on Iesta Veracrux these days. Here out in the ranges of the Ultima Segmentum, across the span of the galaxy from the Throne of Terra, the planet and its people felt distant and unprotected while wars were being fought, lines of battle drawn over maps their home world was too insignificant to grace. The Emperor and his council seemed so far away, and the oncoming storm of the insurrection churning sightless and unseen in the nearby stars laid a pall of creeping apprehension over everything. In every shadowed corner, people saw the ghosts of the unknown.

They were afraid; and people who were afraid easily became people who were angry, directing their terror outwards against any slight, real or imagined. Today's killing was only the newest of many that had rolled across Iesta Veracrux in recent months; murders spawned from trivialities, suicides, panicked attacks on illusory threats. While life went on as it ever did, beneath the surface there lay a black mood infecting the whole populace, even as they pretended it did not exist. Had Jaared Norte become a victim of this as well? Yosef thought it likely.

They moved around a tall corner of containers and into a small courtyard formed by lines of crates. Overhead, another cargo ballute drifted slowly past, for a moment casting a broad oval shadow across the proceedings. A handful of other jagers were at work conducting fingertip sweeps of the location, a couple from the documentary office working complex forensic picters and sense-nets, another talking into a bulky wireless with a tall whip antenna. Skelta exchanged looks with one of the docos, and she gave him a rueful nod in return. Behind them all, there was a narrow but high storage shed with its doors splayed wide open. The reeve immediately spotted the patches of brown staining the metal doors.

He frowned, looking around at the identical rust-coloured greatcoats and peaked caps of the Sentine officers. 'The Arbites are inside?' Yosef nodded towards the shed.

Skelta gave a derisive sniff. 'The Arbites are not here, sir. Called it in, as per the regulations. Lord Marshal's office was unavailable. Asked to be kept informed, though.'

'I'll bet they did.' Yosef grimaced. For all the grand words and high ideals spouted by the Adeptus Arbites, at least on Iesta Veracrux that particular branch of the Adeptus Terra was less interested in the policing of the planet than they were in *being seen* to be interested in it. The officers of the Sentine had been the lawmen and wardens of the Iestan system since the days of the colony's founding in the First Establishment, and the installation of an office of the Arbites here during the Great Crusade had done little to change that state of affairs. The Lord Marshal and his staff seemed more than happy to remain in their imposing tower and allow the Sentine to function as they always had, handling all the 'local' matters. Quite what the Arbites considered to be *other* than local had never, in twenty years of service, been made clear to Yosef Sabrat. The politics of the whole thing seemed to orbit at a level far beyond the reeve's understanding.

He glanced at Skelta. 'Do you have a read on the murder weapon?'

Skelta glanced at the doco officer again, as if asking permission. 'Not exactly. Bladed weapon, probably. For starters. There might have been, uh, other tools used.' What little colour there was on the jager's face seemed to ebb away and he swallowed hard.

Yosef stopped on the threshold of the shed. A slaughterhouse stink of blood and faeces hit him hard and his nostrils twitched. 'Witnesses?' he added.

Skelta pointed upwards, towards a spotlight tower. 'There are security imagers on the lighting stands, but they didn't get anything. Angle was too shallow for the optics to pick up a likeness.'

The reeve filed that information away; whoever had made the kill knew the layout of the airdocks, then. 'Canvass every other imager in a half-kilometre radius, pull the memory coils and have some of the recruits sift them. We might get lucky.' He took a long inhalation, careful to breathe through his mouth. 'Let's see this, then.'

He went in, and Skelta hesitantly followed a few steps behind. Inside, the shed was gloomy, lit only by patches of watery sunshine coming in by degrees through low windows and the hard-edged glares of humming portable arc lamps. On splayed tripod legs, a quad of gangly field emitters stood at the corners of an ill-defined square, a faint yellow glow connecting each to its neighbours. The permeable energy membrane allowed objects above a certain mass or kinetic energy to pass through unhindered, but kept particulates and other micro-scale matter *in situ* to aid with on-site forensics.

Yosef's brow creased in a frown as he approached the field; the area of open, shadowed floor between the emitters seemed at first glance to be empty. He stepped through the barrier and the stench in the air intensified. Glancing over his shoulder he saw that Skelta had not followed him through, instead remaining outside the line at stiff attention, his gaze directed anywhere but at the scene of the crime.

The stone floor was awash in dark arterial blood, and there were fleshy shapes scattered randomly in the shallow little sea of rippling crimson. Ropes of what had to be intestine, shiny lumps of organ meat that caught the light, and other things pasty-white and streaked with fluid. An array of butcher slab remnants, discarded not in haste but with disinterest.

The reeve felt disgust and confusion in equal measure, but he reined them in and let his sharp eye take the lead. He looked for patterns and impressions. It had been done with care and precision, this. No crime of passion, no murder of opportunity. Cool, calm and without fear of discovery. Yosef peered into the shadows, the first questions forming in his mind.

How had this been done and kept silent enough that no one had heard it? With so much blood shed, had the killer been tainted, left a trace? And where...? Where was...?

Yosef stopped short and blinked. The pool of blood was in gentle motion, small swells crossing it back and forth. He heard tiny hollow splashes here and there. 'The remains...' he began, glancing back at Skelta. 'There's not enough for a corpse. Where's Norte's body?'

The jager had one hand to his mouth, and with the other he gingerly pointed upwards. Yosef raised his eyes to the roof and there he found the rest of Jaared Norte.

The drivesman's body had been opened in a manner that the reeve had only seen in use by morticians – or rather, in a manner that was an extreme variation on the cuts used for a post-mortem examination. Iron impact rods, the kind of heavy bolts used by building labourers to secure construction work to sheer cliff sides, had been used to nail Norte to the ceiling of the shed. One through each ankle, another through the meat of the forearms, the limbs splayed out in an X-shaped stance. Then, slices across the torso at oblique angles had enabled the killer to peel back the epidermis of the torso, the neck and face. These cuts created pennants of skin that each came to a point; one to the right and to the left, another down across the groin and the last torn up over the bloody grinning mess of the skull to rise over the dead man's head. Four more impact rods secured the tips of these wet rags of meat in place. From the opened confines of the man's body, loops of dislodged muscle and broken spars of bone pointed down towards the blood pool, weeping fluid.

'Have you ever seen anything like that?' managed Skelta, his voice thick with revulsion. 'It's horrific.'

Yosef's first thought was of a sculpture, of an art-work. Against the dark metal plates of the shed's roof, the drivesman had been made into a star with eight points.

'I don't know,' whispered the reeve.

# TWO

### The Shrouds
### Masked
### A Common Blade

THE IMPERIAL PALACE was more city than stronghold, vast and ornate in the majesty of its sprawling scope, towers, pinnacles and great monoliths of stone and gold that swept from horizon to jagged horizon. Landscapes that in millennia past had been a patchwork of nation-states and sovereignties were now buried beneath the grand unity of the Empire of Humanity, and its greatest monument. The dominions of the palace encompassed whole settlements and satellite townships, from the confines of the Petitioner's City to the ranges of the Elysium Domes, across the largest star-port in the Sol system and down to the awesome spectacle of the Eternity Gate. Millions toiled within its outer walls in service to the Imperium, many living their lives without ever leaving the silver arcology ziggurats where they were born, served, and died.

This was the shining, beating heart of all human endeavour, the throne and the birthplace of a species

that stood astride the galaxy, its splendour and dignity
vast enough that no one voice could ever hope to
encompass them with mere words. Terra and her
greatness were the jewel in the Imperial crown, bright
and endless.

And yet; within a metropolis that masqueraded as a
continent, there were a myriad of ghost rooms and
secret places. There were corners where the light did
not fall – some of them created for just that purpose.

There was a chamber known as the Shrouds. Inside
the confines of the Inner Palace, if one could have
gazed upon the schematics of those bold artisans who
laid the first stones of the gargantuan city-state, no
trace of the room or its entrances would have been
apparent. To all intents and purposes, this place did
not exist, and even those who had need to know of its
reality could not have pinpointed it on a map. If one
could not find the Shrouds, then one was not meant
to.

There were many ways to the chamber, and those
who met there might know of one or two – hidden
passageways concealed in the tromp l'oeil artworks of
the Arc Galleries; a shaft behind the captured waterfall
at the Annapurna Gate; the blind corridor near the
Great Orrery; the Solomon Folly and the ghost switch
in the sapphire elevator at the Western Vantage; these
and others, some unused for centuries. Those sum-
moned to the Shrouds would emerge into a labyrinth
of ever-shifting corridors that defied all attempts to
map them, guided by a mech-intellect that would navigate them to the room and never twice by the same
route. All that could be certain was that the chamber
was atop a tower, one of thousands ranged in sentry

rows across the inner bulwarks of the Palace, and even
that was a supposition, based on the weak patina of
daylight allowed to penetrate the sailcloth-thick
blinds that forever curtained the great oval windows
about the room. Some suspected that the light might
be a deception, a falsehood filtered through trick glass
or even totally simulated. Perhaps the chamber was
deep underground, or perhaps there were more than
one of them, a suite of dozens of identical rooms so
exacting in similarity that to tell them apart would be
impossible.

And once within, there was no place on Earth more
secure, save for the Emperor's Throne Room itself.
None could listen in upon words spoken in a place
that did not exist, that could not be found. The walls
of the chamber, dark mahogany panels adorned with
minimalist artworks and a few lume-globes, concealed layers of instrumentality that rendered the
room and everything in it completely dead to the eyes
and ears of any possible surveillance. There were
counter-measures that fogged radiation detection frequencies, devices that swallowed sound and heat and
light, working alongside slivers of living neural matter
broadcasting the telepathic equivalent of white noise
across all psychic spectra. There was even a rumour
that the chamber was cloaked by a field of disruption
that actually dislocated local space-time by several
fractions of a second, allowing the room to exist a
heartbeat into the future and out of reach of the rest
of the universe.

In the Shrouds there was a table, a long octagon of
polished rosewood, and upon it a simple hololithic
projector casting a cool glow over the assembled men

and women gathered there. In deep, comfortable seats, six of them clustered around one end of the table, while a seventh sat alone at the head. The eighth did not sit, but instead stood just beyond the range of the light, content to be little more than a tall shape made up of shadows and angles.

The seven at the table had faces of porcelain and precious metals. Masks covered their countenances from brow-line to neck, and like the room they were in, these outer concealments were far more than they appeared. Each mask was loaded with advanced technologies, data-libraries, sensoria, even microweapons, and each had a different aspect that was the mirror of its wearer; only the man at the head of the table wore a face with no affectation. His mask was simple and silver, as if it had been carved from polished steel, with only the vaguest impression of a brow, eyes, a nose and mouth. Reflected in its sheen, the panes of information shown by the hololith turned slowly, allowing everyone in the room to read them.

What was written there was damning and disappointing in equal measure.

'Then he is dead,' said a woman's voice, the tone filtered through a fractal baffle that rendered her vocal pattern untraceable. Her mask was black and it fit skin-close, almost like a hood made of silk; only the large oval rubies that were her eyes broke the illusion. 'The report here makes that clear.'

'Quick to judge, as ever,' came a throaty whisper, similarly filtered, from a motionless mask that resembled a distended, hydrocephalic skull. 'We should hold for certainty, Siress Callidus.'

The ruby eyes glared across the table. 'My esteemed Sire Culexus,' came the terse reply. 'How long would you have us wait? Until the revolt reaches our door?' She turned her jewelled gaze on the only other woman seated at the table, a figure whose face was hidden behind an elegant velvet visor of green and gold, vaned with lines of droplet pearls and dark emeralds. 'Our sister's agent has failed. As I said he would.'

The woman in the green mask stiffened, and leaned back in her chair, distancing herself from the ire of Callidus. Her reply was frosty and brittle. 'I would note that none of you have yet been able to place an operative so close to the Warmaster as Clade Venenum did. Tobeld was one of my finest students, equal to the task he was set upon–'

That drew a derisive grunt from a hulking male behind a grinning, fang-toothed rictus made of bone and gunmetal. 'If he was equal to it, then why isn't the turncoat dead? All that time wasted and for what? To give the traitors a fresh corpse at Horus's doorstep?' He made a spitting sound.

Siress Venenum's eyes narrowed behind their disguise. 'However little you think of my clade, dear Eversor, your record to date gives you no cause to preen.' She drew herself up. 'What have you contributed to this mission other than a few messy and explosive deaths?'

The fanged mask regarded her, anger radiating out from the man behind it. 'My agents have brought fear!' he spat. 'Each kill has severed the head of a key insurrectionist element!'

'Not to mention countless collaterals,' offered a dry, dour voice. The comment emerged from behind a standard-issue spy mask, no different from the kind issued to every one of the sniper operatives of Clade Vindicare. 'We need a surgeon's touch to excise the Archtraitor. A scalpel, not a firebomb.'

Sire Eversor let out a low growl. 'When the day comes that someone invents a rifle you can fire from the safety of your chair and still hit Horus half a galaxy away, you can save us all. But until then, hide behind your gun sight and stay silent!'

The sixth figure at the far end of the table cleared his throat, cocking his head. His mask, a thing made of glassy layers that reflected granulated, randomised images, flickered in the dimness. 'If I might address Sire Culexus and Siress Callidus?' said Sire Vanus. 'My clade's predictive engines and our most diligent infocytes have concluded, based on all available data and prognostic simulations, that the probability of Tobeld's survival to complete his mission was zero point two percent. Margin of error negligible. However, it did represent an improvement in proximity-to-target over all Officio Assassinorum operations to date.'

'A mile or an inch,' hissed Culexus, 'it doesn't matter if the kill was lost.'

Siress Callidus looked up the table towards the man in the silver mask. 'I want to activate a new operative,' she began. 'Her name is M'Shen, she is one of the best of my clade and I–'

'Tobeld was the best of the Venenum!' snapped Sire Vindicare, with sudden annoyance. 'Just as Hoswalt was the best of mine, just as Eversor sent his best and so on and so on! But we're throwing our most gifted students into a meat-grinder, sending them in blind and half-prepared! Every strike against Horus breaks, and he shrugs it off without notice!' He shook his head grimly. 'Is this what we have been reduced to? Every time we meet, listening to a catalogue of each other's failures?' The masked man spread his arms, taking in his five cohorts. 'We all remember that day on Mount Vengeance. The pact we made in the shadow of the Great Crusade, the oath that breathed life into the Officio Assassinorum. For decades we have hunted down the enemies of our Emperor through stealth and subterfuge. We have shown them there is no safe place to hide.' Sire Vindicare shot a look at Sire Vanus. 'What did he say that day?'

Vanus answered immediately, his mask shimmering. *'No world shall be beyond my rule. No enemy shall be beyond my wrath.'*

Sire Culexus nodded solemnly. 'No enemy…' he repeated. 'No enemy but Horus, so it seems.'

'No!' snarled Callidus. 'I can kill him.' The man in the silver mask remained silent and she went on, imploring. 'I will kill him, if only you will give me leave to do so!'

'You will fail as well!' snarled Eversor. 'My clade is the only one capable of the deed! The only one ruthless enough to end the Warmaster's life!'

At once, it seemed as if every one of the masters and mistresses were about to launch into the same tirade, but before they could begin, the silver mask resonated with a single word of command. *'Silence.'*

The chamber became quiet, and the Master of Assassins took a breath before speaking again. 'This rivalry and bickering serves no purpose,' he began, his voice level and firm. 'In all the history of this group, there has never been a target whose retirement required more than one mission to prosecute. To date, the Horus problem has claimed eight Officio operatives across all six of the primary clades. Each of you are the first of your clade, the founders... And yet you sit here and jostle for supremacy over one another instead of giving me the kill we so desperately want! I demand a solution to rid us of the Emperor's turbulent and wayward son.'

Sire Eversor spoke. 'I will commit every active agent in my clade. All of them, all at once. If I must spend the lives of every last Eversor to kill Horus, then so be it.'

For the first time since the group had assembled, the silent figure in the hooded robes made a sound; a soft grunt of disagreement.

'Our visitor has something to add,' said Sire Vanus.

The Master of Assassins inclined his head towards the shadows. 'Is that so?'

The hooded man moved slightly, enough that he became better defined by the glow-light, but not so much that his face could be discerned inside the depths of the robe. 'None of you are soldiers,' he rumbled, his deep tones carrying across the room. 'You are so used to working alone, as your occupation demands, that you forget a rule of all conflict. Force doubled is force squared.'

'Did I not just say such a thing?' snapped Sire Eversor.

The hooded man ignored the interruption. 'I have heard you all speak. I have seen your mission plans. They were not flawed. They were simply not *enough*.' He nodded to himself. 'No single assassin, no matter how well-trained, no matter which clade they come from, could ever hope to terminate the Archtraitor alone. But a collective of your killers...' He nodded again. 'That might be enough.'

'A strike team...' mused Sire Vindicare.

'An Execution Force,' corrected the Master. 'An elite unit hand-picked for the task.'

Sire Vanus frowned behind his mask. 'Such a suggestion... There is no precedent for something like this. The Emperor will not approve of it.'

'Oh?' said Callidus. 'What makes you so certain?'

The master of Clade Vanus leaned forward, the perturbations of his image-mask growing more agitated. 'The veils of secrecy preserve all that we are,' he insisted. 'For decades we have worked in the shadows of the Imperium, at the margins of the Emperor's knowledge, and for good reason. We serve him in deeds that he must never know of, in order to maintain his noble purity, and to do so there are conventions we have always followed.' He shot a look at the hooded man. 'A code of ethics. Rules of conflict.'

'Agreed,' ventured Siress Venenum. 'The deployment of an assassin is a delicate matter and never one taken lightly. We have in the past fielded two or three on a single mission when the circumstances were most extreme, but then always from the same clade, and always after much deliberation.'

Vanus was nodding. 'Six at once, from every prime clade? You cannot expect the Emperor to sanction such a thing. It is simply... not done.'

The Master of Assassins was silent for a long moment; then he steepled his fingers in front of him, pressing the apex of them to the lips of his silver face. 'What I expect is that each clade's Director Primus will obey my orders without question. These "rules" of which you speak, Vanus... Tell me, does Horus Lupercal adhere to them as strongly as you do?' He didn't raise his voice, but his tone brooked no disagreement. 'Do you believe that the Archtraitor will baulk at a tactic because it offends the manners of those at court? Because it is *not done*?'

'He bombed his sworn brethren, his own men even, into obliteration,' said Sire Vindicare. 'I doubt anything is beyond him.'

The Master nodded. 'And if we are to kill this foe, we cannot limit ourselves to the moral abstracts that have guided us in the past. We must dare to exceed them.' He paused. 'This will be done.'

'My lord—' began Vanus, reaching out a hand.

'It is so ordered,' said the man in the silver mask, with finality. 'This discussion is at an end.'

WHEN THE OTHERS had taken their leave through the doorways of the Shrouds, and after the psyber eagles nesting hidden in the apex of the ceiling had circled the room to ensure there were no new listening devices in place, the Master of Assassins allowed himself a moment to give a deep sigh. And then, with care, he reached up and removed the silver mask, the dermal pads releasing their contact from the flesh of his face. He shook his head, allowing a grey cascade of hair to emerge and pool upon his shoulders, over the pattern of the nondescript robes he wore. 'I think I need a drink,' he muttered. His voice sounded nothing like the one that had issued from the lips of the mask;

but then that was to be expected. The Master of Assassins was a ghost among ghosts, known only to the leaders of the clades as one of the High Lords of Terra; but as to which of the Emperor's council he was, that was left for them to suspect. There were five living beings who knew the true identity of the Officio's leader, and two of them were in this room.

A machine-slave ambled over and offered up a gold-etched glass of brandy-laced black tea. 'Will you join me, my friend?' he asked.

'If it pleases the Sigillite, I will abstain,' said the hooded man.

'As you wish.' For a brief moment, the man who stood at the Emperor's right hand, the man who wore the rank of Regent of Terra, studied his careworn face in the curvature of the glass. Malcador was himself once more, the cloak of the Master of Assassins gone and faded, the identity shuttered away until the next time it was needed.

He took a deep draught of the tea, and savoured it. He sighed. The effects of the counter-psionics in the room were not enough to cause him any serious ill-effect, but their presence was like the humming of an invisible insect, irritating the edges of his witch-sight. As he sometimes did in these moments, Malcador allowed himself to wonder which of the clade leaders had an idea of who he might really be. The Sigillite knew that if he put his will to it, he could uncover the true faces of every one of the Directors Primus. But he had never pursued this matter; there had never been the need. The fragile state of grace in which the leaders of the Officio Assassinorum existed had served to keep them all honest; no single Sire or Siress could ever know if their colleagues, their subordinates, even their lovers were not behind the masks they saw about the table. The group had been born in darkness and secrecy, and now it could only live there as long as the rules of its existence were adhered to.

Rules that Malcador had just broken.

His companion finally gave himself up to the light and stepped into full visibility, walking around the table with slow, steady steps. The hooded man was large, towering over the Sigillite where he sat in his chair. As big as a warrior of the Adeptus Astartes, out of the darkness the man who had observed the meeting was a threat made flesh, and he moved with a grace that caused his rust-coloured robes to flow like water. A hand, tawny of skin and scarred, reached up and pulled back the voluminous hood over a shorn skull and queue of dark hair, to reveal a face that was grim and narrow of eye. At his throat, gold-flecked brands in the shapes of lightning bolts were just visible past the open collar.

'Speak your mind, Captain-General,' said Malcador, reading his aura. 'I can see the disquiet coming off you like smoke from a fire pit.'

Constantin Valdor, Chief Custodian of the Legio Custodes, spared him a glance that other men would have withered under. 'I have said all I need to say,' Valdor replied. 'For better or for worse.' The warrior's hand dropped to the table top and he absently traced a finger over the wood. He looked around; Malcador had no doubts that the Custodian Guardsman had spent his time in this chamber working out where the room might actually be located.

The Sigillite drowned the beginnings of a waxen smile in another sip of the bittersweet tea. 'I confess, I had not expected you to do anything other than observe,' he began. 'But instead you broke open the pattern of the usual parry and riposte that typically comprises these meetings.'

Valdor paused, looking away from him. 'Why did you ask me here, my lord?'

'To watch,' Malcador replied. 'I wanted to ask your counsel after the fact–'

The Custodian turned, cutting him off. 'Don't lie to me. You didn't ask me to join you in this place just for my silence.' Valdor studied him. 'You knew exactly what I would say.'

Malcador let the smile out, at last. 'I… had an inkling.'

Valdor's lips thinned. 'I hope you are pleased with the outcome, then.'

The Sigillite sensed the warrior was about to leave, and he spoke again quickly to waylay him. 'I am surprised in some measure, it must be said. After all, you are the expression of Imperial strength and nobility. You are the personal guard of the Lord of Earth, as pure a warrior-kindred as many might aspire to become. And in that, I would have thought you of all men would consider the tactics of the Assassinorum to be…' He paused, feeling for the right word. 'Underhanded. Dishonourable, even?'

Valdor's face shifted, but not towards annoyance as Malcador had expected. Instead he smiled without humour. 'If that was a feint to test me, Sigillite, it was a poor one. I expected better of you.'

'It's been a long day,' Malcador offered.

'The Legio Custodes have done many things your assassins would think beyond us. The sires and siresses are not the only ones who have marque to operate under... special conditions.'

'Your charter is quite specific on the Legio's zone of responsibility.' Malcador felt a frown forming. This conversation was not going where he had expected it to.

'If you wish,' Valdor said, with deceptive lightness. 'My duty is to preserve the life of the Emperor of Mankind above all else. That is accomplished through many different endeavours. The termination of the traitor-son Horus Lupercal and the clear and present danger he represents, no matter how it is brought to pass, serves my duty.'

'So, you really believe that a task force of killers could do this?'

Valdor gave a slight shrug of his huge shoulders. 'I believe they have a chance, if the pointless tensions between the clades can be arrested.'

Malcador smiled. 'You see, Captain-General? I did not lie. I wanted your insight. You have given it to me.'

'I haven't finished,' said the warrior. 'Vanus was right. This mission will not please the Emperor when he learns of it, and he will learn of it when I tell him every word that was spoken in this room today.'

The Sigillite's smile vanished. 'That would be an error, Custodian. A grave misjudgement on your part.'

'You cannot have such hubris as to believe that you know better than he?' Valdor said, his tone hardening.

'Of course not!' Malcador snapped in return, his temper flaring. 'But you know as well as I do that in order to protect the sanctity of Terra and our liege-lord, some things must be kept in the dark. The Imperium is at a delicate point, and we both know it.

All the effort we have spent on the Great Crusade, and the Emperor's works, all of that has been placed in most dire jeopardy by Horus's insurrection. The conflicts being fought at this very moment are not just on the battlefields of distant worlds and in the void of space! They are in hearts and minds, and other realms less tangible. But now, here is the opportunity to fight in the shadows, unseen and unremarked. To have this bloody deed done without setting the galaxy ablaze in its wake! A swift ending. The head of the snake severed with a single blow.' He took a long breath. 'But many may see it as ignoble. Use it against us. And for a father to sanction the execution of his son… Perhaps it may be beyond the pale. And *that* is why some things cannot be spoken of outside this chamber.'

Valdor folded his muscular arms over his chest and stared down at Malcador. 'That statement has all the colour of an order,' he said. 'But who gives it, I wonder? The Master of Assassins, or the Regent of Terra?'

The Sigillite's eyes glittered in the gloom. 'Decide for yourself,' he said.

BEFORE THE EMPEROR'S enlightenment, the Sentine's precinct house had been a place of idolatry and ancestor worship. Once, the bodies of the rich and those judged worthy had been buried in crypts beneath the main hall, and great garish statuary and other extravagant gewgaws had filled every corner of the building, with cloisters and naves leading here and there to chapels for every deity the First Establishment had brought with them from Old Earth. Now the crypts were cells and memory stacks, armouries and storage lockers. The chapels had different tenants now, icons called security and vigilance, and all the artworks and idols were crushed and gone, a few saved in museums as indicators of a less sophisticated past. All this had taken place a long time before Yosef Sabrat had been born, however. There were barely a handful of living citizens on Iesta Veracrux who could recall any vestiges of a past with religion in it.

The cathedral's second life as a place of justice served the building well. It was just as impressive a home for the Sentine as it had been for the long-departed priests. Sabrat crossed the long axis of the main hall, past the open waiting quad where citizens queued and argued with the luckless jagers on desk duty, and through the checkpoint where an impassive, watchful gun-servitor licked his face with a fan of green laser light before letting him by. He threw a cursory nod to a group of other reeves from the West Catchment, all of them gathered around a nynemen board with tapers of scrip, waving off an invite to join them in a game; instead he took the spiral stairs up to the second level. The upper floors were almost a building inside a building, a multi-storey blockhouse that had been constructed inside the hangar-like confines of the main hall, and retrofitted into the structure. The room was in the same state of shabby, half-controlled clutter as it ever was, with bales of rough vinepaper and starkly shot picts arranged in loose piles that represented some sort of untidy order, if only one knew how to interpret it. In the centre of the room, a pillar studded with brass communication sockets sprouted thick rubber-sheathed cables that snaked to headsets or to hololiths. One of them ended in a listening rig around the head of Yosef's cohort, who sat bent over in a chair, listening with his eyes closed, fingers absently toying with a gold aquila on a chain about his wrist.

'Daig.' Yosef stopped in front of the man and called his name. When he didn't respond, the reeve snapped his fingers loudly. 'Wake up!'

Reeve Daig Segan opened his eyes and let out a sigh. 'This isn't sleep, Yosef. This is deep thought. Have you ever had one of those?' He took off the headset and looked up at him. Yosef heard the tinny twitter of a synthetic voice from the speakers, reading out the text of an incident report in a clicking monotone.

Daig was a study in contrasts to his cohort. Where Sabrat was of slightly above average height, narrow-shouldered, clean-shaven and sandy-haired, Segan was stocky and not without jowls, his hair curly and unkempt around a perpetually dejected expression. He managed another heavy sigh, as if the weight of the world were pressing down upon him. 'There's no point in me listening to this a second time,' he went on, tugging the rig's jack plug from its socket on the pillar with a snap of his wrist. 'Skelta's reports are just as dull with the machine reading them to me as him doing it.'

Yosef frowned. 'What I saw out there wasn't any stripe of dull.' He glanced down and saw a spread of picts from the storage shed crime scene. Even rendered in light-drenched black and white, the horror of it did not lessen. Mirrors of liquid were in every image, and the sight of them brought sense memory abruptly back into the reeve's forebrain. He blinked the sensation away.

Daig saw him do it. 'You all right?' he asked, concern furrowing his brow. 'Need a moment?'

'No,' Yosef said firmly. 'You said you had something new?'

Daig's head bobbed. 'Not so new. More like a confirmation of something we already suspected.' He searched for a moment through the papers and data-slates before he found a sheaf of inky printout. 'Analysis of the cutting gave up a pattern that matches a type of industrial blade.'

'Medical?' Yosef recalled his impression of the almost clinical lines of the mutilation; but Daig shook his head.

'Viticultural, actually.' The other reeve pawed through a box at his feet and produced a plastic case, opening it to reveal a wickedly curved knife with a knurled handle. 'I brought one up from evidentiary so we'd have an example to look at.'

Yosef recognised it instantly, and his hand twitched as he resisted the urge to reach for it. A harvestman's blade, one of the most familiar tools on the planet, made by the millions for Iesta Veracrux's huge army of agricultural workers. Blades exactly like this one were used in every vineyard, and they were as commonplace as the grapes they were used to cut. Being so widespread, of course, they were also the most common tool of murder on Iesta – but Yosef had never seen such a blade used for so ornate a killing as the one at the airdocks. To use the crude tool for so fine a cutting would have required both great skill and no little time to accomplish it. 'What in Terra's name are we dealing with?' he muttered.

'It's a ritual,' said Daig, with a certainty that seemed to come from nowhere. 'It can't be anything else.' He put the blade aside and gestured at the scattered files. As well as the tide of paperwork from the airdock murder, packets of fiche and other picts had arrived from a couple of the sub-precincts in the nearby arroyo territories, automatically flagged by the reports of the incident sent out on the planetwide watch-wire. There had been other deaths, and while the nature of them had not been exactly the same as Jaared Norte's, elements of similar methodology were expressed in each. Daig had suggested that their killer was 'maturing' with each assault, growing more confident in what they wished to convey with their deeds.

This was not Iesta Veracrux's first serial murder spree. But it seemed different from all the others that had gone before it, in a manner that Yosef could not yet fully articulate.

'What I don't fathom,' began a voice from behind them, 'is how in Stars the bugger got the poor fool up on the ceiling.' Yosef and Daig turned to where Reeve Warden Berts Laimner stood, a fan of picts in his meaty paw. Laimner was a big man, dark-skinned and always smiling, even now in a small way at the sight of Norte's grotesque death; but the warm expression was always a falsehood, masking a character that was self-serving and oily. 'What do you think, Sabrat?'

Yosef framed a noncommittal answer. 'We're looking into that, Warden.'

Laimner gave a chuckle that set Yosef's teeth on edge and discarded the images. 'Well, I hope you've got a better reply than that up your sleeve.' He pointed across the room to an entranceway. 'The

High-Reeve is just outside that door. She wants to weigh in on this.'

Daig actually let out a little groan, and Yosef felt himself sag inside. If the precinct commander was putting her hand on this case, then the investigators could be certain that their job was about to become twice as hard.

As if Laimner's words had been a magical summons, the door opened and High-Reeve Kata Telemach entered the office with an assistant trailing her. Telemach's appearance was like a shock going through the room, and every reeve and jager scrambled to look as if they were working hard and being diligent. She didn't appear to notice, instead making a direct line for Yosef and Daig. The woman was wearing a well-pressed dress uniform, and around her neck was a gold rod with one single silver band around it.

'I was just telling Reeves Sabrat and Segan of your interest, ma'am,' said Laimner.

The commander seemed distracted. 'Progress?' she asked. The woman had a sharp face and hard eyes.

'We're building a solid foundation,' offered Daig, equally as good at giving non-answers as his cohort was. He swallowed. 'There are some matters of cross-jurisdictional circumstance that might become an issue later, however.' He was about to say more, but Telemach shot Laimner a look as if to say *Haven't you dealt with this already?*

'That will not be a concern, Reeve. I have just returned from an audience with the Lord Marshal of the Adeptus Arbites.'

'Oh?' Yosef tried to keep any sarcasm out of his voice.

Telemach went on. 'The Arbites have a lot of wine in their glass at the moment. They're engaged in a few operations across the planet. This... case doesn't need to be added to that workload.'

*Operations*. That seemed to be the current word of choice to describe the actions of the Arbites on Iesta Veracrux. A colourless, open term that belied the reality of what they were actually doing – which was quietly dredging the lower cities and the upper echelons alike for the slightest evidence of any anti-Imperial sedition and pro-Horus thinking, ruthlessly stamping out anything that might blossom into actual treason.

'It's only bodies,' noted Laimner, in an off-hand manner.

'Exactly,' said the High-Reeve. 'And quite frankly, the Sentine are better suited for this sort of police work. The Arbites are not native to this world, and we are. We know it better than they ever will.'

'Just so,' offered Yosef.

Telemach graced them with a tight smile. 'I want to deal with this in a swift and firm manner. I think the Lord Marshal and his masters back on Terra could do with a reminder that we Iestans can deal with our own problems.'

Yosef nodded here, partly because he knew he was supposed to, and partly because Telemach had just confirmed for him her real reason for wanting the case closed quickly. It was no secret that the High-Reeve had designs on the rank of Landgrave, head of all Sentine forces across the planet; and for her to get that, the current incumbent – and so the rumours went, her lover – would need to rise to the only role open to him, the Imperial Governorship of the planet. The Landgrave's only real competition for that posting was the Lord Marshal of the Arbites. Showing a decisive posture towards a crime like this one would count for a lot when the time for new installations was nigh.

'We're investigating all avenues of interest,' said Laimner.

The High-Reeve tapped a finger on her lips. 'I want you to pay special attention to any connection with those religious fanatics that are showing up in the Falls and out at Breghoot.'

'The Theoge,' Laimner offered helpfully, with a sniff. 'Odd bunch.'

'With respect,' said Daig, 'they're hardly fanatics. They're just–'

Telemach didn't let him finish. 'Odium spreads wherever it takes root, Reeve. The Emperor did not guide the Great Crusade to us for nothing. I won't have superstition find purchase in this city or any other on my watch, is that clear?' She eyed Yosef. 'The Theoge is an underground cult, forbidden by Imperial law. Find the connection between them and this crime, gentlemen.'

*If it exists or not*, Yosef added silently.

'You have an understanding of my interest, then?' she concluded.

He nodded once more. 'Indeed I do, ma'am. We'll do our best.'

Telemach sniffed. 'Do better than that, Sabrat.'

She walked on, and Laimner fell in step with her, shooting him a weak grin as they moved off.

'*It's only bodies*,' parroted Yosef, in a pinched imitation of the Warden's voice as he watched them go.

'What he means, it's only little people dead so far. No one he has any interest in.' He blew out a breath.

Daig's expression had become more pessimistic than normal. 'Where does that effluent about the Theoge come from?' he muttered. 'What could they possibly have to do with serial murders? Everything Telemach knows about those people comes from rumours, trash based on nothing but hearsay and bigotry.'

Yosef raised an eyebrow. 'You know better, do you?'

He shrugged. 'Clearly not,' said the other man, after a moment.


AFTER HE HAD put Ivak to bed, Yosef returned to the living room and took a seat by the radiator. He smiled to see that his wife had poured a glass of the good mistwater for him, and he sipped it as she set the auto-launder to work in the back room.

Yosef lost himself in the honeyed swirl of the drink and let his mind drift. In the fluids he saw strange oceans, vast and unknown. Somehow, the sight of them rested him, the perturbations soothing his thoughts.

When Renia coughed, he looked up with a start, spilling a drop down the side of the glass. His wife had entered the room and he had been so captured by reverie that he had not even been aware of her.

She gave him a worried look. 'Are you all right?'

'Yes.'

Renia was not convinced. Fifteen years of loving someone gave you that kind of insight as a matter of course. And because of that, she didn't press him. His wife knew his job, and she knew that he did his best to leave it at the precinct every time he came home. Instead she asked him, just once. 'Do you need to talk?'

He took a sip of the wine and didn't look at her. 'Not yet.'

She changed the subject, but not enough for Yosef's comfort. 'There was an incident at Ivak's schola today. A boy taken out of classes.'

'Why?'

'Ivak said it was because of a game some of the older children were playing. *The Warmaster and the Emperor*, they called it.' Yosef put down the glass as she went on. Somehow, he already knew what Renia was going to say. 'This boy, he went on about the Warmaster. Ivak's teachers heard him and they reported it.'

'To the Arbites?'

She nodded. 'Now people are talking. Or else they are not talking at all.'

Yosef's lips thinned. 'Everyone is uncertain,' he said, at length. 'Everyone is afraid of what's behind the horizon... But this sort of thing... It's foolishness.'

'I've heard rumours,' she began. 'Stories from people who know people on other worlds, in other systems.'

He had heard the same thing, hushed whispers in the corners of the precinct from men who couldn't moderate the sound of their voices. Rumour and counter-rumour. Reports of terrible things, of black deeds – sometimes the *same* deeds – attributed to those in service of the Warmaster *and* the Emperor of Mankind.

'People who used to talk freely are going silent to me,' she added.

'Because I'm your husband?' Off her nod he frowned. 'I'm not an Arbites!'

'I think the Lord Marshal's men are making it worse,' she said. 'Before, there was nothing that could not be said, no debate that could not be aired without prejudice. But now... After the insurrection...' Her words lost momentum and faded.

Renia needed something from him, some assurance that would ease what troubled her, but as Yosef searched himself for it, he found nothing to give. He opened his mouth to speak, not sure of what he would tell her, and somewhere outside the house glass shattered against bricks.

He was immediately on his feet, at the window, peering through the slats. Raised voices met him. Down below, where the road snaked past the stairs to his front door, he saw a group of four youths surrounding a fifth. They were brandishing bottles like clubs. As he watched, the fifth stumbled backwards over the broken glass and fell to his haunches.

Renia was already opening the wooden case on the wall where the watch-wire terminal sat. She gave him a questioning look and he nodded. 'Call it in.'

He snatched his greatcoat from the hook in the hall as she shouted after him. 'Be careful!'

Yosef heard feet on the stairs behind him and turned, one hand on the latch, to see Ivak silhouetted in the gloom. 'Father?'

'Go back to bed,' he told the boy. 'I'll just be a moment.'

He put his warrant rod around his neck and went out.

* * *

By the time he got to the road, they had started throwing punches at the youth on the ground. He heard yelling and once again, the name rose up at him, shouted like a blood-curse. Horus.

The fifth youth was bleeding and trying to protect himself by holding his arms up around his head. Yosef saw a particularly hard and fast haymaker blow come slamming in from the right, knocking the boy down.

The reeve flicked his wrist and the baton he carried in his sleeve pocket dropped into his palm. With a whickering hiss, the memory-metal tube extended to four times its length. Anger flared inside him and he shouted out 'Sentine!' even as he aimed a low sweeping blow at the knees of the nearest attacker.

The hit connected and the youth went down hard. The others reacted, falling back. One of them had a half-brick in his hand, weighing it like he was considering a throw. Yosef scanned their faces. They had scarves around their mouths and noses, but he knew railgangers when he saw them. These were young men from the loading terminals, who by day worked the cargo monorails that connected the airdocks to the vineyards, and by night made trouble and engaged in minor crime. But they were out of their normal patch in this residential district, apparently drawn here by their victim.

'Bind him!' shouted one of them, stabbing a finger at the injured youth. 'He's a traitor, that's what he is! Whoreson traitor!'

'No…' managed the youth. 'Am not…'

'Sentine are no better!' snarled the one with the half-brick. 'All in it together!' With a snarl he threw his missile, and Yosef batted it away, taking a glancing hit on his temple that made him stagger. The railgangers took this as a signal and broke into a run, scattering away down the curve of the street.

For a split second, Yosef was possessed by a fury so high that all he wanted to do was race after the thugs and beat them bloody into the cobbles; but then he forced that urge away and bent down to help the injured youth to his feet. The young man's hand was wet where he had cut himself on the broken glass. 'You all right?' said the reeve.

The youth took a woozy step away from him. 'Don't… Don't hurt me.'

'I won't,' he told him. 'I'm a lawman.' Yosef's skull was still ringing with the near-hit of the brick, but in a moment of odd perceptivity, he saw the lad had rolls of red-printed leaflets stuffed in his pocket. He grabbed the youth's hand and snatched one from the bunch. It was a Theoge pamphlet, a page of dense text full of florid language and terms that meant nothing to him. 'Where did you get these?' he demanded.

In the glare of the streetlights, Yosef saw the youth's pale face full on; the fear written large there was worse than that he had shown to the thugs with the bottles and bricks. 'Leave me alone!' he shouted, shoving the reeve back with both hands.

Yosef lost his balance – the pain in his head helping that along the way – and stumbled, fell. Shaking off the spreading ache, he saw the youth sprinting away, disappearing into the night. He cursed and tried to get to his feet.

The reeve's hand touched something on the cobbles, a sharp, curved edge. At first he thought it was part of the scattering of broken glass, but the light fell on it a different way. Peering at the object, Yosef saw what it actually was. Discarded in the melee, dropped from the pocket of... *who*, he wondered?

It was a harvesting knife, worn with use and age.

# THREE

### What Must Be Done
### The Spear
### Intervention

STRIPPED TO THE waist, Valdor strode into the sparring hall with his guardian spear raised high at the crook of his shoulder, the metal of the ornate halberd cool against his bare flesh; but what awaited him in the chamber was not the six combat robots he had programmed for his morning regimen, only a single figure in duty robes. He was tall and broad, big enough to look down at the Chief Custodian, even out of battle armour.

The figure turned, almost casually, from a rack holding weapons similar to the one Valdor carried. He was tracing the edge of the blade that hung beneath the heavy bolter mechanism at the tip of the metal staff, considering its merit in the way that a shrewd merchant might evaluate a bolt of fine silk before a purchase.

For a moment, the Custodian was unsure what protocol he was to observe; by rights, the sparring hall belonged to the Legio Custodes and so it could be considered their territory. For someone, a non-Custodian, to appear there unannounced was... impolitic. But the nature of the visitor – Valdor was loath to consider him an *intruder* – called such a thing into question. In the end, he chose to halt at the edge of the fighting quad and gave a shallow bow, erring on the side of respect. 'My lord.'

'Interesting weapon,' came the reply. The voice was resonant and metered. 'It appears overly ornate, archaic even. One quick to judge might even think it ineffective.'

'Every weapon can be effective, if it is in the right hands.'

'In the right hands.' The figure at last gave Valdor his full attention. In the cold, sharp light tracing through the windows, the face of Rogal Dorn, Primarch of the Imperial Fists, was like chiselled granite.

For a moment, Valdor was tempted to offer Dorn the chance to try the use of the Custodes halberd-gun, but prudence warned him to hold his tongue. One did not simply challenge the master of an entire Astartes Legion to a sparring match, no matter how casually. Not unless one was prepared to take that challenge as far as it would go.

'Why am I here?' said Dorn, asking Valdor's question for him. 'Why am I here and not attendant to my duties out on the Palace walls?'

'You wish to speak to me?'

Dorn continued, as if he had not heard his answer. The primarch glanced up at the ornate ceiling above them, which showed a frieze of jetbike-borne Custodians racing across the skyline of the Petitioner's City.

'I have blighted this place, Valdor. In the name of security, I have made this palace into a fortress. Replaced art with cannonades, gardens with kill zones, beauty with lethality. You understand why?'

Something in Dorn's tone made the Custodian's hand tighten on his weapon. 'Because of the war. To protect your father.'

'I take little pride in my defacement,' Dorn replied. 'But it must be done. For when Horus comes here, as he will, he must be met by our strength.' He advanced a step. 'Our honest strength, Valdor. Nothing less will suffice.'

Valdor remained silent, and Dorn gave him a level, demanding stare. In the quiet moment, the two of them measured one another as each would have gauged the lay of a battlefield before committing to combat.

The Imperial Fist broke the lengthening silence. 'This palace and I… We know each other very well now. And I am not ignorant of what goes on in its halls, both those seen and those unseen.' His heavy brow furrowed, as if a choice had been made in his thoughts. 'We shall speak plainly, you and I.'

'As you wish,' said the Custodian.

Dorn eyed him. 'I know the assassin clades and their shadow-killers are mounting an operation of large scope. I know this,' he insisted. 'I know you are involved.'

'I am not a part of the Officio Assassinorum,' Valdor told him. 'I have no insight into their workings.' It was a half-truth at best, and Dorn knew it.

'I have always considered you a man of honour, Captain-General,' said the Primarch. 'But as I have learned to my cost, it sometimes becomes necessary to revise one's opinion of a man's character.'

'If what you say was true, then you know it would be a matter of utmost secrecy.'

Dorn's eyes flashed. 'Meaning, if I am not informed of such a thing, then I should not know of it?' He advanced again and Valdor stood his ground. The stoic, unchanging expression on the face of the Imperial Fist was, if anything, more disquieting than any snarl of annoyance. 'I question the purpose of anything so clandestine. I am Adeptus Astartes, warrior by blood and by birth. I do not support the tactics of cowardice.'

Valdor let the guardian spear's tip drop to the floor. 'What some consider cowardly others might call expedient.'

Dorn's expression shifted for a second, with a curling of his lip. 'I have crossed paths with the agents of the Officio Assassinorum on the battlefield. Those encounters have never ended well. Their focus is always... too narrow. They are tools best suited for courtly intrigue and the games of empire. Not for war.' He folded his arms. 'Speak, Custodian. What do you know of this?'

Valdor stiffened. 'I... can't say.'

For a moment, the tension on the primarch's face resonated through the room and Valdor's knuckles whitened around the haft of his spear; then Dorn turned away. 'That is unfortunate.'

The Custodian bristled at the warrior-lord's demeaning tone. 'We all want the same thing,' he insisted. 'To preserve the Emperor.'

'No,' Dorn looked up at the windows, and he allowed himself a sigh. 'Your first remit is to safeguard the life of the Emperor of Mankind above all else. Mine, and that of my brothers, is to safeguard the Imperium.'

'The two are the same,' said Valdor. There was a flicker of uncertainty in his words that he did not expect.

'Not so,' Dorn said, as he left. 'A narrow view, Custodian.' The primarch paused on the threshold and spoke one last time, without looking back. 'This conversation is not ended, Valdor.'

CIRSUN LATIGUE LIKED to pretend that the aeronef belonged to him. When he left the Iestan capital of a night and took the languid flight back to his home in the Falls, he liked to place himself by the window of the little gondola slung beneath the cigar-shaped ballute and watch the hab-towers flash past, imagining the workadays from the service industries and the vineyards seeing him cruise along by, their faces lit with envy at someone of such importance. The gondola was no bigger than a monorail carriage, but it was opulently appointed with chaises and recessed automata for beverages and other services. For the most part, it served important clients or the urgent travel needs of upper tier management, but for a lot of the time the craft sat at dock, unused.

The aeronef was not his property, however much he wished it so. It belonged, as his wife often told him *he* did, to the Eurotas Trade Consortium, and while his rank with the company was such that use of the aircraft could be a regular perk of the job, on some level he knew that he would never rise far enough to truly own something of such status.

That wasn't something he liked to think about, though. Rather like his wife, more often than not. All his not-inconsiderable earnings as a senior datum-clerk, their appealing townhouse in the fashionable end of the suburbs, the private schola for the children... She appreciated none of it. Latigue's love of the company flyer was a reaction against that. When he was in the aeronef, he felt free, just for a little while. And thanks to the correct application of some bribery and favours in the shape of a few deliberately misla-belled shipping forms, he had learned from one of the Consortium's technologians how simple it was to adjust the aircraft's docile, unsophisticated machine-brain in order to take the flyer to other destinations that didn't show up on the logs. Places like the White Crescent Quarter, where the company was always agreeable, and for a man of Latigue's means, quite affordable.

He smiled at that, listening to the soft chopping hum of the propeller as the aeronef crossed over Spin-dle Canyon, and he thought about ordering a change of course. The wife was at some interminable gaming event at one of her ridiculous social clubs, so there would be no judgemental hissing and narrowing of eyes when he came home. Why not stay out a little longer, he wondered? Why not take a cruise towards the White Crescent? The daring of the thought made him smile, and he began to warm to the idea. Latigue leaned forward, reaching for the command panel and licking his lips.

It was then he noticed the object for the first time. On the seat across from him, a peculiar little ball that resembled a seed pod. Gingerly, he reached for it, prodded it with a finger – and blanched. The thing was warm to the touch, and it felt like it was made of flesh.

Latigue's gorge rose in his throat and he tasted the sour tang of the half-digested meat dish he had eaten at mid-meal; but still he could not stop himself from reaching out once more, this time carefully gathering up the object from where it lay.

In the light cast through the cabin windows, he saw that the ball was lined and strangely textured. He let it roll in his hand, this way and that, finally bringing it closer to his nose to get a better look.

When it opened he let out a yelp. Splitting along its length, the sphere revealed an eye, horribly human in aspect, hidden behind the fleshy covering. It rotated of its own accord and Latigue became aware that it was looking directly at him, and with something that might have been recognition.

Suddenly overcome with disgust, he threw the orb away, and it vanished under a low couch. Confused and sickened, suddenly all he wanted was to be down on the ground. The interior of the gondola was hot and stifling, and Latigue felt sweat gathering around the high collar of his brocade jacket.

He was still trying to process what had just happened when one of the cabin walls began to move. The velvet patterning, the rich claret-red and spun gold of the adornment, flowed and shifted as oil moved on water. Something was extruding itself out of the side of the cabin, making its shape more definite and firm with each passing instant.

Latigue saw a head and a torso emerging, saw hands ending in long-fingered digits. In the places where the shape-thing grew out of the walls, there was a strange boiling effect, and the light caught what appeared to be something like lizard-skin, rippling and throbbing.

Latigue's reason fled from him. Rather than seek escape, he forced himself into the corner formed by the couch and the far side of the aeronef's cabin, the window at his back. The head turned to him, drawn by the motion. The skin-camouflage of the velvet walls faded into a tanned, rich crimson that looked like stained leather or perhaps flayed flesh: as the figure pulled itself free of the wall with spindly legs, its head came up to show a patterned skull pointed into a snout, with a peculiar, plough-shaped lower jaw. Teeth made of silver angled back in long, layered rows. There were no eyes in the sockets above, only dark pits.

Latigue coughed as a smell like blood and sulphur enveloped him, emanating from the apparition. He vomited explosively and began to cry like a child. 'What do you want?' he begged, abruptly finding his voice. 'Who are you?'

The reply was husky, distant, and strangely toned, as if it had been dragged up from a great depth. 'I... am Spear.' It seemed more like a question than an answer.

The creature took a first step towards him, and in one hand it had a curved blade.

THE TRANSPORT RUMBLED through the thermals rising from the surface of the Atalantic Plain, and inside the aircraft's cargo bay, the bare ribs of the walls creaked and flexed under the heavy power of the thruster pods. Beneath the transport's belly, a blur of feature-less desert raced past, torrents of windborne rust-sand reaching up from the dusty ground to snatch at it. In the distant past, thousands of years gone, this region would have been deep beneath the surface of a vast ocean, one of many that stretched across the surface of Terra; all that was left now were a few minor inland seas that barely deserved the name, little more than shrinking lakes of mud ringed by caravan townships. Much of the vast plainslands had been absorbed by the masses of the Throneworld's city-sprawls, but there were still great swathes of it that were unclaimed and lawless, broken with foothills sculpted by the long-forgotten seas and canyons choked with the wrecks of ancient ships. There were precious few places on Terra that could still truly be considered a wilderness, but this was one of them.

The flyer's pilot was deft; isolated in the cockpit pod at the prow, she lay wired into a flight couch that translated her nerve impulses into the minute flexions of the transport's winglets and the outputs of the engine bells. The aircraft's course was swift and true, crossing the barren zone on a heading towards the distant city-cluster crowded around the peaks of the Ayzor Ridge; she was following a well-traced course familiar to many of the more daring pilots. Those who played it safe flew at much higher altitudes, in the officially-sanctioned sky corridors governed by the agents of the Ministorum and the Adeptus Terra – but that cost fuel and time, and for fringer pilots working on tight margins, sometimes the riskier choice was the better one. The hazards came from the rust storms and the winds – but also from more human sources as well. The vast erg of the Atalantic was also home to bandit packs and savage clans of junkhunters.

At first glance, the cargo being carried by the flyer was nothing remarkable – but one who looked closer would have understood it was only a make-weight, there to bulk out the transport's flimsy flight plan. The real load aboard the craft was the two passengers, and they were men so unlike to one another, it could hardly be believed they had both been dispatched by the same agency.

Constantin Valdor sat in a gap between two cube-containers of purified water, cross-legged on the deck of the cargo bay. His bulk was hidden beneath the ill-defined layers of a sandcloak which concealed an articulated suit of ablative armour. It was by no means a relative to the elaborate and majestic Custodian wargear that was his normal garb; the armour was unsophisticated, scarred and heavily pitted with use. Over Valdor's dense form it strained to maintain its shape, almost as if it were trying to hold him in. At his side was a careworn long-las inscribed with Techno-mad tribal runes and an explorer's pack containing survival gear and supplies, the latter for show. With his enhanced physiology, Valdor would have been able to live for weeks on the plains on drops of mois-ture he sucked from the dirt or the sparse meat of insects. The rifle he could use, though. Everything about Valdor's disguise was there to tell a vague fic-tion, not enough to hide from a deep analysis but enough to allow him to go on his way without arous-ing too much suspicion. The Custodian had done this many times before, in blood games and on missions of other import. This was no different, he reflected.

Across the cargo bay, sitting uncomfortably upon a canvas seat that vibrated each time the transport forded a pocket of turbulence, Valdor's companion on this journey was bent forwards over his right arm. Wearing a sandcloak similar to the Custodian's, the smaller man was busy with a pane of hololithic text projected from a cybernetic gauntlet clasped around his wrist. With his other hand he manipulated shapes in the hologrammatic matrix, his attention on it total and complete. His name was Fon Tariel; the light of the text threw colour over his pale olive skin and the dark ovals of his eyes. A tight nest of dreadlocks drawing over Tariel's head did their best to hide discreet bronze vents in the back of his skull, where interface sockets gleamed alongside memory implants and dataphilia. Unlike the cohorts of the Mechanicum, who willingly gave themselves fully to the marriage of flesh and machine, Tariel's augmentations were discreet and nuanced.

Valdor studied him through lidded eyes, careful to be circumspect about it. The Sigillite had presented Tariel to him in a manner that made it clear no questioning of his choice would be allowed. The little man was Sire Vanus's contribution to the Execution Force, one of the clade's newest operatives, with a skull crammed full of data and a willingness to serve. They called Tariel's kind 'infocytes'; essentially they were human computing engines, but at the very far opposite of the spectrum from the mindless meat-automata of servitors. In matters of strategy and tactics, the insight of an infocyte was unparalleled; their existence cemented Clade Vanus as the intelligence-gathering faction of the Officio Assassinorum. It was said they had never been known to make an error of judgement. Valdor considered that as little more than disinformation, however; the creation and dissemination of propaganda was also a core strength of the Vanus.

From the corner of his eye, the Custodian saw the movement of a monitor camera high up on the roof of the cargo bay. He had noted earlier that it appeared to be dwelling on him more than it should have, and now the device's attention seemed solely fixed on him. Without turning his head, Valdor saw that Tariel had moved slightly so that his holoscreen was now concealed by the bulk of his body.

The Custodian's lip curled, and with a quick motion he was on his feet, crossing the short distance between the two of them. Tariel reacted with a flash of panic, but Valdor was on him, grabbing his arm. The hololith showed the monitor's point of view, locked onto the Custodian. Data streams haloed his image, feeding out bio-patterns and body kinestics; Tariel had somehow invaded and co-opted the flyer's internal security systems to satisfy his own curiosity.

'Don't spy on me,' Valdor told the infocyte. 'I value my privacy.'

'You can't blame me,' Tariel blurted. 'I wondered who you were.'

Valdor considered this for a moment, still holding him in an immobile grip. They had both boarded the transport in silence, neither speaking until this moment; he was not surprised that the other man had let his inquisitiveness outstrip his caution. Tariel and his kind had the same relationship with raw information that an addict did with their chosen vice; they were enrapt by the idea of new data, and would do whatever they could to gather it in, and know it. Quite how that balanced with the Assassinorum's obsessive need for near-total secrecy he could not imagine; perhaps it went some way towards explaining the peculiar character of the Vanus clade and its agents. 'Then who am I?' he demanded. 'If I caught you staring at me through that camera, then surely you have been doing that and more since we first left the Imperial City.'

'Let go of my hand, please,' said Tariel. 'You're hurting me.'

'Not really,' Valdor told him, but he released his grip anyway.

After a moment, the infocyte nodded. 'You are Constantin Valdor, Captain-General of the Custodian Guard, margin of error less than fourteen percent. I parsed this from physiological data and existing records, along with sampling of various other information streams.' Tariel showed him; inputs from sources as diverse as traffic routings, listings of foodstuffs purchased by the Palace consumery, the routes of cleaning automata, renovation files from the forges that repaired the robots Valdor had smashed during his morning exercises… To the warrior it seemed like a wall of white noise, but the infocyte manipulated it effortlessly.

'That is… impressive,' he offered. 'But not the work of an assassin, I would think.'

Tariel's expression stiffened at that. 'Clade Vanus has removed many of the Imperium's enemies. We do our part, as you do, Captain-General.'

Valdor leaned in, looming over the man. 'And how many enemies of Terra have *you* killed, Fon Tariel?'

The infocyte paused, blinking. 'In the way that you would consider it a termination? None. But I have been instrumental in the excision of a number of targets.'

'Such as?'

For a moment, he thought Tariel would refuse to answer, but then the infocyte began to speak, quickly and curtly, as if he were giving a data download. 'I will provide you with an example. Lord-Elective Corliss Braganza of the Triton-B colony.'

'I know the name. A delinquent and a criminal.'

'In effect. I discovered through program artefacts uncovered during routine information-trawling that he was in the process of embezzling Imperial funds as part of a plan to finance a move against several senior members of the Ministorum. He was attempting to build a powerbase through which to influence Imperial colonial policy. Through the use of covert blinds, I inserted materials of an incendiary nature into Braganza's personal datastacks. The resultant discovery of these fabrications led to his death at the hands of his co-conspirators, and in turn the revelation of their identities.'

Valdor recalled the incident with Braganza; he had been implicated in the brutal murder of a young noblewoman, and after ironclad evidence had come to light damning him despite all his protestations to the contrary, the Triton electorate that had voted him into office had savagely turned against him. Braganza had apparently died in an accident during his transport to a penal asteroid. 'You leaked the details of his prison transfer.'

Tariel nodded. 'The cleanest kill is one that another performs in your stead with no knowledge of your incitement.'

The Custodian allowed him a nod. 'I can't fault your logic.' He stepped back and let the infocyte have room to relax. 'If you have so much data to hand, perhaps you can tell me something about the man we have been sent to find?'

'Eristede Kell,' Tariel answered instantly. 'Clade Vindicare. Currently on an extended duration deployment targeted at the eventual eradication of exocitizen criminal groups in the Atalantic Delimited Zone. Among the top percentile of field-deployed special operatives. Fifty-two confirmed kills, including the Tyrant of Daas, Queen Mortog Haeven, the Eldar general Sellians nil Kaheen, Brother-Captain–'

Valdor held up his hand. 'I don't need to know his record. I need to know *him*.'

The Vanus considered his words for a long moment; but before Tariel could answer, a flash of fire caught Valdor's eye through one of the viewports, and the Custodian turned towards it, his every warning sense rushing to the fore.

Outside, he glimpsed a spear made of white vapour, tipped with an angry crimson projectile; it described a corkscrew motion as it homed in on the aircraft. Alert sirens belatedly screamed a warning. He had barely registered the light and flame before the transport suddenly resonated with a colossal impact, and veered sharply to starboard. Smoke poured into the cargo bay, and Valdor heard the shriek of torn metal.

Unsecured, the two of them tumbled across the deck as the aircraft spun into the grip of the rusty haze.

* * *

A VISIT TO the valetudinarium always made Yosef feel slightly queasy, as if the proximity to a place of healing was somehow enough to make him become spontaneously unwell. He was aware that other people – people who didn't work in law enforcement, that was – had a similar reaction being around peace officers; they felt spontaneously guilty, even if they had committed no crime. The sensation was strong, though, enough that if ever Yosef felt an ache or a pain that might best have been looked at by a medicae, a marrow-deep revulsion grew strong in him, enough to make him bury it and wait for the issue to subside.

Unfortunate then that a sizeable portion of his duties forced him to visit the capital's largest clinic on a regular basis; and those visits were always to the most forbidding of its halls, the mortuarium. Winter-cold, the pale wooden floors and panelled walls were shiny with layers of heavy fluid-resistant varnishes, and harsh white light thrown from overhead lume-strips filled every corner of the chamber with stark illumination.

Across the room, the dead stood upright in liquid-filled suspensor tubes that could be raised from compartments in the floor or lowered from silos in the ceiling. Frost-encrusted data-slates showed a series of colour-coded tags, designating which were new arrivals, which had been kept aside for in-depth autopsy and which were free to be released so that their families could perform final rites of enrichment.

Daig took off his hat as they crossed the chamber, weaving in between the medicae servitors and subordinate clinicians, and Yosef followed suit, tucking his brown woollen toque under an epaulette.

They were here to see Tisely, a rail-thin woman with hair the colour of straw, who served as the senior liaison between the mortuarium and the Sentine. She threw them a glance as they approached and gave a glum nod. An accomplished doctor and a superlative pathlogia investigator, Tisely was nevertheless one of the most joyless people Yosef Sabrat had ever met. He struggled to remember a single moment where she had expressed any mood to him but negativity.

'Reeves,' she said, by way of greeting, and immediately kept to form. 'I'm surprised you made it in today. The traffic was very dense this morning.'

'It's the weather,' offered Daig, equally downbeat. 'Cold as space.'

Tisely nodded solemnly. 'Oh yes.' She tapped one of the suspensor tubes. 'We'll be filling more of these with those who can't buy fuel for the winter.'

'Governor ought to lower the tithe,' Daig went on, matching her tone. 'It's not fair to the elderly.'

The clinician was going to follow on, but before the two of them could enter into a mutually-supporting spiral of circular complaining about the weather, the government, the harvest or whatever subject would come next, Yosef interrupted. 'You have another body for us?'

Tisely nodded again and changed conversational gears seamlessly. 'Cirsun Latigue, male, fifty years Terran reckoning. Gutted like a cliffgull.'

'He died of that?' Yosef asked, examining the face behind the glass. 'The cutting?'

'Eventually.' Tisely sniffed. 'It was done slowly, by a single blade, like the others.'

'And he was laid out like the Norte case? In the star-shape?'

'Across a very expensive chaise longue, in an aeronef gondola. Not nailed down this time, though.' She reported the horrific murder in exactly the same tone she had used to complain about the traffic. 'Quite a troubling one, this.'

Yosef chewed his lip. He'd gone over the abstract of the crime scene report on the way to the valetudinarium. The victim's wife, who was now somewhere several floors above them in a drugged sleep after suffering a hysterical breakdown, had returned home the previous evening to find the flyer parked on the lawn of their home, the machine-brain pilot diligently waiting for a return-to-hangar command that had never come. Inside the aeronef's cabin, every square metre of the walls, floor and ceiling was daubed with Latigue's blood. The eight-point star was repeated everywhere, over and over, drawn in the dead man's vitae.

Daig was looking at the data-slate, fingering his wrist chain. 'Latigue had rank, for a civilian. Important, but not too much so. He worked for Eurotas.'

'Which complicates matters somewhat,' said Tisely.

She made it sound like a minor impediment, but in fact the matter of Cirsun Latigue's employer had the potential to send Yosef's serial murder investigation spiralling out of control. He had hoped that the sketchy report made by the jager on the scene might have been in error, even as some part of him knew that it was not. *My luck is never that good*, he told himself. Bad enough that the High-Reeve had put her measure into the bottle for all this, but with this latest

victim now revealed as a ranking member of the Eurotas Consortium, a whole new layer of problems was
opening up for the investigators.

Latigue and all those like him were on the planetside
staff of an interstellar nobleman, who was quite possibly the richest man for several light years in any
direction. His Honour the Void Baron Merriksun Eurotas was the master of a rogue trader flotilla that plied
the spaceways across the systems surrounding Iesta
Veracrux. Holding considerable capital and trading
concerns on many planets, his consortium essentially
controlled all local system-to-system commerce and
most interplanetary transportation into the bargain.
Eurotas counted high admirals, scions of the Navis
Nobilite and even one of the Lords of Terra among his
circle of friends; his business clan could trace its roots
back to the time of Old Night, and it was said that the
hereditary Warrant of Trade held by his family had
been personally ratified by the Emperor himself. Such
was his high regard that the man served the Adeptus
Terra as an Agentia Nuntius, the Imperial Court's
attaché for every human colony in the Taebian Sector.

'Tisely,' Yosef lowered his voice and stepped closer,
becoming conspiratorial. 'If we could keep the
identity of this victim under wraps, just for a few days,
it would help–'

But she was already shaking her head. 'We tried to
keep the information secure, but…' The clinician
paused. 'Well. People talk. Latigue's staff saw it all.'

Yosef's heart sank. 'So the Consortium know.'

'It's worse than that, actually,' she told him. 'They've
reclaimed the aeronef directly from evidentiary after
using some pull with the Landgrave.'

'They can't do that…' said Daig, with a grimace.

'It's already done,' Tisely went on. 'And there are Consortium clinicians on the way to take custody of the luckless Cirsun here.' She tapped the mist-wreathed tube. 'They're probably caught in that cursed traffic, otherwise they'd have been here already and removed him.'

Yosef's eyes narrowed. 'This is a Sentine matter. It's an *Iestan* matter.' His annoyance burned cold and slow as he remembered Telemach's words in the precinct; and yet a day later her superior was sweeping all that aside in favour of doing everything possible to appease the Consortium; because Iesta Veracrux supplied wines to the entire Ultima Segmentum, and without Eurotas, the planet's economy would die on the vine.

Daig finally swore under his breath, earning him a censorious glare from Tisely. 'It doesn't stop there,' she went on, as if to chastise him. 'Latigue's seniors sent an astropathic communiqué to the Void Baron himself. He's apparently taking a personal interest in the incident.'

Yosef felt the colour drain from his face. 'Eurotas… He's coming here?'

'Oh, I don't doubt it,' Tisely told him. 'In fact, I hear a whisper that some of his personal agents are already in the warp, on their way.'

In spite of himself, that queasy feeling returned to Yosef's gut and he took a breath of the chilled, antiseptic air. With a sudden jolt of anger, he snatched the data-slate from Daig's hand and glared at it. 'This isn't an investigation any more, it's a bloody poison chalice.'

\* \* \*

VALDOR SNAPPED BACK to awareness with a jerk, and he stifled a reflexive cough. He felt a heavy weight across his torso and thick drifts of sandy matter all around him. There was heat, too, close and intense, searing his skin. He tasted the stink of burning fuel on his lips.

Checking himself, the Custodian found nothing more serious than a minor dislocation among the contusions he had suffered in the crash. With care, he rotated his forearm back into its socket and tested it, the flash of pain ebbing. Valdor placed both hands against the weight holding him down – a section of hull plate, he noted – and forced it up and away.

He came to his feet surrounded by flames and grey smoke. Valdor remembered the moment of the impact only in fleeting impressions; sparks of pain and the spinning of the cargo bay all around him as the wounded flyer slammed into the sand. He had heard Tariel cry out; there was no sign of the infocyte nearby. Valdor moved forward, picking his way over steaming mounds of wreckage, heated by the blazing slick of liquid promethium that had spilled out across the landscape. Sections of the transport lay in a line that vanished off across the ruddy plains, surrounding a black trail carved in the dirt by the craft as it had skidded to a halt, losing pieces of itself along the way.

He saw something that looked familiar; the cockpit pod, the egg-shape of it stove in and crumpled. Blood painted the canopy from the inside, and Valdor knew that the pilot would not have survived the landing. He turned this way and that. The encroaching flames were high and swift, and he had little room to manoeuvre. Sweeping around, he found what seemed to be the thinnest part in the wall of fire and ran at it, his legs pumping. At the last possible second, Valdor leapt into the flames and punched through, the sandcloak around him catching alight.

He landed hard on the other side of the wreckage and came up in a crouch. Snatching at the cloak, he tore it from himself as the fire took hold and threw it as hard as he could. Panting, Valdor looked up; and it was then he realised he was not alone.

'Well,' said a rough voice, 'what have we got here?'

He counted eight of them. They wore the patchwork gear of a junkhunter gang, armour cobbled together from a dozen disparate sources, faces hidden behind breath filters and hoods. All of them were armed with large-gauge weapons – different varieties of stubber guns mostly, but he also spied a couple with twin-barrelled laser carbines, and one with the distinctive shape of a plasma gun held at the ready. Their collection of vehicles was as motley as everything else, a pair of four-legged walker platforms along with fast duneriders on fat knobbled tires, and a single ground-effect truck.

Valdor considered them with the cold tactical precision of a trained warrior. Only eight, eight humans, some of them likely to have reflex enhancements, perhaps even dermal plating, but still only eight. He knew with complete certainty that he would be able to kill them all in less than sixty seconds, and that was if he took his time about it.

There were only two things that gave him a moment's pause. The first was the figure standing up through a hatch in the GEV's cab, behind the pintle mount of a quin-barrel multilaser. The gunner had an

unobstructed arc of fire that was directly centred on
Valdor, and as resilient as he was, without his usual
wargear to protect him the heavy weapon would put
the Custodian down before he took ten paces.

The second thing was Fon Tariel, his face a mess of
blood and bruises, on his knees in front of one of the
walkers, with the muzzle of a junkhunter's rifle
pressed to his back.

'Hah,' he heard the infocyte say, labouring the words
up past his injuries. 'You're all going to be sorry now.'

Valdor frowned, and continued to glance around,
ignoring the gang and looking off in all directions,
squinting towards the near horizon. It was difficult
through the low sheen of rust-sand in the air, but his
eyes were gene-altered for acuity.

'Put up your hands,' buzzed the junkhunter with the
plasma gun. Valdor had guessed possession of the
powerful weapon made that one the leader, and this
confirmed it. He ignored the command, still looking
away. 'Are you deaf, freak?'

In the distance, perhaps a kilometre away, maybe
more, the Custodian thought he saw something brief
and bright. A glint off a metallic object atop a low
butte. He resisted the urge to smile and turned back to
the junkhunters, casually positioning himself in such
a way that he could see both the flat-topped hill and
the bandit crew. 'I hear you,' he told the gang leader.

'He's a big one,' ventured one of the riflemen. 'Some
kinda aberrant?'

'Could be,' said the leader. 'That what you are,
freak?'

Tariel shouted at him, his voice high with fright.
'What are you waiting for, man? Help me!'

'Yeah, help him,' mocked the GEV gunner. 'I dare you.'

'You've made a very serious error,' Valdor began, speaking slowly and carefully. 'I had hoped we could make a landing in the erg, scout you out for ourselves. But you took the initiative, and I must admire that. You saw prey and you attacked.' Looking again, the Custodian could see a second, unmanned weapon mount on the rear of the hover-truck. Untended, it pointed the mouth of a surface-to-air missile tube skyward. 'Lucky shot.'

'Nothing lucky about it,' said the leader. 'You're not the first. Won't be the last.'

'I beg to differ,' Valdor told him. 'As I said, you made an error. You've drawn the attention of the Emperor.'

The use of the name sent a ripple of fear through the group, but the gang leader stamped on it quickly. 'Rust and shit, you're some kind of liar, freak. No one cares what goes on out here, not a one, not a man, not the bloody Emperor hisself. If he cared, he'd come here and share a little of that glory of his with us.'

'Let's just kill them,' said the gunner.

'Valdor!' Tariel blurted out his name in fear. 'Please!'

Unseen by everyone else, the glimmer from the distant hill blinked once, then twice. 'Let me tell you who I am,' said the Custodian. 'My name is Constantin Valdor, Captain-General of the Legio Custodes, and I hold the power of the Emperor's displeasure in my hands.'

The gang leader snorted with cold amusement. 'Your brain is broke, that's what you have!'

'I will prove it to you.' Valdor raised his arm and pointed a finger at the gunner behind the multilaser.

'In the Emperor's name,' he said, his tone calm and conversational, '*death*.'

A heartbeat later, the gunner's upper torso exploded into chunks of meat on a blast of pink fluids.

The fear that the Emperor's name had briefly conjured returned tenfold. Valdor pointed to the rifleman standing over Tariel. 'And death,' he went on. The junkhunter's body bifurcated at the spine with a wet chug, collapsing to the sand. 'And death, and death, and death…' The Custodian let his arm fall, and stood still as three more of the gang were torn apart where they stood.

Tariel dived into the dirt and the rest of the junkhunters broke apart in a terrified scramble, some of them racing towards a vehicle, others desperately trying to find cover. Valdor saw one of them leap into a dunerider and gun the engine, the vehicle surging away. The windscreen shattered in a red blink of blood and the rover bounded into a shallow gulley, crashing to a halt. The others died as they ran.

A furious snarl drew Valdor's attention back and he looked up as the gang leader came speeding towards him – too fast for a normal human, quite clearly nerve-jacked as he had first suspected. The junkhunter had the plasma gun aimed at the Custodian's chest; at this close a range, a blast from it would be a mortal wound.

Valdor did nothing, stood his ground. Then, like the work of an invisible trickster god, the gun was ripped from the gang leader's hand and it spun away into the air, the mechanism torn open and spitting great licks of blue-white sparks.

Only then did Valdor step in and break the man's neck with a short chopping motion to his throat. The last of the junkhunter band dropped and was still.

THE SUN WAS dipping towards the horizon when a piece of the desert seemed to detach itself and transform into the shape of a man. A cameoline cloak shimmered from the colours of the rust-sand to a deep night-black, revealing a muscular figure in a stealthsuit that was faceless behind a gunmetal spy mask. The mask's green eye-band studied Valdor and Tariel, where the two of them had sought shelter in the lee of the parked GEV truck. A spindly rifle, easily as long as the man was tall, lay across his back.

Valdor gave him a nod. 'Eristede Kell, I presume?'

'You are out of uniform, Captain-General,' said the marksman. 'I hardly recognised you.' His voice was low.

Valdor raised an eyebrow. 'Have we met before?'

The sniper shook his head. 'No. But I know you. And your work.' He glanced at the infocyte.

'Vindicare,' said Tariel, by way of terse greeting.

'Vanus,' came the reply.

'I'm curious,' said Kell. 'How did you know I would be watching?'

'You've been in this sector for some time. It stood to reason you would have seen the crash.' The Custodian gestured around. 'I had intended to find some of your prey in order to find you. It seems events altered the order of that but not the result.'

Tariel shot Valdor a look. 'That's why you didn't attack them? You could have dealt with them all, but you did nothing.' He grimaced. 'I might have been killed!'

'I considered letting that happen,' said the sniper, with a casual sniff. 'But I dismissed the idea. If a pair as unlikely as you two had come out here, I knew there had to be good reason.'

'You almost missed that thug with the plasma gun!' snapped the infocyte.

'No,' said Valdor, with a half-smile, 'he did not.'

The sniper cocked his head. 'I never miss.'

'You came to the Atalantic zone without your vox rig,' Valdor went on.

'Comm transmissions would have been detected,' said Kell. 'It would have given me away to the bandits.'

'Hence our somewhat unconventional method of locating you,' continued the Custodian.

Tariel's eyes narrowed. 'How did you know when to fire?'

'His weapon's scope contains a lip-reading auspex,' Valdor answered for the sniper. 'Your assignment was open-ended, I believe.'

'I've been systematically terminating the raider gangs as I find them,' said Kell. 'I still have work to do. And it makes good exercise.'

'You have a new mission now,' said Tariel. 'We both do.'

'Is that so?' Kell reached up and took off the spy mask, revealing a craggy face with close-cut black hair, sharp eyes and hawkish nose. 'Who is the target?'

Valdor stood up, and pulled a mag-flare tube from a compartment in his chest plate, aiming it into the sky. 'All in good time,' he said, and fired.

Kell's eyes narrowed. 'You are leading this mystery mission then, Captain-General?'

'Not I,' said the Custodian, shaking his head as the flare ignited, casting jumping shadows all around them. '*You*, Eristede.'

# FOUR

### Blood
### Weapons
### Face and Name

THE COLEOPTER'S CHATTERING rotors made it impossible to have a conversation at normal levels in the cabin, and Yosef was reduced to growling into Daig's ear in order to get something approximating privacy. 'It's the pattern I'm not certain about,' he said.

Daig had a fan-fold file open on his lap, one hand holding in the slips of vinepaper, the other gripping a thick data-slate. 'What pattern?'

'Exactly,' Yosef replied. 'There isn't one. Every time we've had a crazed lunatic go on a killing spree like this, there's been some kind of logic to it, no matter how twisted. Someone is murdered because they remind the killer of their abusive stepfather, or because the voices in their head told them that all people who wear green are evil...' He pointed a finger at the file. 'But what's the link here? Latigue, Norte and the others? They're from all different walks of life, men and women, old and young, tall and short...'

Yosef shook his head. 'If there's a commonality between them, I haven't seen it yet.'

'Well, don't worry,' Daig said flatly, 'there will be plenty of people willing to throw in their half-baked theories about it. After Latigue's death, you can bet the watch-wire will be buzzing with this.'

Yosef cursed under his breath; with everything else that had been on his mind, he hadn't stopped to think that if the Eurotas Consortium had become involved with the case, then of course the Iestan news services would have got wind of it into the bargain. 'As if they don't have enough doom and gloom to put on the watch-wire already,' he said. 'By all means, let's add to everyone's woes with the fear of a knife in the belly from every dark alleyway.'

Daig shrugged. 'Actually, it might take people's minds off the bigger issues. Nothing like a killer of men on the loose in your own backyard to keep you focussed.'

'That all depends on how large your backyard is, don't you think?'

'Good point.' Yosef's cohort paged through the panes of data installed on the slate with solemn slowness. He paused on one slab of dense text, his eyes narrowing. 'Hello. This is interesting.' He handed the device over. 'Look-see.'

'Blood work,' noted Yosef. It was the analysis reports from the site of the Latigue murder, multiple testing on samples that confirmed, yes, the fluids all over the walls of the gondola had once been contained inside the unfortunate clerk. At least, *almost* all of them. There was a rogue trace right in the middle of the scan reports, something picked up by chance from one of the medicae servitors. A single blood trace that did not match the others.

Yosef felt a slight thrill as he absorbed this piece of information, but he stamped down on it immediately. He didn't dare jinx the chance that Daig might have just pointed out something that could be their first important break.

'It doesn't tally with any of the previous deaders, either,' said the other reeve. He reached for the intercom horn. 'I'll comm the precinct, get them to run this up to the citizen database…'

But just as quickly as it had lit, Yosef's brief spark of excitement guttered out and died as he read a notation appended to the bottom of the information pane. 'Don't waste your time. Tisely got her people to do that already.'

'Ah,' Daig's expression remained neutral. 'Should have expected that. She's efficient that way. No joy, then?'

Yosef shook his head. The notification for a citizen ident read *Not Found*. That meant that the killer was unregistered, which was a rare occurrence on Iesta Veracrux, or else they were from somewhere else entirely. He chewed on that thought for a moment. 'He's an off-worlder.'

'What?'

'Our cutter. Not an Iestan.'

Daig eyed him. 'That's a bit of a leap.'

'Is it? It explains why his blood's not in the database. It explains how he's doing this and leaving no traces.'

'Off-world technology?'

Yosef nodded. 'I admit it's thin, but it's a direction. And with Telemach breathing down our necks, we need to be seen to be proactive. It's that or sit around waiting for a fresh kill.'

'We could just hold off,' suggested the other man. 'I mean, if Eurotas has his own operatives inbound... Why not let them come in and take a pass over it? They're bound to have better resources than we do.'

He gave his cohort an acid look. 'Remember that engraving on your warrant rod that talks about "to serve and protect"? We're called *investigators* for a reason.'

'Just a thought,' said Daig.

Yosef sensed something unsaid in his cohort's words and studied him. To anyone else, Segan's dour expression would have seemed no different from any of the other dour expressions he wore day in and day out; but the other reeve had been partnered with him for a long time, and he could read moods in the man that others missed completely. 'What aren't you telling me, Daig?' he asked. 'Something about this case has been gnawing at you since we had it dropped on us.' Yosef leaned closer. 'You didn't do it, did you?'

Daig made a brief spluttering sound that was the closest he ever came to a laugh, but then he sobered almost instantly. After a moment of silence he looked away. 'We've seen some things, you and I,' he said. 'This is different, though. It feels different. Don't ask me to be objective about it, because I can't. I think there's more here than just... *human* madness.'

Yosef made a face. 'Are you talking about xenos? There's not an alien alive in this entire sector.'

Daig shook his head. 'No.' He sighed. 'I'm not sure what I'm talking about. But... After *Horus*...'

Once more, the reeve felt the sudden tension that the name brought with it. 'If I'm sure of anything, I'm damned sure that *he* didn't do it.'

'There are stories, though,' Daig went on. 'People talk about worlds that have declared for the Warmaster, worlds that go silent soon after. Those who make it out before the silence comes down, they've said things. Talked about what happened on those planets.' He tapped a sheaf of crime scene picts. 'Things like this. I know you've heard the same.'

'It's just stories. Just scared people.' Yosef wondered if he sounded convincing. He took a breath. 'And it has no bearing on what we're doing here.'

'We'll see,' Daig said darkly.

A thought occurred to Yosef and he reached for the intercom horn. 'Yes, we will.' He pressed the stud that would allow him to talk to the coleopter's pilot. 'Change of plans,' he said briskly, 'we're not going back to the precinct house. Take us to the Eurotas compound.'

The pilot acknowledged the command and the flyer pivoted into a banking turn, the pitch of the rotors deepening.

Daig gave him a confused look. 'The trader's men won't be here for another couple of days yet. What are you doing?'

'Everyone wants to keep Eurotas happy, so it seems,' Yosef told him. 'I think we should use that to our advantage.'

THEY LANDED ON a tree-lined transit pad just within the walls of the Consortium's compound. In a definite attempt to stand out from the more typical Iestan

architectural styles of the other great manses in the
area, the Eurotas house was modelled on the Cygnus
school of design, reminiscent of many reunification-
era colony palaces from the early decades of the Great
Crusade. It was an open, summery building, full of
courtyards and cupolas, with fountains and small
pocket gardens that were at odds with the cool pre-
winter chill of the day.

The two reeves were barely to the foot of the
coleopter's drop-ramp when they were met by a narrow woman in the bottle-green and silver of the rogue
trader's livery. Standing behind her at a discreet distance were two men in the same garb, but both of
them were twice her body mass with faces hidden
behind the blank glares of info-visors. Yosef saw no
weapons visible on them, but he knew they had to be
carrying. One of the many tenets of the Consortium's
corporate sovereignty throughout the Taebian Sector
allowed Eurotas to ignore planetside laws the Void
Baron considered to be detrimental to his business,
and that included Iestan weapon statutes.

The woman spoke before Yosef could open his
mouth, firmly determined to set the rules of the
impromptu visit immediately. 'My name is Bellah
Gorospe, I'm a Consortium liaison executive. We'll
need to make this quick,' she told him, with a fake
smile. 'I'm afraid I have an important meeting to attend
very shortly.' The woman had the kind of silken Ultima
accent that automatically categorised her as non-native.

'Of course,' Yosef said smoothly. 'This won't take
long. The Sentine require access to the Consortium's
database of passenger and crew manifests for incom-
ing starships to Iesta Veracrux.'

Gorospe blinked. She was actually startled by the directness of his demand, and didn't say no straight away. 'Which ship?'

'All of them,' Daig added, following his lead.

The automatic denial that she was trained to give came next. 'That's impossible. That data is proprietary material under ownership of the Eurotas Trade Consortium. It cannot be released to any local jurisdictional bodies.' Gorospe said the word *local* as if it rhymed with *irrelevant*. 'If you have a specific request regarding any data pertaining to Iestan citizens, I may be able to accommodate you. Otherwise, I'm afraid not.' She started to turn away.

'Did you know Cirsun Latigue?' said Yosef.

That brought the woman to a halt. She covered her hesitation well. 'Yes. We had cause to work together on occasion.' Gorospe's lips thinned. 'Is that pertinent?'

'We're investigating the possibility that whoever murdered him is following a vendetta against employees of Baron Eurotas.' That was an outright lie, but it got Yosef the response he wanted. The woman blinked, and she was clearly wondering if she could be next. The reeve had no doubt that by now everyone in the compound, no matter if they were supposed to know or not, knew exactly how horribly Latigue had died. 'We believe the killer may have arrived on planet aboard a Eurotas-operated vessel,' he added.

If the murderer was from another planet, then that was undeniable; the Consortium ran every inter-system ship that came to Iesta Veracrux, and as a part of Imperial transit law, all travellers were required to submit to cursory medical checks in order to prevent the spread of any potential biosphere-specific contagions from world to world. That data would exist in the Consortium's records.

Gorospe was uncertain how to proceed. Her plan to dismiss the Sentine officers and return to whatever her other tasks were had crumbled. Yosef imagined that she was now thinking of a way to deal with this by invoking some higher authority. 'Sanctioned Consortium security operatives will be arriving in fifty hours. I suggest you return at that time and make your request to them.'

'It wasn't a request,' Yosef told her. 'And given the frequency of the murders to date, there could be two, perhaps even three more deaths before then.' He kept his voice level. 'I think that even the Baron himself would agree that time is of the essence.'

'The Baron is coming here,' Gorospe noted, in an absent, distant manner that seemed to be half disbelief.

'I'm sure he would want as much done as possible towards dealing with this unfortunate circumstance,' said Daig. 'And quickly.'

She glanced back at Yosef. 'Please tell me again what it is that you need, reeve?'

He resisted the urge to smile and instead offered her the data-slate. 'There's an unidentified blood trace listed here. I require it to be cross-referenced with the Consortium's database for any matches.'

Gorospe took the slate and her practised smile reappeared. 'The Consortium will of course do anything possible to assist the Sentine in the pursuit of their lawful duties. Please wait here.' She walked swiftly away, leaving the two silent men standing watch.

After a moment, Daig glanced at his cohort. 'When Laimner finds out you brought us here without authorisation, the first thing he's going to do is rip you down to foot patrol in the slums.'

'No,' said Yosef, 'the first thing he's going to do is cover his ample backside with Telemach so she won't blame him for any fallout. But he won't be able to pull out anything about jurisdiction if we bring him some actual evidence.'

Daig watched Gorospe vanish into the main house. 'There is a large chance that she may not have anything we can use, you know.'

Yosef shot him a glare. 'Well, in that case, our careers are over.'

Daig nodded grimly. 'Just so we're both clear on that.'


THE NIGHT AIR was as warm as blood, and humid with it. It was still and oppressive, almost a palpable thing surrounding and pressing down on Fon Tariel. He sighed and used a micropore kerchief to dab at his head before returning to the nested layers of hololith panes floating above his cogitator gauntlet.

Across the sparse room, in a pool of shadow at the far window, the sniper sat cross-legged, his longrifle resting across the crook of his arm. Without turning, Kell spoke to him. 'Are you really in so much discomfort that you cannot sit still for more than a moment? Or is that twitching something common to all Vanus?'

Tariel scowled at the Vindicare. 'The heat,' he said, by way of explanation. 'I feel... soiled by it.' He glanced around; judging by the detritus scattered all about them, the room had once been the central space of a small domicile, before what appeared to be a combination of fire and structural collapse had ruined it. There were great holes in the roof allowing in the light, tepid rain from the low clouds overhead, and other rents in the floor that emitted smells Tariel's augmetic scent-sensors classified as human effluent, burned rodent meat and contaminated fusel oils. The building was deep in the ghetto shanties of the Yndenisc Bloc, where low-caste citizens were piled atop one another like rats in a nest.

'I'm guessing you don't leave your clade's sanctum very often,' said Kell.

'There hasn't been the need,' Tariel said defensively. He and his fellow infocytes and cryptocrats had taken part in many operations, all of them conducted through telepresent means directly from the sanctum, or from aboard an Officio-sanctioned starship. The thought of actually physically deploying *into the field* was almost an impossibility. 'This is my, uh, second sortie.'

'The first being when Valdor brought you looking for me?'

'Yes.'

Kell gave a sarcastic grunt. 'What wild stories you'll have to tell when you go home to your hive, little bee.'

Tariel's grimace hardened. 'Don't mock me. I'm only here because you need me. You won't find the girl without my assistance.'

The sniper still refused to look his way, eyes locked on the sights of his longrifle. 'That's true,' he offered. 'I'm just wondering why you have to be here with me to do it.'

Tariel had been asking himself the same thing ever since Captain-General Valdor had given mission command to the Vindicare and ordered them out to the tropics. As far as he could be certain, it seemed that operational confidence for this mission was of such paramount importance that detection of any live in-theatre signals transmitted from the Yndenisc Bloc to the Vanus sanctum could not be risked. He wondered what kind of foe could threaten to defeat the finest information security in the Imperium and found he had no answer; and the fact that such a threat could even exist troubled him in no small degree. 'The quicker we get it done, then, the quicker we can leave this place and each other's company,' he said, with genuine feeling.

'It will take as long as it takes,' Kell replied. 'Wait for the target to come to you.'

The infocyte disagreed but did not voice it. Instead, he returned to the hololiths, leafing through them as if they were pages made of glass hanging suspended in the air. Anyone watching him would have only seen the motions of his hands and nothing else; Tariel had tuned the images to a visual frequency only readable by his enhancile retinal lenses.

The penetration of the local sensor web had presented him with a minor impediment, but nothing that he would have considered challenging. The infocyte sent a small swarm of organic-metal netfly automata out to chew into any opti-cables they found, and parse what rich data flows they located back to him. Each fly was by itself a relatively unsophisticated device, but networked en masse, the information the swarm returned could be cohered into a dense picture of what was happening in the surrounding area. Tariel had already assembled maps of the nearby structures, the flows of foot and vehicular traffic, and he was currently worming his way into the encoding of several hundred monitor beads scattered throughout the zone.

The Yndeniscs called this locale the Red Lanes, and the area was a centre for what one might tactfully describe as hedonistic pursuits. The local confederation of warlords allowed the place a great degree of latitude from their already lax legal codes, and in return reaped a sizeable percentage of profit from the patronage of pleasure-tourists from all across Terra and the Sol system. Quite how a place like this was allowed to exist on the Throneworld was a mystery to Tariel, as much so as the tribes of bandits he had encountered out in the Atalantic Plain. His understanding of Imperial Terra was of a nation-world united and glorious – that was what he saw through the glassy lenses of his monitors from the safety of his workpod in the sanctum. But now, *outside*... He was quickly realising that there were many dirty, messy, dark corners that did not conform to his view of the Imperium.

A soft chime sounded from the gauntlet. 'Are you through?' asked Kell.

'Working,' he replied. The netflys had bored into a deep sub-web of imaging coils hidden several layers beneath the more obvious ones, and all at once he was assailed by a storm of images from the shielded rooms in a tall building across the square; images of men, women and other humans of indeterminate gender performing acts upon one another that were as fascinating as they were repulsive. 'I have... access,' he muttered. 'Commencing, uh, image match sweep.'

The facial pattern Valdor had provided to Tariel phased through the images, one after another, like looking for like. The infocyte tried to maintain an objective viewpoint, but the feeds he was seeing made him uncomfortable; if anything, he felt more soiled by them than by the dirt and humidity of the night air.

And then suddenly, she was there, the tawny skin of the girl's face dark in the lamplight of a red-lit room as the trace program found its target. 'Location confirmed,' he said.

'Good,' said Kell. 'Now find me a way to contact her before she gets killed.'


AND SO IOTA found herself in the room after opening her eyes. She had wondered if it would still be there when she looked again, and it was. This confirmed her earlier hypothesis, that the sensations she was experiencing were not hallucinatory but actually real. On some level, that was troubling to accept; perhaps, if she had understood her state more correctly, Iota would not have allowed some of the liberties that had been taken with her physical form to occur. But then again, they had been necessary to secure her cover in the Red Lanes. She remembered those activities distantly, like a half-recalled dream. The persona-implants that had been used to bolster the cover identity were crumbling like sand, and recollection of any particular point of them was difficult.

It wasn't important. The false overlay was drifting away, and beneath was revealed her real self; such as it was. Iota was not a blank slate, as those who did not fully understand the works of her clade might think. No. She was a fluid in the bottle of herself, a shape without definition, a form needing direction, a space to fill.

She surveyed the crimson room, the walls covered with rich velvet hangings sketched with erotic detail in gold threads, the great oval bed emerging from the deep carpeting. Floating lume-globes provided sultry lighting, with a shuttered window the only entrance for any natural illumination.

The men who ran the doxy-house seemed caught in some peculiar kind of attract-repel balance with her. Iota's gift made them uncomfortable without them ever knowing exactly why. Perhaps it was the hollow distance in her dark eyes, or the silence that was her habitual mien. However the gift manifested, it was enough to unsettle them. Some liked that, taking pleasure from the thrill of it as they might the tread of a scorpion across their naked flesh; most avoided her, though. She scared them without ever giving form to their fear.

Iota touched the ornamental torc around the dusky flesh of her throat. If only they knew how little of her they really sensed. Without the dampener device concealed in the necklet, the icy void inside her would have spread wide.

She sniffed the perfumed air. Iota felt odd to be out of her suit, but then she always did. The silken shift dress that covered her body was gossamer-thin, and she continually forgot that she was wearing it. Of its own accord, her right hand – her killing hand – reached up and buried itself in the tight cornrows of her shiny black hair. The hand toyed absently with the plaits dangling off her scalp, and she wondered how long it would be until the murder came. Her eyes wandered to the wooden box on the bed, and that was when she had her answer.

The other woman came into the room striding like a man, and around the back of her scalp she wore an emitter crown, the delicate filigree of crystalline psyber-circuits and implant tech glowing with soft light. She towered over the diminutive Iota, nearly two metres tall in elevated boots of shiny blue leather, a full and well-shaped body showing through a bustier-affair outfit that could only have been a few strips of hide if taken off and laid end to end. She carried a device that resembled a bulbous tonfa in one hand, one end of it bladed, the other crackling with energy.

The woman sneered at Iota. The expression was ugly and ill-fitting on her face, and Iota saw the small twitches of the nerves around her lips and nostrils as the crown worked on her. 'You're new,' said the woman. The words were slightly slurred.

Iota nodded, remaining downcast and passive.

'They tell me there's something odd about you,' she said, reaching for Iota's hand. 'Different.' The ugly sneer widened. 'I do enjoy things that are different.'

Then she knew for certain. There was a small chance it wasn't going to be him, but the clade had invested too much time and effort into inserting Iota into the right place at the right time for a mistake to happen at this late stage. The voice belonged to the woman, but the words – and the personality animating her at this moment – belonged to Jun Yae Jun, scion of one of the Nine Families of the Yndenisc Bloc and warlord-general. He was also, as intelligence had proven, a deceiver who was disloyal to the Imperial Throne, in violation of the Nikaea Edict, and suspected of involvement in a counter-secular cult.

'We will play.' Jun made the woman say the words. He was on the other end of the emitter crown, somewhere nearby, his body in repose while he forced his consciousness onto the flesh of the proxy. It was a game the warlord-general liked a great deal, working a meat-puppet in order to slake his desires. Iota was aware that many of her guardians back at her clade's holdfast viewed what Jun did with disgust, but she only felt a vague curiosity about him, the same clinical detachment that coloured almost all her interactions with other humans.

Iota wondered if the woman Jun controlled was conscious during the activities, and dispassionately considered the psychological effects that might have; but such thoughts were trivia. She had a murder to focus on. 'Wait,' she said. 'I have something for you,' Iota nodded at the box. 'A gift.'

'Give it to me,' came the demand.

Iota let the shift dress fall from her shoulders, and with Jun's second-hand gaze all over her, she picked up the box and brought it closer. Bloodlock sensors released the latches and she presented it, holding it up with one hand like a server offering a tray of food. The killing hand went to the torc and unfastened it.

'What is this?' A clumsy echo of Jun's confusion crossed the woman's face. 'A mask?'

The lume light fell over the shape of a metallic skull. One eye was a glittering ruby, but the other was a cluster of lenses made from milky sapphire, spiked with stubby vanes and strange antennae. 'Of a sort,' Iota explained.

The torc released with a delicate click and Iota felt a sudden rush of cold move through her, as if a floodgate inside her had opened. At least for the moment, she no longer needed to hold it all in, to keep the emptiness inside her bottled up.

Jun made a strange noise through the woman that was half-cry, half-yelp, and then the psychoactive matrix of the crown began to fizz and pop, the tonfa falling from the proxy's nerveless fingers. With a disordered, tinkling peal, the psionic crystals in the headdress began to shatter and the woman tottered on her spiked heels, stumbling over herself to fall upon the bed. She made moaning, weeping sounds.

Iota cocked her head to listen; the same chorus of wailing was coming from room after room down the corridor of the change-brothel, as the nulling effect of her raw self spread out.

Before the link could fully die, she sprang onto the bed and brought her face to the anguished woman's, staring into her eyes. 'I want to kiss you,' she told Jun.

Through the window, across the companionway from the brothel building, the doors of a nondescript residential slum block had broken open and a tide of panicked figures was spilling onto the street, all of them half-dressed in clothes that marked them too rich to be locals.

Iota nimbly leapt back to the floor and unfurled the stealthsuit lying beneath the skull-helm, stepping into it with careless ease. The mask went on last, and it soothed her as it did so.

The weeping woman coughed out a last, stuttered word as Jun's hold on her finally disintegrated. 'Cuh. Cuh. *Culexus.*'

But Iota did not wait to hear it; instead she threw herself through the window in a crash of glass and wood, spinning towards the other building.

WHILE THEY WAITED for Gorospe, Yosef glanced around the landing pad's surroundings. The fountains, which were usually gushing with coloured water, were silent; and when he looked closer, he noted that the well-tended gardens seemed, if anything, considerably unkempt. There were even dead patches in the otherwise flawless lawns; the Consortium appeared to be slacking on matters of minor maintenance. He wondered what that small detail could mean in the greater scheme of things.

Daig had made an attempt to engage one of the security men in conversation, resorting to his usual gambit of complaining about the weather, but the guard had been disinterested in talking. 'Nice outfits they have,' he opined, wandering back to the parked coleopter. 'Do you think they have to buy their own uniforms?'

'Considering a career change, then?'

Daig shrugged. 'Or maybe a sabbatical. A very long one, to somewhere quiet.' He glanced up into the sky, then away again.

Yosef sensed something in his cohort and found himself asking the question that had been preying on his mind for a time. 'Do you think he will come here?'

'The Warmaster?'

'Who else?' The air around them seemed suddenly still.

'The Arbites say the situation will be dealt with by the Astartes.' Daig's manner made it clear he didn't believe that.

Yosef frowned. Now he had asked the question, he found he couldn't stop thinking about it. 'I still find it hard to grasp. The idea of one of the Emperor's sons plotting a rebellion against him.' The concept seemed unreal, like the rain rebelling against the clouds.

'Laimner says there is no mutiny at all. He says it's a disinformation ploy by the Adeptus Terra to keep the planets out in the deeps off-balance, keep them loyal to the Throneworld. After all, a fearful populace is a compliant one.'

'Our esteemed Reeve Warden is a fool.'

'I won't argue that point,' Daig nodded. 'But then, is that any more shocking than the idea that the War-master would turn against his own father? What possible reason could he have to do that, unless he has some sort of sickness of the mind?'

Yosef felt a chill move through him, as if a shadow had passed over the sun. 'It's not a matter of lunacy,' he said, uncertain as to where the words were coming from. 'And fathers can be fallible, after all.'

He caught a flash of irritation on Daig's face. 'You're talking about ordinary men. The Emperor is far more than that.'

Yosef considered an answer, but then his attention was drawn away by the return of the Gorospe woman. Her carefully prepared expression of superior neutral-ity had been replaced by a severe aspect, concern and irritation there in equal measure. He had to wonder what she had found to instigate so profound a shift in her manner. She held the data-slate in her hand, along with a page of vinepaper. 'You have something for us?' he asked.

Gorospe hesitated, then tersely dismissed the two security men. When it was just the three of them, she gave the lawmen a firm stare. 'Before we go any further, there are a number of assurances that I must have from you. No information will be forthcoming if you refuse any of the following conditions, is that understood?'

'I'm listening,' said Yosef.

She ticked off the stipulations on her long, elegantly manicured fingers. 'This meeting did not occur; any attempt to suggest it did at a later date will be denied and may be considered an attempt at slander. Under no account are you to refer to the method in which this information was brought to you in any official records of investigation, now or at a later date in any legal setting. And finally, and most importantly, the name of the Eurotas Trade Consortium will in no way be connected to the suspect of your investigation.'

The two men exchanged glances. 'I suppose I have no choice but to agree,' said Yosef.

'Both of you,' she insisted.

'Aye, then,' said Daig, with a wary nod.

Gorospe handed back the data-slate and unfolded the vinepaper. On it, Yosef saw file text and an image of a thuggish man with heavy stubble and deep-set eyes. 'There was a match between the blood trace you provided and a single subject listed in our biomedical records. His name is Erno Sigg, and he is known to be at large on Iesta Veracrux.'

Yosef reached for the paper, but she held it away. 'He was a passenger on one of your ships?'

When the woman didn't answer straight away, Daig made the connection. 'That's a bondsman's record you have there, isn't it? Sigg isn't a passenger. He works for you.'

'Ah,' nodded Yosef, suddenly understanding. 'Well, that clears the mist, doesn't it? The last thing the Void Baron would want is the good name of his clan being connected to a murderous psychotic.'

'Erno Sigg is *not* an employee of the Consortium,' Gorospe insisted. 'He has not been a member of our staff for the last four lunars. His bond and his shares were cancelled in perpetuity with the clan, following an… incident.'

'Go on.'

The woman glanced at the paper. 'Sigg was cashiered after a violent episode on one of the Consortium's deep space trading stations.'

'He stabbed someone.' Yosef tossed out the guess and the widening of her eyes told him he was right. 'Killed them?'

Gorospe shook her head. 'There was no fatality. But a… a weapon was used.'

'Where is he now?'

'We have no record of that.'

Daig's lip curled. 'So you decided to throw him out, just dump a violent offender on our planet without so much as a warning to the local law enforcement? I think I could find a judiciary who would classify that irresponsible endangerment.'

'You misunderstand. Sigg was released after a period of detention commensurate with the severity of his misbehaviour.' Gorospe looked at the paper again. 'According to notations made by our security staff, he was genuinely remorseful. He voluntarily went into the custody of a charitable rehabilitation group here on Iesta Veracrux. That's why he asked to be released on this planet.'

'What group?' said Daig.

'The file notes it was part of an informal organisation called the Theoge.'

Yosef swore under his breath and snatched the paper from the woman's hand. 'Give me that. We'll take this from here.'

'Remember our arrangement!' she insisted, her cheeks colouring; but the reeve was already stalking away towards the coleopter.


THE WARLORD JUN Yae Jun bolted upright from the ornate couch where he lay, his robe falling open, scattering the attendants from his sides. He spluttered and snarled, tearing at the web of golden mechadendrites that were wrapped about his head, winding into his ear canals, nostrils and mouth. 'Get these things off me!' he bellowed, flailing around, knocking over a hookah and table piled with wine goblets and ampoules.

With an agonised wrench he finally freed himself and glared around, looking for his guardian. Jun could hear the sounds of violence and panic in the halls beyond the room. Something had gone very wrong, and a tide of terror was welling up inside him. He turned it into fury as he found the guardian on his hands and knees, staring into a pool of vomit.

Jun gave him a violent kick. 'What are you doing down there? Get up! Get up and protect me, you worthless wretch!'

The guardian stood, as shaky as a drunkard. 'There is darkness,' he muttered. 'Black curtains falling.' The man choked and coughed up bile.

Jun kicked him again. 'You were supposed to protect me! Why did you fail me?' His face was crimson with anger. In defiance of Imperial law, without grant or sanction from the Adeptus Terra, the warlord had secured himself a guardian who not only had combatant skills, but was also possessed of a measure of psychic ability. For months, his pet killer had been his most closely-guarded confidence, but now it seemed that his secret was out. 'There's a Culexus here! Do you know what that means?'

The guardian nodded. 'I know.'

When he had first heard the name of the assassin clade spoken, when the story of what the word meant had been told to him, the warlord did not believe it. He understood psykers, the humans gifted – some said *cursed* – by the touch of the warp. A psyker's essence burned bright in the realm of the immaterium, forever connecting the world of flesh with the world of the ethereal; but if psykers reflected the far extreme of a spectrum, and ordinary men and women the brief candles of life in the middle ground, then what could represent the opposite end of that balance? The darkness?

They were called *pariahs*. Chance births, less than one in a billion, children born, so it was said, without a soul. Where a psyker burned sun-bright, they were a black hole. They were antithesis, made manifest. Ice to the fire, darkness to the light.

And as with so many things, the Imperium of Man had found a use for such aberrations. The Clade Culexus harvested pariahs wherever they were found, and rumour suggested that they might even grow them wholesale from synthesis tanks in some secret fleshworks in the wilds of Terra. Jun Yae Jun had never believed in them until this moment, dismissed the very idea as a fiction created to instil fear in the kings and regents who ruled under the aegis of the Emperor. He knew fear now, though, and truth with it.

Jun stumbled towards the doorway, and hands pulled at his robes. 'Warlord, please,' said the attendant. The spindly man was speaking rapidly. 'Stop! The game has not been completed. There is the letting of fluids to be gathered, the sacrament!'

The warlord turned and glared at the attendant. Like all the others who ran this sordid diversion for the masters of the Red Lanes, he was draped in strips of silk and painted with bright inks. He had numerous daubs across his skin, repeating the shape of a disc, a rod and opposed crescents. The design was meaningless to Jun. He tried to shove the man away, but he would not let go.

'You must not leave!' snarled the attendant. 'Not yet!' He gripped the warlord's arm and held on tightly.

Jun spat and produced a push-dagger from a pocket. 'Get off me!' he roared, and stabbed the man in the throat with three quick moves. Leaving him to die, the warlord forced his way out into the corridor. The guardian stayed with him, his face pale and sweaty. He was mumbling to himself with every step. 'Vox!' shouted Jun. 'Give me your vox!'

The guardian obeyed. A line of blood was seeping from his right eye, like red tears.

Barging his way through the change-brothel's other clients, slashing a path with the push-dagger, the warlord barked a command string into the mouthpiece of the communicator. 'Air Guard,' he shouted. 'Deploy mobiles for zone strike, now now *now*!'

'*Location?*' asked the worried voice of the coordinator, back at the Yae clan compound.

'The Red Lanes!' he replied. 'Wipe it off the map!'

'*Lord, are you not in that area?*'

'Do it now!' It was the only way to be certain of killing the Culexus. He had no other option open to him.

IN THE RUINED apartment, Kell held his breath and listened. Over the disarray in the street below them, his spy mask's audial sensors had detected the sound of gravity-resist motors. 'Vanus,' he said. 'Do you hear that?'

'Gunships,' said Tariel, studying his hololiths. 'Cyclone-class. I read an attack formation.'

Kell's face twisted in a grimace, and he ejected the magazine from his weapon, quickly reloading it with a different kind of ammunition.

CROSSING THE COURTYARD, the warlord looked up into the rainy night as the first salvo of rockets slammed into the buildings surrounding the square. A massive fist of orange fire and black smoke engulfed the tallest of the shanty-towers, and curls of flame spun away, lighting new infernos wherever they landed.

His guardian was behind him, blinded by a roaring headache, barely able to stagger in a straight line, and with a monumental effort, the psyker bodyguard hauled himself to the groundcar parked near the gates. Dead bodies lay in a circle around the vehicle, shocked to death by the vehicle's autonomic security system. Recognising him, the car's driver-servitor opened the gull wing doors to allow the guardian and the warlord inside. Another strike hit home nearby, blasting tiles off the brothel's roof, sending them down to shatter harmlessly against the vehicle's armoured skin.

'Get me out of here,' demanded Jun. 'Stop for nothing.'

The guardian, half in and half out of the door, coughed suddenly and blood spluttered from his mouth. He turned, the pain in his skull burning like cold fire, as a figure in glistening black fell the distance from the roof to the courtyard floor. A ring of invisible force radiated out from it, causing a halo of rain to vaporise into mist.

'Kill her!' shouted the warlord, his voice high and filled with terror. 'Kill her!'

The psyker took a foot in the spine and Jun shoved him out of the safety of the car, onto his knees. The gull wing door slammed shut and sealed tight.

The Culexus assassin stepped forwards as the guardian got up again, catching sight of the rain rolling down the contours of her skull-helm, dripping from the orbit of the single ruby eye as if she were weeping. The guardian reached inside himself and went deep, past the blazing pain, past the horrific wave of nothingness that threatened to drown him. He found a breath of fire and released it.

The pyrokinetic pulse chugged into existence, streaming from his twitching fingertips. The blast hit the Culexus dead on, and she backed away, shaking her distended steel head; but the tiny flare of hope the guardian experienced died a second later as the fire ebbed, almost as if it had been pulled into the ribbing of the assassin's sinister garb.

He was aware of the car moving forwards in fits and starts, but his attention could not stray from the grinning, angular skull. The sapphire eye-clutch shimmered and the punishing gaze of the weapon known as the animus speculum was turned upon him.

Power, raw and inchoate, sucked in from the fabric of the warp and from the guardian's abortive attack, drawn in like light from the event horizon of a singularity, was now unleashed. A pulse of energy flashed from the psychic cannon and blasted the warlord's bodyguard backward, slamming him into the wall of the courtyard. As he tumbled to the ground, he combusted from within, the fire consuming his flesh and his screams.

JUN YAE JUN was shouting incoherently at his driver-servitor as it used the bull-bars on the groundcar's prow to shoulder pedestrians out of the way. The vehicle made it onto the street as fresh salvos of rocket fire tore the Red Lanes into rubble. The servitor gunned the engine and aimed the car towards the bridge that led back towards the Yae compound.

A black blur fluttered in the light of an explosion and the armoured windscreen cracked and crazed as indigo fire lashed across it. Great gobs of polymer glass denatured and collapsed, smothering the servitor in a suffocating blanket of superheated plastic. The car spun out and collided with a bollard.

Jun pulled wildly at the door's locking handle, then stabbed it with the push-dagger. He was operating on blind panic.

Taking her time, the Culexus clambered in through the destroyed window and disarmed him, almost as an afterthought. The warlord soiled himself as the skull came closer. 'I'm sorry I'm sorry I'm sorry I'm sorry–'

'Kiss me,' she said, her voice devoid of all emotion.

Jun's lips were pressed to the cold steel of the mask, and agony spiked through him. He fell back, and spat dust. Raw pain boiled at his extremities as his flesh blackened and became thick ash, crumbling before his eyes until those too rotted in their sockets and shrivelled to nothing. Jun Yae Jun's very energy of life was drawn from him, leached into the force matrix webbing the assassin's stealthsuit, until there was nothing left of him but a slurry of indeterminate matter.

IOTA LEFT THE target's vehicle and the area around her was suddenly drenched in brilliant white light. The downdraught from a gravity drive beat at the ground, stirring up debris and what remained of the warlord. The sensor suite inside her helm registered a gunship's weapons grid locking on to her silhouette, and she paused, wondering if it were possible for her to die.

In the next moment, she saw a line of light across the infrared spectrum as a single high-impact bullet passed through the armoured canopy of the gunship, beheading both the pilot and the gunner. Suddenly unguided, the Cyclone's autoflight system kicked in and brought it down to a soft landing.

Presently two men, one in the operations gear of the Vindicare clade and another in a more basic stealth rig, emerged from one of the smouldering buildings. Iota glanced at them, then went back to watching the spreading fires.

As the sniper tipped the corpses from the flyer's cockpit, the other man warily approached her. 'Iota?' he asked. 'Protiphage, Clade Culexus?'

'Of course it's her,' said the Vindicare. 'Don't be obtuse, Tariel.'

'You have to come with us,' said the one called Tariel. He indicated the gunship as the sniper took the controls.

Iota ran a finger over the grinning teeth of her skull-mask. 'Will you kiss me too?'

The man went pale. 'Perhaps later?'

# FIVE

**Fears**
**Release**
**Innocence**

'HUSBAND?'

Renia's hand on Yosef's shoulder shocked him out of the dreamless doze he had fallen into at the kitchen table; so much so that he almost knocked over the glass of black tea by his hand. Before it could tip, he snatched it back upright without spilling a drop.

He gave her a weak smile. 'Heh. Quicker this time.'

Yosef's wife gathered her thick housecoat around her and took the seat across from him. It was late, deep into the evening, and the house was unlit except for a single lume over the table. It had a sharp-edged shade around it that forced the cast light into a cone, reducing everything beyond it to vague shapes in the shadows.

'Is Ivak up as well?'

'No. He's still asleep, and I'm pleased to see it. With everything that's been going on, he's had a lot of bad dreams.'

'Has he?' Yosef asked the question and immediately felt a flicker of guilt. 'I've been absent a lot
recently...'

'Ivak understands,' Renia said, cutting him off. 'I
didn't hear you come in,' she noted.

Yosef nodded and resisted the urge to yawn. 'You
and the boy had already turned in. I didn't want to
wake you, so I made tea...' He sipped at the glass and
found the contents had gone cold.

'And fell asleep in the chair?' She tutted quietly.
'You're doing this too often these days, Yosef.' Renia
brushed some stray threads of copper-coloured hair
out of her eyes.

He nodded. 'I'm sorry. It's the investigation.' Yosef
sighed. 'It's... troubling.'

'I've heard,' she said. 'The watch-wire was running
stories about it for a while, before the news from
Dagonet came in. Now that is all anyone is talking
about.'

Yosef blinked. 'Dagonet?' he repeated. The planet
was a trading partner with Iesta Veracrux, a few light
years distant down the spine of the Taebian Sector's
mercantile routes, in a system orbiting a pale yellow
sun. By the interstellar scales of the Imperium of Man,
Dagonet was practically a neighbour. He asked his
wife to explain; Yosef and Daig had both been buried
in research on the serial murders all day long, fruit-
lessly looking for information about Erno Sigg, and
neither of them had seen anything that wasn't a case
file or medical report.

For the first time since she had broken his dozing,
Yosef realised that Renia was hiding something, and as
she talked it became clear. She was worried.

'Some ships came into the system from Dagonet,' Renia began. 'The Planetary Defence Force monitors couldn't catch them all, there were so many.'

Yosef felt a peculiar thrill of fear in his chest. 'Warships?'

She shook her head. 'Transports, liners, that sort of thing. All Dagoneti ships. Some of them barely made it out of the warp in one piece. They were all overloaded with people. The ships were full of *refugees*, Yosef.'

'Why did they come here?' Even as he asked the question, he knew what the answer was most likely to be. Ever since stories of the galactic insurrection had broken out across the sector, Dagonet's government had been noticeably reticent to commit on the subject.

'They were running. Apparently, there's an uprising going on out there. The population are split over their... loyalty.' She said the word as if it was foreign to her, as if the idea of being *disloyal* to Terra was a totally alien concept. 'It's a revolt.'

Yosef frowned. 'The Governor on Dagonet won't let things run out of control. The noble clans won't let the planet fall into anarchy. If the Imperial Army or the Astartes have to intervene there–'

Renia shook her head and touched his hand. 'You don't understand. It's the Dagoneti clans who *started* the uprising. The Governor issued a formal statement of support for the Warmaster. The nobles have declared in favour of Horus and rejected the rule of Terra.'

'What?' Yosef felt suddenly giddy, as if he had stood up too quickly.

'The common people are the ones fighting back. They say there is blood in the streets of the capital. Soldiers fighting soldiers, militia fighting clan guards. Those who could flee filled every ship they could get their hands on.'

He sat quietly, letting this sink in. There was, he had to admit, a certain logic to the chain of events. Yosef had visited Dagonet in his youth and he recalled that Horus Lupercal was second only to the Emperor in being celebrated by the people of the planet; statues in the Warmaster's honour were everywhere, and the Dagoneti spoke of him as 'the Liberator'. As the historic record went, in the early years of the Great Crusade to reunite the lost colonies of humanity, Dagonet languished under the heel of a corrupt and venal priest-king who ruled the planet through fear and superstition. Horus, at the head of his Luna Wolves Legion, had come to Dagonet and freed a world – accomplishing the deed with only one round of ammunition expended, the single shot he fired that dispatched the tyrant. The victory was one of the Warmaster's most celebrated triumphs, and it ensured he would be revered forever as Dagonet's saviour.

Small wonder then, that the aristocratic clans who now ruled the planet would give their banners to him instead of a distant Emperor who had never set foot on their world. Yosef's brow creased in a frown. 'If they follow Horus...'

'Will Iesta follow suit?' said Renia, completing his question for him. 'Terra is a long way from here, Yosef, and our Governor is no stronger-willed than the rulers of Dagonet. And if the rumours are true, the Warmaster may be closer than we know.' His wife reached out again and took both his hands, and this time he noticed that she was trembling. 'They say that the Sons of Horus are already on their way to Dagonet, to take control of the entire sector.'

He tried to summon a fraction of his firm, steady voice, the manner he had been trained to display as a reeve when the citizens looked to him in time of danger. 'That won't happen. We have nothing to be afraid of.'

Renia's expression – her love for him for trying to protect her there, but intermingled with stark fear – told him that for all his efforts, he did not succeed.


THE CHEMICAL SNOWS of the Aktick Zone, thick feathery clumps tainted a sickly yellow from thousands of years of atmospheric contaminants, beat at the canopy of the aircraft. Out beyond the bullet-shaped nose of the transport, there was only a featureless cowl of grey sky and the whirling storm. Eristede Kell gave it a glance and then turned away, stepping back from the raised cockpit deck to the small cabin area behind it.

'How much longer?' said Tariel, who sat strapped into a thrust couch, a half-finished logica puzzle in his soft, thin fingers.

'Not long,' Kell told him, deliberately giving him a vague answer.

The Vanus's face pinched in irritation, and he fiddled with the complex knot of the logica without really paying attention to it. 'The sooner we get there, the happier I will be.'

'Nervous passenger?' the sniper asked, with mild amusement.

Tariel heard it in his voice and fired him an acid look. 'The last aircraft I was in got shot down over the desert. That hasn't exactly made me well-disposed to the whole experience.' He discarded the logica – which, to his surprise, Kell realised the Vanus had completed without apparent effort – and pulled up his sleeve to minister to his cogitator gauntlet. 'I still don't understand why I am needed here. I should have returned with Valdor.'

'The Captain-General has duties of his own to attend to,' said Kell. 'For now on, we're on our own.'

'So it would seem.' Tariel threw a wary look to the far end of the cabin, where the girl Iota was sitting. Tariel had placed himself as far away from her as it was possible to get and still be inside the aircraft's crew compartment.

For her part, the Culexus appeared wholly occupied with the pattern of the rivets on the far bulkhead, running her long fingers over the surface of them, back and forth. She seemed lost in the repeated, almost autistic actions.

'Operational security,' said Kell. 'Valdor's orders were quite clear. We assemble the team he wants, and no one must learn of it.'

Tariel paused, and then leaned closer. 'You know what she is, don't you?'

'A pariah,' sniffed the Vindicare. 'Yes, I know what that means.'

But the Vanus was shaking his head. 'Iota is designated as a protiphage. She's not human, Kell, not like you or I. The girl is a replicae.'

'A clone?' The sniper looked back at the silent Culexus. 'I would not think it beyond the works of

her clade to create such a thing.' Still, he wondered
how the genomasters would have gone about it. Kell
knew that the Emperor's biologians were greatly
skilled and possessed of incredible knowledge – but
to make a living person, whole and real, from cells in
a test tube…

'Exactly!' insisted Tariel. 'A being without a soul.
She's closer to the xenos than to us.'

A smile pulled briefly at Kell's lips. 'You're afraid of
her.'

The infocyte looked away. 'In all honesty, Vindicare,
I am afraid of most things. It's the equilibrium of my
life.'

Kell accepted this with a nod. 'Tell me, have you ever
been face to face with one of the Eversor?'

Tariel's face went ashen, the tone of his cheeks pal-
ing to match the polar snows outside the flyer's
viewports. 'No,' he husked.

'When that happens,' Kell went on, 'then you'll truly
have something to be afraid of.'

'That's where we're going,' offered Iota. Both of
them had thought the girl to be wrapped up in whatever private reality existed inside her mind, but now
she turned away from the bulkhead and spoke as if
she had been a part of the conversation all along. 'To
fetch the one they call the Garantine.'

Kell's eyes narrowed. 'How do you know that
name?' He had not spoken of the next assassin on Valdor's list.

'Vanus are not the only ones who know things.' She
cocked her head to stare at Tariel. 'I've seen them.
Eversor.' Iota's hand strayed to her skull-helm, where
it rested nearby on a vacant passenger couch. 'Like and

like.' She smiled at the infocyte. 'They are rage distilled. Pure.'

Tariel glared at the sniper. 'That's why we're out here in this icy wilderness? To get one of *them*?' He shuddered. 'A primed cyclonic warhead would be safer!'

Kell ignored him. 'You know the Garantine's name,' he said to Iota. 'What else do you know?'

'Pieces of the puzzle,' she replied. 'I've seen what he left behind. The tracks of blood and broken meat, the spoor of the vengeance killer.' She pointed at Tariel. 'The infocyte is right, you know. More than any one of us, the Garantine is a weapon of terror.'

The matter-of-fact way she said the words made Kell hesitate; ever since Valdor had appeared out there in the deserts with his commands and his authority handed down from the Master of Assassins himself, the Vindicare's sense of unease had grown greater by the day, and now Iota cut to the heart of it. They were lone killers, all of them in their own ways. This gathering together sat wrongly with him; it was not the way in which things were to be done. And somewhere, deep in the back of his thoughts, Eristede Kell found he was also afraid of what such orders boded.

'Vindicare!' He turned as the transport pilot called out his clade's name. 'Approach control doesn't answer. Something is wrong!'

Tariel muttered something about his cursed luck and Kell brushed past him, back into the cockpit. The pilot was already pushing the transport into a steep turn. Below them, distinguished only by a slight change in the tone of the chem-snow, he spotted the mottled lifeless landscape of the Aktick ranges through the spin and whirl of the blizzard-borne ice.

There, beneath the craft, was a low blockhouse of heavy ferrocrete, distinguishable only by stripes of weather-faded crimson outlining the edges of it, and the steady blink of locator beacons. But where there should have been the hex-shape of a landing silo, there was only a maw belching black smoke and flickers of fire.

Kell caught the tinny sound of panicked voices coming through the pilot's vox-bead, and as they banked, he thought he saw the blink of weapons discharges down inside the silo proper. His jaw stiffened; this was no chance accident. He knew exactly what had happened.

'Oh. They woke him,' said Iota, from behind, giving voice to his thoughts. 'That was a mistake.'

'Take us in,' Kell snapped.

The pilot's eyes widened behind his flight goggles. 'The silo is on fire and there's nowhere else to set down! We have to abort!'

The Vindicare shook his head. 'Land us on the ice!'

'If I put this craft down there, it might never lift again,' said the pilot, 'and if–'

Kell silenced him with a look. 'If we don't deal with this right now, by sunrise tomorrow every settlement within a hundred kilometre radius will be a slaughterhouse!' He pointed at the snow fields. 'Land this thing, *now*!'

INSTEAD OF RETURNING home to the small apartment cluster where he lived alone, out near the western edge of the radial park, Daig Segan took a public conveyor to the old market district. At this time of night, none of the stalls were open to make sales but they were still hives of activity; men and women loaded produce and prepared for the dawn shift, moving crates on dollies this way and that across shiny tiled floors that were slick with sluice-water.

Daig crossed the covered market to the other conveyor halt and took the first ride that came in, irrespective of its destination. As the monorail moved along the line embedded in the cobbled street bed, he gave the carriage a long, careful sweep, running over the faces of the other passengers with a policeman's wary eye. There were only a handful of people. Three teenagers in loader's hoods, tired and serious-looking. An old couple, bound for home. Men and women in work-cloaks. None of them spoke. They either stared into the middle distance, or looked blankly out the windows of the conveyor. Daig could sense the tension in them, the unfocussed fear. It manifested in short tempers and hollow gazes, brittle silences and morose sighs. All these people and everyone like them, all were looking to a horizon lit by the distant fires of war, and they wondered – *when will it reach us?* It seemed as if Iesta Veracrux was holding its collective breath as the shadow of the rebellion drew ever closer. Daig looked away and watched the streets roll by.

He rode for three stops before disembarking once more. He took another conveyor back the way he came, this time stepping off the running board just as it pulled away from the halt before the market. The reeve jogged across the road, throwing a glance over his shoulder to be certain he had not been followed. Then, his toque pulled low to his brow line, Daig vanished into an ill-lit alleyway and found his way to an unmarked metal door.

A shutter opened in the door and a round, florid face peered out at him. Recognition split the face in a broad smile. 'Daig. We haven't seen you in a good while.'

'Hello, Noust.' He nodded distractedly. 'Can I come in?'

The door creaked open in reply and he stepped through.

Inside it was warm, and Daig blinked a few times, his eyes watering as the chilled skin of his face thawed a little. Noust handed him a tin cup with a measure of mulled wine in it and the reeve followed the other man down a steel staircase. A breath of gentle music wafted up on the warm air as they descended.

'I wondered if you might have changed your mind,' said Noust. 'Sometimes that happens. People question things after they take on the belief. It's like buyer's remorse.' He gave a dry chuckle.

'It's not that,' said Daig. 'It's just that I haven't been able to get here. It's the work.' He sighed. 'I have to be careful.'

Noust shot him a look over his shoulder. 'Of course you do. We all do, especially in the current climate. He understands.'

Daig sighed, feeling guilty. 'I hope so.'

The staircase deposited them in a cellar with a low ceiling. Lumes had been glued to the walls along the long axis of the chamber, and in rough rows there were a collection of seats – some plastiformed things pilfered from office plexes, others threadbare sofas from lost homes, a few little more than artfully cut packing crates – all of them arranged in a semi-circle around a cloth-covered table. Red-printed leaflets lay on some of the chairs.

High-Reeve Kata Telemach would have given much to find this place. It was one of a handful, each concealed in plain sight across Iesta Veracrux. There was no identifying symbol to show it was here, no secret passwords to be spoken or special sign that would grant access. It was simply that those who were called to know these places found them of their own accord, or else they were brought here by the like-minded; and despite what the High-Reeve insisted, despite all the hearsay and foolish gossip that was spread about what took place in such cellars and hidden spaces, there were no horrors, no murderous blood rites or dark ceremonies. There were only ordinary souls that made up the membership of the Theoge, that and nothing more. He thought on this as he rubbed his thumb over the smoothed gold of the aquila talisman about his wrist.

On the table, there was an elderly holographic projector that flickered and hummed; a blue-tinted image of Terra floated above it, a time-lapse loop of the planet's day-night cycle. At the side of the projector was a book, open at a page of dense text. The book was made of common-quality vinepaper and it had been bound without a cover; Daig understood that a friend of Noust's who worked the nightshift at an inkworks had used cast-offs from other jobs and downtime between the print runs of paying customers to run out multiple copies of the document.

The pages were careworn from many sets of hands upon them, and he wanted to pick them up and leaf through them, draw comfort from the writings. Daig knew that he only had to ask, and Noust would give him a copy of his own to keep, but to have the book in his home, somewhere it could be discovered by mistake or worse, used to incriminate him by people who didn't understand the true meaning contained in it... He couldn't take the risk.

Noust was at his side. 'You timed it well. We were just about to have a reading. You'll join us, yes?'

Daig looked up. There were only a few other people in the cellar, some of whom he knew, others not so familiar. He spotted a new face and recognised him as a jager from the precinct; the man returned a wary look, but Daig gave him a nod that communicated a shared confidence. 'Of course,' he said to Noust.

A youth with a bandaged hand picked up the book and handed it to Daig's friend. On the front was the only element of adornment on the otherwise Spartan document.

Picked out in red ink, the words *Lectitio Divinitatus*.

IF THE GARANTINE had once possessed a true name, that time was long ago and of little consequence. The entire concept of a *past* and a *future*, these were strange abstracted notions to the Eversor. They were things that – if he had been able to stop to dwell on them – would have only brought tics of confusion; and as with all things about him, *rage*.

The Eversor existed only in a permanent state of the furious *now* and matters of before and after were limited to the most transitory of elements. Before, just heartbeats earlier, he had beheaded a guard attempting to down him with some kind of heavy webber cannon. In a moment more, he would leap the distance across the open space where the handling gantry for the flyers did not reach, in order to land among

the group of technicians who were fleeing towards a
doorway. In these small ways, the Garantine allowed
himself to comprehend the nature of past and future,
but to go beyond that was pointless.

It was the manner of his life that he existed in the
thick of the killing. He had a dim understanding of
the other times, the times when he would lie in the
baths of amnio-fluids as the patient machines of his
clade healed his wounds or upgraded the stimjectors
and drug glands throughout his body. The times
when, in the dreamless no-sleep between missions,
hypnogoge data streams would unfold in his head like
blossoms of information, target profiles linked to
mood-triggers that would give him bursts of elation
for every kill, jolts of pleasure for each waypoint
reached, jerks of pain if he deviated off-programme.

These things had not happened here, though. He
reflected on that as he completed his leap, his aug-
mented muscles relaxing to take the impact of
landing, the sheer force of his arrival killing one of the
fleeing technicians immediately. As he spun about,
the knife-claws on his hands and feet opening veins,
the grinning rictus of his steel skull-mask steaming
with splashes of blood, he searched for a programme,
for a set of victory conditions.

There was none. Digging deeper, he reached for his
stunted *past*. He remembered back as far as he could –
an hour, perhaps? He replayed the moment. A sudden
awakening. The transit cocoon that held him in its
silent, womb-like space, where he could wait out the
non-time until his next glorious release; suddenly broken. An error, or something else? Enemy action? That
assumption was the Garantine's default setting, after

all. He reasoned – as much as he was able – that surely if he had been awakened for any other reason, the hypnogoges would have ensured he knew why.

But there was nothing. No parameters, only wakefulness. And for an Eversor, to be awake was to be in the glory of killing. A cocktail of stimulants and battle drugs boiled through his bloodstream, heavy doses of Fury, Spur and Psychon synthesised to order by the compact biofac implants in his abdomen. Under normal circumstances, the Garantine would have been armed with more than just his skinplanted offensive weapons and helm-mask; he would have been sheathed in armour and arrayed with a suite of servo-systems. That he did not have these only served to modify the killer's approach to his targets. He had taken and employed several light stubber guns, using each until the ammo drum ran dry, then making the weapons into clubs he used to beat his kills to the floor; but the stubbers were only good for a few hits before his violence broke them across the frame and he was forced to discard them.

He punched a man with enough energy that it shattered his skull, and then he vaulted a makeshift barricade, moving faster than the men hiding behind it could aim. He killed them with their own guns and ran on, deeper through the complex.

Parts of the building might have looked familiar to him, if the Garantine had been able to stop the racing pace of his thoughts, if he had been able to slow his kill-need for just a moment; but he could do neither.

In the absence of orders, with no target to aim for, the Eversor did what he was trained to do; and he would go on, killing here and then moving on to the

next set of targets, and the next and the next, forever
in the moment.

AFTERWARDS, DAIG FELT refreshed by his experience,
but he had not come to the meeting for personal reasons. While some of the others talked amongst
themselves, the reeve took Noust to one side and the
two men shared cups of the warm wine, and questions.

Noust listened in silence to Daig's explanation of
his caseload, and at length, he gave a nod. 'I know
Erno Sigg. I guessed that might be why you'd come to
see me. His face was on the public watch-wire. Said
that he was sought after to assist in your "enquiries".'

Daig suppressed a wince. Laimner, on Telemach's
orders, had deliberately leaked Sigg's image to the
media in a ham-fisted attempt to flush him into the
open; but if anything, it appeared to have driven the
man deeper into hiding.

Noust continued. 'He's a troubled fellow, to be certain. Someone without a compass, you could say. But
that's where the Theoge can be of help to a man. He
learned of the text while he was incarcerated, from a
ship-hand. Erno found another path with us.' He
looked away. 'At least, for a time he did.'

Daig leaned in. 'What do you mean?'

Noust eyed him. 'Is that you asking, Daig Segan? Or
is it the Sentine?'

'Both,' he replied. 'This is important. You know I
wouldn't ask if it wasn't.'

'Aye, that's so.' Noust sighed. 'Here's the thing. For a
while, Erno was a regular fixture here, and he was trying to make something of himself. He wanted to make

amends. Erno was working to become a better man than the angry, frustrated thug he'd left out there in space. It's a long road, but he knew that. But then he started to come around less often.'

'When did this happen?'

'A few demilunars ago. Two, maybe. When I did see him, he was twitchy. He said that he was going to have to pay for what he had done.' Noust paused, sorting through his thoughts. 'I got the impression that some- one was... I don't know, following him? He was irritable, paranoid. All the old, bad traits coming back to the fore.'

Daig rubbed his chin. 'He may have killed people.'

Noust gave the reeve a shocked look. 'No. *Never*. Maybe once upon a time, but not now. He's not capa- ble of that, not any more. I'd swear that to the God-Emperor himself.'

'I need to find Erno,' said Daig. 'If he's innocent, we need to prove it. We... *I* need to protect all this.' He gestured around. 'I found my path here. I can't lose it.' Daig imagined what might happen if Telemach or Laimner got hold of Sigg, broke him in interrogation and then found the door to this place. In their secu- lar, clinical world there was no place for the revelation of the Imperial Truth, the undeniable real- ity of the Emperor's shining divinity. The church, such as it was, and all the others like it would be torn down, burned away, and the words of the *Lectitio Divinitatus* that had so transformed Daig Segan when he read them would be erased and left unheard. They would use Sigg and the crimes to excuse them as they put a torch to it all.

'The Emperor protects,' said Noust.

'And I'll help Him do it, if you give me the chance,' insisted the reeve. 'Just tell me where Erno Sigg is hiding.'

Noust finished his drink. 'All right, brother.'

BEHIND HER, SHE heard the clattering thunder of auto-fire and more screams. Iota skidded to a halt on the cold metal floor and cocked her head, letting her skull-helm's autosenses take readings and pass the analysis back to her. He was very close; she had attracted his interest by appearing in the middle of a companionway, letting him see her clearly, and then breaking into a run. The Eversor knew another assassin when he saw one, and she was without doubt the most serious threat vector the rage-killer had encountered since his awakening. He was coming for her, but that didn't stop him from pausing along the way to dispatch any of the facility's staff who were unlucky enough to cross his path. The murderers of the Clade Eversor were like that; for all their bloody violence and instinct-driven brutality, they were still methodical. They left no witnesses, nothing but corpses.

Iota waited, rocking on her heels, ready to break into a run the moment he spotted her again. From what the infocyte had managed to piece together from the base's cogitators, it seemed that there had been a catastrophic accident during the retrieval of the Garantine from one of the deep cold iso-stores beneath the mantle of the Aktick ice. The cryopod containing the assassin in his dormant state had cracked a fluid line; the burst conduit sprayed super-chilled methalon across the handlers, flash-freezing them all in an instant. By the time another team had made it down to the transfer area, the pod had drained and the Garantine was already awake. Even in his semi-dormant, unarmed state, they were easily cut down by him.

The clade's technologians made the fatal mistake of addressing the problem of the coolant leak first – an easy choice to understand, given that this particular facility housed another nine Eversor field operatives down in the iso-stores. Left unchecked, the Garantine's brethren would have eventually followed him into wakefulness. But the time spent stabilising the storage compartments had allowed the Garantine to fully thaw and begin the business of terminating every living being in the facility.

'*Culexus? Where are you?*' said Tariel, his voice a hiss in her helmet vox.

'Area eight, tier one, facing west,' she replied. 'Waiting.'

'*I've accessed the main systems library,*' he told her, clearly impressed with his own achievement. '*I'm closing the pressure hatches behind him as he moves.*'

Iota glanced down at the multi-barrelled combineedler fixed to her right wrist, considering it. 'He's not an animal, Vanus. He'll know if you're trying to herd him.'

'*Just keep him reactive,*' came the reply.

She didn't say any more, because at that moment the Garantine came storming around the bend in the corridor, his thickset, densely-muscled body rippling with exertion. Chugs of white vapour puffed into the cold air from behind his metal mask, and as he moved, Iota saw the places where his bare skin showed and the shapes of implants beneath. The

Garantine was covered from head to toe with daubs of human blood. He halted, rumbling like an engine, and eyed her with a low chuckle. In one hand he had a stubber carbine, liquid dripping from the blunt maw of the barrel.

She thought for a fleeting instant about attempting to reason with him, then dismissed the idea just as quickly. There were rumours that every Eversor had an abeyance meme encoded into their brains, a nonsense string of words that would lull them into inaction, or even send them into neuro-death if spoken aloud; but if this were so, Iota was sure that the rage-killer would have made certain any technologians in the base who knew the code were no longer able to voice it.

The Garantine pointed the broken gun at her. 'You,' he said thickly. 'Quick.'

Perhaps it was a threat – a promise that he was going to end her swiftly – or perhaps it was a compliment on her agility, acknowledging Iota as the first real challenge he had come across since awakening. It mattered little; in the next second he was coming at her, charging like an enraged grox.

She fired a blast of glassaic needles at him, describing a seamless back flip to open the distance between them. The glittering shots clattered across the Eversor's torso, burying themselves in the meat of his chest, but the rage-killer only grunted and batted them away.

Iota spun to a halt in front of a large oval exterior hatchway, as Tariel's voice reached her once more. *'Is he there?'* came the urgent question. *'I... I am having difficulty reading the location of the Garantine...'*

She nodded to herself. Among the many implants beneath the flesh of an Eversor were passive sensing baffles that could confuse the detector heads of many conventional scanners. 'Oh, he's here,' Iota told him. 'He will murder me in less than one hundred and ten seconds.' The prediction was based on observing the other kills the Garantine had made.

'*Working,*' said the infocyte, a new urgency in his words.

'Take your time,' she replied.

The Eversor halted and cocked his head, considering her. Iota took a breath and drew in on herself. She let the force matrix built into the structure of her stealth-suit come alive, allowing it to reach its web of influence beyond the real and into the etherium of the warp; but the process was slow. Had she been fighting a psyker, she could have drained them dry in a moment, siphoned off their power for herself. But here and now, there was nothing but the common-place energy of air and heat and life. She felt the eye of the animus speculum slowly iris open – but even as it did she knew it would not be ready in time.

The other assassin grunted out a laugh and stooped to rip a short stanchion pole from a support pillar, tearing it off in a flutter of sparks. He brandished the steel rod like a club and went for her.

At once, the hatch at Iota's back groaned on heavy hydraulics and fanned open with a clatter of fracturing ice. A blast of polar air and windborne snow thundered in around her from outside. For a moment, the snowstorm whirled into the corridor, filling the space with whiteness.

The energy inside the animus was approaching readiness, but as she had predicted, the Garantine killer had her range and he did not hesitate again.

Before Iota could release even a fraction of the psy-weapon's potential, he slammed the bar into her chest with such force that she flew backwards, out into the snow-filled courtyard. Iota noted the snapping of several of her ribs with a disconnected understanding. She landed badly in a shallow drift of white and coughed up a stream of bloody spittle into her helmet. The fact she wasn't dead made it clear he wanted to toy with her first.

They called him the Garantine because it was said he hailed from the Garant Span, an Oort cloud collective on the near side of the Perseus Null. A natural psychotic, he had killed everyone on his home asteroid, and all this as a child barely able to read. It was no wonder the Clade Eversor had been delighted to take ownership of him.

Iota struggled to get up, and through the optics of her skull-helm she looked to see another grinning rictus come into view. The Garantine grabbed her by the ankle and effortlessly threw her across the courtyard. This time the impact was lessened by a deep snow bank, but still the shock vibrated through her. She let out a tiny cry of pain. In her ear, the Vanus was jabbering something about closing the hatch, but that had no consequence to her. Iota focussed on bringing the animus to a firing state. If their plan failed, she would have to be the one to kill him, crushing his fevered mind with a blast of pure warp energy.

The Eversor bounded towards her, laughing, and at the last moment he leapt into the air. Time seemed to thicken and slow, the hazy man-shape falling down towards her; then she was distantly aware of a heavy report and suddenly the Garantine's fall was deflected.

He jerked away at a right angle, as if pulled on an invisible cord.

Iota saw the steaming wound in the rage-killer's chest as he stumbled back to his clawed feet, shaking off the strike. Her head swimming, the Culexus searched and then found the source of the attack. A shimmering white figure stood up atop one of the nearby blockhouses, a longrifle in his grip. The white colouration faded into ink-black as the Vindicare deliberately reset his cameoline cloak to a null mode, allowing the Eversor to see him clearly. He raised the rifle to his shoulder as the rage-killer roared at him, and for the moment Iota was apparently forgotten.

The Eversor charged again, and the rifle shouted. The first shot had been a kinetic impact round, the kind of bullet that could shatter the engine block of a hover truck or reduce an unarmoured man to meat; that had been enough to attract the Garantine's attention. The next shot whistled through the frigid air, blurring as it impacted the Eversor's chest. The round was a heavy dart, fashioned from high-density glas-saic. It contained a reservoir of gel within, pressure-injected into the target's flesh on impact; but it was not a drug or philtre. An Eversor's body was a chemical hell of dozens of interacting combat medicines, and no poison, no sedative could have been enough to slow it. The gel-matter in the rounds was a myofluid with a very different function; when exposed to oxygen it created a powerful bioelectric charge, a single hit strong enough to stun an ogryn.

It was a non-lethal attack, and the Garantine seemed incensed by that, as if he were insulted that so trivial a weapon was being used on him. He tore out

the dart and came on. Kell fired again, flawlessly striking the same spot, and then again, and then a third
time. The Eversor did not falter, even as crackles of
blue sparks erupted from the weeping wound in his
chest.

For one moment, Iota felt a rare stab of fear. How
many rounds did the Vindicare have in the magazine
of his longrifle? Would it be enough? She ignored the
Vanus shouting in her ear and watched, as the crash of
shot after shot was swallowed up by the hush of the
falling snows.

The Eversor leapt up to where the Vindicare stood
and swung a taloned hand at him, but his balance faltered, the warshot of a dozen darts pinning his flesh.
The blow smashed Kell's rifle in two and sent the
pieces spinning. Iota was on her feet, aiming the animus; if she fired now, the Vindicare would be caught
in the nimbus of the psi-blast.

But then the fight ebbed from the Eversor assassin,
and the Garantine staggered backward, finally suc-
cumbing to all the hits he had taken. He made a last
swipe at Kell and missed, the force of the blow carrying him back off the roof of the blockhouse and down
into the courtyard.

Iota approached him carefully, loping low across
the ground. She was not convinced. Behind her, the
marksman came in to survey his work.

'Is he down?' she heard Tariel ask.

'For our sake,' Kell muttered, 'I bloody hope so.'


DAIG HALTED THE groundcar at the foot of the hill and
killed the engine. 'We walk from here,' he said, the
weak pre-dawn light giving his face a ghostly cast.

Yosef studied him. 'Tell me again how you came across this lead?' he said. 'Tell me again why you had to drag me out of my bed – a bed I've hardly had leave to be in these last few days, mind – to come out to a derelict vineyard while the rest of the city is sleeping?'

'I told you,' Daig said, with uncharacteristic terseness, '*a source*. Come on. We couldn't risk coming in by flyer in case Sigg gets spooked… and he may not even be here.'

Yosef followed him out into the cold air, pausing a moment to check the magazine in his pistol. He looked up the low hill. On the other side of heavy iron gates, what had once been the Blasko Wine Lodge was now a tumbledown husk of its former self. Gutted by fire a full three seasons ago, the site on the southerly ridges had yet to be reopened, and it stood empty and barren. In the dampness of the dawn air, the tang of fire-damaged wood could still be scented, drawn out by the moisture. 'If you think Sigg is in there,' Yosef went on, 'we should at least have some support.'

'I don't know for sure,' Daig replied.

'Not an overly reliable source, then,' said Yosef.

That earned him a sullen look. 'You know what will happen if I breathe a word of this at the precinct. Laimner would be all over it like a blight.'

He couldn't disagree with that; and if Laimner was involved and Daig's tip came to nothing, it would be the two reeves who would suffer for it. 'Fine. But don't keep me in the dark.'

When Daig looked at him again, he was almost imploring him. 'Yosef. I don't ask much of you, but I'm asking now. Just trust me here, and don't question it. All right?'

He nodded at length. 'All right.'

They got into the vineyard through a broken stand of fencing, and followed the driveway up to the main building. Small branches and drifts of wet leaves dotted the ground. Yosef glanced to his right and saw where unkempt, blackened ground ranged away down the steep terraces. Before the fire, those spaces had been thick with greenery, but now they were little more than snarls of wild growth. Yosef frowned; he still had a ten-year bottle of Blasko caskinport at home. It had been a good brand.

'In here,' whispered Daig, motioning him towards an outbuilding.

Yosef hesitated, his eyes adjusted to the dimness now, and his sight picking out what did not fit. Here and there he saw signs of recent motion, places where dirt had been disturbed by human movement. Looking up from the gates, an observer would have seen nothing, but here, close up, there was evidence. Yosef thought about the Norte and Latigue murders, and he reached into the pocket of his coat for the butt of his gun, comforting himself with the steady presence of the firearm.

'We take him alive,' he hissed back.

Daig shot him a look as he drew a thermal register unit from inside his jacket, panning it around to scan for a heat return. 'Of course.'

They found their suspect asleep inside the cooper's shack, lying in the curve of a half-built barrel. He heard their approach and bolted to his feet in a panic. Yosef put the brilliant white glare of his hand lantern on him and took careful aim with the pistol.

'Erno Sigg!' he snapped, 'We are reeves of the Sentine, and you are bound by law. Stand where you are and do not move.'

The man almost collapsed, so great was his terror. Sigg flailed and stumbled, falling against the side of his makeshift shelter, before catching himself with an obvious physical effort. He held up his shaking hands, in the right gripping the handle of an elderly fuel-lamp. 'H-have you come to kill me?' he asked.

It wasn't the question Yosef had expected. He had faced killers of men before, more often than he might have liked, but Sigg's manner was unlike any of them. Dread came off him in waves, like heat from a naked flame. Yosef had once rescued a young boy held prisoner for weeks in a wine cellar; the look on the boy's face as he saw light for the first time was mirrored now in Erno Sigg's expression. The man looked like a victim.

'You are suspected of a high crime,' Daig told him. 'You're to come with us.'

'I paid for what I did!' he retorted. 'I've done nothing else since!' Sigg looked in Daig's direction. 'How did you find me? I hid well enough so even *he* couldn't know where I was!'

Yosef wondered who *he* might be as Daig answered. 'Don't be afraid. If you are innocent, we will prove it.'

'Will you?' The question was weak and fearful, like the words of a child.

Then Daig said something that seemed out of place in the moment, and yet the words were like a calmative, immediately easing the tension in Sigg's taut frame. Daig said 'The Emperor protects.'

When Yosef looked back to Sigg, the man was staring directly at him. 'I've done many things I'm not proud of,' he told him. 'But no longer. And not those things the wire accuses me of. I've never taken a man's life.'

'I believe you, Erno,' said Yosef, the words leaving his mouth before he was even aware of them forming in his thoughts; and the strangeness of it was, he *did* believe him, with a totality that surprised the reeve with its strength. On some instinctual level, he knew that Erno Sigg was telling the truth. The fact that Yosef could not fathom where this abrupt conviction had come from troubled him deeply; but he did not have time to dwell upon it.

The roof of the cooper's shack was a shell of corrugated metal and glass, some of it warped or shattered by the passage of the old inferno. From nowhere, as the dawn wind changed direction, the musty air was suddenly full of noise. Yosef recognised the rattling hum of coleopter rotors a split-second before harsh sodium light drenched the floor with white, the glare from spotlamps blazing down through the smoke-dirty glass and the holes in the roof. An amplified voice echoed Yosef's original challenge to Sigg, and then there was movement.

The reeve looked up, shielding his eyes, and made out the blurs of jagers dropping from the hovering fly-ers, heavy guns in their grips at they fell on descender lines.

He looked back and saw pure fury on Sigg's face. '*Bastards*!' he spat venomously, 'I would have come! But you lied! You lied!'

Daig was reaching out to him. 'No, wait!' he cried out. 'I didn't bring them! We came alone–'

Sigg cursed them once again and threw the fuel-lamp in his hand with a savage jerk. The lantern hit the ground and split in a crash of glass and fire, even as overhead the intact portions of the roof were breached by the jagers. As pieces of the roof rained down from above, the lamp's burning oils kissed the soiled matter and old spills on the floor and a pulse of smoky flame erupted. Yosef pushed Daig aside as the new blaze rolled out, chewing on the piles of rotting wood and discarded sacks all around them.

Daig tried to go after Sigg, but the fire had already built a wall between them, and the droning throb of the coleopter blades fed it, raising it high. Sigg vanished into the heat and the smoke.

The jagers were disentangling themselves from their ropes as Yosef stormed over to them; one was already on the wireless for a firefighter unit. The reeve saw Skelta's face among the men and grabbed him by his collar.

'Who ordered you in?' he shouted, over the sound of the rotors. 'Who's the shit who ruined this?'

But he knew the answer before he heard it.

# SIX

*Ultio*
**Lies and Murder**
**The Death of Kings and Queens**

THE OFFICIO PRESENTED the ship to them without ceremony. Like those it served, the vessel had a fluid
identity; at the present moment, as it made its way
towards the orbit of Jupiter, its pennants and beacons
declared it to be the *Hallis Faye*, an oxygen tanker out
of Ceres registered to a Belter Coalition habitat. Its
codename, revealed to Kell and the others as they
boarded, was *Ultio*.

Outwardly, the *Ultio* resembled the class of light bulk
transport ships that travelled a thousand different sublight intrasystem space lanes across the Imperium. It
was a design so commonplace that it became almost
invisible in its ubiquity; a perfect blind for a craft in service to the Officio Assassinorum. Small by the
standards of the mammoth starcruisers that comprised
the fleets of the Imperial Navy and the rogue trader
baronage, the *Ultio* was every inch a lie. A stubby tri-
dent, the shaft of the main hull – what appeared to be

space for cargo – was in fact filled with the mechanisms and power train for an advanced design of interstellar warp motor. The craft had been constructed around the old engine, the origins of which were lost to time, and it was only the forward arrowhead-shaped section of the ship that was actually given over to cabins and compartments. This module, swept back and curved like an aerodyne, was capable of detaching itself from the massive drives to make planetfall like a guncutter. Inside, the crew sections of the *Ultio* were cramped and narrow, with sleeping quarters no larger than prison cells, hexagonal corridors and a flight deck configured with advanced gravity simulators so that every square centimetre of surface area could be utilised.

The ship had three permanent crewmembers, in addition to the growing numbers of the Execution Force, but none of them were what could be considered wholly human. As Kell walked towards the stern, he was aware that beneath his feet the ship's astropath lay sleeping inside a null chamber, having deliberately shocked itself into a somnambulant state; similarly, the *Ultio*'s Navigator, who habitually remained far back among the systemry of the drive section, had also opted to drop into sense-dep slumber inside a similar contrapsychic chamber. Both of them had expressed grave displeasure at Iota's arrival on board, but their requests that she be sequestered or drugged into stasis were denied. Kell could only guess at how the delicate psionic senses of the warp navigator and the astro-telepath would be perturbed by the ghostly negative aura cast by the Culexus; even he, without a taint of the psyker about him, found it profoundly unsettling to be around the pariah girl for too long. She had agreed to wear her dampener torc for the duration, but even that device could not block the eerie air that followed Iota wherever she went.

The third member of the *Ultio*'s crew was the least human of them all. Kell could still see the strange look of mingled horror and fascination on Tariel's face as they had met the starship's pilot. There was no body to the pilot, not any more; like the venerable dreadnoughts of the Adeptus Astartes, a being that had once been a man many centuries ago was now only a few pieces of flesh interred inside a body of iron and steel. Somewhere deep inside the block of computational hardware that filled the rear section of the crew deck, parts of a brain and preserved skeins of nerve ganglia were all that remained. Now he was the *Ultio*, and the *Ultio* was him, the hull his skin, the fires of the fusion core his beating heart. Kell tried to comprehend what it might be like to surrender one's self to the embrace of a machine, but he could not. He was, on some base level, appalled by the very idea of such a merging; but what he thought counted for nothing. The pilot, the Navigator, the astropath and all the rest of them, they were here to serve the interest of the Assassinorum – to do, and not to question.

He halted outside a hatchway, his boots ringing on the metal-grilled deck. '*Ultio*,' he asked the air, 'Is the Garantine awake?'

'Confirmed.' The pilot-cyborg's voice came from a speaker grille above his head. It had the flat tonality of a synthetic vocoder.

'Open it,' he ordered.

'Complying,' came the reply. 'Hazard warning. Increased gravity field ahead. Do not enter.'

The hatch fell into the deck, and a waft of stale air, reeking of chemical sweat, wandered into the corridor. Inside, the Eversor sat uncomfortably on the floor, his breathing laboured. With visible effort, the rage-killer lifted his head and glared at Kell. 'When I get out of here,' he said, forcing the words from his mouth, 'I am going to rip you apart.'

Kell's lips thinned. He didn't approach any closer. Although the Garantine was not tethered to the deck by any chains or fetters, there was no way he could have come to his feet. The gravitational plates beneath the floor of the Eversor's compartment were operating well above their standard setting, confining the assassin to the floor with the sheer weight of his own flesh. Veins stood out from his bare skin as his bio-modified physiology worked to keep him alive; an unaugmented human would have died from collapsed lungs or crushed organs within an hour or so.

The Garantine had been in the room for two days now, enduring a regimen of anti-psychotics and neural restoratives.

Kell studied him. 'It must be difficult for you,' he began. 'The doubt. The uncertainty.'

'There's no hesitation in me,' gasped the Eversor. 'Let me up and you'll see.'

'The mission, I mean.' That got him the smallest flash of hesitation from behind the Garantine's skull-face. 'To wake without direction... That can't have been easy on you.'

'I will kill,' said the Eversor.

'Yes,' agreed the Vindicare. 'And kill and kill and kill, until you are destroyed. But it will be for nothing. Worthless.'

With an agonised grunt, the Garantine tried to lurch forward, clawing towards the open doorway. 'I'll kill *you*,' he grated. 'Worth something.'

Kell resisted the reflex to step back. 'You think so?'

'Broke your gun, back there,' muttered the Eversor, the sweat thick on his bare neck. 'Pity. Were you... attached to it?'

Kell didn't rise to the bait; his prized longrifle had been custom-made by Isherite weaponsmiths, and it had served him well for years. 'It was just a weapon.'

'Like me?'

He spread his hands. 'Like all of us.' Kell paused, then went on. 'The accident that woke you early... The Vanus Tariel tells me that it would take too long to put you under again, to go through all the hypno-programming and conditioning. So we either vent you to space and start anew with another one of your kindred, or we find–'

'A different way?' The rage-killer gave a coughing chuckle. 'If I was chosen by my clade for whatever is planned, I'm the one you need. Can't do it without me.'

'I'm compelled to agree.' Kell gave a thin smile. The Garantine was no mindless thug, appearances to the contrary. 'I was going to say we would find an understanding.'

The other assassin laughed painfully. 'What can you offer me that would be richer than tearing your head from your neck, sniper?'

The Vindicare stared into the Eversor's wide, blood-shot eyes. 'Nothing has been said yet, but the directors can only be bringing us together for one reason. One target. And I think you'd like to be there when he dies.'

He said the name, and behind his fanged mask the Garantine grinned.

* * *

YOSEF'S HANDS WERE tight fists, and it was all he could do not to haul back and smack that weak half-smile off the face of Reeve Warden Laimner. For a giddy moment, he pictured himself with Laimner's greasy curls in his hand, smashing his face against the tiled floor of the precinct house, beating him into a broken ruin. The potency of the anger was startlingly strong, and it took an effort to rein himself in.

Laimner was waving his hand in Daig's face and going on and on about how all of this was Segan's fault for not following proper channels, for not calling in backup units. He had been singing the same song all the way back from the Blasko lodge.

'You lost the suspect,' the warden bleated, 'you had him and you lost him.' Laimner glared at Yosef. 'Why didn't you take a shot? Leg hit? Put him down, even?'

'I could have walked Sigg in through the front door,' Daig grated. 'He was going to surrender!'

Laimner rounded on him. 'Are you an idiot? Do you really believe that?' He stabbed at a pile of crime scene picts on the desk before him. 'Sigg was playing you. He wanted to make meat-toys out of you both, and you almost let him do it!'

Yosef found his voice and bit out a question. 'How did you know where we were?'

'Don't be stupid, Sabrat,' said the warden. 'Do you think the High-Reeve would let you off on a major case like this without having you tracked every second?'

Yosef saw Daig go pale at that, but he didn't remark on it. Instead, he pressed on. 'We had a solid lead, from a… a reliable source! We could have brought Sigg to book, but you came in mob-handed and ruined it!'

'Watch your tone, reeve!' Laimner shot back. He ran a deliberate finger down his warrant rod to emphasise his rank. 'Remember who you're talking to!'

'If you want to run this case, then do it,' Yosef continued. 'But otherwise don't second-guess the investigating officers!'

The warden's sneering smile returned. 'I was following Telemach's orders.'

Yosef's lip curled. 'Well, thanks for making that clear. I thought it was just your impatience and poor judgement that would make this case fall apart, but it seems like the problem is further up the line.'

'You insubordinate–!'

'Sir!' Skelta burst into the wardroom before Laimner could finish his sentence. 'He's here! The, uh, man. The baron's man.'

Laimner's attitude transformed in the blink of an eye. 'What? But they're not supposed to be here until tomorrow morning.'

'Um,' Skelta gestured at the door. 'Yes. No.'

Yosef turned to see two figures entering behind the jager. The first was an ebon-skinned man who matched Sabrat for height, but was broader across the chest, with the thickset look of a scrumball player. He had ash-coloured hair that fell to his shoulders and an oblong data monocle that almost hid a faint scar over his right eye. At his side was a pale, thin woman with a bald head covered in intricate tattoos. Both of them wore the same green and silver livery Yosef had seen on Bellah Gorospe, but the man's cuffs bore some kind of ornate flashing that had to be indicative of rank. The woman had a golden brooch, he noted, in the shape of an open eye. As he looked at her she raised her head to meet his gaze and he saw the unmistakable shape of an iron collar around her neck, like one that might be used to tether a dangerous animal. It seemed crude and out of place on her.

The man surveyed the room; something in his manner told Yosef he had heard every word of the argument that had preceded his entrance. The woman – it was hard to determine her age, he noted – continued to stare at him.

Laimner recovered well and gave a shallow bow. 'Operatives. It's a pleasure to have you here on Iesta Veracrux.'

'My name is Hyssos,' said the man. His voice was solemn. He indicated his companion. 'This is my associate, Perrig.'

Daig was gawking at the woman. 'She's a psyker,' he blurted. 'The eye. That's what it means.' He tapped his lapel in the same place where Perrig's brooch was pinned.

Yosef saw that the eye design was subtly repeated in among the woman's tattoos. His first reaction was denial; it was common knowledge, even on the most parochial of worlds, that psykers were forbidden. The Emperor himself, at a council called on the planet Nikaea, had outlawed the use of psionic sensitives, even among the Legions of his own Space Marines. While some stripes of psyker were approved under the tightest reins of Imperial control – the gifted Navigators who guided ships through the immaterium or the telepaths who carried communications between worlds, for example – most were considered mind-witches, dangerous and unstable aberrants to be corralled and neutered. Yosef had never been face to face with a psyker before this day, and Perrig unnerved him greatly. Her gaze upon him made him feel like he was made of glass. He swallowed hard as at last she looked away.

'My lord baron has sanction from the Council of Terra to employ an indentured psionic,' Hyssos explained. 'Perrig's talents are extremely useful in my line of work.'

'And what work is that?' said Daig.

'Security, Reeve Segan,' he replied. Hyssos's manner made it clear he knew the name of every person in the room.

Yosef nodded to himself. He knew that the Eurotas clan wielded great power and influence across the Ultima Segmentum, but he had never guessed it had such reach. To be granted dispensation against so rigid a ruling as the Decree of Nikaea was telling indeed; he couldn't help but wonder what other rules the Void Baron was free to ignore.

'I had expected you to go straight to the Eurotas compound,' Laimner ventured, trying to recover control of the conversation. 'You've had a long journey–'

'Not so long,' replied Hyssos, still sweeping the room with his gaze. 'The baron will arrive very soon. He will want a full accounting of the situation. I see no reason to delay.'

'How… soon?' managed Skelta.

'A day,' Hyssos offered, his answer drawing Laimner up short. 'Perhaps less.'

The Reeve Warden licked his lips. 'Well. In that case, I'll have a briefing prepared.' He gave a weak smile. 'I will make myself available to the baron on his arrival for a full and thorough–'

'Forgive me,' Hyssos broke in. 'Reeves Sabrat and Segan are the lead investigators in the case, are they not?'

'Well, yes,' said Laimner, clearly uncertain of how he should behave towards the Eurotas operative. 'But I am the senior precinct officer, and–'

'But not an *investigating* officer,' Hyssos went on, his tone level and firm. He gave Yosef a brief glance through his monocle. 'The baron prefers to have information delivered to him as directly as possible. From the men closest to it.'

'Of course,' the warden said tightly, catching up to the realisation that he was being dismissed. 'You must proceed as you see fit.'

Hyssos nodded once. 'You have my promise, Reeve Warden. Perrig and I will help Iesta Veracrux to bring this murderer to justice in short order. Please pass that assurance on to the High-Reeve and the Landgrave in my stead.'

'Of course,' Laimner repeated, his smile weak and false. Without another word, he left the room, shooting Yosef a final, acid glare as he closed the door behind him.

Yosef felt wrung out by the events of the day even though it had hardly begun. He sighed and looked away, only to find the woman Perrig watching him again.

When she spoke, her voice had a melody to it that was at odds with the fire in her eyes. 'There is a horror here,' she told them. 'Darkness clustering at the edges of perception. Lies and murder.' The psyker sighed. 'All of you have seen it.'

Yosef broke her gaze with no little effort on his part and gave Hyssos a nod. 'Where do you want to start?'

'You tell me,' said the operative.

* * *

ULTIO DRIFTED INTO the gravity well of the gas giant, crossing the complex web of orbits described by Jupiter's outer moons. It was almost a solar system in miniature, with the gas giant at its core rather than the blazing orb of a sun. The cloud of satellites and Trojan asteroids surrounding it were full of human colonies, factories and forges, powered by drinking in the radiation surging from the mammoth planet, feeding on mineral riches that in centuries of exploitation had yet to be fully exhausted. Jupiter was Terra's shipyard, and its sky was forever filled with vessels. Centred around Ganymede and a dozen other smaller moons, spacedocks and fabricatories worked ceaselessly to construct everything from single-crew Raven interceptors up to the gargantuan hulls of mighty Emperor-class command-carrier battleships.

In a zone so dense with spacecraft and orbitals of every kind, it should have been easy for the *Ultio* to become lost in the shoals of them; but security was tight, and suspicion was at every point of the compass. In the opening moves of the insurrection, an alliance of turncoats, men of the Mechanicum and traitors from the Word Bearers Legion, had assembled in secret a dreadnought called the *Furious Abyss*, constructing it in a clandestine berth on the asteroid-moon Thule. The small Jovian satellite had been obliterated during the ship's explosive departure and the ragged clump of its remains still orbited far out at the edges of the planetary system; but the shockwave from Thule's destruction and the *Abyss* incident was still being felt.

Thus, the *Ultio* moved with care and raised no uncertainties, doing nothing to draw attention to itself. Secure in its falsehood, the vessel passed under the shadow of the habitats at Iocaste and Ananke and then deeper into the Galiliean ranges, passing the geo-engineered ocean-moon of Europa and Io's seething orange mass. It followed a slow and steady course in across the planet's bands of dirty orange, umber and cream-grey clouds, down towards the Great Red Spot.

A vast spindle floated there, bathed in the crimson glow; Saros Station resembled a crystal chandelier severed from its mountings and cast free into the void, turning and catching starlight. Unlike the majority of its industrial and colonial cohorts, Saros was a resort platform where the Jovian elite could find respite and diversion from the works of the shipyards and manufactories. It was said that only the Venus orbitals could surpass Saros Station for its luxury. Avenues of gold and silver, acres of null-g gardens and auditoriums; and the finest opera house outside the Imperial Palace.

THE STATION FILLED the view through the *Ultio*'s canopy as the ship drifted closer.

'Why are we here?' asked Iota, with an idle sullenness.

'Our next recruit,' Tariel told her. 'Koyne, of the Clade Callidus.'

At the rear of the flight deck, the Garantine bent his head to avoid slamming it against the ceiling. He made a rasping, spitting noise. 'What do we need one of *them* for?'

'Because the Master of Assassins demands it,' Kell replied, without turning.

The Vanus glanced up from the displays fanned out around his gauntlet. 'According to my information, there is an important cultural event taking place. A recital of the opus *Oedipus Neo*.'

'The what?' sniffed the Eversor.

'A theatrical performance of dance, music and oratory,' Tariel went on, oblivious to his derision, 'It is a social event of great note in the Jovian Zone.'

'Must have lost my invite,' the Eversor rumbled.

'And this Koyne is down there?' Iota wandered to the viewport and pressed her hands to it, staring at Saros. 'How will we know a faceless Callidus among so many faces?'

Kell studied the abstract contact protocols he had been provided and frowned. 'We are to... send flowers.'

GERGERRA REI WEPT like a child as Jocasta went to her death.

His knuckles turned white as he held on to the balustrade around the edge of the roaming box the theatre had provided. Behind him, the machine-sentries in his personal maniple stood motionless and uncomprehending as their master's lips trembled in a breathy gasp. Rei leaned forward, almost as if he could will her not to take the steel noose and place it over her supple neck. A cry was filling his throat; he wanted to call to her, but he could not.

The nobleman had seen the opera before, and while it had always held his attention, it had never touched him as much as it had this night. Every biannual performance of *Oedipus Neo* was a lavish, sumptuous affair orbited by dozens of stately dinners, parties and gatherings, but at the core it was about the play.

Everyone in the Jovian set shared the same fears about this year's act; at first it had only been dreary naysayers who claimed it should not be put on because of the conflicts, but then after the diva Solipis Mun had perished in a tragic airlock accident… Many more had felt the opera should not have continued, as a mark of respect to her.

But if he was honest, Rei did not miss Mun onstage. As Jocasta, she had played the part with gusto and power, indeed, but after so many repetitions her investment in the character had grown careworn and flat. But now this new queen, this new Jocasta – a woman from the Venusian halls, as he understood it – had taken the part and breathed new life into it. In the first act, she seemed to mimic Mun's style, but soon she blossomed into her own interpretation of the role, and with it, she eclipsed the late diva so completely that Rei had all but forgotten her predecessor as the opera rolled towards its conclusion. The new actress had also brought with her new direction, and the performance had been shifted from the usual modern-dress style to a strangely timeless mode of costume, all in metallic colours and soft curves that Rei found quite alluring.

And now, with the stage drenched in blood-coloured light and flickers of lightning from the Red Spot beyond the skylights, the character of Jocasta took her own life as the orchestra struck an ominous chord. Against reason, Rei hoped that the play might suddenly diverge from the story he knew so well; but it did not. As the actress's body melted away into the wings and the final scenes of the opera unfolded, he found he could not focus on the fate of poor, blinded Oedipus, the lead actor giving his all in a finale that brought the audience to its feet in a storm of applause.

It was only as the floating viewing box returned to the high balcony with a silken thud that Rei regained a measure of composure, pulling himself back from a daze.

She had truly *moved* him. It had almost been as if this new Jocasta were performing only to Rei; he could swear that even in the moment of her drama's suicide, she had looked directly to him and wept in unison.

Rei's ranking meant that he had, as a matter of course, an invitation to the post-show gathering in the auditorium proper. Usually he declined, preferring the company of his machines to those of the venal peacocks who drifted about Jupiter's entertainment community. Tonight, however, he would not decline. He would meet *her*.

THE PARTY WAS jubilant, high with the thrill of the performance's energy as if it still resonated around the theatre even after the last note of music had faded. Critics from the media took turns to congratulate the director and the actor who had played the tortured king, but all of them did so while looking about in hopes of catching a glimpse of the true star of the show; the queen of this night, the new Jocasta.

Under the aegis of this, the invited nobles alternated between praising the opera and discussing the matters of the moment; and the latter meant discussion of the rebellion and of the pressures upon Jupiter and her shipyards. The wounds opened by the incident at Thule had not been healed, despite assurances from the Council of Terra, despite the quiet purges and the laying of blame. But accusations still crossed back and forth, some decrying the Warmaster for such perfidy and base criminality, others – those who spoke in hushed tones – wondering if the Emperor had let this thing occur just so he might tighten his grip on the Jovians. Every heartbeat of their forges was now turned to the construction of a military machine designed to break the turncoat advance, but many felt it was bleeding Jupiter white. Those who questioned this questioned other things as well; they asked exactly *how* it was that a force of Mechanicum Adepts and Astartes with traitorous intentions had been able to build a warship of the scope of the *Furious Abyss*, without alerting anyone to their duplicity.

Was it possible that Jupiter harboured rebel sympathisers? It had happened with the Mechanicum of Mars, and so some whispered, even among the warlords of Earth's supposedly united nation-states. The questions turned and turned, but they faded when Gergerra Rei entered the room.

Resplendent in the circuit-laced robes of a Mech-Lord, Rei's high status as master of Kapekan Sect of the Legio Cybernetica was known to all. Two full cohorts of combat mechanoids were under his personal command, and they had fought in many battles of note during the Great Crusade alongside the Luna Wolves and the Warmaster.

Like many of the Cybernetica, Rei eschewed the gross cyborg augmentations of his colleagues in the Mechanicum in favour of subtle enhancements that did not disfigure or dilute his outwardly human aspect; but those who knew Rei knew that whatever humanity he did show was rare and fleeting.

Behind him, moving with fluidity, his bodyguards were a three-unit maniple of modified Crusader-class

robots. Painted as works of art, each insect-like
machine was a stripped-down variant of its battlefield
standard, armed with a discreetly sheathed power-
rapier and a lasgun. A fourth mechanical, this one
custom-built to resemble a female form rendered in
polished chrome, walked at his side and served as his
aide.

No one asked questions about loyalty when Rei was
nearby. His machines could hear a whisper among a
roaring crowd, and those who dared to suggest aloud
that Rei was anything less than the Emperor's obedi-
ent servant lived to regret it.

THE MECH-LORD TOOK a schooner of an indifferent
Vegan brandy and pecked at a few small sweetmeats
from ornamental serving trays offered by menials,
allowing his mechanoid aide to delicately sniff at each
before he ingested it; the robot's head was filled with
sensing gear capable of picking up any particulate
trace of poison. The machine shook its head each
time, and so he ate and drank but none of the rich
foodstuffs sated the real hunger in him. Rei engaged
in a moment or two of small talk with the director of
the opera house, but it was a perfunctory and hollow
exchange. Neither of them wanted to spend time with
one another – Rei was simply uninterested and the
director was doubtless wracked with worry over the
reason why the Kapekan general had decided to take
up his long-ignored invite – but both of them had to
fake the genial nothings of greeting, for the sake of
propriety.

'My Lord Rei?' He turned as a servant approached, a
young man in the Saros livery with a wary cast to his

face. He nervously side-stepped the Crusaders and offered a card to the Mech-Lord; and that was his error. The servant did not wait to be addressed, but instead proffered the card before it was acknowledged.

Rei's aide stepped in to meet him with a faint hiss of hydraulics, and in one fluid motion took the hand holding the card and broke it at the wrist. The bone cracked wetly and the servant went white with shock, staggering. He would likely have fallen if the machine had not been holding him up.

'What is this?' he asked.

The servant spoke through gritted teeth. 'A… A message for you, sir…' He gasped and gave him a pleading look. 'Please, I only did as the lady asked me to…'

'The lady?' Rei's heart thumped in his chest. 'Give it to me.'

His aide took the card and held it to her chromium lips. She licked it with a disconcertingly human-looking tongue, paused, then handed it on to her master. Had there been any contact toxins on the surface, she would have destroyed it.

The Mech-Lord fought off a tremor in his hands as he read the languid, flowing script written across the white card. It was a single word: 'Come'. He turned it over and saw it listed a location in the apartments reserved for the opera house's performers.

'Is something amiss?' said the director, his face pinched in concern.

Rei pressed his half-empty brandy glass into the man's hand and walked away. His robots followed, and behind them the servant staggered down to his knees, clutching at his ruined wrist.

\* \* \*

THE APARTMENTS WERE a short pneu-car ride up three levels to Saros Station's most exclusive residential decks. Rei had his own orbital out by Callisto and did not keep rooms here, but he had visited the chambers in the past during one of his many affairs and so he knew where to go. The presence of his maniple made sure that no one dared to waylay him, and presently he reached the room. His aide knocked on the door and it opened on silent servos.

From within came that silken voice. 'Come,' she said.

Rei took a step – and then hesitated. He pulse was racing like that of a giddy youth in the first blush of infatuation, and he had to admit, as much as he was enjoying the sensation of it, he was still the man he was. Still distrustful of everything on some deep level. His enemies had tried to use women as weapons against him before, and he had buried them; could this be one more attempt to do the same? His throat went dry; he hoped it would not be so. The strange, ephemeral connection he felt with the actress seemed so very real, and the thought that it might be a thing brought into existence just to hurt him cut deeply.

For a long moment, he wavered on the threshold, contemplating turning about and leaving, taking the pneu-car back to the docks and his yacht, leaving and never coming back.

Just making the thought felt like razors in his gut; and then she spoke again. 'My lord?' He heard the mirror of his own questions and fears in her words.

His aide walked in ahead of him and Rei went to follow, but again he hesitated. Even if what he hoped for would come about in this glorious evening, he could not afford to lose sight of the realities of his life. He turned to the Crusaders and spoke a string of command words. The robots immediately took up sentry positions around the door to the apartment, weapons ready, bowing their mantis-like heads low so that they would not damage the lamps hanging from the ceiling above.

Rei entered the room and became overcome by a vision.

His first thought was; *she is not dead!* But of course that was true. It had only been a play, and yet it had seemed so real to him. The woman stood, still dressed in her queenly costume, the sweep of her lithe and flawless skin visible through the diaphanous silver of the dress. Metallic glitter accented her cheekbones and the almond curves of her dark eyes. She bowed to him and looked away shyly. 'My lord Rei. I feared you would not visit me. I feared I might have presumed too much…'

'Oh no,' Rei said, dry-throated. 'No. It is my honour…' He managed a smile. 'My queen.'

She looked up at him, smiling too, and it was magnificent. 'Will you call me that, my lord? May I be your Jocasta?' She toyed with a thin drape of silk that curtained off one section of the apartments from another.

He was drawn to her, crossing the white pile of the anteroom's rich carpeting. 'I would like that very much,' he husked.

The woman – his Jocasta – threw a look towards his mechanoid. 'And will she be joining us?'

The open invitation in her reply made Rei blink. 'Uh. No.' He turned and spoke tersely to the robot. 'Wait here.'

His Jocasta smiled again and vanished into the room beyond. Grinning, Rei paused and unbuttoned his tunic. Glancing around, he saw a spray of fresh Saturnine roses still in their delivery wrappings; he tossed his jacket down next to them and then followed her into the bedchamber.

JOCASTA DID NOT weep as Gergerra Rei went to his death.

The queen enveloped him in long, firm arms as he stepped in, bringing her body up to meet his, pressing her breasts to his chest, moulding herself to him. The Mech-Lord's dizzy smile was shaky and he gasped for air. His reactions were perfect; his flawless new love for Jocasta – for that was what it was, the most pure and exact rendition of neurochemical release – was the final product of weeks of carefully tailored pheromone bombardment. Tiny amounts of meta-dopamine and serotonin analogues had been introduced to Rei over time, the dosages light enough that even the ultra-sensitive scanners of his machine-aide would not detect them. The cumulative amounts had pushed him into something approaching obsession; and combined with a physiological template based on his taste in female bed partners, the trap had been set and laden with honey.

Jocasta bent Rei's head down to meet hers and pressed her lips to his. He shuddered as she did it, surrendering to her. It was so easy.

Gergerra Rei had been involved in the creation of the *Furious Abyss*. Not in a way that could be proven without doubt in a court of law, not in a way that connected him through any direct means, but enough that the guardians of the Imperium were certain of it. Whatever his crime, perhaps the transfer of certain bribes, the diversion of materials and manpower, the granting of passage to ships that should have been denied, the Kapekan Mech-Lord had done the bidding of the traitor Horus Lupercal.

The small weapon concealed between Jocasta's tongue and the base of her mouth was pushed up, held in place by clenched teeth. A lick of the trigger plate was all that was needed to fire the kissgun. The needle-sized round penetrated the roof of Rei's mouth and fragmented, allowing the threads of molecule-thin wire to explode outward. The threads whirled through the meat of his nasal cavity and up into his forebrain, shredding everything they touched. He lurched backwards and fell to the bed, blood and brain matter drooling from his lips and nostrils. Rei sank into the silken sheets, his corpse dragging them awry, revealing beneath the body of the actress whose face he had loved so ardently.

His killer moved quickly, shrugging off the illusion of the dead woman even as the target's corpse began to cool.

Flesh shifted in small ways, the Jocasta-face slipping to become less defined, more like a sketch upon paper. The killer spat out the kissgun and discarded it, then drew sharp nails along the inside of a muscular thigh. A seam in the skin parted to allow a wet pocket to open, and long fingers drew out a spool and handle affair from within. The killer gently shook the device and padded towards the silk curtains. Rei had died silently but the machine-aide was clever enough to run a passive scan for heartbeats every few seconds; and if it detected one instead of two...

The spool unwound into a thin taper of metal, which rolled out to the length of a metre. Once fully extended, the weapon became rigid; it was known as a memory sword, the alloy that comprised the blade capable of softening and hardening at the touch of a control.

Koyne liked the memory sword, liked the gossamer weight of it. Koyne liked what it could do, as well. With a savage slash, the blade sliced down the thin silk curtain and the motion alerted the mechanoid – but not quickly enough. Koyne thrust the point into the aide's chromium chest and through the armour casing around the biocortex module that served as the robot's brain. It gave a faint squeal and became a rigid statue.

Leaving the sword in place, Koyne took a moment to prepare for the next template. Koyne knew Gergerra Rei as well as the actress who played Queen Jocasta, and would adopt him just as easily. The Callidus despised the term 'mimicry'. It was a poor word that could not encompass the wholeness with which a Callidus would become their disguises. To mimic something was to ape it, to pretend. Koyne became the disguise; Koyne *inhabited* each identity, even if it was for a short while.

The Callidus was a sculpture that carved itself. Bio-implants and heavy doses of the shapeshifter drug polymorphine made skin, bone and muscle become supple and motile. Those who could not control the freedom it gave would collapse and turn into monstrosities, things like molten waxworks that were little more than heaps of bone and organs. Those with the gift of the self, though, those like Koyne, they could become anyone.

Concentrating, Koyne shifted to neutrality, a grey, sexless form that was smooth and almost without features. The Callidus did not recall any birth-gender; that data was irrelevant when it was possible to be man or woman, young or old, even human or xenos if the will was there.

It was then Koyne saw the flowers. They had been delivered by courier shortly before Rei had arrived. The assassin picked at the plants and noted the colour and number of the petals on the roses. Something like irritation crossed the killer's no-face and Koyne paused at the vox-comm alcove in the far wall, inputting the correct sequence of encoding that the flower arrangement signified.

The reply was almost immediate, meaning that there was a ship nearby. '*Koyne?*' A male voice, gruff with it.

The Callidus immediately copied the tonality and replied. 'You have broken my silent protocol.'

'*We're here to help you conclude your mission as quickly as possible. You have new orders.*'

'I have no idea who you fools are, or what authority you may think you have. But you are compromising my operation and getting in my way.' Koyne grimaced. It was an ugly expression on the grey face. 'I don't require any help from you. Don't interrupt me again.' The Callidus cut the channel and turned away. Such behaviour was totally unprofessional. The clade knew that once committed, an assassin's cover should not be compromised except in the direst of circumstances – and someone's impatience was certainly not reason enough.

Koyne sat and concentrated on Gergerra Rei, on his voice, his gait, the full sense of the man. Skin puckered and moved, thickening. Implants slowly expanded to add mass and dimension. Moment by moment, the killer changed.

But the task was still incomplete when the three Crusaders crashed in through the doorway, searching for a target.

KELL GLARED AT the vox pickup before him. 'Well. That was discourteous,' he muttered.

'Arrogance is a noted character trait of many of the Clade Callidus,' Iota offered.

The Garantine looked at Kell from across the *Ultio*'s cramped bridge. 'What are we supposed to do? Take in a show? Have a little dinner?' The hulking killer growled in irritation. 'Put me down on the station. I'll bring the slippery changer freak back here in pieces.'

Before Kell could reply, a sensor telltale on one of the consoles began to blink. Tariel motioned at the hololiths around his gauntlet and his expression grew grave. 'The ship reads energy weapon discharges close to Koyne's location.' He looked up, out past the nose of the ship to where the hull of Saros Station drifted nearby. 'The Callidus may be in trouble.'

'We should assist,' said Iota.

'Koyne didn't want any help,' Kell replied. 'Made that very clear.'

Tariel gestured at his display. 'Auspex magno-scan shows multiple mechanoid units in the area. War robots, Vindicare. If the Callidus becomes trapped–'

Kell held up a hand to silence him. 'The Master of Assassins chose this one for good reason. Let's consider this escape a test of skill, shall we? We'll see how good this Koyne is.'

The Garantine gave a rough snort of amusement.

KOYNE MADE IT into the enclosed avenue outside the apartments with only minor injuries. The Callidus had been able to recover the memory sword from the steel corpse of the aide, realising far too late that there had to have been a failsafe backup biocortex inside the machine, one that broadcast an alert to the rest of Rei's bodyguard maniple. Koyne did not doubt that other robots were likely vectoring to this location from the Mech-Lord's ship, operating on a kill-switch protocol that activated with the death of their master. The core directive would be simple – seek and destroy Gergerra Rei's murderer.

If only there had been more time. If Koyne could have completed the change into Rei, then it would have been enough to fool the auto-senses of the machines, long enough to reach the extraction point and exfiltrate. Rei and the actress would have been found days later, along with all the evidence that Koyne had prepared to set the scene for a murder-suicide shared by a pair of doomed lovers. It had a neatly theatrical tone that would have played well to Saros Station's intelligentsia.

All that was wasted now, though. Koyne limped away, pain burning from a glancing laser burn in the leg. The Callidus looked like an unfinished model in pinkish-grey clay, caught halfway between the neutral self-template and the form of the Mech-Lord.

There was a cluster of revellers coming the other way, and Koyne made for them, fixing the nearest with a hard gaze and imagining their identity as the assassin's own. The Callidus heard the heavy stomp of the spindly Crusader robots as they scrambled in pursuit, chattering to one another in machine code.

The small crowd reacted to the new arrival, the merriment of the group dipping for a moment in collective confusion. Koyne pressed every grain of mental control into adopting the face of the civilian – or at least something like it – and swung into the mass of the group.

The robots stood firm and blocked the avenue, guns up, the faceted eyes of their sensor modules sweeping the crowd. The revellers lost some of their good humour as the threat inherent in the maniple of machines became clear.

Koyne knew what would happen next; it was inevitable, but at least the hesitation would buy the assassin time. The Callidus searched for and found a side corridor that led towards an observation cupola, and began pushing through the people towards it.

This was the moment when the machines opened fire on the crowd. Unable to positively identify their target among the group of people, yet certain that their master's murderer was in that mass, the Crusaders made the logical choice. Kill them all and leave no doubt.

Koyne ran through the screaming, panicking civilians, laser bolts ripping through the air, cutting them down. The assassin vaulted into the corridor and ran to the dead end of it. Red light from the giant Jovian storm seeped in through the observation window, making everything blurry and drenched in crimson.

Time, again. Little enough time. The Callidus concentrated and retched, opening a secondary stomach to vomit up a packet of white, doughy material. With shaking hands, Koyne ripped open the thin membrane sheathing it and allowed air to touch the pasty brick inside. It immediately began to blacken and melt, and quickly the assassin pressed it to the glassaic of the cupola.

The robots were still coming. The shooting had stopped and the Crusaders were advancing down the corridor. Koyne saw the shadows of them jumping on the curved walls, lurching closer.

The assassin sat down in the middle of the room and drew up into a foetal ball, forgetting the face of the civilian, forgetting Gergerra Rei and the Queen Jocasta, remembering instead something old. Koyne let the polymorphine soften flesh into waxen slurry, let it flow and harden into something that resembled the chitin of an insect. Air was expunged, organs pressed together. By turns the body became a mass of dark meat; but still not quickly enough.

The Crusader maniple advanced into the observation cupola just as the package of thermo-reactive plasma completed its oxygenation cycle and self-detonated. The blast shattered the glassaic dome and everything inside the cupola was blown out into space. Rei's guardian machines spun away into the vacuum even as safety hatches fell to seal off the corridor. Koyne's body, now enveloped in a cocoon of its own skin, went with them into the dark.

Outside, the *Ultio* hove closer.

# SEVEN

**Storm Warning**
**An Old Wound**
**Target**

YOSEF SABRAT WAS out of his depth.

The audience chamber was big enough that it would have swallowed the footprint of his home three times over, and decorated with such riches that they likely equalled the price of every other house in the same district put together. It was a gallery of ornaments and treasures from all across the southern reaches of the Ultima Segmentum – discreet holographs labelled sculptures from Delta Tao and Pavonis, tapestries and threadwork from Ultramar, art from the colonies of the Eastern Fringes, triptychs of stunning picts in silver frames, glass and gold and steel and bronze... The contents of this one chamber alone shamed even the most resplendent of museums on Iesta Veracrux.

Thinking of his home world, Yosef reflexively looked up at the oval window above his head. The planet drifted there in stately silence, the dayside turning as dawn passed over the green-blue ribbons of ocean near the equator. But for all its beauty, he couldn't shake the sense of it hanging over him like some monumental burden, ready to fall and crush him the moment his focus slipped. He looked away, finding Daig by his side. The other reeve glanced at him, and the expression on his cohort's face was muted.

'What are we doing up here?' Daig asked quietly. 'Look at this place. The light fittings alone are probably worth a governor's ransom. I've never felt so common in my entire life.'

'I know what you mean,' Yosef replied. 'Just stay quiet and nod in the right places.'

'Try not to show myself up, you mean?'

'Something like that.' A few metres away, Hyssos was mumbling quietly to the air; Yosef guessed that the operative had to have some sort of communicator implant that allowed him to subvocalise and send vox messages as easily as the jagers of the Sentine used a wireless. It had been clear to him the moment the Consortium shuttlecraft had landed in the precinct courtyard, the elegant swan-like ship making a point-perfect touchdown that barely disturbed the trees; Eurotas's riches clearly bought the baron and his clan the best of everything. Still, that didn't seem to sit squarely with the neglect he'd seen at the trader's compound a day ago. He thought on that for a moment, making a mental note to consider it further.

The shuttle had swiftly brought them into deep orbit, there to meet the great elliptical hulk of the *Iubar*, flagship of the Eurotas Consortium and spaceborne palace of the rogue trader who led it. A handful of other smaller ships attended the *Iubar* like handmaidens around a queen; and Yosef only thought of them as smaller because the flagship was so huge. The support craft were easily a match for the tonnage of the largest of the system cruisers belonging to the Iestan PDF.

The psyker Perrig remained on the surface, having insisted on being taken to the Blasko lodge to take a sensing. Hyssos explained that the woman had the ability to divine the recent past of objects by the laying on of hands, and it was hoped that she would find Erno Sigg's telepathic spoor at the location. Skelta drew the job of being her escort, and the silent panic on the jager's face had been clear as daylight. The reeve marvelled how Hyssos seemed completely unconcerned by Perrig's preternatural powers. He spoke of her as Yosef or Daig would discuss the skills of the documentary officers at a crime scene – as no more than a fellow investigator with unique talents all their own.

In the hours after his arrival – and his blunt dismissal of Laimner – Hyssos had thrown himself fully into the serial murder case, absorbing every piece of information he could get his hands on. Yosef knew that the man had already been briefed as fully as the Eurotas Consortium could – how else could he have known the names of everyone in the precinct without prior instruction from Gorospe and her offices? – but he was still forming his view of the situation.

Daig took a few hours to sleep in the shift room, but Yosef was caught up by Hyssos's quiet intensity and sat with him, repeating his thoughts and impressions to him. The operative's questions were all insightful and without artifice. He made the reeve think again

on points of evidence and supposition, and Yosef
found himself warming to the man. He liked Hyssos's
lack of pretence, his direct manner… and he liked the
man for the way he had seen right through Berts Laimner at first glance.

'There's more to this,' Hyssos had said, over a steaming cup of recaf. 'Sigg murdering and playing artist
with the corpses… That doesn't add up.'

Yosef had agreed; but then the message had come
down from command. The Void Baron had arrived,
and the Governor was in a fit. Normally, a visitation
from someone of Baron Eurotas's rank would be a day
of great import, a trade festival for Iesta's merchants
and moneyed classes, a diversion for her workers and
commoners – but there had been no time to prepare.
Even as the shuttle had taken them up to meet Hyssos's summons, the government was in turmoil trying
to throw together some hasty pomp and ceremony in
order to make it seem like this had been planned all
along.

Laimner tried one last time to get a foot on the shuttle. He said that Telemach had ordered him to give the
baron the briefing, that he could not in good con-
science remain behind and let a lesser officer take the
responsibility. He'd looked at Yosef when he said
those words. Yosef imagined that Telemach was probably unaware of the shuttle or the summons, probably
too busy fretting with the Landgrave and the Imperial
Governor and the Lord Marshal to notice. But again,
Hyssos had firmly blocked the Reeve Warden from
using this as any way to aggrandise himself, and left
him behind as he took the two lowly reeves up into
orbit.

It was an experience that Daig was never to forget; it was his first time off-world, and his usual manner had been replaced with something that approximated stoic dread.

Hyssos beckoned them towards the far end of the wide gallery, where a dais and audience chairs were arranged before a broad archway. Inside the arch was a carved frieze made of red Dolanthian jade. The artwork, easily the size of the front of Yosef's house, showed a montage of interstellar merchants about their business, travelling from world to world, trading and spreading the light of the Imperium. In the centre, a sculpture of the Emperor of Mankind towered over everything. He was leaning forward, holding out his hand with the palm down. Kneeling before him was a man in the garb of a rogue trader patriarch, who held up an open book beneath the Emperor's hand.

Daig saw the artwork and gasped. 'Who... Who is that?'

'The first of the Eurotas,' said Hyssos. 'He was the commander of a warship that served the Emperor many centuries ago, a man of great diligence and courage. As a mark of respect for his service, the Emperor granted him the freedom of space and made him a rogue trader.'

'But the book...' said Daig, pointing. 'What is he doing with the book?'

Yosef looked closer and saw what Daig was talking about. The artwork clearly showed what could only be a cut upon the Emperor's downturned palm and a drip of blood – rendered here from a single faceted ruby – falling down towards the page of the open tome.

'That is the Warrant of Trade,' said a new voice, as footsteps approached from behind them. Yosef turned to see a hawkish, imperious man in the same cut of robes as the figure in the frieze. A group of guardsmen and attendants walked in lockstep behind him, but the man paid them no mind. 'The letter of marque and statement granting my clan the right to roam the stars in the name of humanity. Our liege lord ratified it with a drop of his own blood upon the page.' He gestured around. 'We carry the book in safety aboard the *Iubar* as we have for generation after generation.'

Daig glanced about him, as if for a moment thinking he might actually *see* the real thing; but then disappointment clouded his face and his jaw set in a thin line.

'My lord,' said Hyssos, with a bow that the reeves belatedly imitated. 'Gentlemen. Allow me to introduce his lordship Merriksun Eurotas, Void Baron of Narvaji, Agentia Nuntius of the Taebian Sector and master of the Eurotas Trade Consortium–'

'Enough, enough,' Eurotas waved him into silence. 'I will hear that a thousand times more once I venture down to the surface. Let us dispense with formality and cut to the meat of this.' The baron gave Yosef and Daig a hard, measuring stare before he spoke again. 'I will make my wishes clear, gentlemen. The situation on Iesta Veracrux is delicate, as it is on many worlds among the Taebian Stars. There is a storm coming. A war born of insurrection, and when it brushes these planets with the heat of its passage there will be fire and death. There will be.' He blinked and paused. For a moment, a note of strange emotion crept into his words, but then he flattened it with a breath of air.

'These… killings. They serve only to heap tension and fear upon a populace already in the grip of a slow terror. People will lash out when they are afraid, and that is bad for stability. Bad for business.'

Yosef gave a slow nod of agreement. It seemed the rogue trader understood the situation better than the reeve's own commanders; and then he had a sudden, chilling thought. Was the same thing happening on *other* planets? Had Eurotas seen this chain of events elsewhere in the Taebian Sector?

'I want this murderer found and brought to justice,' Eurotas concluded. 'This case is important, gentlemen. Complete it, and you will let your people know that we… that the Imperium… is still in power out here. Fail, and you open the gateway to anarchy.' He began to turn away. 'Hyssos will make available to you any facilities you may need.'

'Sir?' Daig took a step after the rogue trader. 'My, uh, lord baron?'

Eurotas paused. When he looked back at the other reeve, he did so with a raised eyebrow and an arch expression. 'You have a question?'

Daig blurted it out. 'Why do you care? About Iesta Veracrux, I mean?'

The baron's eyes flashed with a moment of annoyance, and Yosef heard Hyssos take a sharp breath. 'Dagonet is falling, did you know that?' Daig nodded and the baron went on. 'And not only Dagonet. Kelsa Secundus. Bowman. New Mitama. All dark.' Eurotas's gaze crossed Yosef's and for a moment the nobleman appeared old and tired. 'Erno Sigg was one of my men. I bear a measure of responsibility for his conduct. But it is more than that. Much more.' Yosef felt the rogue trader's gaze pinning him in place. 'We are alone out here, gentlemen. Alone against the storm.'

'The Emperor protects,' said Daig quietly.

Eurotas gave him an odd look. 'So they tell me,' he replied, at length; and then he was walking away, the audience at an end and Yosef's thoughts clouded with more questions than answers.

WHEN THE GULL wing hatch of the flyer opened, the first thing that Fon Tariel experienced was the riot of smells. Heady and potent floral scents flooded into the interior of the passenger compartment, buoyed on warm air. He blinked at the daylight streaking in, and with wary footsteps he followed Kell out and into... wherever this place was.

Unlike the Eversor, who had not been afraid to provide the group with the location of one of their Terran facilities, the Clade Venenum made it clear in no uncertain terms that the members of the Execution Force would not be free to come to them of their own accord. The Siress had been most emphatic; only two members of the group were granted passage to the complex, and both were required to be unarmed and unequipped.

Tariel was learning Kell's manner by and by, and he could see that the Vindicare was ill at ease without a gun on him. The infocyte was sympathetic to the sniper; he too had been forced to leave his tools behind on board the *Ultio*, and he felt strangely naked without his cogitator gauntlet. Tariel's hand kept straying to his bare forearm without his conscious awareness of it.

The journey aboard the unmarked Venenum flyer had done nothing to give them any more clue to the whereabouts of the complex called the Orchard. The passenger compartment had no windows, no way for them to reckon the direction of their flight. Tariel had been dismayed to learn that his chronometer and mag-compass implants were being suppressed, and now as he stepped out of the craft they both flickered back to life, giving him a moment of dizziness.

He glanced around; they stood on a landing pad at the top of a wide metal ziggurat, just shy of the canopies of tall trees with thick leaves that shone like dark jade. The jungle smells were stronger out here, and the olfactory processor nodes in his extended braincase worked furiously to sift through the sensoria. Tariel guessed that they were somewhere deep in the rich rainforests of Merica, but it was only a speculative deduction. There was no way to know for sure.

A man in a pale green kimono and a domino mask emerged from a recessed staircase on the side of the ziggurat and beckoned them to follow him. Tariel was content to let Kell lead the way, and the three of them descended. The sunshine attenuated as they dropped below the line of the upper canopy, becoming shafts of smoky yellow filled with motes of dust and the busy patterns of flying insects.

A pathway of circular grey stones awaited them on the jungle floor, and they picked their way along it, the man in the kimono surefooted and confident. Tariel was more cautious; his eyes were drawn this way and that by bright, colourful sprays of plants that grew from every square metre of ground. He saw small worker mechanicals moving among them; what seemed at first glance to be wild growth was actually some sort of carefully random garden. The robotics were ministering to the plants, harvesting others.

He paused, studying one odd spindly blossom he did not recognise emerging from the bark of a tall tree. He leaned closer.

'I would not, Vanus.' The man in the kimono placed a gentle hand on his shoulder and reeled him back. Before he could ask why, the man made an odd knocking noise with his lips and in response the blossom grew threadlike legs and wandered away, up the tree trunk. 'Mimical spiders, from Beta Comea III. They adapt well to the climate here on Terra. Their venom causes a form of haemorrhagic fever in humans.'

Tariel recoiled and blinked. Looking again, he drew up data from his memory stacks, classifying the plant life. Castor, nightshade and oleander; *Cerbera odollam*, digitalis and Jerusalem cherry; hemlock and larkspur and dozens of others, all of them brimming with their own particular strains of poisons. He kept his hands to himself from then on, not wavering at all from the pathway until it deposited them in a clearing – although clearing was hardly the word, as the place was overgrown with vines and low greenery. In the middle of the area was an ancient house, doubtless thousands of years old; it too was swamped by the jungle's tendrils, and Tariel noted that such coverage would serve well as a blind for orbital sensors and optical scopes.

'Not what I expected,' muttered Kell, as they followed the man in the kimono towards an ivy-covered doorway.

'It appears to be a manse,' said the infocyte. 'I can only estimate when it was built. The rainforest has reclaimed it.'

Inside, Tariel expected the place to show the same level of disarray as the exterior, but he was mistaken. Within, the building had been sealed against the elements and wildlife, and care had been taken to return it to its original form. It was only the gloom inside, the weak and infrequent sunlight through the windows, that betrayed the reality. The Vanus and the Vindicare were taken to an anteroom where a servitor was waiting, and the helot used a bulbous sensing wand to scan them both, checking everything down to their sweat and exhalations for even the smallest trace of outside toxins. The man in the kimono explained that it was necessary in order to maintain the balance of poisons in the Orchard proper.

From the anteroom, they went to what had once been a lounge. Along the walls there were numerous cages made of thin glassaic, rank upon rank of them facing outward. Tariel's skin crawled as he made out countless breeds of poisonous reptiles, ophidians and insects, each in their own pocket environment within the cases. The infocyte moved to the middle of the room, instinctively placing himself at the one point furthest from all the cage doors.

A thing with a strange iridescent carapace flittered in its confinement, catching his eye, and the sheen of the chitin recalled a recent memory. The flesh of the Callidus had looked just the same when they had pulled Koyne out of the vacuum over Jupiter; the shapeshifting assassin had done a peculiar thing, turning into a deformed, almost foetus-like form in order to survive in the killing nothingness of space. Koyne's skin had undergone a state change from flesh to something like bone, or tooth. Tariel recalled the disturbing sensation of touching it and he recoiled once again.

He looked away, towards Kell. 'Do you think the Callidus will live?'

'His kind don't perish easy,' said the Vindicare dryly. 'They're too conceited to die in so tawdry a manner.'

Tariel shook his head. 'Koyne is not a "he". It's not male or female.' He frowned. 'Not any more, anyway.'

'The ship will heal... it. And once our poisoner joins us, we will have our Execution Force assembled...' Kell trailed off.

Tariel imagined he was thinking the same thing as the sniper; *and what then?* The question as to what target they were being gathered to terminate would soon be answered – and the Vanus was troubled by what that answer might be.

*It can only be–*

The thought was cut off as the man in the kimono returned with another person at his heels. Tariel determined a female's gait; she was a slender young woman of similar age to himself.

'By the order of the Director Primus of our clade and the Master of Assassins,' said the man, 'you are granted the skills of secluse Soalm, first-rank toxin artist.'

The woman looked up and she gave a hard-edged, defiant look at the Vindicare. Kell's face shifted into an expression of pure shock and he let out a gasp. '*Jenniker?*'

The Venenum drew herself up. 'I accept this duty,' she said, with finality.

'No,' Kell snarled, the shock shifting to anger. 'You do not!' He glared at the man in the kimono. 'She does *not*!'

The man cocked his head. 'The selection was made by Siress Venenum herself. There is no error, and it is not your place to make a challenge.'

Tariel watched in confused fascination as the cool, acerbic mien Kell had habitually displayed crumbled into hard fury. 'I am the mission commander!' he barked. 'Bring me another of your secluses, now.'

'Are my skills in question?' sniffed the woman. 'I defy you to find better.'

'I don't want her,' Kell growled, refusing to look at Soalm. 'That's the end of it.'

'I am afraid it is not,' said the man calmly. 'As I stated, you do not have the authority to challenge the assignment made by the Siress. Soalm is the selectee. There is no other alternative.' He pointed back towards the doorway. 'You may now leave.' Without another comment, the man exited the room.

'Soalm?' Kell hissed the woman's surname with undisguised anger. 'That is what I should call you now, is it?'

It was slowly dawning on Tariel that the two assassins clearly shared some unpleasant history together. He looked inward, thinking back over what he had managed to learn about Eristede Kell since the start of their mission, looking for some clue. Had these two been comrades or lovers, he wondered? Their ages were close enough that they could have both been raised in the same schola before the clades drew them for individual selection and training...

'I accepted the name to honour my mentor,' said the woman, her voice taking on a brittle tone. 'I started a new life when I joined my clade. It seemed the right thing to do.'

Tariel nodded to himself. Many of the orphan children selected for training by the Officio Assassinorum entered the clades without a true identity to call their own, and often they took the names of their sponsors and teachers.

'But you dishonoured your family instead!' Kell grated.

And then, for a brief moment, the woman's mask of defiance slipped to reveal the regret and sadness behind it; suddenly Tariel saw the resemblance.

'No, Eristede,' she said softly, 'you did that when you chose to kill innocents in the name of revenge. But our mother and father are dead, and no amount of bloodshed will ever undo that.' She walked by Kell, and past a stunned Tariel, stepping out into the perfumed jungle.

'She's your sister,' Tariel blurted it out, unable to stay silent, the data rising up from his memory stack in a rush. 'Eristede and Jenniker Kell, son and daughter of Viceroy Argus Kell of the Thaxted Duchy, orphaned after the murder of their parents in a local dispute–'

The Vindicare advanced on him with a livid glare in his eyes, forcing Tariel back against a cage filled with scorpions. 'Speak of this to the others and I will choke the life from you, understand?'

Tariel nodded sharply, his hands coming up to protect himself. 'But... The mission...'

'She'll do what I tell her to,' said Kell, the anger starting to cool.

'Are you sure?'

'She'll follow orders. Just as I will.' He stepped back, and Tariel glimpsed a hollowness, an uncertainty in the other man's eyes that mirrored what he had seen in the Vindicare's sister.

* * *

THE IUBAR HAD decks filled with cogitator engines that hummed and whirred like patient cats, gangs of progitors moving back and forth between them with crystalline memory tubes and spools of optic coil. According to Hyssos, the devices were used to gather financial condition data from the various worlds along the Eurotas trade routes, running prognostic models to predict what goods a given planet might require months, years, even decades into the future.

'What are we to do with these things?' asked Daig. He'd never been comfortable with the thought of machines that could do a man's job better.

Hyssos nodded at one of the engines. 'I've been granted use of this module. Various information sources from Iesta Veracrux's watch-wire are being collated and sifted by it.'

'You can do that from up here?' Yosef felt an odd stab of concern he couldn't place.

The operative nodded. 'The uptake of data is very slow due to the incompatibility of the systems, but we have some level of parity. Enough to check the capital's traffic patterns, compare information on the suspect with the movements of his known associates, and so on.'

'We have jagers on the ground doing that,' Daig insisted. 'Human eyes and ears are always the best source of facts.'

Hyssos nodded. 'I quite agree. But these machines can help us to narrow our fields of inquiry. They can do in hours what would take your office and your jagers weeks to accomplish.' Daig didn't respond, but Yosef could see he was unconvinced. 'We'll tighten the noose,' continued the operative. 'Sigg won't slip the net a second time, mark my words.'

Yosef shot him a look, searching the comment for any accusation – and he found none. Still, he was troubled, and he had to voice it. 'Assuming Sigg is our killer.' He remembered the man's face in the cooper's shack, the certainty he had felt when he read Erno Sigg's fear and desperation. *He looked like a victim.*

Hyssos was watching him. 'Do you have something to add, Reeve Sabrat?'

'No.' He looked away and found Daig, his cohort's expression unreadable. It wasn't just Sigg he was having his doubts about; Yosef thought back to what the other man had said in the ruined lodge, and the recent changes in his manner. Daig was keeping something from him, but he could not think of a way to draw it out. 'No,' he repeated. 'Not now.'

WHAT THE OTHERS called the 'staging area' was really little more than a converted storage bay, and Iota saw little reason why the name of it made so much difference. The *Ultio* was a strange vessel; she was still trying to know it, and it wasn't letting her. The ship was one thing pretending to be another, an assemblage of rare technologies and secrets that had been stitched into a single body; given a mission, thrown out into the darkness. It was like her in that way, she mused. They could almost have been kin.

The mind inside the ship spoke to her when she spoke to it, answering some of her questions but not others. Eventually, Iota became bored with the circular conversations and tried to find another way to amuse herself. As a test of her stealth skills, she took to exploring the smallest of the crawlspaces aboard the *Ultio* or spying on the medicae compartment where the Callidus was recovering inside a therapy pod. When she wasn't doing this or meditating, Iota spent the time hunting down spiders in shadowed corners of the hull, catching and collecting them in a jar she had appropriated from the ship's mess. So far, her hopes of encouraging the arachnids to form their own rudimentary society had failed.

She spotted another of the insects in the lee of a console and deftly snared it; then, with a cruelty born of her boredom, she severed its legs one by one, to see if it could still walk without them.

Kell entered the chamber; he was the last to arrive. The infocyte Tariel had been working at the hololith projector and he seemed uncharacteristically muted. The Vanus's mood had been like this ever since he and the Vindicare had returned from Terra with the last of the recruits, the woman who called herself Soalm. The new arrival didn't speak much either. She seemed rather delicate for an assassin; that was something that many thought of Iota when they first laid eyes on her, but the chill of her preternatural aura was usually enough to destroy that illusion within a heartbeat. The Garantine's bulk took up a corner of the room, like an angry canine daring any one of them to crowd into his space. He was playing with a sliver of sharpened metal – the remains of a tool, she believed – dancing the makeshift blade across his thick fingers with a striking degree of dexterity. He was bored too, but annoyed with it; then again, Iota had come to understand that every mood of the Eversor was some shade of anger, to a greater or lesser extent. Koyne sat in a wire-frame chair, the Callidus's smoothed-flat features like an unfinished carving in soapstone. She watched the shade for a few moments, and Koyne offered Iota a brief smile. The Callidus's skin darkened, taking on a tone close to the tawny shade of Iota's own flesh; but then the moment was broken by Kell as he rapped his gloved hand on the support beams of the low ceiling.

'We're all here,' said the Vindicare. His gaze swept the room, dwelling briefly on all of them; all of them except Soalm, she noted. 'The mission begins now.'

'Where are we going?' asked Koyne, in a voice like Iota's.

Kell nodded to Tariel. 'It's time to find out.'

The infocyte activated a code-key sequence on the projector unit and a haze of holographic pixels shimmered into false solidity in the middle of the chamber. They formed into the shape of a tall, muscular man in nondescript robes. He had a scarred face and a queue of close-cut hair over an otherwise bare skull, and if the image was an accurate representation, then he was easily bigger than the Garantine. The hologram crackled and wavered, and Iota recognised the tell-tale patterns of high-level encoding threading through it. This was a real-time transmission, which meant it could only be coming from another ship in orbit, or from Terra itself.

Kell nodded to the man. 'Captain-General Valdor. We are ready to be briefed, at the Master's discretion.'

Valdor returned the gesture. 'The Master of Assassins has charged me with that task. Given the... unique nature of this operation, it seems only right that there be oversight from an outside party.' The Custodian

surveyed all of them with a measuring stare; at his end
of the communication, Iota imagined he was standing
among a hololithic representation of the room and
everyone in it.

'You want us to kill *him*, don't you?' the Garantine
said without preamble, burying his makeshift knife in
the bulkhead beside his head. 'Let's not be precious
about it. We all know, even if we haven't had the will
to say it aloud.'

'Your insight does you credit, Eversor,' said Valdor,
his tone making it clear his compliment was anything
but that. 'Your target is the former Warmaster of the
Adeptus Astartes, Primarch of the Luna Wolves, the
Archtraitor Horus Lupercal.'

'They are the Sons of Horus now,' muttered Tariel,
disbelief sharp in his words. 'Throne's sake. It's true,
then...'

The Venenum woman made a negative noise in the
back of her throat. 'If it pleases my lord Custodes, I
must question this.'

'Speak your mind,' said Valdor.

'Every clade has heard the rumours of the missions
that have followed this directive and failed it. My
clade-cohort Tobeld was the last to be sent on this
fool's errand, and he perished like all the others. I
question if this can even be achieved.'

'Cousin Soalm has a compelling point,' offered
Koyne. 'This is not some wayward warlord of which
we are speaking. This is Horus, first among the
Emperor's sons. Many call him the greatest primarch
that ever lived.'

'You're afraid,' snorted the Garantine. 'What a surprise.'

'Of course I am afraid of Horus,' replied Koyne, mimicking the Eversor's gruff manner. 'Even an animal would be afraid of the Warmaster.'

'An Execution Force like this one has never been gathered,' Kell broke in, drawing the attention of all of them. 'Not since the days of the first masters and the pact they swore in the Emperor's service on Mount Vengeance. We are the echo of that day, those words, that intention. Horus Lupercal is the only target worthy of us.'

'Pretty words,' said Soalm. 'But meaningless without direction.' She turned back to the image of Valdor. 'I say again; how do we hope to accomplish this after so many of our Assassinorum kindred have been sacrificed against so invulnerable an objective?'

'Horus has legions of loyal warriors surrounding him,' said Tariel. 'Astartes, warships, forces of the Mechanicum and Cybernetica, not to mention the common soldiery who have come to his banner. How do we even get close enough to strike at him?'

'He will come to you.' Valdor gave a cold, thin smile. 'Perhaps you wondered at the speed with which this Execution Force has been assembled? It has been done so as to react to new intelligence that will place the traitor directly in your sights.'

'How?' demanded Koyne.

'It is the judgement of Lord Malcador and the Council of Terra that Horus's assassination at this juncture with throw the traitor forces into disarray and break the rebellion before it can advance on to the Segmentum Solar,' said Valdor. 'Agents of the Imperium operating covertly in the Taebian Sector report a strong likelihood that Horus is planning to bring his flagship, the *Vengeful Spirit*, to the planet Dagonet in order to show his flag. We believe that the Warmaster's forces will use Dagonet as a foothold from which to secure the turning of every planet in the Taebian Stars.'

'If you know this to be so, my lord, then why not simply send a reprisal fleet to Dagonet instead?' asked Soalm. 'Send battle cruisers and Legions of Astartes, not six assassins.'

'Perhaps even the Emperor himself...' muttered Koyne.

Valdor gave them both a searing glare. 'The Emperor's deeds are for him alone to decide! And the fleets and the loyal Legions have their own battles to fight!'

Iota nodded to herself. 'I understand,' she said. 'We are to be sent because there is *not* certainty. The Imperium cannot afford to send warfleets into the darkness on a mere "likelihood".'

'We are only six,' said Kell, 'but together we can do what a thousand warships have failed to. One vessel can slip through the warp to Dagonet far easier than a fleet. Six assassins... the best of our clades... can bring death.' He paused. 'Remember the words of the oath we all swore, regardless of our clades. *There is no enemy beyond the Emperor's wrath.*'

'You will take the *Ultio* to the Taebian Sector,' Valdor went on. 'You will embed on Dagonet and set up multiple lines of attack. When Horus arrives there, you will terminate his command with extreme prejudice.'

'MY LORD.' EFRIED bowed low and waited.

The low mutter of his primarch's voice was like the distant thunder over the Himalayan range. 'Speak, Captain of the Third.'

The Astartes looked up and found Rogal Dorn standing at the high balcony, staring into the setting sun. The golden light spilled over every tower and crenulation of the Imperial Palace, turning the glittering metals and white marble a striking, honeyed amber. The sight was awesome; but it was marred by the huge cube-like masses of retrofitted redoubts and gunnery donjons that stood up like blunt grey fangs in an angry mouth. The palace of *before* – the rich, glorious construct that defied censure and defeat – was cheek-by-jowl with the palace of *now* – a brutalist fortress ranged against the most lethal of foes. A foe that had yet to show his face under Terra's skies.

Efried knew that his liege lord was troubled by the battlements and fortifications the Emperor had charged him to build over the beauty of the palace; and while the captain could see equal majesty in both palace and fortress alike, he knew that in some fashion, Great Dorn believed he was diminishing this place by making it a site fit only for warfare. The primarch of the Imperial Fists often came to this high balcony, to watch the walls and, as Efried imagined, to wait for the arrival of his turncoat brother.

He cleared his throat. 'Sir. I have word from our chapter serfs. The reports of preparations have been confirmed, as have those of the incidents in the Yndenisc Bloc and on Saros Station.'

'Go on.'

'You were correct to order surveillance of the Custodes. Captain-General Valdor was once again witnessed entering closed session at the Shrouds, with an assemblage of the Directors Primus of the Assassinorum clades.'

'When was this?' Dorn did not look at him, continuing to gaze out over the palace.

'This day,' Efried explained. 'On the conclusion of the gathering a transmission was sent into close-orbit space, likely to a vessel. The encryption was of great magnitude. My Techmarines regretfully inform me it would be beyond their skills to decode.'

'There is no need to try,' said the primarch, 'and indeed, to do so would be a violation of protocols. That is a line the Imperial Fists will not cross. Not *yet*.'

Efried's hand strayed to his close-cropped beard. 'As you wish, my lord.'

Dorn was silent for a long moment, and Efried began to wonder if this was a dismissal; but then his commander spoke again. 'It begins with this, captain. Do you understand? The rot beds in with actions such as these. Wars fought in the shadows instead of the light. Conflicts where there are no rules of conduct. No lines that cannot be crossed.' At last he glanced across at his officer. 'No honour.' Behind him, the sun dipped below the horizon, and the shadows across the balcony grew.

'What is to be done?' Efried asked. He would obey any command his primarch had cause to utter, without question or hesitation.

But Dorn did not answer him directly. 'There can only be one target worth such subterfuge, such a gathering of forces. The Officio Assassinorum mean to kill my errant brother Horus.'

Efried considered this. 'Would that not serve our cause?'

'It might appear so to those with a narrow view,' replied the primarch. 'But I have seen what the assassin's bullet wreaks in its wake. And I tell you this, brother-captain. We will defeat Horus… but if his death comes in a manner such as the Assassinorum intend, the consequences will be terrible, and beyond our capacity to control. If Horus falls to an assassin's hand there will be a gaping vacuum at the core of the turncoat fleet, and we cannot predict who will fill it or what terrible revenges they will take. As long as my brother lives, as long as he rides at the head of the traitor Legions, we can predict what he will do. We can match Horus, defeat him on even ground. We know him.' Dorn let out a sigh. 'I know him.' He shook his head. 'The death of the Warmaster will not stop the war.'

Efried listened and nodded. 'We could intervene. Confront Valdor and the clade masters.'

'Based on what, captain?' Dorn shook his head again. 'I have only hearsay and suspicion. If I were as reckless as Russ or the Khan, that might be enough… But we are Imperial Fists and we observe the letter of Imperial law. There must be proof positive.'

'Your orders, then, sir?'

'Have the serfs maintain their observations,' Dorn looked up into the darkening sky. 'For the moment, we watch and we wait.'

# EIGHT

### Cinder and Ash
### Toys
### Unmasked

THE ROOM IN the compound they had given over for
Perrig's use was of a reasonable size and dimension,
and the last of four that had been offered. The other
three she had immediately rejected because of their
inherent luminal negativity or proximal locations to
undisciplined thought-groupings. The second had
been a place where a woman had died, some one hundred and seven years earlier, having taken her own life
as the result of an unplanned pregnancy. The adjutant,
Gorospe, had looked at Perrig with shock and no little
amount of dismay at that revelation; it seemed that no
one among the staff of the Eurotas Consortium had
had any idea the building on Iesta had such a sordid
history.

But this room was quiet, the buzzing in her senses
was abating and Perrig was as close to her equilibrium
as she could be in a place so filled with droning, self-
absorbed minds. Running through her alignment

exercises, Perrig gently edited them out of her thoughtscape, eliminating the disruption through the application of a gentle psionic null-song, like a counter-wave masking an atonal sound.

She absently touched the collar around her neck as she did this. It was just metal, just a thing, secured only with a bolt that she herself could undo with a single twist. It had meaning, though, for those who looked upon it, for those who might read the words from the Nikaea Diktat acid-etched into the black iron. It was a slave's mark, after a fashion, but one she wore only for the benefit of the comfort of others. It was not a nullifier, it could not hold her back; it was there so those who feared her ability could have her at their side and still sleep soundly, convinced by the lie that it would protect them from her unearthliness. The texture of the cool metal gave her focus, and she let herself draw inward.

The last thing she looked at before she closed her eyes was the chronometer on a nearby desk; Hyssos and the local lawmen had returned from the *Iubar* several hours ago, but she hadn't seen any of them since the audience with the Void Baron. She wondered what Hyssos would be doing, but she resisted the urge to extend a tendril of thought out to search for him. Her telepathic abilities were poor and it was only her familiarity with his mind that allowed her to sense him with any degree of certainty. In truth, Perrig's desire to be close to Hyssos only ever brought her melancholy. She had once looked into his thoughts as he slept, once when he had let down his guard, and there she saw that he had no inkling of the strange devotion the psyker had for her guardian; no understanding of this peculiar attachment that could not be thought of as love, but neither as anything else. It was better that way, she decided. Perrig did not wish to think of what might happen if he knew. She would be taken away from him, most likely. Perhaps even returned to the Black Ships from where Baron Eurotas had first claimed her.

Perrig suffocated the thoughts and returned to her business at hand, eyes tightly shut, her calm forced back into place like a key jammed into a lock.

The psyker knelt on the hard wooden floor of the room. Arranged in a semi-circle around her were a careful line of objects she had picked from the debris of the old wine lodge. Some stones, a brass button from a greatcoat, sticky grease-paper wrapping from a meat-stick vendor and a red leaflet dense with script in the local dialect of Imperial Gothic. Perrig touched them all in order, moving back and forth, lingering on some, returning to others. She used the items to build a jigsaw puzzle image of the suspect, but there were gaping holes in the simulacra. Places where she could not sense the full dimension of who Erno Sigg was.

The button had fear on it. It had been lost as he fled the fire and the howl of the coleopters.

The stones. These he had picked up and turned in his hands, used them in an idle game of throws, tossing them across the shack and back again, boredom and nervous energy marbling their otherwise inert auras.

The grease-paper was laden with hunger, panic. The image here was quite distinct; he had stolen the food from the vendor while the man's back was turned. He had been convinced he would be caught and arrested.

The leaflet was love. Love or something like it, at least in the manner that Perrig could understand. Dedication, then, if one were to be more correct, with almost a texture of righteousness about it.

She dithered over the piece of paper, looking through her closed lids at the emotional spectra it generated. Sigg was complex and the psyker had trouble holding the pieces she had of him in her mind. He was conflicted; buried somewhere deep there was the distant echo of great violence in him, but it was overshadowed by two towering opposite forces. On one hand, a grand sense of hope, even redemption, as if he believed he would be saved; and on the other, an equally powerful dread of something hunting him, of his own victimhood.

Perrig's psychometry was not an exact science, but in her time as an investigator she had developed a keen sense of her own instincts; it was this sense that told her Erno Sigg did not kill for his pleasures. As that thought crystallised inside her mind, Perrig felt the first fuzzy inklings of a direction coming to her. She allowed her hand to pick up the stylus at her side and moved it to the waiting data-slate on the floor. It twitched as the auto-writing began in spidery, uneven text.

Her other hand, though, had not left the leaflet. Her fingers toyed with the edges of it, playing with the careworn paper, seeking out the places where it had been delicately folded and unfolded, time and time again. She wondered what it meant to Sigg that he cared so much for it, and sensed the ghost of the anguish he would feel at its loss.

That would be how she would find him. The sorrow, fluttering from him like a pennant in the wind. The scribbling stylus moved of its own accord, back and forth across the slate.

Confidence rose in her. She would find Erno Sigg. *She would*. And Hyssos would be pleased with her–

Her heart jumped in her chest and she gasped. The stylus, gripped beyond its tolerances, snapped in two and the broken ends dug into her palm. Perrig was suddenly trembling, and she knew why. At the back of her mind there had been a thought she had not wanted to confront, something she took care to avoid as one might favour an ugly, painful bruise upon the skin.

But now she was drawn to it, touching the discoloured edges of the psychic contusion, flinching at the tiny ticks of pain it gave off.

She had sensed it after their arrival on Iesta Veracrux. At first, Perrig imagined it was only an artefact of the transition of her mind, from the controlled peace of her domicile aboard the *Iubar* to the riotous newness of the planet's busy city.

*Correction*; she had *wanted* to believe it was that.

The trembling grew as she dared to focus on it. A dark shadow at the edges of her perception, close at hand. Closer than Erno Sigg. Much, much closer, more so than Hyssos or any of the Iestan investigators suspected.

Perrig felt a sudden wetness at her nostrils, on her cheek. She smelled copper. Blinking, she opened her eyes and the first thing she saw was the leaflet. It was red, deep crimson, the words printed on it lost against the shade of the paper. Panting in a breath, Perrig looked up from where she knelt and saw that the room, and everything in it, was red and red and red.

She let the broken stylus fall and wiped at her face. Thick fluid came away from the corners of her eyes. Blood, not tears.

Propelled by a surge of fright, she came to her feet, her boot catching the data-slate and crushing the glassy screen beneath the heel. The room seemed humid and stifling, every surface damp and meat-slick. Perrig lurched towards the only window and reached for the pull to drag back the curtains so she might open it, get a breath of untainted air.

The drapes were made of red and shadows, and they parted like petals as she came closer. Something approximating the shape of a human being opened up there, suspended by spindly feet from the ceiling overhead. The heavy velvets thumped to the wooden floor and the figure unfolded, wet and shiny with oils. Its name impressed itself on the soft surfaces of her mind and she was forced to speak it aloud just to expunge the horror of it.

'Spear...'

A distended maw of teeth and bone barbs grew from the head of the monstrosity. Stygian flame, visible only to those with the curse of the witch-sight, wreathed the abstract face and the black pits that were its eyes. In an instant, Perrig knew what had made all those kills, what hands had delicately cut into Jaared Norte, Cirsun Latigue and all the others who had perished at its inclination.

She backed away, her voice lost to her. More than anything, Perrig wanted to cover her eyes and look away, find somewhere to hide her face so that she would not be forced to see the Spear-thing; but there was nowhere for her to turn. Even if she clawed the orbs from her sockets, her witch-sight would still remain, and the aura of this monstrous creature would continue to smother it.

Horribly, she sensed that the killer *wanted* her to look upon it, with all the depth of perception her psychic talents allowed. It projected a need for her to witness it, and that desire drew her in like the pull of gravity from a dark sun.

Spear muttered to itself. When Perrig had touched the minds of other killers in the past, she had always flinched at the awful joy with which they pursued their craft; she did not see that here, however. Spear's psyche was a pool of black ink, featureless and undisturbed by madness, lust or naked fury. It was almost inert, moving under the guidance of an unshakable certainty. It reminded her for one fleeting instant of Hyssos's ordered mindset; the killer shared the same dogged, unflinching sense of direction towards its goals... almost as if it were following a string of commands.

And still it let her in. She knew if she refused it, Spear would tear her open then and there. She tried desperately to break past the miasma of cold that lay around her, projecting as best she could a panicked summons towards her absent guardian; but as she did this, she also let her mind fall into Spear, stalling for time, on some level repulsed and fascinated by the monster's true nature.

Spear was not coy; it opened itself to her. What she saw in there sickened her beyond her capacity to express. The killer had been made this way, taken from some human stock now so corrupted that its origin could not be determined, sheathed with a skein of living materials that seemed cut from the screaming depths of the warp itself. Perhaps a fluke of cruel nature, or perhaps a thing created by twisted genius, Spear was soulless, but unlike any stripe of psionic null Perrig had ever encountered.

It was a Black Pariah; the ultimate expression of negative psychic force. Perrig had believed such things were only conjecture, the mad nightmare creations of wild theorists and sorcerous madmen – yet here it stood, watching her, breathing the same air as she wept blood before it.

And then Spear reached out with fingers made of knives and took Perrig's hand. She howled as burning pain lanced through her nerves; the killer severed her right thumb with insolent ease and drew it up and away, toying with its prize. Perrig gripped her injured hand, vitae gushing from the wound.

Spear took the severed flesh and rolled it into its fanged maw, crunching down the bone and meat as if it were a rare delicacy. Perrig sank back to the blood-spattered floor, her head swimming as she caught the edges of the sudden psionic shift running through the killer.

The black voids of its eyes glared down at her and they became smoky mirrors. In them she saw her own mind reflected back at her, the power of her own psionic talents bubbling and rippling, copied and enhanced a thousandfold. Spear had tasted her blood, the living gene-code of her being – and now it knew her. It had her imprint.

She scrambled backwards, feeling the humming chorus of her mind and that of the killer coming into shuddering synchrony, the orbits of their powers

moving towards alignment. Perrig cried out and
begged it to stop, but Spear only cocked its head and
let the power build.

It had not killed in this manner for a long time, she
realised. The other deaths had been mundane and
unremarkable. It wanted to do this just to be sure it
was still capable, as a soldier might release a clip of
ammunition to test the accuracy of a firearm. Belatedly Perrig understood that she was the only thing for
light years around that could have been any kind of
threat to it; but now, too late.

And then, they met in the non-space between them.
Beyond her ability to stop it, Perrig's psionic ability
unchained itself and thundered against Spear's waiting, open arms. The killer took it all in, every last
morsel, and did so with the ease of breathing.

In stillness, Spear released its burden and reflected
back all that Perrig was, the force of her preternatural
power returning, magnified into a silent, furious hurricane.

The woman became ashes and broke apart.

THROUGH THE CORUSCATING, unquenchable fires of
the immaterium, the *Ultio* raced on, passing through
the corridors of the warp and onwards beyond the
borders of the Segmentum Solar. The ship's sight-
blind Navigator took it through the routes that were
little known, the barely-charted passages that the
upper echelons of the Imperial government kept off
the maps given to the common admiralty. These
were swift routes but treacherous ones, causeways
through the atemporal realm that larger ships would
never have been able to take, the soul-light glitter of

their massive crews bright enough that they would attract the living storms that wheeled and turned, while *Ultio* passed by unnoticed. The phantom-ship was barely there; its Geller fields had such finely-tuned opacity and it engines such speed that the lumbering, predatory intelligences that existed inside warp space noted it only by the wake it left behind. As days turned and clocks spun back on Terra, *Ultio* flew towards Dagonet; by some reckonings, it was already there.

On board, the Execution Force gathered once more, this time in a compartment off the spinal corridor that ran the length of the starship's massive drives.

KELL WATCHED, AS he always did.

The Garantine was still toying with his makeshift blade. He had continued to craft it into a wicked shiv that was easily the length of a man's forearm. 'What do you want, Vanus?' he asked.

Tariel gave a nervous smile and indicated a large cargo module that replaced one whole wall of the long, low compartment. 'Uh, thank you for coming.' He glanced around at Kell, Iota and the others. 'As we are now mission-committed, I have leave to continue with the next stage of my orders.'

'Explain,' said Koyne.

The infocyte rubbed his hands together. 'I was given a directive by the Master of Assassins himself to present these materials to you only after the group had been completely assembled and only after the *Ultio* had left the Sol system.' He moved to a keypad on the cargo module and tapped in a string of symbols. 'I am to address the matter of your equipment.'

The Eversor assassin's head snapped up, his mood instantly changing from insolence to laser-like intensity. 'Weapons?' he asked, almost salivating.

Tariel nodded. 'Among other things. This unit contains the hardware for our mission ahead.'

'Did you know about this?' demanded the Garantine, glaring at Kell. 'Here I am playing with scraps and there's a war-load right here on board with me?'

Kell shook his head. 'I assumed we'd be equipped on site.'

'Why did someone fail to tell me there was an armoury aboard this tub?' Tariel ducked as the Garantine threw his shiv and it buried itself in a stanchion close by. 'Give me a weapon, *now*! Feels like I'm bloody naked here!'

'What a delightful image,' murmured Soalm.

'He needs it,' said Iota, distractedly. 'He actually feels a kind of emotional pain when separated from his firearms. Like a parent torn from its child.'

'I'll show you *torn*,' grated the hulking killer, menacing the Vanus. 'I'll do some *tearing*.'

'Open!' Tariel fairly shouted the word and the mechanism controlling the lock hissed on oiled hydraulics. The pod split along its length and rolled back, presenting brackets of guns, support equipment and other wargear.

The Garantine's face lit up with something approximating joy. 'Hello, pretty pretty,' he muttered, drawn to a rack where a heavy pistol, ornate and decorated with metallic wings and sensor probes, lay waiting. He gathered it up and hefted it in one hand. Cold laughter fell from his lips as gene-markers tingled through him, briefly communing with the lobo-chips implanted in his brain, confirming his identity and purpose.

'The Executor combi-pistol,' said Tariel, blinking rapidly as he drew the information up from a mnemonic pool in his deep cortex. 'Dual function ballistic bolt weapon and needle projectile–'

'I know what it is!' snarled the Garantine, before he could finish. 'Oh, we are very well acquainted.' He stroked the gun like it was a pet.

Kell spoke up. 'All of you, take what you need but make sure you use what you take. Go back to your compartments and prepare your gear for immediate deployment. We have no idea how long we may have between our arrival and the target's.'

'He may already be there waiting for us,' offered Koyne, drifting towards a different rack of weapons. 'The tides of the warp often flow against the ebb of time.'

The Garantine greedily gathered armfuls of hardware, taking bandoliers of melta-grenades, a wickedly barbed neuro-gauntlet and the rig for a sentinel array. With another guttural laugh, he snagged a heavy, blunt-ended slaughterer's sword and placed it under his arm. 'I'll be in my bunk,' he sniggered, and wandered away under his burden.

Iota watched the Eversor go. 'Look at him. He's almost… happy.'

'Every child needs its toys,' said Soalm.

The Culexus gave the racks a sideways look, and then turned away. 'Not me. There's nothing here that I need.' She shot the Venenum poisoner a look, tapping her temple. 'I have a weapon already.'

'The animus speculum, yes,' said Soalm. 'I've heard of it. But it is an ephemeral thing, isn't it? Its use depends on the power of the opponent as much as that of the user, so I am led to believe.'

Iota's lips pulled tight in a small smile. 'If you wish.'

Tariel nervously approached them. 'I... I do have an item put aside for your use, Culexus,' he said, offering an armoured box covered with warning runes. 'If you will?'

Iota flipped open the lid and cocked her head. Inside there were a dozen grenades made of black metal. 'Oh,' she said. 'Explosives. How ordinary.'

'No, no,' he insisted. 'This is a new technology. An experimental weapon not yet field-tested under operational conditions. A creation of your clade's senior scienticians.'

The woman plucked one of the grenades from the case and sniffed it. Her eyes narrowed. 'What is this? It smells like the death of suns.'

'I am not permitted to know the full details,' admitted the infocyte. 'But the devices contain an exotic form of particulate matter that inhibits the function of psionic ability in a localised area.'

Iota studied the grenade for a long moment, toying with the activator pin, before finally giving Tariel a wan look. 'I'll take these,' she said, snatching the box from his hand.

'What do you have for the rest of us in your delightful toy box?' Koyne asked lightly, playing with a pair of memory swords. They had curved, graceful blades that shifted angles in mid-flight as the Callidus cut the air with them.

'Toxin cordes.' The Vanus pressed a control and a belt threaded with glassy stilettos extended from a sealed drum marked with biohazard trefoils.

Koyne put up the swords and reached for them, only to see that Soalm was doing the same. The Callidus gave a small bow. 'Oh, pardon me, cousin. Poisons are of course your domain.'

Soalm gave a tight, humourless smile. 'No. After you. Take what you wish.'

Koyne held up a hand. 'No, no. After *you*. Please. I insist.'

'As you wish.' The Venenum carefully retrieved one of the daggers and turned it in her fingers. She held it up to the light, turning it this way and that so the coloured fluids inside the glass poison blade flowed back and forth. At length, she sniffed. 'These are of fair quality. They'll work well enough on any man who stands between us and Horus.'

The Callidus picked out a few blades. 'But what about those who are not men? What about Horus himself?'

Soalm's lips thinned. 'This would be the bite of a gnat to the Warmaster.' She gave Tariel a look. 'I will prepare my own weapons.'

'There's also this,' offered the Vanus, passing her a pistol. The weapon was a spindly collection of brass pipes with a crystalline bulb where a normal firearm might have had an ammunition magazine. Soalm took it and peered at the mesh grille where the muzzle should have been.

'A bact-gun,' she said, weighing it in her hand. 'This may be useful.'

'The dispersal can be set from a fine mist to a gel-plug round,' noted Tariel.

'Are you certain you know how to use that?' said Kell.

Soalm's arm snapped up into aiming position, the barrel of the weapon pointed directly at the Vindicare's face. 'I think I can recall,' she said. Then she wandered away, turning the pistol over in her delicate, pale hands.

Meanwhile, Koyne had discovered a case that was totally out of place among all the others. It resembled a whorled shell more than anything else, and the only mechanism to unlock it was the sketch of a handprint etched into the bony matter of the latch – a handprint of three overlong digits and a dual thumb.

'I have no idea what that may be,' Tariel admitted. 'The container, I mean, it looks almost as if it is–'

'Xenos?' said Koyne, with deceptive lightness. 'But that would be prohibited, Vanus. Perish the thought.' There was a quiet cracking sound as the Callidus's right hand stretched and shifted in shape, the human digits reformed and merging until they became something more approximate to the alien handprint. Koyne pressed home on the case and it sighed open, drooling droplets of purple liquid on to the decking. Inside the container, the organic look was even more disturbing; on a bed of fleshy material wet with more of the liquid rested a weapon made of blackened, tooth-like ceramics. It was large and off-balance in shape, the front of it grasping a faceted teardrop crystal the sea-green colour of ancient jade.

'What is it?' Tariel asked, his disgust evident.

'In my clade it has many names,' said Koyne. 'It rips open minds, tears intellect and thought to shreds. Those it touches remain empty husks.' The Callidus held it out to the Vanus, who backed away. 'Do you wish to take a closer look?'

'Not in this lifetime,' Tariel insisted.

A pale tongue flickered out and licked Koyne's lips as the assassin returned the weapon to the shell. Gathering it up, the Callidus bowed to the others. 'I will take my leave of you.'

As Koyne left, Kell glanced back at the Vanus. 'What about you? Or do those of your clade choose not to carry a weapon?'

Tariel shook his head, colour returning to his cheeks. 'I have weapons of my own, just not as obvious as yours. An electropulse projector, built into my cogitator gauntlet. And I have my menagerie. The psyber eagles, the eyerats and netfly swarms.'

Kell thought of the pods he had seen elsewhere aboard the *Ultio*, where Tariel's cybernetically-modified rodents and preybirds and other animals slept out the voyage in dormancy, waiting for his word of command to awaken them. 'Those things won't keep you alive.'

The Vanus shook his head. 'Ah, believe me, I will make sure that nothing ever gets close enough to kill me.' He sighed. 'And in that vein... There are also weapons for you.'

'My weapon was lost,' Kell said, with no little venom. 'Thanks to the Eversor.'

'It has been renewed,' said Tariel, opening a lengthy box. 'See.'

Every Vindicare used a longrifle that was uniquely configured for their biomass, shooting style, body kinetics, even tailored to work with the rhythm in which they breathed. When the Garantine had smashed Kell's weapon into pieces out in the Aktick snows, it was like he had lost a part of himself; but there inside the case was a sniper rifle that resembled the very gun that had been his constant companion for years – resembled it, but also transcended it. 'Exitus,' he breathed, stooping to run a hand over the flat, non-reflective surface of the barrel.

Tariel indicated the individual components of the weapon. 'Spectroscopic polyimager scope. Carousel ammunition loader. Nitrogen coolant sheath. Whisperhead suppressor unit. Gyroscopic balance stabiliser.' He paused. 'As much of your original weapon as possible was salvaged and reused in this one.'

Kell nodded. He saw that the grip and part of the cheek-plate were worn in a way that no newly-forged firearm could have been. As well as the longrifle, a pistol of similar design lay next to it on the velvet bedding of the weapon case. Lined up along the lid of the container were row after row of individual bullets, arranged in colour-coded groups. 'Impressive. But I'll need to sight it in.'

'We'll doubtless all have many opportunities to employ our skills before Horus shows his face,' said Soalm. She hadn't left the room, but stood off to one side as the sniper and the infocyte talked.

'We will do what we have to,' Kell replied, without looking at her.

'Even if we destroy ourselves doing it,' his sister replied.

The marksman's jaw hardened and his eyes fell to a line of words that had been etched into the slender barrel of the rifle. Written in a careful scrolling hand was the Dictatus Vindicare, the maxim of his clade; *Exitus Acta Probat*.

'The outcome justifies the deed,' said Kell.

* * *

WHAT HE SAW in the room was like no manner of death Yosef Sabrat had ever conceived of. The killings of Latigue in the aeronef and Norte at the docks, while they were horrors that sickened him to his core, had not pressed at his reason. But not this, not this... deed.

Black ashes were scattered in a long pool across the middle of Perrig's room, cast out of a set of clothes that lay splayed out where they had fallen. At the top of the cascade of cinders, a small hill of the dark powder covered an iron collar, the bolt holding it shut still secure, and in among the pile there were the silver needles of neural implants glittering in the lamplight.

'I... don't understand.' The Gorospe woman was standing a few steps behind the investigators, outside in the corridor with Yosef where the jagers milled around, uncertain how to proceed. 'I don't understand,' she repeated. 'Where did the... the woman go to?'

She had almost said *the witch*. Yosef sensed the half-formed word on her lips, and he shot her a look filled with sudden fury. Gorospe looked up at him with wide, limpid eyes, and he felt his hands contract into fists. She was so callous and dismissive of the dead psyker; he fought back a brief urge to grab her and slam her up against the wall, shout at her for her stupidity. Then he took a breath and said 'She didn't go anywhere. That's all that is left of her.'

Yosef walked away, pushing past Skelta. The jager gave him a wary nod. 'Heard from Reeve Segan, sir. They called him in from his off-shift. He's on his way.'

He returned Skelta's nod and took a wary step through the field barrier and into the room, careful not to disturb the cluster of small mapping automata that scanned the crime scene with picters and ranging lasers. Hyssos was crouching, looking back and forth around the walls, staring towards the windows, then back to the ashen remains. He had his back to the doorway and Yosef heard him take a shuddering breath. It was almost a sob.

'Do you... need a moment?' As soon as he said the words, he felt like an utter fool. Of *course* he did; his colleague had just been brutally murdered, and in an abhorrent, baffling manner.

'No,' said Hyssos. 'Yes,' he said, an instant later. 'No. *No*. There will be time for that. *After*.' The operative looked up at him and his eyes were shining. 'Do you know, I think, at the end... I think I actually heard her.' He fingered one of the braids among his hair.

Yosef saw the semi-circle of objects on the floor, the stones and the paper. 'What are these?'

'Foci,' Hyssos told him. 'Objects imbued with some emotional resonance from the suspect. Perrig reads them. She read them.' He corrected himself absently.

'I am sorry.'

Hyssos nodded. 'You will let me kill this man when we find him,' he told Yosef, in a steady, measured voice. 'We will make certain, of course, of his guilt,' he added, nodding. 'But the death. You will let me have that.'

Yosef felt warm and uncomfortable. 'We'll burn that bridge after we cross it.' He looked away and found the places on the far wall behind him where the markings had been made. On his entry into the room, he hadn't seen them. Like the paintings in blood inside the aeronef or the shape that Jaared Norte's body had been cut into, there were eight-point stars all over the light-coloured walls. It seemed that the killer had used the residue of Perrig as his ink, repeating the same pattern over and over again.

'What does it mean?' Hyssos mumbled.

The reeve licked his lips; they were suddenly dry. He had a strange sensation, a tingling in the base of his skull like the dull headache brought on by too much recaf and not enough fresh air. The shapes were all he could see, and he felt like there was an answer there, if only he could find the right way to look at them. They were no different from the mathematical problems in Ivak's schola texts, they just needed to be *solved* to be *understood*.

'Sabrat, what does it mean?' said Hyssos again. 'This word?'

Yosef blinked and the moment vanished. He looked back at the investigator. Hyssos had removed something from among the ashen remains; a data-slate, the screen spiderwebbed and fractured. Incredibly, the display underneath was still operating, flickering sporadically.

Gingerly, Yosef took it from him, taking care to avoid touching the powder-slicked surfaces of the device. The touch-sensitive screen still remembered the words that had been etched upon it, and flashed them at him, almost too quickly to register.

'One of the words is "Sigg",' Hyssos told him. 'Do you see it?'

He did; and beneath that, there was a scribble that appeared to be the attempt to form another string of letters, the shape of them lost now. But above the name, there was another clearly-lettered word.

'Whyteleaf. Is that a person's name?'

Yosef shook his head, instantly knowing the meaning. 'Not a person. A place. I know it well.'

Hyssos was abruptly on his feet. 'Close?'

'In the low crags, a quick trip by coleopter.'

The investigator's brief flash of grief and sorrow was gone. 'We need to go there, right now. Perrig's readings decay over time.' He tapped the broken slate. 'If she sensed Sigg was in this place, every moment we waste here, we run the risk he will flee again.'

Skelta had caught the edge of their conversation. 'Sir, we don't have any other units in the area. Backup is dealing with a railganger fight that went bad out at the airdocks and security prep for the trade carnival.'

Yosef made the choice then and there. 'When Daig gets here, tell him to take over the scene and keep Laimner occupied.' He moved towards the door, not looking back to see if Hyssos was following. 'We're taking the flyer.'

THE OPERATIVE HAD lost colleagues before, and it had been difficult then as it was now; but Perrig's death was something more than that. It came in like a bullet, cutting right into the core of Hyssos's soul. Losing himself in the rush of the dark, low clouds outside the windows of the coleopter, he tried to parse his own emotional reactions to the moment without success. Perrig had always been a good, trusted colleague, and he liked her company. She had never pressured him to talk about his past or tried to worm more information out of him than he wanted to give. Hyssos had always felt respected in her presence, and rewarded by her competence, her cool, calm intelligence.

Now she was dead; worse than dead, not a corpse even, just dark cinders, just a slurry of matter that did not bear any resemblance to the human being he had known. He felt a hard stab of guilt. Perrig had always given him her complete and total trust, and he had not been there to protect her when she needed it. Now this investigation had crossed from the professional to the personal, and Hyssos was uncertain of himself.

Looking from the outside in, had he been a passive observer, Hyssos would have immediately insisted that an operative in his circumstances be withdrawn from the case and a new team assigned from the Consortium's security pool. And that, he knew, was why he had not yet sent an official report on Perrig's death to the Void Baron, because Eurotas himself would say the same.

But Hyssos was here, now, and he knew the stakes. It would take too long to bring another operative up to speed. As competent as locals like Sabrat were, the reeve's seniors couldn't be trusted to handle this with alacrity.

*Yes.* All those were good lies to tell himself, all gilded with the ring of truth, when in fact all he wanted at this moment was to put Perrig's killer down like a rabid animal.

Hyssos clasped his hands together to stop them making fists. Outwardly his icy calm did not shift, but inside he was seething. The operative glanced at Sabrat as the flyer began to circle in towards a landing. 'What is this Whyteleaf?'

'What?' Sabrat turned suddenly, snapping at him with venom, as if Hyssos had called out some grave

personal insult. Then he blinked, the strange anger
ebbing for a moment. 'Oh. Yes. It's a winestock. Many
of the smaller lodges store vintage estufagemi here,
holding barrels of it for years so it can mature undisturbed.'

'How many staff?'

Sabrat shook his head distractedly. 'It… It's all
automated.' The flyer's skids bumped as the craft
landed. 'Quickly!' said the reeve, bolting up from his
seat. 'If the coleopter dwells, Sigg will know we're on
to him.'

Hyssos followed him down the drop ramp, into a
cloud of upswept dust and leaves caught in the wake
of the aircraft. He saw Sabrat give the pilot a clipped
wave and the coleopter rattled back into the sky, leaving them ducking the sudden wind.

As the noise died away, Hyssos frowned. 'Was that
wise? We could use another pair of eyes.'

The reeve was already walking on, across the top of
the shallow warehouse where they had been
deposited. 'Sigg ran the last time.' He shook his head.
'Do you want that to happen again?' Sabrat said it
almost as if it had been the operative's fault.

'Of course not,' Hyssos said quietly, and drew his
gun and a portable auspex from the pockets inside his
tunic. 'We should split up, then. Search for him.'

Sabrat nodded, crouching to open a hatch in the
roof. 'Agreed. Work your way down the floors and
meet me on the basement level. If you find him, put a
shot into the air.' Before Hyssos could say anything in
reply, the reeve dropped through the hatch and into
the dark.

Hyssos took a deep breath and moved forward, finding another accessway at the far end of the warehouse. Pausing to don a pair of amplifier glasses, he went inside.

THERE WAS LITTLE light inside the winestock, but the glasses dealt with that for him. The pools of shadow were rendered into a landscape of whites, greys, greens and blacks. Reaching the decking of the uppermost tier, Hyssos saw the shapes of massive storage tanks rising up around him, the curves of towering wooden slats forming the walls of the great jeroboams. The smoky, potent smell of the wine was everywhere, the air thick and warm with it.

He walked carefully, his boots crunching on hard lumps of crystallised sugar caught in the gaps between the planks of the floor, the wood giving with quiet, moaning creaks. The auspex, a small device fashioned in the design of an ornate book, was open on a belt tether, the sensing mechanism working with a slow pulse of light. The unchanged cadence indicated no signs of human life within its scan radius. Hyssos wondered why Sabrat wasn't registering; but then this building was dense with metals and the scanner's range was limited.

The operative's thoughts kept returning to the dataslate that Perrig had left behind. From the positioning of it among the psyker's ashes, he supposed that it might have been in her hand when she met her end. She had seen Erno Sigg through the foci objects gathered from the Blasko Wine Lodge and tracked him here through the etherium – but the other word, the third line of letters on the slate… What meaning did they have? What had she been trying to say? How had she died in such a manner?

Finally, he could not let the question lie and he used his free hand to pull the smashed slate from his pocket.

*Another error in judgement*, said a voice in the back of his thoughts. The data-slate was evidence, and yet he had taken it from a crime scene. Pushing back the glasses to his forehead, Hyssos studied the broken screen in the dimness. The scribble of letters there were barely readable, but he knew Perrig's steady, looping handwriting of old. If he could just find a way to see it afresh, to look with new eyes, perhaps he could intuit what she had been trying to write–

*Spear.*

It hit him like a splash of cold water. A sudden snap of comprehension. Yes, he was sure of it. The spin of the consonants and the loop of the vowels… *Yes.*

But what did it mean?

The next step he took made a wet ripping noise and something along the line of his boot dragged at him, as if a thick layer of glue carpeted the floor.

Hyssos sniffed the air, wondering if one of the mammoth wine casks had leaked; but then the stale, metallic smell rose up to smother the cloying sweetness all around. He dropped the slate back into his pocket and gingerly slid the goggles down over his eyes once more.

And there, rendered in cold, sea-green shades, was a frieze made of meat and bones. Across the curve of a wooden storage tank, beneath a wide stanchion and in shadow where the light of Iesta's days would never have fallen, the display of an eviscerated corpse was visible to him.

The body was open, the skin cut so that the innards, the skeleton and the muscle were free for removal. The fleshy rags that remained of the victim were nailed up in the parody of a human shape; organs and bones had been taken and arranged in patterns, some of them reassembled together in horrible new fusions. Ribs, for example, fanned like daggers sticking into the wet meat of a pale liver. A pelvic bone dressed with intestines. The spongy mass of a lung wrapped in coils of stripped nerve. All about him, the blood was a matted, dried pool, a sticky patina that had mixed with wine spillages and doubtless seeped down through the floor of this level and the next. Thousands of gallons of carefully matured liquor was tainted, polluted by what had been done here.

At the edges of the ocean of vitae where the fluid ran away, eight-point stars dotted the bland wooden panels. Amid it all, Hyssos's eyes caught a shape that focussed his attention instantly; a face. He gingerly stepped closer, his gorge rising as his boots sucked at the flooring. Narrowing his eyes, the operative drew up the auspex, turning its sensoria on the blood slick.

It was Erno Sigg's face, cut from the front of his skull, lying like a discarded paper mask.

The chime of the auspex drew his gaze from the horror. Hyssos had been trained by the Consortium's technologians on the reading of its outputs, and he saw datums unfurl on its small screen. The blood, it told him, was days old; perhaps even as much as a week. This atrocity had been done to Erno Sigg well before Perrig's execution, of that there was no doubt. The auspex could not lie.

Swallowing his revulsion, Hyssos let the scanning device drop on its tether and raised his gun upwards, finger tightening on the trigger. His hand was trembling, and he could not seem to steady it.

But then the footsteps reached him. From across the other side of the lake of dried blood, a shadow detached from the darkness and came closer. Hyssos recognised the purposeful gait of the Iestan reeve; but he moved without hesitation, straight across the middle of it, boots sucking at the glutinous, oily mess.

'Sabrat,' called the operative, his voice thick with repugnance, 'What are you doing, man? Look around, can't you see it?'

'I see it,' came the reply. The words were paper-dry.

The amplifier glasses seemed like a blindfold around his head and Hyssos tore them off. 'For Terra's sake, Yosef, step back! You'll contaminate the site!'

'Yosef isn't here,' said the voice, as it became fluid and wet, transforming. 'Yosef went away.'

The reeve came out of the dimness and he was different. There were only black pits glaring back at Hyssos from a shifting face that moved like oil on water.

'My name is Spear,' said the horror. The face was eyeless, and no longer human.

# NINE

### Dagonet
### Assumption
### Falling

THE ORBITS ABOVE Dagonet were clogged with the wreckage of ships that had tried too hard to make it off the surface, vessels that were built as pleasure yachts or shuttlecraft, suborbitals and single-stage cargo barges for the runs to the near moons. Many of them had fallen foul of the system frigates blockading the escape vectors, torn apart under hails of las-fire; but more had simply failed. Ships that were over-loaded or ill-prepared for the rigours of leaving near-orbit space had burned out their drives or lost atmosphere. The sky was filled with iron coffins that were gradually spiralling back to the turning world below them. At night, those on the planet could see them coming home in streaks of fire, and they served as a reminder of what would happen to anyone who disagreed with the Governor's new order.

The *Ultio* navigated in on puffs of thruster gas, hav-ing left the warp in the shadow of the Dagonet system's

thick asteroid belt. Cloaked in stealth technologies so
advanced they were almost impenetrable, it easily
avoided the ponderous turncoat cruisers and their nervous crews, finding safe harbour inside the empty shell
of an abandoned orbital solar station. Securing the
drive section in a place where it – along with *Ultio*'s
astropath and Navigator – would be relatively safe, the
forward module detached and reconfigured itself to
resemble a common courier or guncutter. The pilot's
brain drew information from scans of the traitorous
ships to alter the electropigments of the hull, and by
the time the assassin craft touched down at the capital's star-port, it wore the same blue and green as the
local forces, even down to the crudely crossed-out
Imperial aquila displayed by the defectors.

Kell had Koyne stand by the vox rig, ready to talk
back to the control tower. The Callidus had already
listened in on comm traffic snared from the airwaves
by Tariel's complex scanning gear, and could perform
a passable imitation of a Dagoneti accent – but challenge never came.

The tower was gone, blown into broken fragments,
and all across the sprawling landing fields and smoke-
wreathed hangars, small fires were burning and
wrecked ships that had died on take-off lay atop crumpled departure terminals and support buildings.
Gunfire and the thump of grenade detonations
echoed to them across the open runways.

Kell advanced down the ramp and used the sights
on his new longrifle to sweep the perimeter.

'Fighting was recent,' said the Garantine, following
him down. The hulking rage killer took a deep
draught of air. 'Still smell the blood and cordite.'

'They've moved on,' said the sniper, sweeping his gaze over corpses of soldiers and civilians who lay where they had fallen. It was difficult to be sure who had been shooting at who; Dagonet was in the middle of a civil war, and the lines of loyalist and turncoat were not yet clear to the new arrivals. A blink of laser fire from inside one of the massive terminals caught his eye and he turned to it as the crack of broken air reached them a moment later. 'But not too far. They're fighting through the buildings. Lucky for us the place is still contested. Leaves us with less explaining to do.'

He shouldered the rifle as Tariel ventured a few wary steps down the ramp. 'Vindicare? How are we to proceed?'

Kell walked back up a way. The rest of the Execution Force were gathered on the lower deck, watching him intently. 'We need to gather intelligence. Find out what's going on here.'

'Dagonet's extrasolar communications went dark some time ago,' noted Tariel. 'Perhaps if you could secure a prisoner for interrogation…'

Kell nodded and beckoned to Koyne. 'Callidus. You're in charge until we get back.'

'*We?*' said Soalm pointedly.

He nodded towards the Garantine. 'The two of us. We'll scout the star-port, see what we can find.'

'Ah, good,' said the Eversor, rubbing his clawed hands together. '*Exercise.*'

'Are you sure two will be enough?' Soalm went on.

Kell ignored her and moved closer to Koyne. 'Keep them alive, understand?'

Koyne made a thoughtful face. 'We're all lone wolves, Vindicare. If the enemy come knocking, my first instinct might be to run and leave them.'

He didn't rise to the bait. 'Then consider that order a test of your oath over your instincts.'

Sabrat's longcoat whirled as the horror coiled, leaping into the air towards Hyssos. The operative heard it snapping like sailcloth in a stiff breeze and recoiled, firing shots that should have struck centre-mass but instead hit nothing but air.

The thing that called itself Spear landed close to him and he took a heavy blow that threw him off his feet. Hyssos slammed into a tall pile of Balthazar bottles that tumbled away with the impact, rolling this way and that. Pain raced up his spine as he twisted and tried to regain his footing.

Spear tossed the coat away and then, with care that seemed strange for something so abhorrent in appearance, deftly unbuttoned the white shirt beneath and set it aside. Bare from the waist up, Hyssos could see that the creature's flesh was writhing and changing, cherry-red like tanned leather. He saw what looked like hands pressing out from inside the cage of the monster's chest, and the profile of a screaming face. *Yosef Sabrat's face.*

The bare arms distended and grew large, their proportions ballooning. Fingers merged into flat mittens of meat, grew stiff and glassy. Hands became bone blades, pennants of pinkish-black nerve tissue dangling from them.

Hyssos aimed the gun and fired at the place where a man's heart would have been, but down came the arms and the shot was deflected away. He smelled a slaughterhouse stink coming off the creature, saw the sizzling pit in the limb from the impact as it filled with ooze and knit itself shut.

The body of the thing was in chaos. It writhed and throbbed and pulsed in disgusting ways, and the operative was struck by the conviction that something was *inside* the meat of it, trying to get out.

As the eyeless face glared into him, the distended jaws opening wide to let droplets of spittle fall free, Hyssos found his voice. 'You killed them all.'

'Yes.' The reply was a gurgling chug of noise.

'Why?' he demanded, retreating back until he was trapped against the fallen bottles. 'What in Terra's name are you?'

'There is no Terra,' it bubbled, horrible amusement shading the words. 'Only *terror*.'

Hyssos saw the shape of the face again, this time pressing from the meat of Spear's bloated shoulders. He was sure it was crying out to him, imploring him. *Run*, it mouthed, *run run run run*–

He raised the gun, shaking, his blood turning to ice. Hands tightening on the grip, aiming for the head. In his time, Hyssos had seen many things that defied easy explanation – strange forms of alien life, the impossible vistas of warp space, the darkest potentials of the human character – and this creature was first among them. If hell was a place, then this was something that had been torn out of that infernal realm and thrust into the real world.

Spear raised its sword-arms and rattled their hard surfaces off one another. 'One more,' it intoned. 'One step closer.'

'To what?' The question was a gasp. It came at him again, and Hyssos shot it in the face.

Spear shrugged it off. The first downward slash cut away Hyssos's right hand across the forearm, the gun falling with it. The second stabbing motion pierced skin, ribcage and lung before emerging from his back in a splatter of dark arterial crimson.

Hyssos was not quite dead as Spear began to cut him into pieces. His last awareness was of the sound of his own flesh being eaten.


Shots and cries of pain sounded distantly as they drew closer to the engagement. The crackling drone of an emplaced autocannon sounded every few moments from down in the open plaza.

They had found plenty of dead along the way, and to begin with the Eversor paused at the sight of each clash, looking around to see if any of the combatants had perished carrying weapons of any particular note. But he found nothing he wanted to salvage, all of it basic Nire-pattern stubbers and the occasional lasgun. The Garantine didn't like lasers; too fragile, too light-weight, too prone to malfunction when worked hard. He liked the heavy certainty of a ballistic gun, the comforting shock of recoil when it fired, the deep bass note of the shells crashing from the muzzle or the whickering sizzle of needle rounds. The bulky combi-weapon in his mailed fist was a perfect fit; it was his intention rendered in gunmetal.

Crouching in the lee of a tall, broken terracotta urn, he studied the Executor pistol and worked his fingers around the grip. The desire to use it on some target, *any target*, was almost too much to hold in. The

anticipation tingled in his lobo-chips, and he felt the
chemoglands in his neck grow cool as they produced
a calmative to regulate the hammering pace of his
heartbeat.

'*Eversor.*' The sniper's voice issued out from the ear-
piece of his skull-mask. '*There's a group of irregulars to
the south, under the broken chronograph near the monorail
entrance. They're dug in with a heavy gun.*' The Garantine took a look around the urn and saw the shattered
clock face. He grunted an affirmative and Kell went
on. '*They're holding off a unit of Defence Force troopers.
Not many of the PDFs left. Hold and observe.*'

That last sentence actually drew a laugh from the
Eversor. 'Oh, no.' He jumped to his feet, the hissing of
stimjectors sounding in his ears, and rolling fire
flooded through him. The Garantine's eyes widened
behind his mask and his body resonated like a struck
chord. Kell was saying something over the vox, but it
seemed like the chattering of an insect.

The Garantine leapt into the air from the balcony
overlooking the ticketing plaza and fell two storeys to
land on the top of the smashed clock, where it hung
from spars extending from the ceiling. The weight of
his arrival dislodged the whole construction and he
dropped with it, riding it to the tiled floor below to
land behind the makeshift gun emplacement. The
clock exploded into fragments as it struck the ground,
ejecting cogwheels and bits of the fascia in all directions, the shock of it staggering the men behind the
autocannon.

Kell had called them *irregulars*; that meant they were
not soldiers, at least in an official sense. His drug-
sharpened perception took in all details of them at

once. They were garbed in pieces of armour, some of it PDF or Arbites issue, and the weapons they carried were an equally random assortment. At the sight of the towering, skull-masked monster that had fallen from the skies above them, the men on the autocannon hauled the weapon around on its tripod, swinging it to bear on the Garantine.

He roared and threw himself at them, his shout lost in the scream of the Executor. Bolt shells broke the bodies of the men in wet, red bursts, and he fell into their line, raking others with the spines of his neuro-gauntlet. The barbs of the glove bit into flesh and sent those it touched reeling to a twitching, frenzied death. Those on the autocannon he killed by punching, putting his fist through their ribcages. As an afterthought, he kicked the tripod gun away, and it rolled to the tiled floor.

Shivering with the rush, he laughed again. Through his adrenaline haze, he saw the men in the PDF uniforms warily peer out of cover, and then finally advance towards him with laser carbines ready.

He gave a theatrical bow and addressed them. 'A rescue,' he snapped. 'Consider it a gift from the ruler of Terra.'

'*Idiot.*' Kell's words pierced the veil of his racing thoughts. '*Look at their chest plates!*'

He did so; all of the PDF soldiers wore the etched-out aquila that signified their rejection of the Emperor's dominion. They started firing, and the Garantine laughed once more, diving into the beam salvo with the Executor at his lead.

* * *

SPEAR'S MEAL WAS methodical. All the eating of the human foodstuffs while it had been in quietus had been enough to fuel the camouflage aspect's biology, but the layers of the killer's true self were starting to starve. Sipping at the meat of the dockworker and the clerk had served to hold off the hunger pangs, but they had not been enough for true satisfaction; and the destruction of the telepath had taken a lot of energy from him.

Still; feeding now, and a full meal with it. Bones ground between razor teeth, organs still hot and wet bitten into like ripe fruits, and blood by the bucket for the drinking. Thirst slaked, for a while. *Yes*. It would do.

Deep in the canyons of his mind, Spear could hear the echo of the camouflage's ghost-mind as it wept and screamed, forced to watch these deeds from the cage where it was held. It could not understand that it was only noise now, no longer a being with life and power to influence the outside world. For as long as Spear remained in control, it would always be so.

Yosef Sabrat was only the last in a long line of coatings painted over Spear's malleable aspect, like a dye poured on silk. The killer's flesh, infused with the living skin of a warp-predator, was more daemon than man and it obeyed no laws of the conventional universe. It was a shape with no shape, but not like those human fools who used chemical philtres to manipulate their skin and bone and think themselves clever. What Spear was went beyond the nature of disguise, beyond transformation. There was a word for it that the ancient banned theologies used to talk of their deities taking on human form; they called it *assumption*.

When he was sated, he gathered what remained of Hyssos and cautiously filled a barrel with the leavings. The operative's clothing and gear he had stripped with care, placing it to one side for later use. The corpse-meat would be hurled from the roof of the winestock, where it would fall to the floor of the narrow crags far below, and into the rapids that would wash the left-overs out to sea; but first he had the final steps to perform.

From one of the giant tanks given over to the maturation of the wines, Spear dragged out a fleshy egg and used his teeth to open it. Foul gases discharged from within and a naked man dropped out on to the wooden flooring. The sac had grown from a seed Spear planted in the lung of a homeless drunkard shortly after arriving on Iesta Veracrux. Conjured by the sorcery of his masters, the seed consumed the vagrant to make the egg, giving birth to a stasis caul where Spear had been able to store Yosef Sabrat's body for the past two months.

As the sac dissolved into vapour, he dressed Sabrat in the clothes he had worn while the aspect had been at the fore. The caul had done its work. The dead reeve looked as if he had been freshly killed; no human means of detection would say otherwise. The stab wound through the man's heart began to bleed again, and Spear artfully arranged the body, finding the harvesting knife in a flesh pocket and applying it to the wound.

He paused to ensure that the puncture on the roof of Sabrat's mouth was not visible. The iron-hard proboscis that penetrated there had licked at the matter of the lawman's brain and siphoned off the chains of chemicals that were his memories, his persona. Then,

Spear's daemonskin had patterned itself on those markers, shifting and becoming. The change was so strong, so deep, that when Spear surrendered control to it, the camouflage aspect was not merely a mask that the murderer wore; it was a living, breathing identity. A persona so perfect that it believed itself to be real, resilient enough that even a cursory psionic scan would not see the lie of it.

Still, it had made sense to murder the psyker woman as soon as possible, if not only to protect the truth but also to force the hand of the investigators. Now the next phase was complete, and the Yosef Sabrat identity had played its role flawlessly. Soon Spear would begin the purgation of the disguise, and finally be rid of the man's irritatingly moral thought processes, his disgustingly soft compassion, the sickening attachment to his colleagues, brood-child and bed partner. From this point on, Spear would only wear a face, and never again give himself over to another man's self. He was almost giddy with anticipation. Just a few more steps, and he would be within striking distance of his target.

The murderer knelt next to Hyssos's head, severed at the neck by a slicing cut, and gathered it up. With a guttural choke, Spear spat the proboscis from the soft palate of his mouth and into the skull through its right eye. Seeking, penetrating, it dug deep and found the regions of the dead man's brain where his self was growing cold.

Spear drank him in.

KOYNE PUT AWAY the monocular and hid it inside a pocket of the officer's tunic the infocyte had recovered from one of the airfield's dead. It fit snugly, but the adjustment of the fluid-filled morphing bladders layered underneath the Callidus's skin allowed the assassin to alter body mass and dimension to accommodate it a little better.

'How do you propose we get inside?' said Iota. The Culexus was almost invisible in the shadows by the broken window, with only the steel-grey curve of her grinning helmet visible in the moonlight. Her voice had a peculiar, metallic timbre to it when she spoke from inside the psyker-hood, as if it were coming to Koyne's ears from a very great distance.

'Through the front door.' The Callidus watched the men walking back and forth in front of the communicatory, considering the cautious motions in their steps, analysing the cues of their body language not just for infiltration's sake, but to parse their states of mind. Data-slates, recovered from what remained of the corpses of the turncoat patrol murdered by the Garantine, had provided the Execution Force with a lead on this facility. It was the nearest thing to a garrison for kilometres around, and at this stage Kell wasn't ready to send the group out from the relative safety of the *Ultio* and down the long highway to the capital city, several kilometres to the south. The metropolis itself, the largest of all on Dagonet, could be seen clearly against the darkening sky. Some of the taller towers were still smoking, some had half-collapsed and fallen like drunkards suspended on each other's shoulders; but no snakes of tracer lashed at the skies, there were no mushroom clouds or flights of assault craft buzzing overhead. It seemed calm, or at least as calm as a city on a world at war with itself had any right to be.

When Koyne had asked the Vindicare what he had learned on his scouting mission, the Eversor had just grinned and the sniper replied with a terse dismissal. 'It's complicated,' he said.

Koyne did not doubt that. The Callidus had learned through many hundreds of field operations, a lot of them in active zones of conflict, that what generals in their places of comfort and control called 'ground truth' was often anything but true. For the soldier as much as the assassin, the only equation of truth that always worked was the simple vector between a weapon and a target. But now they were here, Koyne and the pariah girl Iota, the Culexus's skin-crawling null ability brought along to protect the shade from any possible psionic interception.

'Tariel was correct in his evaluation,' said Iota, as a rotorplane chattered past overhead. 'There is an astropath inside that building.'

'Is it aware of you?'

She shook her head, the distended skull-helm moving back and forth. 'No. I think it may be under the influence of chemical restraints.'

'Good.' Koyne stood up. 'We don't want the alarm to be raised before we are done here.' Concentrating on a thought-shape and impressing that on flesh, the Callidus altered the dimension of its vocal chords, mimicking the tonality of an officer caught on one of the intercepted vox broadcasts. 'We will proceed.'

THE SHAPESHIFTER WAS as good as its word.

Keeping to the shadows and the low rooftops along the star-port's blockhouses, Iota followed the Callidus and watched Koyne become a simulacrum of a turncoat PDF commander, advancing through the outer guard post of the communicatory without raising even a moment of concern. At one point, Iota lost sight of the Callidus, and when a man in Dagoneti colours approached her hiding place, she made ready the combi-needler about the wrist of her killing hand in order to silently end him.

'Iota,' called an entirely different voice. 'Show yourself.'

She stepped into the light. 'I like your tricks,' said Iota.

Koyne smiled with someone else's face and opened a door. 'This way. I relieved the guards at the elevator in here so we won't have much time. They're holding the astropath on one of the sublevels.'

'Why did you change it?' Iota asked as they moved through the ill-lit corridors. 'The face?'

'I bore easily,' replied Koyne, halting at a lift shaft. 'Here we are.'

As the Callidus reached for the switch, the doors opened, flooding the corridor with light; inside the elevator two troopers saw the dark shape of the Culexus and went for their guns.

SPEAR SWALLOWED HYSSOS'S one undamaged eye before depositing the dead man's reamed head among the rest of him; and then with a swift spin of his body, he pitched the remains into the canyon and watched them fall away.

Returning to the tank room, he skirted the beauty of the blood-art he had made from Erno Sigg's corpse. He had used poor Erno as his stalking horse, tormenting him, pushing him to the edge of sanity before destroying him. The man had served his purpose perfectly. Spear moved on, checking once more that the body of Yosef Sabrat had been arranged *just so*. The evidence he had fabricated over the past few weeks was also scattered around, arranged so that when it was discovered, it would lead the investigators of the Sentine towards one undeniable conclusion – the killer of Jaared Norte, Cirsun Latigue, Perrig and Sigg and the rest of them was none other than their fellow lawman.

He made a mock-solemn expression with the new face he wore, trying the look on for size; but he had no mirror to see how it seemed on his new guise. Spear pawed at a face that now resembled that of the Eurotas operative. It felt odd and incomplete. The churn of new memories and personality sucked in from Hyssos was curdling where it mixed with those of Sabrat, making him thought-sick. It seemed it would be necessary to purge the stolid reeve's self sooner rather than later.

With a deep sigh, Spear dropped to the floor and sat cross-legged. He drew on the disciplines that had been beaten into him by his master and focussed his will, seeing it like a line of poison fire laced with ink-black ice.

Reaching into the deeps of his thoughts, Spear found the cage and tore it open, clawing inside to gather up the mind-scraps that were all that remained of Yosef Sabrat. He grinned as fear resonated up from the shuddering persona as some understanding of its final end became clear. Then he began the purge, ripping and tearing, destroying everything that had been the man, vomiting up every nauseating, cloying skein

of emotion, little by little sluicing Sabrat's cloying self
away.

Spear gave this deed such focus that it was only
when he heard the voice he realised he was no longer
alone.

KOYNE'S HAND FLICKED up and the toxin-filled stiletto
hidden in a wrist sheath flew out in a shallow arc,
piercing the stomach of the man on the left. The liquid inside was a consumptive agent that feasted on
organic matter, even down to natural fibres and cured
leather. He fell to the floor and began to dissolve.

The other man was briefly wreathed in white light
that glowed down the hallway as Iota pressed a hand
into his chest and shoved him back into the elevator.
Koyne watched with detachment as the Culexus's dark
power enveloped the man and destroyed him. His
silent scream resonated and he became a mass of
material like burned paper. In moments, a curl of
damp smoke was all that marked the man's passing;
the other hapless soldier was now a puddle of fluids
leaking away through the gridded decking of the elevator floor.

Content that the toxin had run its course and consumed itself into the bargain, the Callidus kicked at
the collection of inert tooth fillings, metal buttons
and plastic buckles that had gathered and brushed
them away with the passage of a boot. Koyne took a
moment to break the biolume bubble illuminating
the interior of the elevator, and then pressed the control to send it downwards.

They travelled in dark and silence for a few
moments, and for Koyne the Culexus seemed to melt

away and disappear, even though she was standing at her shoulder.

'His name was Mortan Gautami,' Iota said suddenly. 'He never told anyone of it, but his mother had been able to see the future in dreams. He had a measure of postcognitive ability, but he indulged in narcotics, preventing him from accessing his potential.' The skull head turned slightly. 'I used that untapped energy to destroy him.'

'I'll bet you know the names of everyone you've terminated,' said Koyne, with a flicker of cruelty.

'Don't you?' said the Culexus.

The Callidus didn't bother to grace that with an answer. The elevator arrived at the sublevel, and the guards standing outside fell to quick killing blows.

There was a spherical containment chamber in the middle of a room made of ferrocrete, festoons of cables issuing from every point on its surface. A heavy iron iris hatch lay facing them like a closed eye, a short gantry reaching it from the sublevel proper. Koyne stepped up and worked the lever to open it; there was a thin, high-pitched sound coming from inside, and at first the Callidus thought it was a pressure leak; then the iron leaves retracted and it became clear it was reedy, shrill screaming.

Koyne peered into the depths and saw the corpse-grey astropath. It was pressed up against the back of the sphere's inner wall, glaring sightlessly towards Iota. 'Hole-mind,' it babbled, between howls. 'Black-shroud. Poison-thought.'

The Callidus rapped a stolen pistol against the threshold of the hatch. 'Hey!' Koyne snarled in the officer's voice. 'Stop whining. I'll make this simple.

Give up the information I need, or I'll lock her in there with you.'

The astropath made the sign of the aquila, as if it were some kind of ancient rite of warding that would fend off evil. The shrieking died away, and crack-throated, the psychic spoke. 'Just keep it at a distance.'

Iota took her cue and wandered away, moving back towards the elevator shaft but still within earshot. 'Better?'

That earned Koyne a weak nod. 'I will tell you what you want to know.'

The assassin learned quickly that the astropath was one of only a handful of its kind still alive in the Dagonet system. In the headlong melee of revolution, in the process of isolating itself from the galaxy and the Imperium, the planet had begun to rid itself of all lines of connection back to Terra – but some of the newly empowered nobles had thought otherwise and made sure that at least a few telepaths capable of interstellar sending were kept alive. This was one of them, cut off from all means of speaking to its kindred, locked up and isolated. It was starved of communication, and once it began to talk in its papery monotone, the astropath seemed unable to stop.

The psychic spoke of the state of the civil war. As the brief given by Captain-General Valdor had said, Dagonet was a keystone world in the politico-economic structure of the Taebian Sector, and if it fell fully under the shadow of the Warmaster, then it would mark the beginning of a domino effect, as planet after planet along the same trade axis followed suit. Every loyalist foothold in this sector of space would be in jeopardy. In the first moments of the insurrection, desperate signals had been sent to the Adeptus Astartes and the Imperial Navy; but these had gone unanswered.

Koyne took this in and said nothing. Both the ships of the admiralty and the Legions of the Emperor's loyalist Astartes had battles of their own to fight, far from the Taebian Stars. They would not intervene. For all the fire and destruction the collapse of Dagonet and its sister worlds might cause, there were larger conflicts being addressed at this very moment; no crusade of heroes was coming to ride to the rescue. Then the astropath began to lay out the lines of the civil war as it had spread up until this point, and the Callidus thought back to something said aboard the *Ultio* on their way to Dagonet.

The civil war was a rout, and it was those who stood in the Emperor's name who were dying. Across the planet, the forces that carried Horus's banner were only days away from breaking the back of any resistance.

Dagonet was already lost.

REEVE DAIG SEGAN. Through Sabrat's memories, Spear recalled that the man was as dogged as he was dour, and for all his apparently slow aspect, he was troublingly perceptive.

'Yosef?' said the reeve, moving through the gloom with a torch in one hand and a gun in the other. 'What is that stench? Yosef, Hyssos… Are you in here?'

Segan had followed them to Whyteleaf, despite the orders Sabrat had given, the persona unaware of Spear's subtle guidance bubbling beneath the surface.

In his thoughts, the murderer heard the dim resonance of Sabrat's essence crying out to be heard.
Impossibly, the persona was trying to *defy* him. It was
fighting its own erasure.

Spear's body, cloaked in Hyssos's proxy flesh, trembled. The purge was a complicated, delicate task that
required all of his concentration. He could not afford
to deal with any interruption, not now, not when he
was at so critical a juncture...

'Hello?' Segan was coming closer. At any moment,
he would come across Spear's carefully constructed
crime scene. But it was too soon. *Too soon!*

Very clearly, Spear heard Sabrat laughing at him. With
sudden annoyance, he punched himself in the head and
the pain of the blow made the ghost of the voice fall
silent. His cheek and the orbit of his right eye sagged as
they tried to retain the shape of Hyssos's imprint.

Spear got up and went to meet Segan as he
approached. The other reeve's torch caught him and
he heard the man gasp in shock.

'Hyssos? Where's Yosef?' Segan peered at him.
'What's wrong with your face?'

'Nothing,' said the operative's voice. 'Everything is
fine.'

The reeve seemed doubtful. 'Can you smell that?
Like blood and shit and all kinds of–' Segan's torch-
light illuminated part of the operative's coat, still wet
with vitae. 'Are you hurt?'

Spear was close to him now. 'I had a job for you,' he
said. 'A part to play. Why did you come here when I
told you to stay in the city?'

'Yosef told me to stay, not you,' Segan retorted,
becoming wary. 'I don't follow your orders, even if

everyone else jumps each time your damn baron cough.'

'But you should have stayed,' Spear insisted. 'Now I'll have to rewrite the scenario.'

'What are you on about?' said the reeve.

'Come and see.' Spear lashed out and grabbed him by the collar. Caught off-guard, Segan stumbled and that was all the murderer needed to destroy his balance and throw him down the length of the room.

Segan slammed into the floor, his gun skittering away into the shadows, sliding to a halt at the edge of the blood pool; he reacted with a sharp yelp. 'Throne!' He saw Sabrat's body and Spear felt a moment of victory as something perished inside the other man. A little bit of his will shrivelled to see his friend so violated. 'Yosef…?'

'He did it all,' said Spear. 'How terrible.'

Segan shot a venomous glare in his direction. '*Liar!* Never! Yosef Sabrat is a good man, he would never… never…'

Spear frowned. 'Yes. I knew you wouldn't accept it. That was your role. There had to be one person in the Sentine who would fight this explanation, or else it would seem false. But now you've ruined that. I'll have to compensate.'

At last, understanding dawned on the other man's face. '*You.* You did this.'

'I did it all,' Spear chuckled. He let his face shift and transform, his eyes become black and dark. 'I did it all,' he repeated.

The blood drained from Segan's face as Spear came closer, letting the change happen slowly. With trembling fingers, the reeve pulled something shiny and gold from inside his cuff and clung to it, as if it were the key to a door that would spirit him away from the horror all around him. The dour little man was pinned to the spot, transfixed with fright.

'The Emperor protects,' Segan said aloud. 'The Emperor protects.'

Spear opened his spiked jaws. 'He really doesn't,' said the murderer.

THE DISTANT HUM-AND-CRACK of mortar shells could be heard on the *Ultio*'s flight deck, through the opened vents in the canopy that let in wet, grimy air.

Koyne's encrypted report, burst-transmitted via tight-beam vox, had reached them just after sunset and confirmed Tariel's worst fears. The mission was over before it had even begun. He said as much to Kell and the others, earning himself a feral snarl from the Garantine.

'Weakling,' growled the Eversor. 'You're gutless. Afraid to get your robes dirty in the field!' The hulking killer leaned towards him, looming. He had his mask off, and his scarred, broken face was if anything more ugly than the metal skull. 'Mission circumstances always change. But we adapt and burn through!'

'Burn through,' repeated the Vanus. 'Perhaps you misunderstood the meaning of Koyne's report? Did the larger words confuse you?'

The Garantine rose to his feet, eyes narrowing. 'Say that again, piss-streak. I dare you.'

'This war is over!' Tariel almost shouted it. 'Dagonet is as good as conquered! Horus has won this world, don't you see?'

'Horus has not even set foot on Dagonet,' countered Soalm.

He rounded on her. 'Exactly! The Warmaster is not even here, and yet still *he is here*!'

'Make him speak sense,' the Eversor said to Kell, 'or I'll cut out his tongue.'

'It's not Horus,' Kell explained. 'It's what he represents.'

Tariel nodded sharply. 'The turncoat nobility on this planet don't need to see Horus. His influence hangs over Dagonet like an eclipse blotting out the sun. They're fighting in his name in fear of him, and that is enough. And when they win, the Warmaster's work will be done for him. This same thing is happening all across the galaxy, on every world too far from the Emperor and the rule of Terra.' He trembled a little with the sudden frustration he felt deep inside him. 'When Dagonet falls, Horus will turn his face from this place and move on, his advance one step closer to the gates of the Imperial Palace...'

'Horus will not come to Dagonet,' said Soalm, catching on. 'He will have no need to.'

The infocyte nodded again. 'And everything we've prepared for, the whole purpose of this mission, will be worthless.'

'We'll lose our chance to kill him,' said Kell.

'Aye,' snapped Tariel, and he shot the Garantine a glare. 'Do you see now?'

The Eversor's expression shifted; and after a moment, he nodded. 'Then, we must make sure he *does* come to Dagonet.'

Soalm folded her arms. 'How do you propose to do that? Once this planet's Governor makes his allegiance known to the insurrectionists, perhaps the Warmaster may send some delegate to plant the flag, but no more than a starship admiral or some such. He won't waste a single Space Marine's time on matters of dispensation.'

The Garantine grunted with callous humour. 'You all think I'm the slow one here, don't you? But you miss the obvious answer, woman. If Horus won't come to a fight that has ended, then we make sure the fight does not end.'

'Deliberately prolong the civil war.' Kell said the words without weight.

'We draw him to us,' said the Eversor, warming to his theme, showing teeth. 'We make the taking of Dagonet such a thorn in his side that he has no choice but to come here and deal with it himself.'

Tariel considered the idea; it was blunt and crude, but it had merit. And it could work. 'Dagonet has a personal resonance with the Warmaster. It was the site of one of his very first victories. That, and its strategic value… It could be enough. It would be a dishonour for him to let this planet slip from his control.' Hearing footsteps across the deck, he glanced up to see Iota step on to the flight deck; behind her was a man he did not recognise in a PDF uniform.

'Relax, Vanus,' said the man, in a cynical tone that could only be Koyne's. 'I take it you found my report to be compelling reading. So; what have we missed?'

'You exfiltrated without any complications?' said Kell.

Iota nodded. 'What is the local time?'

'Fourteen forty-nine.' Tariel answered automatically, his chronoimplant already synched to the Dagonet clock standard.

'There's six of us,' the Garantine went on. 'Each has destroyed rulers and broken kingdoms all on their own. How hard could it be to add some fuel to this little blaze?'

'And what about the Dagoneti?' Soalm demanded. 'They'll be caught in the crossfire.'

The other assassin looked away, unconcerned. 'Collateral damage.'

'What is the local time?' Iota said again.

'Fourteen fifty. Why do you keep asking–?' Tariel's reply was cut off by a flash of light in the distance, followed seconds later by the report of an explosion.

'What in Hades was that?' said Kell. 'The... communicatory?'

'A power generator overload. I made it look like the commoner freedom fighters did it,' said Koyne. 'We couldn't afford to leave any traces. Or survivors.'

The Garantine's grin grew even wider. 'See? We've already started.'

# TEN

**Matters of Trust**
**Breakout**
**False Flag**

'DON'T RUN,' SNARLED Grohl. 'They see you running and they'll know.'

Beye shot him a narrow-eyed look from beneath her forage cap. 'This isn't running. Believe me, you'd know if it was running. This is a purposeful walk.'

He snorted and clamped a hand around her arm, forcibly slowing her down. 'Well, dial it back to a meander. Look casual.' Grohl glanced around at the marketplace stalls as they passed through them. 'Look like you want to buy something.'

At their side, Pasri made a face. 'Buy *what*, exactly?' asked the ex-soldier, her scarred nose wrinkling.

She had a point. Most of the stalls were bare, abandoned by owners who were either too afraid to leave their homes, or lacking for produce to offer after the nobles had instituted martial law and imposed checkpoints on all the out-of-city highways. Beye couldn't help but glance over her shoulder. In the distance, what had once been a precinct tower for the capital's regiment of Adeptus Arbites was now wreathed in thin smoke. The crossed-out Imperial aquila on its southerly face was visible through the haze, and the harsh croaks of police sirens wafted towards them on the wind.

'Don't stare,' Grohl snapped.

'You want us to blend in,' she replied. 'Everyone else is staring.' Not that there were many people around. The few daring to venture out onto the streets of Dagonet's capital kept off the rubble-strewn roads or minded their own business. No one assembled in groups of more than four, fearful of the edicts that threatened arrest and detention for anyone suspected of 'gathering for reasons of sedition'.

Beye almost laughed at the thought of that. Sedition was the act of treason against an existing order, and if anything, she, Grohl, Pasri and the handful of others were the absolute antithesis of that. They were the ones championing the cause of rightful authority, of the Emperor's rule. It was the noble clans and the weakling Governor who were the rebels here, rejecting Terra and siding with...

Her eyes flicked up as they passed into a crossroads. There on the island in the centre of the highway, a statue of the Warmaster stood untouched by the street fighting. He towered over her, standing tall with one hand reaching out in a gesture of aid, the other holding a massive bolter pistol upwards to the sky. Beye noticed with a grimace that votive candles and small trinkets had been left at the foot of the plinth by those eager to show their devotion to the new regime.

Grohl paused at the intersection, rubbing at his thin beard, his eyes flicking this way and that. Finally, he made a choice. 'Over here.'

Beye and Pasri followed him across the monorail lines towards an alleyway between two shuttered storefronts. She managed not to flinch as a patrol rotorplane shrieked past over the rooftops, klaxons hooting.

'It's not looking for us,' Pasri said automatically; but in the next moment, Beye heard a change in the aircraft's engine note as it circled, looking for a place to put down.

'Are you sure about that?'

Grohl swore. This entire operation had been a cascade of errors from start to finish. Firstly, the man who was meant to drive the GEV truck did not arrive at the rendezvous, forcing them to improvise with rods and ropes to hold down the steering yoke and throttle – because of course, Grohl would *never* have considered sacrificing himself for the cause on a target so ordinary. Then, at the approach, they found the barricades placed by the clanner troops had been moved, making their straight shot at the precinct doors impossible. And finally, as the payload of crudely-cooked chemical explosives had at last detonated in a wet blast of noise and light, Beye saw that the damage it inflicted on the building was superficial at best.

She had at least hoped they could escape the security dragnet. But if they were captured, their failure would be total and complete. Beye knew that the patrol flyers carried nine-man teams with cyber-mastiffs and spy drones. The first icy surges of panic bubbled up in her chest as she imagined the interior

of a dank interrogation cell. She would never see
Capra again.

Grohl broke into a run and she followed him with
Pasri at her heels, listening for the metallic barks of
the enhanced dogs. He slipped through a gap between
two waste skips and down towards a side road. Ahead
of him, a woman in a sun-hood and sarong stepped
out from a doorway and looked up at them. Beye was
struck by the paleness of her face; Dagonet's bright
sunshine tanned everyone on the planet's temperate
zone, which meant she was either a shut-in noblewoman or an off-worlder; and neither were likely to
be seen in this part of the inner city.

'Pardon,' she began, and her accent immediately
confirmed her non-Dagoneti status. 'If I could trouble
you?'

Grohl almost missed a step, but then he pressed on,
pushing past the stranger. 'Get out of my way,' he
growled.

Beye came after him. She heard the yelps of the mas-
tiffs in the distance and saw Pasri looking back the
way they had come, her expression unreadable.

'As you wish,' the woman said, spreading her hands.
Beye saw the glint of metal nozzles at her wrists just as
she pursed her pale lips and blew out a long breath. A
vaporous mist jetted from the nozzles and engulfed
them all.

The ground beneath Beye's feet suddenly became
the consistency of rubber and she stumbled, dimly
aware of Grohl doing the same. Pasri let out a weak cry
and fell.

As Beye collapsed in a heap, her limbs refusing to
do as she told them, she saw the pale woman smile

and lick beads of the spray off her fingertips. 'It's done,' she heard her say, the words drawing out into a liquid, humming echo.

Beye's senses went dark.

THE ACRID CHEMICAL stink of smelling salts jolted her back to wakefulness and Beye coughed violently. Blinking, she raised her head and peered at the room she found herself in, expecting the pale green walls of an Arbites cell; instead, she saw the gloomy interior of some kind of storehouse, shafts of daylight reaching down through holes in a sheet-plas roof.

She was tied to a chair, hands secured behind her back, ankles tethered to the support legs. Grohl was in a similar state to her right, and past him, Pasri looked back at her with an expression of tight fear. Grohl met her gaze, his face a mask of rigid, forced calm. 'Say nothing,' he told her. 'Whatever happens, say nothing.'

'Right on schedule,' said a new voice. 'As you said.'

'Of course.' That was the pale woman. 'I can time the actions of my toxins to the second, if need be.'

Beye focussed and saw the woman in the sarong talking with an odd-looking youth wearing what looked like some form of combat gear. He was working a device mounted on his forearm, a gauntlet that grew a flickering holoscreen. Both of them glanced at their prisoners – for that was what they were, Beye realised belatedly – and then past their heads.

She heard motion behind her and Beye sensed someone standing at her back. 'Who's there?' she said, before she could stop herself.

A third figure moved around the captives and came into view. He was tall, clad in a black oversuit with

armour patches and gear packs. A heavy pistol of a
design Beye had never seen before hung at his hip. He
had a hawkish face that might have been handsome if
not for the hardness lurking in his gaze. 'Names,' he
said.

Grohl made a derogatory sound deep in his throat.
The youth with the wrist-device sniffed and spoke
again. 'Liya Beye. Terrik Grohl. Olo Pasri.'

'The nobles have files on all of you,' said the hawkish man. 'We took these copies of their database on
the resistance when we destroyed the Kappa Six Communicatory.'

'You did that?' said Pasri.

'Shut up,' Grohl snarled. 'Don't talk!'

Beye kept silent. Like the rest of them, she'd been
wondering just what had happened at Kappa Six ever
since the newsfeeds had announced the 'cowardly,
treacherous attack by terrorist militants' a few days
earlier. In the end, Capra had suggested that it was
either the work of an independent cell they weren't
aware of, or just some accident the nobles had
decided to blame on them.

'We're nothing to do with those resistance radicals,'
insisted Pasri. 'We're just citizens.'

The youth sneered. 'Please don't insult my intelligence.'

'Things are going badly for you, aren't they?' said the
man, ignoring the interruption. 'They're getting close
to finding your hideaway. Close to finding Capra and
all his cell leaders.'

Beye tried not to react when he said the name, and
failed. He turned to her. 'How many of your people
have surrendered in the past few weeks? Fifty? A

hundred? How many have taken the offer of amnesty for themselves and their families?'

'It's a lie,' Beye blurted out, ignoring Grohl's hiss of annoyance. 'Those who give up are executed.'

'Of course they are,' said the man. He nodded towards the youth. 'We even have picts of the firing squads.' He paused. 'Your entire resistance network–'

'Such as it is,' said the youth, with an arch sniff.

'Your network is on the verge of collapse,' continued the other man. 'Capra and his trusted core of freedom fighters are the only things holding it together. And the nobles know that all they really need to do is wait.' He walked down the line of them. 'Just wait, until you run out of supplies, of ammunition. Of *hope*. You're all exhausted, pushed beyond your limits. Hungry and tired. None of you want to say it, but you all know it's true. You've already lost, you just can't admit it.'

That was enough for Grohl to break his own rules. 'Go screw yourself, clanner bastard!'

The man raised an eyebrow. 'We're not... clanners, is it? We are not in the employ of the nobles.' He leaned down and pulled something from the neck of his armour; an identity disc on a chain. 'We serve a different master.'

Beye immediately recognised the shape of an Imperial sigil-tag, a bio-active recognition device gene-keyed to its wearer. An etching of the two-headed aquila glittered there on its surface. It could not be forged, duplicated or removed from the person of its user without becoming useless. Anyone wearing such a tag was a soldier in service to the Emperor of Mankind.

'Who are you?' Pasri was wary.

The man indicated himself. 'Kell. These are Tariel and… Soalm. We are agents of the Imperium and the authority of Terra.'

'Why tell us your names?' hissed Grohl. 'Unless you're going to kill us?'

'Consider it a gesture of trust,' said the pale woman. 'We already know who you are. And in all honesty, knowing what to call us hardly makes you a threat.'

Beye leaned forward. 'Why are you here?'

Kell nodded to Tariel, and the youth produced a mollyknife. He moved to where Pasri was sitting and cut her loose, then proceeded to do the same with Grohl.

'We have been sent by the Emperor's command to aid the planet Dagonet and its people in this time of crisis.' Beye was certain that she saw a loaded look pass between Soalm and Kell before the man spoke again. 'We are here to help you oppose the insurrection of Horus Lupercal and anyone who takes his side.'

Grohl rubbed at his wrists. 'So, of course you would like us to take you to the secret retreat of the resistance. Introduce you personally to Capra. Open ourselves up so you can murder us all in one fell swoop?' He turned his head and spat. 'We're not fools or traitors.'

Tariel cut Beye loose and offered a hand to help her to her feet, but she refused. Instead, he gave her a data-slate. 'You know how to read these, correct? Your file says that you served the Administratum as a datum clerk in the office of colonial affairs, prior to the insurrection.'

'That's right,' she said.

Tariel indicated a text file in the slate's memory. 'I
think you'll want to look at this document. And please
check the security tags so you are sure it has not been
tampered with.'

Kell walked closer to Grohl. 'I believe you when you
say you're not a traitor, Terrik Grohl. But you have
been fooled.'

'What in Stars' name are you talking about?' snarled
the other man.

'Because there *is* a traitor in this room,' Kell went on;
and then faster than Beye's eye could follow, the Imperial agent's hand flicked up from his belt with the
blocky, lethal-looking pistol in its grip, and he shot
Pasri dead through the heart at point-blank range.

Beye let out a cry of shock as Grohl started forward.

Tariel tapped the slate. 'Read the file,' he repeated.

'And then search your good friend Olo,' added
Soalm.

Grohl did that as Beye read on. By the time she had
finished, the colour had drained from her cheeks, and
Grohl had discovered the wireless listening device
concealed on the other woman. The files, as Tariel
said, unaltered from their original form, were reports
from the clanners about an informant in the resistance. Capra had suspected they had a leak for some
time, but he hadn't been able to discover who.
According to the last entry, Olo Pasri had agreed to
give up the location of the main freedom fighter safe
zone, but was stalling for a larger finder's fee and the
guarantee of passage off-world.

All of this she told to Grohl, who listened with a
stony, rigid expression. After a long moment, he
spoke. 'I don't trust you,' he said to Kell. 'Even this,

you could have faked it. Did it all just to get close to
us.'

'Grohl–' Beye began, but Kell held up a hand, silencing her.

'No, he's right. Given time and effort, we could have
engineered something like this. And if I were in your
place, I would share your suspicions.' He paused
again, thinking. 'So, then. We need to earn your trust.'

'A demonstration,' suggested Soalm.

Kell nodded. 'Give us a target.'


SPEAR RAN HIS hand up and down the arm of the grox-
leather chair where he sat, guiding fingers moulded in
fleshy echo of Hyssos's body over the lustrous, tanned
hide. The sensation was pleasing; it made him realise
he had spent too long in quietus, denied the simple
pleasures of awareness, allowing his consciousness to
go dormant while the mind-ghost of Yosef Sabrat ran
his flesh. Puppet and the puppeted, master and per-
former, their roles intermingled. He was tired of it.

At least now he had only to look the part, rather
than literally *become* it. He glanced up and saw a
reflection in the glass cabinet behind the desk of
High-Reeve Kata Telemach; the ebon face of Hyssos
staring back at him.

Telemach swivelled in her deep, wing-backed chair
from the watch-wire console on her desk and replaced
the bulky handset. Standing nearby like an overweight
sentinel, the doughy figure of Reeve Warden Berts
Laimner was uncharacteristically still. Spear imagined
he was still trying to process all the possible outcomes
of the revelation that Yosef Sabrat was the serial killer
in their midst, looking for the results where he would

come off best. He felt a particular kind of hate for the man, but when he concentrated on the shape of it, Spear could not be certain if it had originated in him, or in Yosef Sabrat. More than once, the reeve's own temper had brushed against the killer's, and in those moments threatened to awaken the dormant murderer.

He sucked in a breath and dismissed the thoughts as trivial, refocussing on Telemach, who sat glaring at the vinepaper documents before her.

'How could something like this happen in my precinct, under my governance?' she demanded. Typical of the woman, Spear thought. Her first consideration was not *How could this tragedy have happened?* or *A good man like Sabrat a killer? Impossible!* No, for all the death and bloodshed and fear that had swept across her city, her first impulse was to worry about how it would make her look. Telemach glared at Laimner. 'Well?'

'He… We never suspected for a moment that the killer could be a peace officer.'

The High-Reeve was about to spit out something else, but Spear intervened. In Hyssos's voice he said 'In fairness, how could your men have known, milady? Sabrat was a decorated member of the Sentine with over a decade of service under his belt. He knew your procedures and protocols intimately. He knew all the loopholes and blind spots.'

Laimner nodded. 'Aye, yes. I have teams from the documentary office going over everything in his caseload, back years and years. They've already found incidences of file tampering, evidence manipulation…'

All of which Spear had been planting, little by little over the last few weeks. Very soon they would discover more killings that he had laid at the late reeve's feet, from the deaths of minor citizens to shopkeepers and even a junior jager from this very precinct; every one of them Spear had murdered and impersonated for brief periods of time, working his way up to this identity. Step by step.

'It was only a matter of time before he was caught,' Spear-as-Hyssos went on, and he tapped the evidence bag on the desk that contained the harvesting knife. 'I've encountered these kinds of criminals several times. They all become careless after a while, convinced of their own superiority.'

Telemach grabbed one of the more gory picts of the murder scene at the airdocks, waving it at him, and Spear resisted the urge to lick his lips. 'But what about... all this?' She jabbed at the beautiful perfection of the eightfold sigils drawn in the blood of the dead. 'What does it mean?'

He sensed the edge of fear in her words, and relished it. Yes, she understood the common, squalid manners of death, when humans ended one another over trivialities like money and power, anger and lust; but she could not conceive of the idea that one might take life in the name of something greater... to *appease* something. Spear wanted to tell her. He wanted to tell her that her insect's-eye view of the cosmos was pathetically naïve, blind to the realities that he had been made privy to at the Delphos on Davin and later, at his master's hand.

He made Hyssos's face grow grave and concerned. 'Sabrat wasn't alone in all this. His cohort, Segan... They were a partnership.'

'That fits the facts,' said Laimner. 'But I'm not sure why Yosef killed him.'

'A disagreement?' offered Spear. 'All I know is, the two of them conspired to get me alone with them at Whyteleaf. Then I was forced to watch as Sabrat ended Segan's life, before he tried to do the same to me. I almost...' At this point, he gave a staged shudder. 'He almost killed me too,' he whispered.

'And the... symbols?' Telemach asked.

'These were ritualistic murders.' He paused for the drama of it. 'What do you know of this group called the Theoge?'

He had barely said the word before the High-Reeve's face split in a sour sneer. 'Those throwback religionists? This is their doing?' She shot a look at Laimner. 'I said they were part of this. Didn't I say so? I knew it!'

Spear nodded. 'They are some sort of fundamentalist cult, if I understand correctly. It seems that Daig Segan was the go-between for the Theoge, and in turn the murders committed by Sabrat with his help were likely motivated by some twisted set of beliefs.'

'Human sacrifices?' said Laimner. 'On a civilised world like this? This is the thirty-first millennium, not primitive prehistory!'

Telemach answered immediately. 'Religion is like a cancer. It can erupt without warning.' For a moment, Spear wondered what great hurt in the woman's past had occurred because of someone else's belief; something scarring, no doubt, to make her hate any thought of such things with that undiluted venom.

'I would advise you move against this group as soon as possible,' he went on, getting to his feet. 'Your media services have already learned of some elements of this case. I imagine those involved with the Theoge will quickly become targets for vigilantism.'

Laimner nodded. 'Sabrat's wife and child have already been attacked. I sent Skelta to the house... He said they were hounded and stoned.'

'Find out if they were involved,' Telemach insisted. 'And by nightfall I want every single Theoge suspect on the books hauled in for questioning.'

Spear drew himself up, smoothing down the front of Hyssos's tunic in a reflexive gesture copied from the operative's own muscle-memory. 'I see you have everything in hand. You have my report. I will take my leave of you now this matter is concluded.'

Laimner shook his head. 'But, wait. There are proceedings... Testimony to be made, a tribunal. You will need to remain on Iesta to give statements.'

'The Void Baron does not wish me to stay.' All it took was a look from Hyssos's eyes to the High-Reeve, and she buckled immediately.

'Of course, operative,' she said, the thought of defying Eurotas or one of his agents never occurring to her. 'If any questions arise, a communiqué can be sent via the Consortium. We caught the killer. That's all that is important.'

He nodded and made for the door. Behind him, he heard Laimner speak again. 'The people will feel safer,' he said. It seemed less like a statement of fact, and more like something the man was trying to convince himself of.

A brief smile crossed Spear's changed face. The fear that he had unleashed on the streets of Iesta Veracrux would not be so easily dispelled.

* * *

GOEDA RUFIN WAS enjoying the difference in things.

Before, back when the Governor was still kowtowing to Terra and the nobles did nothing but grumble, Rufin had been destined to remain a low ranked noncommissioned officer in the Dagonet PDF. His life consisted largely of shirking his responsibilities – such as they were – and putting his workload on the junior ratings unlucky enough to be under his supervision at the vehicle pool. Since the day he had enrolled after a justicar gave him the choice between borstal or service, Rufin had never looked back to civilian life, but in all that time he hadn't been able to shake the longing for a day when he could wear a coveted officer's braid. It didn't occur to him that his general level of ignorance outstripped any small measure of ability he had; Rufin was simply unable to grasp the idea that he had never risen in rank because he was a poor soldier. He was a makeweight in the city garrison, and everyone seemed to know it but him. To hear Rufin talk, it would seem like there was a huge conspiracy among the senior officers to keep him down, while other men were promoted up the ladder – men that he considered less deserving, despite copious evidence to the contrary. But Rufin wasn't one to let facts get in the way of his opinions.

He was snide and demeaning to the back of every man who wore the braid. He amused himself by scribbling anonymous obscenities about them on the walls of the barracks washroom, dragging his heels over every order they gave him, this and a dozen other petty revenges.

It was because of that Goeda Rufin was in the office of his commander when the liberation took place.

That's what they were calling it now, 'The Liberation', the bloody day of upheaval that left Dagonet declared free of Imperial rule and true to the banner of the War-master Horus.

Rufin had been there, waiting, forgotten. He had been there for a disciplinary review – someone had heard him bad-mouthing his superiors one time too many – and if it had just been any other day, he would likely have ended up dismissed from the PDF for his troubles.

But then the shooting started, and he saw soldiers fighting soldiers in the courtyard. Warriors from the palace garrison, their uniforms marred by crossed-out aquila sigils, cutting down all the men he never liked. He was hiding in his commander's office when the officer came running in, barking orders at him. At his heels were a pair of the palace men, and seeing them, Rufin at last caught up to what was going on. When his commander bellowed at him to come to his aid, Rufin took up the ornamental dagger the man used as a letter opener and stabbed him with it. Later, the leader of the invading troops shook his hand and offered him a marker with which to scratch out his own Imperial emblems.

He got his officer braid because of that, and all the men who surrendered with him took it too, that or the buzz of a las-round to the back of the head. After the dust settled the new regime needed officers to fill the ranks they had culled. Rufin was happy to accept; Emperor or Warmaster, he didn't give a damn whose name he had to salute. He had no respect for any of them.

Rufin left the motor pool behind. His new com-mand was the 'emergency circumstances security camp' established on the site of the capital terminus monorail station. Ever since the nobles had shut down the networks, the passenger trains had lain idle; but now they had a new duty, serving as prison accommodations for the hundreds of civilians and idiot rebels who had dared to defy the new order.

Rufin lorded it over them, walking back and forth across the high gantries above the choked platforms, making sure each inmate knew he held the power of life and death with random beatings and executions. When he wasn't exercising his dull brutality and boredom on them, Rufin was prowling the ammo stores on the lower levels, in what used to be the maintenance wells for the engines. He liked being down there, among the smells of cordite and gunmetal. It made him feel like a real soldier to be surrounded by all that firepower.

Entering the observation cupola above what was once the station's central plaza, he caught the watch officer sipping a mug of black tea and gave him a glowering stare. 'Status?' he barked.

The officer looked at his chronograph. 'Check-in at the top of the hour, sir. That's another quarter-turn away.' He had barely finished speaking when the intercom grille over their heads crackled into life.

'Early?' said Rufin.

'*Control!*' said a panicked voice over the vox. '*I think… I think there might be a problem.*'

'Post two, say again?' began the watch officer, but Rufin snatched the handset from him and snarled into it.

'This is the base commander! Explain yourself!'

'*Recruit Zejja just… Well, he just fell off the south wall. And Tormol isn't responding to his wireless.*' Then, very distinctly, the open vox channel caught a sound like a quick, low hum, followed a heartbeat later by a wet chug and then the echo of a body falling.

Rufin thrust the handset back at the watch officer, uncertain what to do next. 'Shall I try to raise the other guard posts now, sir?' said the other man, stifling a cough.

'Yes,' He nodded. That sounded like the right sort of thing. 'Do that.'

Then, without warning, the old control board left intact from the station's prior function flickered into life. Lines of colour denoting tracks, blocks of illumination signifying individual carriages, all began to click and chatter as they activated.

Rufin shot a worried look out of the windows of the cupola and heard the mutter of dozens of electric motors coming alive. The sound echoed around the vaulted glass spaces of the station concourse and platforms. Below, the prisoners were scrambling to their feet, energised by the sound. Rufin drew his pistol on impulse and kneaded the grip. 'What's going on?' he demanded.

The watch officer looked at the consoles before him in surprise. 'That... That's not possible,' he insisted, coughing again. 'All remote operations of station systems were locked down, the hard lines were severed...' He swallowed hard, beads of sweat appearing on his high forehead. 'I think someone is trying to move the trains.'

Below, the ornate copper departure boards for all the platforms began whirring in a rattling chorus of noise, each one flashing up destination after destination. With a sharp report, they all stopped at once, all of them showing the same thing; *End Of The Line*.

The prisoners saw the words and let out a ragged cheer. Rufin shouted abuse back at them, and caught sight of one of his men running up the platform with a heavy autogun in his grip. The trooper was perhaps twenty metres from the jeering prisoners when his chest exploded in a silent, red blossom, and he fell.

Finally, the correct words registered in his mind. 'We're under attack!'

When Rufin turned back to the watch officer, the man was lolling in his chair, eyes and mouth open, staring blankly at the ceiling. He caught a strange, floral smell emanating from the officer and gingerly extended a hand to prod his waxy, damp face. The watch officer slumped forward, knocking his tea glass over. The flower-stink grew stronger as the liquid pooled on the floor.

Rufin's hand flew to his mouth. 'Poison!' Without looking back, he ran to the cupola door and raced away, footsteps banging off the metal gantries.

SPEAR REACHED OUT a hand and rubbed the edge of the ornate tapestry between Hyssos's thick fingers. The complex depiction on the hanging was of the Emperor, smiting some form of bull-like alien with a gigantic sword made of fire.

He rolled his eyes at the banal pomposity of the thing and stepped away, carelessly brushing fibres of broken thread from his hands. Touching the object was forbidden, but there was nobody here in the audience chamber to see him do it. The killer idly wondered if the residue left by the daemonskin of his flesh-cloak would poison and shrivel the ancient artwork. He hoped it would; the idea of the humans aboard the *Iubar* running about and panicking as the piece blackened and corroded amused him no end.

He glanced out of the viewing windows as he wandered the length of the chamber. The curve of Iesta Veracrux was slipping away beneath the starship's keel as it turned for open space, and Spear was not sorry to see it go. He had spent too long on that world, living in the inanities of its civilisation, play-acting at a half-dozen different roles. Since his arrival, Spear had been many faces – among them a vagrant, a storeman, a streetwalker, a jager and a reeve, living the lie of their ridiculous, pointless existences. He had stacked their corpses, and all the others, to make the ladder that led him to where he now stood.

*A few more murders. One, perhaps two more assumptions.* And then he would be close to the mark. The greatest prey of them all, in fact. A shiver of anticipation rippled through him. Spear was eager, but he reined the emotion in, pushed it down. Now was not the time to be dazzled by the scope of his mission. He had to maintain his focus.

Before, such a slip might have been problematic; he was convinced that such thoughts were how the psyker wench Perrig had been able to gather a vague sense of him down on Iesta. But with her no more than a pile of ashes in a jar in the *Iubar*'s Chamber of Rest, that threat was gone for the moment. Spear knew from Hyssos's memories that Baron Eurotas had spent much influence and coin in order to bend the Imperium's fear-driven rules about the censure of psychics; and given the present condition of the Consortium's welfare, that would not be repeated. The next time he met a psyker, he would be prepared.

He smirked. That was something unexpected he pulled from the operative's ebbing thoughts. The Void Baron's secret, and the explanation for the shabby appearance of his agency's compound on Iesta; for all the outward glitter and show the merchant clan put on for the galaxy at large, the truth whispered in the corridors of its ships was that the fortunes of Eurotas were waning. Little wonder then that the clan's master was so desperate to hold on to any skein of power he still had.

It made things clearer; Spear had known that sooner or later, if he murdered enough members of the Eurotas staff and made it look like Sigg was the killer, the baron would send an operative to investigate. He never expected him to come in person.

*Matters must be severe…*

Spear halted in front of the red jade frieze, and reached out to touch it, tracing a fingertip over the sculpting of the Warrant of Trade. This place was full of glittering prizes, of that there could be no doubt. A thief in Spear's place could make himself richer than sin – but the killer had his sights set on something worth far more than any of these pretty gewgaws. What he wanted was the key to the greatest kill of his life.

The hubris of the rogue trader irritated Spear. Here, in this room, there were objects that could command great riches, if only they were brought to market. But Eurotas was the sort who would rather bleed himself white and eat rat-meat before he would give up the gaudy trappings of his grandeur.

As if thought of him was a summons, the doors to the audience chamber opened and the Void Baron entered in a distracted, irritable humour. He shrugged off his planetfall jacket and tossed it at one of the squad of servitors and human adjutants trailing behind him. 'Hyssos,' he called, beckoning.

Spear imitated the operative's usual bow and came closer. 'My lord. I had not expected your shuttle to return to the *Iubar* until after we broke orbit.'

'I had you voxed,' Eurotas replied, shaking his head. 'Your communicator implant must be malfunctioning.'

He touched his neck. 'Oh. Of course. I'll have it seen to.'

The baron went for a crystalline cabinet and gestured at it; a mechanism inside poured a heavy measure of wine into a glass goblet, which he snatched up and drank deeply. He gulped it down without savouring it. 'We are done with our visit to this world,' Eurotas told him, his manner veering towards a brooding sullenness. 'And it has taken our dear Perrig along the way.' He shook his head again and fixed Spear with an accusing glare. 'Do you know what she cost me? A *moon*, Hyssos. I had to cede an entire bloody moon to the Adeptus Terra just to own her.' He walked on, across the mosaic floor. The cabinet raised itself up on brass wheels and rolled obediently after him.

Spear searched for the right thing to say. 'She had a good life with us. We all valued her contribution to the clan.'

The baron turned his glare on the vanishing planet. 'The Governor would not stop talking,' he said. 'They wanted our fleet to remain in orbit for another week, something about "helping to stimulate the local economy"...' He snorted with derision. 'But I have little stomach for the festivals they had planned. I walked out on them. More important things to do. Imperial service and all that.'

Spear nodded thoughtfully, deciding to feed the man's mood. 'The best choice, my lord. With the situation as it is in this sector, it makes sense for the clan to keep the flotilla moving. To be in motion is to be safe.'

'Safe from *him*.' Eurotas took another drink. 'But the bastard Warmaster is killing us by inches even so!' His voice went up. 'Every planet he binds to him costs us a weight in Throne Gelt that we cannot recover!' For a moment, it seemed as if the baron was about to give voice to something that might have been considered treasonable; but then he caught himself, like a man afraid he would be overheard, and his expression changed. 'We will head for the edge of this system and then make space to the rendezvous point at the Arrowhead Nebula.'

Spear knew already what their next port of call would be, but he asked anyway. 'What will our intentions be there, lord?'

'We will lay to wait to assemble the clan's full fleet, and while we are there meet a ship from Sotha. Aboard are a party of remembrancers under the Emperor's aegis. I will personally take them home to Terra, as the Council has requested.'

'The security of the remembrancers is of great concern,' said Spear. 'I will make all arrangements to ensure their safety from the moment they board the *Iubar* to the moment we bring them to the Imperial Palace.'

Eurotas looked away. 'I know you'll do what is required.'

Spear had to fight down the urge to grin. The path was open, and now all that he needed to do was follow it all the way to the end. To the very gates of the Emperor's fortress–

*NO*

The voice crackled in his ears like breaking glass, and Spear jerked, startled.

*NO NO NO*

The baron did not appear to have heard it; the killer felt a peculiar twitch in his hands and he glanced down at them. For one terrible moment, the skin there bubbled and went red, before shifting back to the dark shades of Hyssos's flesh. He hid them behind his back.

*NO*

Then the echo made the origin of the sound clear. Spear let his gaze turn inwards and he felt it in there, moving like mercury.

*Sabrat.* Until this moment, Spear had believed the purgation that the idiot reeve's cohort interrupted had gone to plan, but now his certainty crumbled. There was still some fraction of the stolid fool's self hiding in the shadowed depths of the killer's mind, some part of the false self he had worn that had not been expunged. He pushed in and was sickened by the sense of it, the loathsome, nauseating morality of the dead man staining his mind. It was bubbling up like bile, pushing to the top of his thoughts. A scream of recrimination.

'Hyssos?' Eurotas was staring at him. 'Are you all right, man?'

'I...'

*NO NO NO NO NO*

'No.' Spear coughed out the word, his eyes watering, and then with effort took control of himself once more. 'No, lord,' he went on. 'I... A moment of fatigue, that's all.' With a physical effort, the killer silenced the cries and took a shuddering breath.

'Ah.' The baron approached and gave him a kindly pat on the shoulder. 'You were closest to the psyker. There's no shame in being affected by her loss.'

'Thank you,' said Spear, playing into the moment. 'It has been difficult. Perhaps, with your permission, I might take some respite?'

Eurotas gave him a fatherly nod. 'Do so. I want you rested when we reach the rendezvous.'

'Aye, lord,' Spear bowed again and walked away. Unseen by anyone else, he buried the nails of his hand in his palm, cutting the waxy flesh there; but no blood emerged from the ragged meat.

RUFIN FOUND ANOTHER intercom panel on the station's mezzanine level and used it to send out an all-posts alert; but if anything he became even more afraid when the only men that reported back were the ones at the armoury. He told them to hold the line and started on his way to them. If he could get there before any of the terrorist attackers did, he could open the secure locks and drag out all the big, lethal weapons that he had been so far denied the chance to use. There were autocannons down there, grenade launchers and flamers... He'd give these loyalist bastards a roasting for daring to cross him, oh yes...

Descending an enclosed stairwell, he caught sight of the western platforms. Monorails there were filling with prisoners, each one closing its doors and moving off seemingly of its own will, carrying the inmates to freedom. The first few to go had ploughed through the barricades across the lines; now there was nothing to stop a mass exodus. Rufin didn't care, though; he would let them go, as long as he could keep the guns.

Reaching the lowest levels, he found the men at the first guard post were gone. In their place there were piles of clothing and lumps of soggy ash, illuminated by the flickering overhead strip lights. The air here felt cold and oppressive, and Rufin broke into a run again, propelled from the place by a cold pressure that was like a shadow falling over his soul.

He turned the corner and ran towards the armoury post. Six men were there, and all of them were pale and afraid. They saw him coming and beckoned frantically, as if he were being chased by something only they could see.

'What happened back there?' he snapped, turning his ire on the first man he saw. 'Talk, rot you!'

'Screaming,' came the reply. 'Oh, sir, a screaming like you ain't never heard. From Hades itself, sir.'

Rufin's fear bubbled over into anger and he backhanded the man. 'Make sense, you fool! It's the terrorists!'

At that moment, the floor below them exploded upwards, the iron grid-plates spinning away as a hulking figure burst out of the conduits beneath. Rufin saw a grinning, fanged skull made of tarnished silver and then a massive handgun. A single shot from the weapon struck one of the guards with such force it blew him back into another man, the velocity carrying them both into the curved wall where they became a bloody ruin.

Rufin stumbled away as the dark shape blurred, releasing an inhuman snarl. Gunfire sang from the weapons of the guards, but it seemed to make no difference. There were wet, tearing noises, concussive blasts of bolt-fire, the dense sounds of meat under pressure, breaking and bursting. Something whistled through the air and hit Rufin in the chest.

He went to his knees and slumped against the wall, blinking. Like a blood-painted dagger, a broken human femur, freshly ripped from a still-cooling corpse, protruded from his chest. Rufin vomited black, sticky spittle and felt himself start to die.

The skull-faced figure came to him, trembling with adrenaline, and spat through the grille of the mask. 'Oh dear,' it rumbled. 'I think I broke him.'

Rufin heard a tutting sound and a second figure, this one more human than the clawed killer, hove into view. 'This is the base commander. We needed him to open the ammunition store.'

'So?' said the skull-face. 'Can't you do your trick?'

'It's not a parlour game for your amusement, Eversor.' He heard a sigh and then a sound like old leather being twisted.

Through blurry eyes Rufin saw his own reflection; or was it? It seemed to be talking to him. 'Say your name,' said the mirror-face.

'You know... who I am,' he managed. 'We're Goeda Rufin.'

'Yes, that's right.' Now it sounded like him too.

The mirror-face drifted away, towards the locking alcove near the heavy iron hatch that secured the ammo stores. It was impregnable, Rufin remembered. The built-in security cogitator needed to recognise both his features and his vocal imprint before it would open.

*His face and voice…*

'Goeda Rufin,' said the mirror, and with a crunch of gears the armoury hatch began to swing open.

Rufin tried to understand how that could be happening, but the answer was still lost to him when his heart finally stopped.

THE RENDEZVOUS WAS a spur-line outside a storage depot in the foothills, several kilometres beyond the capital. Under Tariel's guiding hand, the simple drive-brains of the monorails had obeyed his command and cut fast routes through the network that confused the PDF spy drones sent to follow them. Now they were all here, emptying their human cargoes as the sun set over the hillside.

Kell watched the rag-tag resistance fighters gather the freed people into groups, some of them welcomed back into the fold as lost brothers in arms, others formed into parties that would split off in separate directions and go to ground, in hopes of riding out the conflict. He saw Beye and Grohl moving among them. The woman gave him a nod of thanks, but all the man returned was a steady, measuring look.

Kell understood his position. Even after they had done what he had charged them to do, and obliterated a major stockpile of turncoat weapons into the bargain, Grohl could still not find the will to trust them.

*Because he is right not to,* said a voice in his thoughts; a voice that spoke with his sister's words. The rebels believed Kell and the others were some kind of advance unit, a scouting party of special operatives sent as the vanguard of an Imperial plan to retake Dagonet in the Emperor's name. Like so many things about the assassins, this too was a lie.

A man in a hood emerged from the midst of the rebels and said something to Beye; but it was Grohl's reaction that gave away his identity, the sudden jerk of the severe man's head, the tensing of his body.

Kell drew himself up as the man came closer, drawing back the hood. He was bald and muscular, with a swarthy cast to his skin, and he had sharp eyes. The Vindicare saw the tips of complex tattoos peeking up from his collar. Kell offered his hand. 'Capra.'

'Kell.' The freedom fighter took it and they shook, palm to wrist. 'I understand I have the Emperor to thank for this.' He nodded at the trains. 'And for you.'

'The Imperium never turns its face from its citizens,' he replied. 'We're here to help you win your war.'

A shadow passed over Capra's face. 'You may be too late. My people are tired, few, scattered.' He spoke in low tones that would not carry. 'It would be more a service to help us find safe passage elsewhere, let some of us come back with the reprisal force as tactical advisors.'

Kell did not break eye contact with the rebel leader. 'We did this in a day. Imagine what we can do together, in the days ahead.'

Capra's gaze shifted to where the rest of the Execution Force stood, waiting silently. 'Beye was right. You are an impressive group. Perhaps... Perhaps with you at our sides, there is a chance.'

'More than a chance,' insisted Kell. 'A certainty.'

Finally, the man's expression changed, the weariness, the doubt melting away. In its place, there was a new strength. New purpose. He wanted so badly for them to be their salvation, Kell could almost taste it. Capra nodded. 'The fate of Dagonet rests with us, my friend. We will not forsake it.'

'No,' he said, as Capra walked away, gathering his men to him as he began to rally them with firebrand oratory.

But the rebels would not know the truth, not until it was too late; that the fate of Dagonet was only a means to a single end.

To place the Archtraitor Horus between Eristede Kell's crosshairs.

# PART TWO

# ATTRITION

# ELEVEN

### Hidden
### Sacrifice
### Cages

THE CAVERNS WERE deep inside the canyons of a rocky and forbidding landscape that the Dagoneti called the Bladecut. From the ground, the real meaning of the name wasn't clear, but up high, when glimpsed through the lenses of one of the aerial drones the rebels had captured, it was obvious. The Bladecut was a massive ravine that moved easterly across the stone wilderness beyond the capital, the shape of it like a giant axe wound in the surface of the landscape. There were no roads, nothing but animal trails and half-hidden hunting routes that meandered into sharp gullies which concealed the mouths of the cave network. Thousands of years ago, this had been the site of the first Dagonet colony, where the new arrivals from Terra had huddled in the gloom while their planetforming technologies, now lost to history, had worked to make the world's harsh environment more habitable for them. The rebels had retaken the old halls of stone, secure in the knowledge that deep inside nothing would be able to dislodge them short of bombing the hills into powder.

Jenniker Soalm walked through the meandering tunnels, her face concealed in the depths of her hood, passing chambers laser-cut from the rock, ragged chainmail curtains hanging over their entrances, others closed off behind heavy impact-welded hatches. Inside the caves everything was in a permanent twilight, with the only constant the watery glow of biolume pods glued to the stone ceiling at random intervals. Capra's people – some of them warriors, many more civilians and even children – passed her as she walked on.

Soalm glimpsed snatches of the everyday life of the resistance through gaps in the curtains or past open doors. She saw Beye and a few others surrounding a chart table piled high with paper maps; across the way, a makeshift armoury full of captured PDF weaponry; a skinny cook who looked up at her, in the middle of stirring a huge iron drum of thick soup; refugees clustered around a brazier, and nearby a pair of children playing, apparently ignorant of the grim circumstances. The latter was no surprise to her; the rebels did not have much choice about where their people could go to ground.

Further on, she saw a side-chamber that had been converted into a drab approximation of an infirmary, right beside a workroom where figures in shadow were bent over a jury-rigged device trailing wires and connectors. Soalm detected the familiar odour of chemical explosives as she moved on.

A hatch was creaking shut as she approached, and she turned to see. As it closed, one of Capra's men gave her a blank look from within; over his shoulder she saw a bloodied trooper in clan colours tied to a chair, a moment before he disappeared out of sight. She paused, and heard footsteps behind her.

Soalm turned and saw a pair of refugee children approach, eyes wide with fear and daring. They were both grimy, both in shapeless fatigues too big for them; she couldn't tell if they were boys or girls.

'Hey,' said the taller of the two. 'The Emperor sent you, right?'

She gave a nod. 'In a way.'

There was awe in their expressions. 'Is he like he is in the picts? A giant?'

Soalm managed a smile. 'Bigger than that, even.'

The other child was about to add something, but an adult turned the corner ahead and gave them both a stern look. 'You know you're not supposed to play down here. Get back to your lessons!'

They broke into a run and vanished back the way they had come. Soalm turned to study the man.

'Are you looking for something?' he asked warily.

'I'm just walking,' she admitted. 'I needed a moment… to think.'

He pointed past her, blocking her path. 'You should probably go back.' The man seemed hesitant, as if he wasn't sure he had the authority to tell her what to do.

The Execution Force fit strangely among the freedom fighter group. In the weeks that had passed since they liberated the prison camp in the city, Soalm and the others had gained a kind of guarded acceptance, but little more. Under Kell's orders, each of them had turned their particular skill-sets towards aiding the rebel cause. Tariel's technical expertise was in constant demand, and Koyne showed a natural aptitude for teaching combat tactics to men and women who had, until recently, been farmers, teachers and shopkeepers. Meanwhile, Iota and the Garantine would go missing for days at a time, and the only evidence of their activities would be intercepted reports from the communication network, stories of destroyed outposts or whole patrols eviscerated by ghostly assailants. As for her brother, he kept his distance from her, working with Capra, Beye and Grohl on battle plans.

Soalm did her part too, but as the days drew on it disturbed her more and more. They were helping the rebels score victories, not just here but through other resistance cells all across the planet; but it was based on a lie. If not for the arrival of the assassins on Dagonet, the war would have been over. Instead they were bolstering it, infusing fresh violence into a conflict that should have already petered out.

The Venenum was precise in what she did; surgical and clean. Collateral damage was a term she refused to allow into her lexicon, and yet here they were, their presence more damaging to the locals than the guns of the nobles.

The man pointed again. 'Back that way,' he repeated. Dispelling her moment of reverie, Soalm realised that he was trying to hide something.

'No,' she said. 'I think not.' Before he could react, she pushed past him and followed the turn of the narrowing corridor as it dropped into a shallow slope. The man reached for her robes to stop her, and she tapped a dot of liquid onto the back of his hand from one of her wrist dispensers. The effect was immediate;

he went pale and fell to the ground, the muscles in his legs giving out.

The corridor opened up into another cavern, this one wide and low. In the middle of the dimly-lit space there was a thermal grate throwing out a warm orange glow; surrounding it were rings of chairs, some scattered cushions and salvaged rugs. A knot of people were there, crowded around an older woman who held an open book in her hand. Soalm had the impression of interrupting a performance in mid-flow.

The older woman saw the assassin and fear crossed her expression. Her audience were a mix of all kinds of people from the camp. Two of them, both fighters, sprang to their feet and came forwards with threats in their eyes.

Soalm raised her hands to defend herself, but the old woman called out. 'No! Stop! We'll have no violence!'

'Milady–' began one of the others, but she waved him to silence, and with visible effort, she drew herself up. Soalm saw the echoes of a lifetime of grace and fortitude there in the old woman's face.

She pushed through the ring of people and faced her interloper. 'I am… I *was* Lady Astrid Sinope. I am not afraid of you.'

Soalm cocked her head. 'That's not true.'

Sinope's aristocratic demeanour faltered. 'No… No, I suppose it is not.' She recovered slightly. 'Ever since Beye told us you were on Dagonet, I knew that this moment would come. I knew one of you would find us.'

'One of us?'

'The Emperor's warriors,' she went on. 'Capra said you were the instruments of his will. So come, then. Do what you must.'

'I don't understand...' Soalm began, but the old woman kept talking.

'I ask only that you show mercy to my friends here.' Sinope held up the heavy book in her hands. 'I brought this to Dagonet. I brought it here, to the resistance, when I fled the treachery of my former noble clan. If anyone must suffer because of that, it should be me alone.' Her eyes glittered with unspent tears. 'If I must beg you, I will. Please do not hurt them because of me.'

No one spoke as Soalm stepped past the two warriors and took the book from the old woman's trembling hands. She read aloud the words on the page. 'The Emperor protects.'

'We only seek solace in His name,' said Sinope, her voice falling to a whisper. 'I know that it is forbidden to speak openly of Him and His divine ways, but we do so only among ourselves, we do not proselytise or seek out converts!' She clasped her hands. 'We are so few. We take in only those who come to us of their own free will. We have hurt no one with our beliefs!'

Soalm ran her fingers over the pages of dense, solemn text. 'You are all followers of the Lectitio Divinitatus. You believe the Emperor is a living god. The only god.'

Sinope nodded. 'And I will die with that belief, if that is what is required. But promise me I will be the only one. Please!'

She understood, finally. 'I have not come to purge you,' Soalm told them. 'I... We did not even know you were here.' There was a strange, giddy sense of events shifting around her.

'But you were sent from Terra...' said one of the men.

'Not for this,' said the Venenum, turning to meet Lady Sinope's gaze, raising her arm as she did so and drawing back her cuff. 'And until this moment, I was not certain why.' Soalm showed them a small golden chain clasped around her wrist, a charm dangling from it in the shape of the Imperial aquila. 'But now... Now I have an inkling.'

'She's one of us,' said the man. 'She *believes*.'

Sinope's expression became one of joy. 'Oh, child,' she said. 'He sent you. He sent you to us.'

Soalm returned the book to her and nodded.


KELL LOOKED UP as the men boiled into the central chamber in a rush of energy and jubilation, weaving through the scattered clumps of hardware and containers, the groups of people who stopped and smiled to see them returning. They still had the smell of cordite, woodsmoke and exertion on them. He scanned the group with a practised eye and saw they had all come back, and only with a few minor injuries. The squad leader, an ex-pilot named Jedda, came over to where Capra was standing at a vox console and enveloped him in a bear hug.

'It's done?' said Capra.

'Oh, it's more than done!' Jedda laughed, the rush of battle still there in his voice. His men shared the moment and laughed with him. 'Tariel's information was dead on! We blew out the supports for the bridge and the whole cargo train went down. Hundreds of clanner troops, a dozen fan-jeeps and armoured GEVs, all of it scrap at the bottom of the Redstone river!'

'They'll feel that,' snorted one of the others. 'The nobles will be tasting blood tonight!'

Capra turned and gave Kell a nod. 'Thank your man for me. In fact, thank them all. A month ago I would never have thought I'd be saying this, but we actually have them on the defensive. The data and guidance you've provided us has enabled the resistance to make coordinated strikes all over the planet. The nobles are reeling.'

'The mistake they made was their arrogance,' said Koyne, wandering up to the group. The men parted to let the Callidus come closer; they were all unnerved by the bland, unfinished cast to the assassin's neutral features. 'They believed they had won, and lowered their guard. They didn't expect you to hit back in synchrony. You've put them off balance.'

'We'll help you keep up the pressure,' Kell told the resistance leader. 'All we've done so far is show you how to find the cracks in their armour. You need to keep widening them until they break.'

Jedda nodded to himself. 'We didn't lose a single man tonight. We keep this up, the commoners who haven't committed will side with us.' He grinned at Kell. 'At this rate, your fleet might get here and find it has nothing to do!'

'We can only hope,' said Koyne, drawing a look from the Vindicare.

'Capra!' Beye crossed the chamber at a jog, 'Grohl's back!'

Kell saw the grim-faced freedom fighter following her, unfurling his overhood and cloak. He had a scuffed carryall over one shoulder.

'From the capital?' said Jedda. 'We made a lot of noise tonight, Terrik! Did they hear it back there in the towers?' His triumphant mood rolled against the other man's stony countenance and rebounded without effect.

'They heard all right,' said Grohl. He dropped the carryall on a crate being used as a makeshift table and threw off his robes with an irritable shake. 'The Governor made a broadcast over all the communications channels. A declaration, he called it.'

The group fell silent. Kell saw the moment radiate out across the cavern to every person within earshot.

'Let's see it, then,' said Capra.

Grohl opened the case and produced a memory spool, the commercial kind that any core world civilian home of moderate means possessed. 'One of our contacts recorded this off the public watch-wire. It's repeating in a loop at the top of each hour.' Jedda went to take it from him, but Grohl didn't give it up. 'Perhaps you should look at this somewhere more… private.'

Capra considered that for a moment, then shook his head. 'No. If it's on the wire, then everyone else knows about it. Our people should too.'

Jedda took the spool and inserted it into a hololithic reader. With a buzzing hum, the device projected the ghostly image of a man in heavy dress uniform, a braided cap upon his head. He was standing before a lectern, and Kell noticed that it bore the sigil of an open, slitted eye; the symbol of the Sons of Horus.

'Governor Nicran,' said Jedda with a sneer. 'I wonder where he recorded this? Cowering in the basement of his mansion?'

'Quiet!' hissed Grohl. 'Listen.'

Kell watched the hololith carefully as the Governor began with empty pleasantries and vapid words of praise for his puppet masters in the noble clans. He read the politician's expressions, for a moment imagining he was seeing that face down the sights of his Exitus longrifle. Nicran had all the look about him of a desperate man. Then he turned to the important part of the announcement.

'Citizens of Dagonet,' he said, 'I have been gravely disturbed to learn of the deaths of many of our brave PDF troopers in the ongoing and ruthless attacks perpetrated by the resistance. Attacks that have also claimed the lives of many innocent civilians...'

'Bollocks they have,' snarled Jedda. 'Clanner blood only!'

'I applaud the vigilance of our troopers and recognise their bravery,' Nicran continued. 'But I also listen when their commanders tell me that the enemy hiding among us is a clear and present danger we have yet to overcome. And so, rather than prolong this terrible fighting and waste more precious Dagoneti lives, I have petitioned for assistance.'

'What does that mean?' muttered one of Jedda's men. Kell kept his expression unchanged, aware that Koyne was watching him closely.

Across the chamber, a hush had fallen as everyone hung on Nicran's words. 'Centuries ago, when Dagonet was beneath the shadow of corrupt priest-kings, we faced a similar crisis. And then, as now, a warrior came to aid us. A *master of war who freed us from fear and terror.'* The Governor blinked and licked his lips; Kell felt an odd tingle of anticipation in his trigger finger. *'Citizens, I have this day received word from the fleet of the Sons of Horus. They are coming to Dagonet to deliver us, and the great hero Horus Lupercal will be with them. Have no fear. The retribution of the Astartes will be swift and terrible, but in its wake the freedom we crave, freedom of liberty, freedom from the stifling rule of a distant and uncaring Emperor, will be ours.'*

Grohl tapped a key on the projector and the image died. 'And there it is.'

It was as if something had sucked all the air from the chamber; Nicran's statement had shocked the rebels into silence.

Jedda spoke first. 'Astartes…' he whispered, all trace of his earlier elation gone. 'Coming here?' He looked to Capra. 'We… We can't fight Space Marines. Clan troopers are one thing, but the Warmaster's elite…'

'They are like nothing we have ever seen,' Grohl said darkly. 'Genetically enhanced superhumans. Living weapons. Angels of death. A handful of them can crush armies–'

'So what should we do, then?' snapped Beye angrily. 'Surrender at once? Shoot ourselves and save them the trouble?'

'They'll destroy us all,' Grohl insisted. 'The only hope we have is to disband our forces and lose ourselves in the general populace, that or flee off-world before their warships arrive.' He glared at Kell. 'Because our salvation won't be here before Horus, will it?'

'He's right, Capra,' said Jedda, his tone bleak. 'Against men, we've got a fighting chance. But we can't beat war gods–'

'They're not gods,' Kell snarled, quieting him. 'They are not invulnerable. They bleed red like any one of us. They can die.' He met Grohl's look. 'Even Horus.'

Capra gave a slow nod. 'Kell's right. The Astartes are formidable, but they can be beaten.' He gave the Vindicare a level stare. '*Tell me* they can be beaten.'

'I killed a Space Marine,' said Kell. Koyne's bland expression flickered as something like surprise crossed the other assassin's face. Kell ignored it and went on. 'And I'm still here.'

'Capra...' Grohl started to speak again, but the rebel leader waved him into silence.

'I need to think on this,' he told them. 'Beye, come with me.' Capra walked away with the woman, and Kell watched him go. Grohl gave the Vindicare a harsh look and left him with Jedda and the other warriors following.

Kell picked up the memory spool and weighed it in his hand.

'Did you really terminate an Astartes?' said Koyne.

'You know the rules,' Kell replied, without looking away. 'A clade's targets are its own concern.'

The Callidus sniffed. 'It doesn't matter. Even if you did, it's just one truth among a handful of pretty lies. That one, Grohl? He's the smartest of all this lot. The Sons of Horus *will* destroy them, and turn this world into a funeral pyre along the way. I've seen how the Astartes fight.'

Kell rounded on the shade and stepped closer. 'The Warmaster is coming here. That's all that matters.'

'Oh, indeed,' said Koyne. 'And by the time Capra and the other ones who have decided to trust you realise that's all we want, it will be too late.' The other assassin leaned in. 'But let me ask you this, Kell. Do you feel any remorse about what we're doing? Do you feel any pity for these people?'

The Vindicare looked away. 'The Imperium appreciates their sacrifice.'

THE QUARTERS ABOARD the *Iubar* belonging to operative Hyssos were as predictably dull as Spear had expected them to be. There were only a few flashes of individuality here and there – a cabinet with a few bottles of good amasec, a shelf of paper-plas books on a wide variety of subjects, and some rather indifferent pencil sketches that the man had apparently drawn himself. Spear's lip curled at the dead man's pretension; perhaps he thought he was some kind of warrior-poet, standing sentinel over the people of the Eurotas clan by day, touching a sensitive artistic soul by night.

The truth was nowhere near as dignified, however. Delving through the morass of jumbled memories he had stolen from Hyssos's dead brain, Spear found more than enough incidents where the security operative had been called upon to use his detective skills to smooth over situations with native law enforcement on worlds along the Taebian trade axis. The Consortium's crews and officers broke laws on other worlds and it was Hyssos who was forced to find locals to take the blame or the right men to bribe. He cleaned up messes left by the Void Baron and his family, and on some level the man had hated himself for it.

Spear had extruded a number of eyes and allowed them to wander the room, sweeping for surveillance devices. Finding nothing, he reconsumed them and then rested, letting his outer aspect relax. The fleshy matter coating his body lost a little definition; to an outside observer, it would have looked like an image slipping out of focus through a lens. He sensed a faint call from the daemonskin. It wanted fresh blood – but then it *always* wanted fresh blood. Spear let some of the remains of Hyssos he had kept in his secondary stomach ooze out to be absorbed by the living sheath, and it quieted.

He sat at the desk across from the sleeping alcove. Laid out over the surface were a half-dozen data-slates, each of them displaying layers of information about the *Iubar*. There were deck plans and security protocols, conduit diagrams, patrol servitor routings, even a copy of the Void Baron's daily itinerary. Spear's long, spidery fingers danced over them, plucking slates from the pile for a moment, putting them back, selecting others. A strategy was forming, and the more he gave it his consideration, the more he realised that it would need to be implemented sooner rather than later.

The rogue trader's flagship had dropped out of the churn of the warp near a neutron star in the Cascade Line, to take sightings and rest the drives before setting off to the rendezvous at Arrowhead. They would be here no more than a day, and once the *Iubar* was back in the immaterium, the energy flux from the vessel's Geller field generators would interfere with Spear's plans to break into Eurotas's personal reliquary. The flux had the unfortunate side effect of causing distress to the daemonskin, rendering some of its more useful traits ineffectual. It would have to be done soon, then–

*NO*

Spear flinched and his whole body rippled with a sudden jolt of pain. The echoing screech lanced through him like a laser.

*NO NO NO NO NO NO*

'Shut up!' he spat, pushing away from the desk, shaking his head. 'Shut up!'

The voice within tried to cry out again, but he smothered it with a sharp exhale of air and a tensing of his will. For a moment, Spear felt it inside himself, deep down in the black depths of his spirit – the flickering ember of light. A tiny piece of Yosef Sabrat's soul, trapped and furious.

The killer dropped to the floor of the room and bowed his head, closed his eyes. He drew inwards, let his thoughts fall into himself. It was akin to sinking into an ocean of dark, heavy oil – but instead of resisting it, Spear allowed himself to be filled by the blackness, relishing the sensation of drowning.

He plunged into the void of his own shattered psyche, searching for the foreign, the human, the thought-colours of a dead man. It was difficult; the faint echoes of every life he had destroyed and then imitated all still lingered here somewhere. But they had all been purged through the ritual rites, and what remained was just a shallow imprint, like the shadows burnt on walls by the flash of a nuclear fireball. Something of Yosef Sabrat was still here, though. Something tenacious that obstinately refused to allow Spear to expunge it, clinging on.

And there it was, a glow in the gloom. Spear's animus leapt at it, fangs out, ready to rip it to shreds. The killer found it cloaked in a memory, a moment –

a terrible burning pain. He laughed as he realised he was experiencing the instant when he had pierced Sabrat's heart with a bone-blade, but this time from his victim's point of view.

The pain was blinding – and *familiar*. Spear hesitated; yes, he knew this feeling, this exact feeling. Sabrat's memory echoed one of his own, a memory from the killer's past.

Too late, Spear understood that the fragment had fled his grasp, cleverly cloaking itself in the similarity; and too late, he was dragged into his own past. Back to an experience that had made him into the monster he was.

BACK TO THE *cage. The pain and the cage…*

Voices outside. The armoured warriors moving and speaking. War-angels and gun-lords, black souls and beasts.

Voices.

'Is this it?' A commander-master, clear from tone and manner. Obeyed, *yes*.

'Aye, my lord,' says the wounded one. 'A pariah, according to the logs left by the Silent Sisterhood. But I have not seen the like. And they didn't know what it was, either. It was bound for destruction, most likely.'

The master-to-be-his-master comes closer. He sees a face filled with wonderment and hatred.

'I smell the witch-stink on it. It did not die with the rest of the crew and cargo?'

'The Emperor's Black Ships are resilient vessels. Some were bound to live beyond our bombardment.'

A pause, during which he takes some sharp breaths, trying to listen to the voices.

'Tell me what it did.'

A sigh, weary and fearful. 'I was attacked. It took a finger from me. With its teeth.'

Mocking laughter. 'And you let it live?'

'I would have destroyed it, lord, but then it... Then it killed the Codicier. Brother Sadran.'

Laughter stopped now. Anger colouring. 'How?'

'Sadran lost an ear to it. Eaten, swallowed whole. Then the witch stood there and waited to be killed. Sadran...' The wounded one is finding it hard to explain. 'Sadran turned his fury on the thing and it reflected it back.'

'Reflected...' The master-voice, different again. *Interested.*

'Fires, lord. Sadran was consumed by his own fires.' The shapes move around in the shadows beyond the cage bars.

'I've never encountered a pariah capable of that...' The master comes close, and he has his first real look at it. 'You're something special, aren't you?'

'It may be a fluke birth,' says the injured one. 'Or perhaps some throwback from the experimentations of the Adeptus Telepathica.'

A smile grows wide in the gloom. 'It may also be an opportunity.'

He presses up towards the bars, allowing himself to reach the ethereal edges of his senses towards the commander-master.

'We should kill it,' says the other voice.

'I'll be the judge of that.'

He touches a mind, and for the first time in his life finds something that is darker than himself. A stygian soul, steeped in blackness, initiated into realms beyond his ability to know.

'My Lord Erebus—' the injured one tries to argue, but the master silences him with a look.

'These are your orders, brother-captain,' says the dark-hearted one. 'Remove all trace that we were ever here, and ensure that this vessel becomes lost to the void. I will gather what we came for... and bring our new friend here into the bargain.' The one called Erebus smiles again. 'I think we will have use for him.'

As the other warrior departs, the master leans in. 'Do you have a name?' he asks.

It has been a long time since he has spoken, and it takes a moment to form the word; but finally he manages. 'Spear.'

Erebus nods. 'Your first lesson, then. I am your master.' Then the warrior is a blur, and there is a blade in his hand, and then the blade is in Spear's chest and the pain is blinding, burning.

'I am your master,' Erebus says once again. 'And from now on, you will kill only who I tell you to kill.'

Spear reels back. He nods, giving his fealty. The pain fills him, fills the cage.

*The pain and the cage...*

THE MOMENT SNAPPED like brittle glass and Spear jerked upright, his foot kicking out and knocking over a chair. He scrambled to his feet, catching sight of his face in a mirror. Hyssos's aspect was pasty, like unfired clay. He grimaced and tried to concentrate; but the encounter with the memory fragment and the flash of his past had cut to his core. He was breathing hard, the daemonskin on his hands rippling crimson.

'Operative?' Someone was knocking on his cabin door. 'I heard a cry. Are you all right in there?'

'I'm fine!' he shouted back. 'It… I fell from my bed. It's nothing.'

'You're sure?' He recognised the voice now; it was one of the duty officers on this deck.

'Go away!' he snapped.

'Aye, sir,' said the officer, after a moment, and he heard footsteps recede.

Spear walked to the mirror and glared at Hyssos's face as it resurfaced. 'You can't stop me,' he told the reflection. 'None of you can. *None of you.*'

IN RECOGNITION OF their help, the rebels had given all the members of the Execution Force quarters in one of the smaller chambers off the main corridor. The rooms were no bigger than holding cells, but they were dry and they had privacy, which was more than could be said for many of the communal sleeping areas.

Soalm didn't knock and wait outside her brother's compartment; instead she slammed the corroded metal door open and stormed into the room.

He looked up from the makeshift table before him, where the disassembled components of his longrifle lay like an exploded technical diagram. Lines of bullets were arranged in rows like tiny sentries on a parade ground. He stopped himself from drawing his Exitus pistol and returned to the work of cleaning his firearm. 'Where are your manners, Jenniker?' he said.

She closed the door and folded her arms. 'We're doing this, then?' she said. 'We're actually going to sacrifice all these people just to complete the mission?'

'What was your first clue?' he asked. 'Was it when I told you that was our plan, on board the *Ultio*? Or when Valdor made it exactly, precisely clear what our objective was?'

'You're manipulating Capra and his people,' she insisted.

'This is what we do,' said her brother. 'Don't pretend you've never done the same thing to get close to a mark. Lied and cheated?'

'I've never put innocents in harm's way. The whole motive for the Officio Assassinorum is to move sightless and unseen, leave no trace but the corpse of our target... But you're cutting a road of blood for us to follow!'

'This isn't the Great Crusade any more, dear sister.' He put down his tools and studied her. 'Are you so naïve that you don't see that? We're not thinning the ranks of a few degenerate bohemian fops in the halls of some hive-world, or terminating a troublesome xenos commander. We're on the front lines of a civil war. The rules of engagement are very different now.'

Soalm was quiet for a moment. It had been many years since she had seen Eristede, and it made her sad to see how he had changed. She could only see the worst of him behind those dark eyes. 'It's not just the resistance fighters whose lives we are threatening. By keeping this conflict alive we will doom countless innocent people, perhaps even threaten the future of this entire planet and the sector beyond.'

'Are you asking me if the death of Horus Lupercal is worth that price? That's a question you should put to Valdor or the Master of Assassins. I am only doing what I was ordered to. Our duty is all that matters.'

She felt a surge of emotion in her chest and crushed it before it could become a snarl or a sob. 'How can you be so cold-blooded, Eristede? We are supposed to protect the people of the Imperium, not offer them up as fodder for the cannons!' Soalm shook her head. 'I don't know who you are…'

With a flash of anger, her brother bolted to his feet. '*You* don't know *me*? I'm not the one who rejected her own name! I didn't turn my back on justice!'

'Is that what you tell yourself?' She looked away. 'We both had a choice all those years ago, Eristede. Escape, or revenge. But you chose revenge, and you condemned us to a life where we are nothing but killers.'

The memory came back to her in a giddy rush. They were both just children then, the scions of their family. The last surviving members of the Kell dynasty, their holdings destroyed and their parents exterminated during an internecine struggle among the aristocrats of the Thaxted Duchy. Orphaned and alone, they had been drawn into the halls of the Imperial schola and there both secretly selected by agents of the Officio Assassinorum.

Brother and sister had shown promise – Eristede was an excellent marksman for one so young, and Jenniker's genius for botany and chemistry was clear. They knew that soon the clade directors would make their decisions, and that they would be split up, perhaps never to see one another again. In the halls of the schola they had made their plans to flee together, to eschew the assassin's path and find a new life.

But then Clade Vindicare offered something that Eristede Kell wanted more than his freedom; the chance to avenge his mother and father. All they asked for in return was his loyalty – and consumed by hate, he gave it willingly. Jenniker had been left behind with nowhere to go but to the open arms of the Venenum.

Months later, she had learned that innocents had been killed in the hit on the man who murdered their parents, and that had been the day when she swore she would no longer go by the name of Kell again.

'I'd hoped you might have changed since I last saw you,' she said. 'And you have. But not for the better.'

Her brother seemed as if he was on the verge of an outburst; but then he drew it back in and looked away. 'You're right,' he told her. 'You *don't* know me. Now get out.'

'As you command,' Soalm said stiffly.

# TWELVE

### A Single Drop
### Messenger
### Wilderness of Mirrors

THE MEN GUARDING the chamber housing the Void Baron's private reliquary had allowed their concentration to falter. Spear listened to them speak as he stood in the shadows beyond their line of sight, a few metres up along the vaulted corridor. News had filtered down through the crew hierarchy aboard the *Iubar*, fractions of the reports from the communicatory that warned of sightings of Adeptus Astartes on the move. No one seemed to know if they were warriors still loyal to the Emperor of Mankind, or if they were those now following the banner of the Warmaster; some even dared to suggest that *all* the mighty Legions of the Astartes had turned their faces from their creator, embarking on a jihad to take for themselves what they had captured for Terra during the Great Crusade.

Spear understood only small elements of the unfolding war going on across the galaxy; and in truth, it mattered little to him. The killer's keyhole view of intergalactic conflict was enough. He cared little about sides or doctrines. All Spear needed was the kill. It was enough that his master Erebus had given him murders to commit; perhaps even the greatest murder in human history.

But before that could happen, he had steps to take. Preparations to be made.

Spear allowed the daemonskin to regain a small amount of control over itself, and the surface of his surrogate flesh shivered. Removing the shipsuit overall he had been wearing, he stepped naked into the deep shadows. Hair-like tendrils emerged from his epidermis, sampling the air and the ambient light all around. In moments Spear's body became wet with sticky processor fluids, changing colour until it was night-dark. His features retreated behind a mask of scabbing crusts, and then he leapt soundlessly to the high ceiling. Secreted oils allowed him to adhere there, and the killer snaked slowly along his inverted pathway, passing over the heads of the guards as they fretted and spoke in low tones about threats they could not understand.

At the entrance to the reliquary there was an intelligent door possessed of a variety of sensory and thought-mechanical systems designed to open only to Merriksun Eurotas, or a member of his immediate family. It was little impediment to Spear. He slapped the daemonskin lightly as it whined in his mind, dragging on him a little as it sensed the guards and expressed a desire to drink their blood. Chastened, it obediently extruded a new, thickly-lipped mouth at his palm. Spear held the mouth over the biometric breath sensor, as the same time sending new hair-tendrils into the thin gaps around the edges of the door. They wormed their way into the locks and teased them open one by one.

It had been easy to sample the Void Baron's breath; simply by standing close to him, Spear's daemonskin sheath had plucked the microscopic particulate matter and DNA traces of his exhalations from the air, and stored them in a bladder. Now the second mouth puffed them out over the sensor.

There was the whisper of well-lubricated cogs and the door opened. Spear slipped inside.

DAGONET'S SUN WAS passing low over the top of the ridgeline, and soon night would fall. Jenniker Soalm stood out on the flat expanse of stone that served as a lookout post, and looked out at the ochre rocks without really seeing them. She knew that the mission clock was winding down towards zero, and at best the Execution Force had only hours until they entered the final phase of the operation.

She could see that the others sensed it too. The Garantine had at last returned from whatever lethality he had been spreading on the clanner forces, menacing all who saw him. Tariel, Koyne and the Culexus waif were all making ready – and her brother…

Soalm knew *exactly* what her brother was doing.

'Hello?' The voice made her turn. With slow, careful steps, Lady Sinope emerged from the cave mouth behind her and approached. 'I was told I might find you here.'

'Milady.' Jenniker bowed slightly.

Sinope smiled. 'You don't need to do that, child. I'm a noblewoman only in name now. The others let me keep the title as a gesture of respect, but the truth is the clans of this world have wiped away any honour we ever had.'

'Others must have rejected the call to join Horus's banner.'

The old woman nodded. 'Oh, a few. All dead now, I think. That, or terrified into compliance.' She sighed. 'Perhaps He will forgive them.'

Soalm looked away. 'I do not believe He is the forgiving kind. After all, the Emperor denies all word of his divinity.'

Sinope nodded again. 'Indeed. But then, only the sincerely divine can do such a thing and be true in it. Those who think themselves gods are always madmen or fools. To be raised to such heights, one must be carried there on the shoulders of faith. One must guide and yet be guided.'

'I would like some guidance myself,' admitted the assassin. 'I don't know where to turn.'

'No?' The noblewoman found a wind-smoothed rock and sat down on it. 'If it is not too impertinent a question, may I ask you how you found your way to the light of the *Lectitio Divinitatus*?'

Soalm sighed. 'After our… after my parents were killed in a conflict between rival families, I found myself isolated and alone in the care of the Imperium. I had no one to watch over me.'

'Only the God-Emperor.'

She nodded. 'So I came to realise. He was the single constant in my life. The only one who did not judge me… Or leave me. I had heard stories of the Imperial Cult… It was not long before I found like-minded people.'

Sinope's head bobbed. 'Yes, that is often the way. Like comes to like, all across the galaxy. Here on Dagonet there are those who do not yet believe as we do – Capra and most of his people, for example – but still we share the same goals. And in the end, there are still many, many of us, child. Under different names, in different ways, everywhere you find human beings. As He led us to greatness and dispelled the fog of all the false gods and mistaken religiosity, the God-Emperor forged the path to the one truth. His truth.'

'And yet we must hide that truth.'

The old woman sighed. 'Aye, for the moment. Faith can be so strong at times, and yet so weak in the same moment. It is a delicate flower that must be nurtured and protected, in preparation for the day when it can truly bloom.' She placed a hand on Jenniker's arm. 'And that day is coming.'

'Not soon enough.'

Sinope's hand fell away and she was quiet for a moment. 'What do you want to tell me, child?'

Soalm turned to look at her, eyes narrowing. 'What do you mean?'

'I've been doing this since before you were born,' said the woman. 'Believe me, I know when someone is holding something back. You're afraid of something, and it isn't just this revolution we find ourselves in.'

'Yes.' The words came of their own accord. 'I am afraid. I am afraid that just by coming to your world we will destroy all of this.' She gestured around.

A brief smile crossed Sinope's lips. 'Oh, my dear. Don't you realise? You have brought hope to Dagonet. That is a precious, precious thing. More fragile than faith, even.'

'No. I did nothing. I am only... a messenger.' Soalm wanted to tell her the truth, in that moment. To explain the full scope of the Execution Force's plans, to reveal the real reasons behind their assistance to Capra's freedom fighters, to cry out her darkest, deepest fear – that in her collusion with it all, she was no better than her bitter, callous brother.

But the words would not come. All she heard in her thoughts was Eristede's challenge, the cold calculation he had laid before her; were the lives of these people worth more than the death of the Warmaster, the living embodiment of the greatest threat to the human Imperium?

Sinope came and sat with her, and slowly the old woman's expression turned darker. 'Let me tell you what *I* am afraid of,' she said. 'And you will understand why the struggle is so important. There are sinister forces at large in the universe, child.'

'The Warmaster...'

'Horus Lupercal is only an agent of that unchecked anarchy, my dear. There are manifestations coming into being on every world that falls into the shadows cast by the Warmaster's ambition. Out in the blackness between the stars, cold hate grows.'

Soalm found the woman's quiet, intense voice compelling, and listened in silence, captured by her words.

Sinope went on. 'You and I, mankind itself and even the God-Emperor... All are being tested by a chorus of ruinous powers. If our Lord is truly divine, then we must know that He will have his opposite, something beyond our understanding of evil... What terrifies me is the dream of what will come if we let that hate overwhelm our glorious Imperium. There will be disorder and destruction. Fire–'

'And chaos,' said Jenniker.

HAD THE CHOICE been his, the killer would have preferred to wait until the *Iubar* and its attendant ships had reached the Sol system before attempting this penetration; but Spear's windows of opportunity were limited, and growing smaller with each passing hour. It was simply the most expedient option to do this now. Once they were within the boundaries of the Segmentum Solar, security around the Eurotas flotilla would increase tenfold and Operative Hyssos would have much to occupy his time and attention.

And then there was the other possibility to consider; that his target, once marked and stored, might be sufficiently powerful that Spear's ability could be released against it from across an interplanetary distance. He hoped that would not prove to be so – Spear relished the moment of great joy when he looked a kill in the eye and saw the understanding of the end upon it. To be denied that in his crowning moment… It would be simply *unjust*.

The killer kept to the lines of tiles that glowed phosphor-green through the gelatinous lenses the daemonskin had grown over his eyes; normal human vision would have noticed nothing to differentiate the tiles on the floor of the reliquary, and so a luckless entrant would wander into one of the zones of contragravity stitched into the chamber – there to float trapped until the guards came with guns and ready trigger-fingers.

He ignored the works of art and objects of incredible value that arrayed the long gallery, each given pride of place in an alcove of its own. The remains of every Eurotas Void Baron since the first were held here, their ashes in urns as tall as a child, the containers made from spun diamond, tantalum, the shells of a Xexet quintal and other materials, each rarer and more expensive than the last. Portraits of lords and ladies from the clan's history dominated every surface, and all of them stared out sightlessly at Spear as he threaded his way past, avoiding the perception spheres of beam sensors and magnetic anomaly detectors. The daemonskin's fronds waved gently as he moved, continually tasting the ambient atmosphere and temperature to keep the intruder cooled in synchrony. The thermal monitors studding every square centimetre of the reliquary walls looked for the glow of body heat, but saw nothing. All the patient, clever machines continued to believe the chamber was still empty.

At the far end of the gallery, inside a glass stasis cage on a plinth made of white marble and platinum, was the Warrant of Trade.

Spear slowed as he approached it, licking his lips behind the bindings of his scab mask. The motion made the oily skin peel back over his cheeks, revealing teeth, a grin.

The book was made of real paper, fabricated from one of the last natural forests on Venus. The ink had been refined from burst-sac fluids harvested from Jovian skimmer rays. Artisans from Merica had assembled the tome, bound it in rich grox-hide. Inlaid on the cover, flecks of gemstones from all the colonised worlds of the Sol system shimmered in the light of the gallery's electrocandles. This book was the physical manifestation of the Eurotas clan's right to travel the stars. More than their fleets of vessels, their armies of staff and crew, more than the fiscal might they wielded over countless worlds and industrial holdings across the Taebian Stars – more than any of those things, the Warrant was what gave Merriksun Eurotas and his kindred the Emperor's permission to trade, to voyage, to expand the Imperium's influence through sheer economic power.

The killer almost laughed at that. As if any being could parcel out sections of the universe to his followers like plots of land or portions of food. What hubris. What monumental arrogance to assume that they had that entitlement. Such power could not be given; it could only be *taken*, through bloodshed, pain and the ruthless application of will.

The glass case had a complex mechanism of suspensors and gravity splines within it, and with the passage of a hand over a ruby sensor pad on the frame, the pages of the book inside could be turned without ever touching them. Spear flicked at the sensor and the Warrant creaked open, leaf after leaf of dense text flickering past.

It fluttered to a halt on an ornately illuminated page lined in gilt, purple ink and silver leaf. Words in High Gothic surrounded a sumptuously detailed picture repeating the image depicted in the jade frieze in the audience chamber – the Emperor granting the first Eurotas his boon. But Spear's hungry gaze ignored the workmanship, turning instead towards a wet, liquid patch of dark crimson captured upon the featureless white vellum of the Warrant's final page.

*A single drop of blood.*

He laid his hand on the edge of the case and let the daemonskin around his fingertips deliquesce, oozing into the weld holding the construction together. The heavy duty armourglass creaked and split down the seam, the malleable flesh pressing on it, shifting it out of true. All at once, a pane gave off a snap of sound, and the killer muffled it with his oily palms. The glass fell out of the frame and into his hand. He greedily reached inside, with trembling fingers.

Spear would rip the page from the ancient book, tear it out of the stasis field that had preserved it for hundreds of years. He would hold the paper to his lips and consume the blood, take it like the kiss of a lover. He would–

His hand reached for the pages of the Warrant of Trade and passed straight through it, as if the book were made of smoke. Inside the glass case, the tome seemed to flicker and grow indistinct, for one blinding moment becoming nothing but a perfect ghost image projected from a cluster of hololithic emitters concealed inside the frame of the cage.

The case was empty; and for a moment so was Spear, his chest hollowed out by the sudden, horrible realisation that his prize *was not here.*

But then he was filled anew with murderous rage, and it took every last fraction of his self-control to stop the killer from screaming out his fury and destroying everything around him.

AFTER LADY SINOPE had left her alone once more, Soalm remained where she was on the ridge and waited for the darkness to engulf her. The night sky, a sight that so often gave her a moment of peace as she contemplated it, now seemed only to veil the threats the old woman had spoken of. She shivered involuntarily and felt a cold, familiar pressure at the edge of her senses.

'Iota.' She turned and found the Culexus standing near the cave entrance, watching her. The dusky-skinned girl's eyes glittered. 'Spying on me?'

'Yes,' came the reply. 'You should not remain outside for too long. There are ships in orbit and satellite systems under the control of the clan forces. They will be sweeping this zone with their long-range imagers.'

'How long have you been watching?'

'*I do not believe He is the forgiving kind,*' she repeated, fingering the nullifier torc around her neck.

Soalm frowned. 'You have no right to intrude on a private conversation!'

If that was meant to inspire guilt in Iota, she gave no such reaction. The pariah seemed unable to grasp the niceties of such concepts as privacy, tact or social graces. 'What did the woman Sinope mean, when she spoke about "forces at large"?' Iota shook her head. 'She did not refer to threats of a military nature.'

'It's complicated,' said Soalm. 'To be honest, I'm not quite sure myself.'

'But you value her words. And the words in the book.'

Soalm's blood ran cold. 'What book?'

'The one in the chamber on the lower levels. Where the others gather with Sinope to talk about the Emperor as a god. You have been there.'

'You followed me?' Soalm took a warning step forwards.

'Yes. Later I returned when no one was there. I read some of the book.' Iota looked away, still toying with the torc. 'I found it confusing.'

Soalm studied the Culexus, her mind racing. If Iota revealed the presence of the hidden chapel inside the rebel base, there was no way to predict what would happen. Many of Capra's resistance fighters followed the staunchly anti-theist Imperial edict that labelled all churches as illegal; and she could not imagine what Eristede might do if he learned she had involvement with the *Lectitio Divinitatus*.

'Kell will not be pleased,' said the other woman, as if she could read her thoughts.

'You won't speak of it,' Soalm insisted. 'You will not tell him!'

Iota cocked her head. 'He is blood kindred to you. The animus speculum reads the colour of your auras. I saw the parity between them the first time I watched you through the eyes of my helm. And yet you keep that a secret too.'

Soalm tried and failed to keep the shock from her face. 'And what other secrets do you know, pariah?'

She returned a level stare. 'I know that you are now considering how you might ensure my silence by killing me. If you make the attempt, there is a chance you may succeed. But you are conflicted by the thought of such an action. It is something your... brother... would not hesitate to do in your place.'

'I am not Eristede,' she insisted.

'No, you are not.' Iota's face softened. 'What is it like?'

'What?'

'Having kindred. Siblings. I have no concept or experience of it. I was matured in an enclosed environment. A research facility. Your experience… fascinates me. What is it like?' she repeated

Strangely, Soalm felt a momentary pang of sadness for the Culexus. 'Difficult,' she replied, at length. 'Iota, listen to me. Please, say nothing to the others about the chapel.'

'If I do not, will you try to kill me?'

'Will you force me?'

The Culexus shook her head. 'No.'

WHERE? WHERE WAS *the Warrant?*

The question thundered through Spear's mind and it would not let him go. He could not find rest, could not find a moment's peace until the document had been located. Everything about his master's careful, intricate plan hinged on the procurement of that one item. Without it, the assassination of the Emperor of Mankind was impossible. Spear was useless, a gun unloaded, a sword blade blunted. His existence had no meaning without the kill. Every single death he had performed, all of them, from the strangling of his birthparents to the ashing of the Word Bearer who came to slit his throat, the fools on Iesta Veracrux, the psy-witch, the investigators and the man whose face he now wore – all of them were only steps on a road towards his ultimate goal.

And now, Merriksun Eurotas had denied him that. The bloody rage Spear felt towards the Void Baron was so all-consuming that the killer feared merely laying eyes on the man would shatter his cover and send him into a berserker frenzy.

Spear had all but the most trivial of Hyssos's memories absorbed within him, and the operative had never known that the Warrant of Trade on display in the reliquary was a fake. There were fewer than a dozen men and women in the entire Eurotas Consortium who outranked the operative in matters of security... Spear wondered if one of them might know the true location of the tome. But how to be sure? He could kill his way through them and never be certain if they had that precious knowledge until he sucked it from their dying minds; but he could not risk such reckless behaviour.

Eurotas himself would know. But murdering the Void Baron here and now, disposing of a body, passing through another assumption so soon after having torn Hyssos's identity from his corpse... This was a course fraught with danger, far too risky to succeed.

*No.* He needed to find another way, and quickly.

'Hyssos?' The nobleman's voice was pitched high and sharp. 'What are you doing here?'

Spear looked up as Eurotas crossed the anteroom of the rogue trader's personal quarters where he stood waiting. 'My lord,' he began, moderating his churning thoughts. 'Forgive my intrusion, but I must speak with you.'

Eurotas glanced over his shoulder as he tied a velvet belt around the day robes he was wearing. Through a half-open door, it was possible to glimpse a sleeping chamber beyond. A naked woman was lying in a doze back there on a snarl of bed sheets. 'I am engaged,' the baron said, with a grimace. He seemed distracted. 'Come to the audience chamber after we enter the warp, and–'

'No sir,' Spear put a little steel into Hyssos's voice. 'This won't wait until we set off for Arrowhead. If I am correct, we may need to return to Iesta Veracrux.'

That got his attention. Eurotas's eyes narrowed, but not enough to hide the flicker of fear in them. 'Why would that be so?'

'I have been retracing my steps, going over my notes and recollections from the Iestan murders.' He fixed the baron with a level gaze and began to pay out the fiction he had created over the last few hours; a fiction he hoped would force the nobleman to give up the information he so desperately needed. 'The two men... Yosef Sabrat and Daig Segan, the ones who did those terrible deeds. There was something they said that did not seem right to me, at the end when I thought I would be killed by them.'

'Go on.' Eurotas went to a servitor and had it pour him a glass of water.

'Sir, they spoke about a warrant.' The baron stiffened slightly at the word. Spear smiled inwardly and went on. 'At the time I thought they meant warrants of arrest... But the thought occurs that they may have been talking about something else.' He nodded towards a painting on the wall, an impressionistic work showing the current Void Baron reading from the Warrant of Trade as if it were some scholarly volume of esoteric knowledge.

'Why would they be interested in the Warrant?' Eurotas demanded.

'I do not know. But these were no ordinary murderers, sir. We still cannot be certain by what exact means they terminated poor Perrig... And the things they did at the sites of their kills in the name of their Theoge cult–'

'They were not part of the Theoge!' snapped the baron, the retort coming out of nowhere. He shook his head and paced away a few steps. 'I always knew...' said the nobleman, after a moment of silence. 'I always knew that Erno Sigg was innocent. That's why I sent you, Hyssos. Because I trusted you to find the truth.'

Spear bowed, allowing his stolen face to grow saddened. 'I hope I did not disappoint you. And you were correct, my lord. Sigg was a dupe.'

'Those murdering swine were not part of the Theoge,' Eurotas repeated, turning to advance on him once more. His face had lost some of its earlier colour and his gaze was turned inwards.

'High-Reeve Telemach seemed to think otherwise,' Spear pressed. 'If I may ask, why do you disagree with her?' The killer saw something ephemeral pass over the other man's face; the shadow of a hidden truth. The understanding was coming up from Hyssos's captured persona, from the operative's instinctive grasp of fragile human nature, his ability to perceive the falsehood in the words of a liar. Spear let it rise; Eurotas was going to incriminate himself, if he could only be encouraged to do so. The Void Baron had known more than he had revealed about this situation all along, and only now was it coming to light.

'I... I will tell you what I... believe,' said the nobleman, moving to the door to close it. 'Those madmen on Iesta Veracrux were not just spree killers tormenting and bloodletting to satisfy their own insanity. I am certain now that they were agents of the Warmaster Horus Lupercal, may he rot. They were part of a plot that casts a shadow over the Taebian Sector, perhaps

over the whole galaxy!' He shuddered. 'We have all
heard the rumours about the... things that happen on
the worlds that have fallen.' Then his tone grew more
intense. 'Discrediting the Theoge and blackening the
name of our clan is just one part of this conspiracy of
evil.'

Spear said nothing, dissembling the man's words in
his thoughts. It was clear now why Eurotas had been
so quick to call the matter closed and depart from
Iesta Veracrux as fast as decorum would allow. The
involvement of Erno Sigg in the murders had been
bad enough, but Eurotas had to be sure that sooner or
later the clan's name would become connected to the
incident in another, more damning way. He was
afraid...

On a swift and sudden impulse, Spear rocked off his
feet from where he stood at attention and snatched at
the Void Baron's robes, pulling the man off-balance.

'What in Terra's name do you think you are doing?'
Eurotas cried out, affronted at the abrupt assault.

But in the next second his flash of anger died in his
throat when Spear pulled up the voluminous sleeve of
his robe to reveal a golden chain tight around his
wrist, and on it the shape of an aquila sigil. This time
he couldn't resist letting a small smile creep out over
Hyssos's lips. 'You're one of them.'

Eurotas shrugged him off and backed away, a guilty
cast coming to his eyes. 'What are you talking about?
Get out. You're dismissed.'

'I think not, sir.' Spear gave him a hard look. 'I think
an explanation is in order.'

For a moment, the man teetered on the verge of
shouting him down, calling in his personal guard

from the corridor outside; but Hyssos's unerring sense for the hidden told Spear that Eurotas would not. The dead man's instincts were correct. The nobleman's shoulders slumped and he planted himself in an ornamental chair, staring into the middle distance.

Spear waited for the confession that he knew would come next; men like the Void Baron lacked the will or the strength to really *inhabit* a lie. In the end, they welcomed the chance to unburden themselves.

'I am not...' He paused, trying to find the right words. 'The people who call themselves the Theoge came after, do you see? It was we who came first. We carried the message from Terra, in safe keeping aboard our ships, across the entire sector. Every son and daughter of the Eurotas family has been a participant in the *Lectitio Divinitatus*, since the day of the boon. We carry the Emperor's divinity with us.' He said the words with rote precision, without any real energy or impetus behind them.

Spear recalled what Daig Segan had said just before he had torn him open. 'The Emperor protects...'

Eurotas nodded solemnly; but it was abundantly clear that the light of true belief, the blind faith that Segan had shown in his dying moments, was in no way reflected in the Void Baron. If the nobleman was a believer in the cult of the God-Emperor, then it was only as one who paid lip service to it, because it was expected of him. Spear's lip curled, his disgust for the man growing by the moment; he did not even have the courage of his convictions.

'It is our hidden duty,' Eurotas went on. 'We spread the word of His divinity in quiet and secrecy. Our clan has been allied to groups like the Theoge on dozens of worlds, for centuries.' He looked away. 'But I never truly... That is, I did not...'

Spear watched and waited, saying nothing. As he expected, Eurotas was compelled to fill the silence.

'Horus is destroying everything. Every thread of power and influence we have, broken one at a time. And now he strikes not only at our holdings, but at the network my forefathers built to carry the word of the *Lectitio Divinitatus*.'

'A network of clandestine authority the Eurotas have used to control the Taebian Sector for hundreds of years.' Spear shook Hyssos's head. The human's arrogance was towering; he actually believed that a being as great as the Warmaster would lower himself to such parlour games as disrupting the ambitions of a single petty, venal rogue trader. The reality was, the slow collapse of the Eurotas clan's fortunes was just a side effect of Horus's advance across the Ultima Segmentum.

Still; it would serve Spear's interests to allow the man to think he was the focus of some interstellar conspiracy, when in fact he and all his blighted clan were little more than a means to an end.

'Ever since the conclusion of the Great Crusade, it has become harder and harder to hold on to things...' Eurotas sighed. 'Our fortunes are on the wane, my friend. I have tried to hide it, but it grows worse every day. I thought perhaps, when we return to Terra, I could petition the Sigillite for an audience, and then–'

'Where is the Warrant of Trade?' Spear was growing tired of the Void Baron, and he struck out with the question.

Eurotas reacted as if he had been slapped. 'It... In the reliquary, of course.' The lie was a poor one at best.

'I am your senior security operative, sir,' Spear retorted. 'Please credit me with some intelligence. Where is the real Warrant?'

'*How did you know?*' He shot to his feet, knocking the water glass to the floor where it shattered. A service mechanical skittered in across the carpet to clean up the breakage, but Eurotas paid it no heed. 'Only three people...' He paused, composing himself. 'When... did you find out?'

Spear studied him. 'That is of no consequence.' After the abortive infiltration of the reliquary, the killer had been careful to ensure that no trace of his entry remained. 'What matters is that you tell me where the real Warrant is now. If you are correct about these agents in the employ of the Warmaster, then we must be certain it is secure.'

'They were looking for it...' whispered Eurotas, shocked by the thought.

When the baron looked up at him with cold fear in his eyes, Spear knew that he had the man in his grasp. 'My sworn duty is to serve the Eurotas clan and their endeavours. That includes your... network. But I cannot do that if the Warrant becomes lost.'

'That must never happen.' The Void Baron swallowed hard. 'It is... not with the fleet. You have to understand, I had little choice. There were certain arrears that could not be paid, favours that were required in order to keep the clan operating–'

'*Where?*' Spear cracked Hyssos's gruff voice like a whip.

Eurotas looked away, abashed. 'The Warrant of Trade was touched by the hand of the God-Emperor of Mankind, and so in the eyes of those who embrace the word of the *Lectitio Divinitatus*, it is a holy object. In exchange for the nullification of a number of very large debts, I agreed to allow an assemblage of nobles involved with the Theoge to take possession of the Warrant for... for an extended period of pilgrimage.'

'What nobles?' Spear demanded. 'Where?'

'They have not answered my communications. I fear they may be dead or in hiding. When Horus's forces find them, they will be wiped out, and the Warrant will be destroyed...' His lip trembled. 'If it has not already been.' Eurotas looked up. 'The Warrant is on the planet Dagonet.'

*Finally. The answer.* For a long moment, Spear considered breaking out of Hyssos's restrictive body and reverting back to his kill-form, just to show Eurotas what sort of fool he was the instant before he ripped him to shreds; but instead he let the rage ebb and gave a sullen nod. 'I will need a ship, then. The fastest cutter available.'

'You cannot go to Dagonet!' Eurotas insisted. 'The government there has already declared for the Warmaster! There is word that the Sons of Horus are on their way to the planet at this very moment... It's suicide! I won't allow it.'

Spear twisted his proxy flesh into a sorrowful smile, and gave a shallow bow. 'I swear to you I will recover the Warrant, my lord. As of this moment, my life has no other purpose.'

At length, the nobleman nodded. 'Very well. And may the Emperor protect you.'

'We can but hope,' he replied.

# THIRTEEN

**Faith or Duty**
**Bonded**
**The Warrant**

THE SUMMONS CAME from the Vindicare, and so Iota joined Kell and the rest of the Execution Force in one of several storage rooms down in the web of caves, away from the more heavily-populated sections of the hideaway. The room smelled of promethium; drums of the liquid fuel were stacked to the ceiling in corners, and the air circulation system worked in fits and starts.

Kell had been careful to time the gathering to coincide with the regular overflights of clan patrol craft; every time it happened, the rebels would fall silent, go dark, and wait for the flyers to make their loop over the Bladecut before heading back to the city. It meant that Capra, Beye, Grohl and the others were all occupied, allowing the assassins to gather unnoticed, at least for a little while.

The Vindicare surveyed the room, looking at them all in turn. Iota noted that he looked to Soalm last of all, and seemed to linger on her. She wondered if his sibling understood the meaning behind that fractional moment. Iota regarded her understanding of human social interaction as an ongoing experiment, but her limited knowledge also afforded her a clarity that others lacked; for all the distance between the brother and sister, it seemed obvious to the Culexus that Kell cared for Soalm more than the woman knew – or *wanted* to know.

'We're entering the final phase,' Kell said, without preamble. 'Beye's contacts in the city have sent word of sightings at the perimeter of the Dagonet system. Warp disturbances. The prelude to the opening of a gateway.'

'How long until we know for sure?' asked Koyne. The Callidus looked like a child's doll the size of a man, all sketched, incomplete features and pale skin.

'We can't stay put and wait for confirmation,' Tariel said, without looking up from his cogitator gauntlet's keyboard. 'By the time the warships enter orbit it will be too late.'

The Garantine made a rumbling noise in the back of his throat that appeared to be an affirmation.

'We commit now,' said Kell. 'The Lance has been concealed, yes?' He looked at Tariel, who nodded.

'Aye,' said the infocyte. 'Grohl supplied transport from the star-port. I supervised the assembly of the component parts myself. It's ready.'

'But there's no way to test it, is there?' Koyne leaned forwards. 'If this doesn't work…'

'It will work,' Kell insisted. 'Everything we've done has been leading up to this moment. We're not going to start second-guessing ourselves now.'

'I was only making an observation,' said the shade. 'As I will be the closest to the target, I think it's fair to say I have the most invested in a trouble-free termination.'

'Don't fret,' said the Eversor. 'You won't get too dirty.'

'We have fall-back options in place.' Kell ignored the comment and nodded towards Iota and Soalm. 'But for now, we concentrate on the primary schema.' He paused and threw Tariel a look.

The Vanus operative consulted a timer window among the panes of hololiths hanging before him, and then glanced up. 'The clanner patrols should be heading back to the capital at any moment.'

'And we'll follow them.' Kell reached for his spy mask where it hung from his gear belt. 'You all have your own preparations to make. I suggest you complete them in short order and then head out. Each of us will go back into the capital individually via different routes, and rendezvous at the star-port. I'll be waiting for you aboard the *Ultio* after sunset.'

The only member of the group who did not move after Kell's dismissal was Soalm. She looked at the Vindicare, her lips thinning. 'Has Capra been informed?'

'Don't be a fool!' snorted the Eversor, before the other man could even speak. 'We may have killed one of the turncoats in this little play-gang of rebels, but there are likely others, watching and waiting for something juicy to report before they betray this place.' The Garantine opened his clawed hands. 'These people are amateurs. They can't be trusted.'

Soalm was still looking at Kell. 'What are they supposed to do after it is done?'

Iota saw colour rise in the Vindicare's cheeks, but he kept his temper in check. 'Capra is resourceful. He'll know what to do.'

'If he has any sense,' muttered Koyne, 'he'll run.'

Soalm turned away and was the first from the chamber.


JENNIKER REACHED THE compartment Beye had assigned to her and went in. What little equipment she had was there, cunningly disguised as a lady traveller's attaché. It seemed strangely out of place among such drab accommodation, on the Imperial Army-surplus bedroll beside a drawstring bag of ration packs. She paused, studying it.

Inside the case, concealed inside clever modules and secret sections, there were vials of powder, flat bottles of colourless fluid, thin strips of metallised chemical compounds, injectors and capsules and dermal tabs. The manner and means to end an entire city's worth of human lives, if need be.

For a while she thought about how simple it would be to introduce a philtre of time-release metasarin into the water system of the rebel hideout. Tailored with the right mix, she could make it painless for them. They would just fall asleep, never to wake. They would be spared the brutal deaths that were fated to them all – the payment that would be exacted no matter if the Execution Force succeeded or failed. She thought about Lady Sinope, of trusting Beye and the ever-suspicious Grohl.

Some might have said it would be a mercy. The Warmaster was not a magnanimous conqueror.

Soalm shook her head violently to dispel the thought, and hated herself in that instant. 'I am not Eristede,' she whispered to the air.

A sharp knock at the rusted metal door startled her. 'Hello?' said a voice. She recognised it as one of the men she had seen in the makeshift chapel. 'Are you in there?'

She slid the door open. 'What is it?'

The man's face was flushed with worry. 'They're coming,' he husked. She didn't need to ask who *they* were. If Beye's contacts in the city had spoken to Capra, then it was logical to assume that others in the rebel encampment knew of what was on the horizon as well.

'I know.'

He pressed something into her palm. 'Sinope gave me this for you.' It was a tarnished voc-locket, a type of portable recording device that lovers or family members gave to one another as a memento. The device contained a tiny, short-duration memory spool and hologram generator. 'I'll be outside.' He pulled the door shut and Soalm was alone in the room again.

She turned the locket over in her hands and found the activation stud. Holding her breath, she squeezed it.

A grainy hololith of Lady Sinope's face, no larger than Jenniker's palm, flickered into life. *'Dear child,'* she began, an urgency in her words that Soalm had not heard before, *'forgive me for not asking this of you in person, but circumstances have forced me to leave the caves. The man who gave you this is a trusted friend, and he will bring you to me.'* The noblewoman paused and she seemed to age a decade in the space of a single breath. *'We need your help. At first I thought I might be mistaken, but with each passing day it has become clearer and clearer to me that you are here for a reason. He sent you, Jenniker.*

*You said yourself that you are only "a messenger"... And now I understand what message you must carry.'* The image flickered as Sinope glanced over her shoulder, distracted by something beyond the range of the locket's tiny sensor-camera. She looked back, and her eyes were intense. *'I have not been truthful with you. The place you saw, our chapel... There's more than just that. We have a... I suppose you could call it a sanctuary. It is out in the wastes, far from prying eyes. I will be there by the time you receive this. I want you to come here, child. We need you. He needs you. Whatever mission may have brought you to Dagonet, what I ask of you now goes beyond it.'* She felt the woman's gaze boring into her. *'Don't forsake us, Jenniker. I know you believe with all your heart, and even though it pains me to do so, I must ask you to choose your faith over your duty.'* Sinope looked away. *'If you refuse... The rains of blood will fall all the way to Holy Terra.'*

The hologram faded and Soalm found her hands were shaking. She could not look away from the locket, grasping it in her fingers as if it would magically spirit her away from this place.

Lady Sinope's words, her simple words, had cut into her heart. Her emotions twisted tight in her chest. She was a sworn agent of the Officio Assassinorum, a secluse of the Clade Venenum ranked at Epsilon-dan, and she had her orders. But she was also Jenniker Soalm – *Jenniker Kell* – a daughter of the Imperium of Man and loyal servant of the divine God-Emperor of Humanity.

Which path would serve Him best? Which path would serve His subjects best?

Try as she might, she could not shake off the power behind Sinope's message. The quiet potency of the noblewoman had bled into the room, engulfing her. Soalm knew that what she was being asked to do was *right* – far more so than a blood-soaked mission of murder that would only lead to death on a far greater scale.

The church of the *Lectitio Divinitatus* on Dagonet needed her. When she had needed help after mother and father – and then Eristede – had been lost to her, it was the word of the God-Emperor that had given her strength. Now that debt was to be answered.

In the end she realised there was no question of what to do next.

THE DOOR OPENED with a clatter, and the rebel soldier started, turning to see the pale assassin woman standing on the threshold. She had an elaborately-etched wooden case over her shoulder on a strap, and was in the process of attaching a holstered bact-gun to her belt. She looked up, her hood already up about her head. 'Sinope said you would take me to her.'

He nodded gratefully. 'Yes, of course. This way. Follow me.' The rebel took a couple of steps and then halted, frowning. 'The others… Your comrades?'

'They don't need to know,' said Soalm, and gestured for him to carry on. The two of them disappeared around a curve in the corridor, heading up towards the surface.

From the shadows, Iota watched them go.

SPEAR LOATHED THE warp.

When he travelled through the screaming halls of the immaterium, he did his best to ensure that he did so in stasis, his body medicated into hibernation – or failing that, if he were forced to remain awake by virtue of having assumed the identity of another, then he prepared himself with long hours of mental rituals.

Both were in order to calm the daemonskin. In the realms of normal space, on a planet or elsewhere, the molecule-thin layer of living tissue bonded to his birth flesh was under his control. Oh, there were times when it became troublesome, when it tried to defy him in small ways, but in the end Spear was the master of it. And as long as it was fed, as long as he sated it with killings and blood, it obeyed.

But in the depths of warp space, things were different. Here, with only metres of steel and the gauzy energy web of a Geller field between him and the thunder and madness of the ethereal, the daemonskin became troublesome. Spear wondered if it was because it sensed the proximity of its kindred out there, in the form of the predatory, almost-sentient life that swarmed unseen in the wake of the starships that passed.

Eurotas had granted him the use of a ship called the *Yelene*, a fast cutter from the Consortium's courier fleet designed to carry low-mass, high-value cargoes on swift system-to-system runs. The *Yelene*'s crew were among the best officers and men the clan had to offer, but Spear barely registered them. He gave the captain only two orders; the first was to make space for Dagonet at maximum speed; the second was not to disturb him during the journey unless the ship was coming apart around them.

The crew all knew who Hyssos was. Among some levels of the Eurotas clan's hierarchy, he was seen as the Void Baron's attack dog, and that reputation served Spear well now, glowering through another man's face at everyone he saw, before locking himself into the opulent passenger cabin provided for his use. The cabin was detailed in rich, red velvet that made the murderer feel like he was drowning in blood. That comforted him, but only for a while.

Once the *Yelene* was in the thick of the warp, the daemonskin awoke and cried in his mind like a wounded, whining animal. It wanted to be free, and for a long moment, so did Spear.

He pushed the thought away as if he were drawing back a curtain, but it snagged on something. Spear felt a pull deep in his psyche, clinging to the tails of the disloyal emotion.

Sabrat.

*NO NO NO NO*

Furious, Spear launched himself at a bookcase along one of the walls and slammed his head into it, beating his malleable face bloody. The impact and the pain forced the remnant of the dead reeve's persona away again, but the daemonskin was still fretting and writhing, pushing at his tunic, issuing tendrils from every square centimetre of bare flesh.

It would not obey him. The moment of slippage, the instant when the corpse-mind shard had risen to the fore, had allowed the daemonskin to gain a tiny foothold of self-control.

'That won't do,' he hissed aloud, and strode over to the well-stocked drinks cabinet. Spear found a bottle of rare Umbran brandy and smashed it open at the neck. He doused the bare skin of his arms with the rich, peaty liquid and the tendrils flinched. Then, he tore open the lid of a humidor on a nearby desk and took the ever-taper from within. At the touch of his thumb, it lit and he jabbed it into the skin. A coating of bluish flame engulfed his hands and he bunched his fists, letting the pain seep into him.

THE FIRE AND *the pain*.

Outside the ship there is nothing but fire. Inside, only pain.

Where he stands, he is shackled to the deck by an iron chain thicker than a man's forearm, heavy double links reaching to a manacle around his right leg. It is so tightly fastened that he would need to sever the limb at the knee to gain his freedom.

His attention is not on this, however. One wall of the chamber in which the master's warriors placed him is not there. Instead, there is only fire. Burning madness. He is aware that a thin membrane of energy separates that inferno from him. How this is possible he cannot know; such science-sorcery is beyond him.

He knows only that he is looking into the warp itself, and by turns the warp looks back into him.

He howls and pulls at the chain. The runes and glyphs drawn all over his naked body are itching and inflamed, cold-hot and torturing him. The warp is pulling at the monstrous, unknowable words etched into him. He howls again, and this time the master answers.

'Be afraid,' Erebus tells him. 'The fear will smooth the bonding. It will give it something to sink its teeth into.'

He can't tell where the voice is coming from. Like so many times before, ever since the opening of the cage, Erebus seems to be inside his thoughts whenever he wishes to be. Sometimes the master comes in there and leaves things – knowledge, ability, thirsts – and sometimes he takes things instead. Memories, perhaps. It's not easy to be certain.

He has questions; but they die in his throat when he sees *the thing* coming from the deeps of the warp. It moves like mercury, shimmering and poisonous. It sees him.

Erebus anticipates his words. 'A minor phylum of warp creature,' explains the master. 'A predator. Dangerous but less than intelligent. Cunning, in a fashion.'

It is coming. The gauzy veil of energy trembles. Soon it will pucker and open, just for the tiniest of moments. Enough to let it in.

'It can be domesticated,' says the Word Bearer. 'If one has the will to control it. Do you have the will, Spear?'

'Yes, master–'

He does not finish his words. The predator-daemon finds the gap and streams through it, into the opened bay of the starship. It smothers him, skirling and shrieking its joy at finding a rich, easy kill.

This is the moment when Erebus allows himself a noise of amusement; this is the moment when the daemon, in its limited way, realises that everywhere it has touched Spear's flesh, across every rune and sigil, it cannot release. It cannot consume.

And he collapses to the deck, writhing in agony as it tries to break free, fails, struggles, and finally merges.

As the hatch closes off the compartment from the red hell outside, Spear hears the master's voice receding.

'It will take you days of agony to dominate it, and failure will mean you both die. The magicks etched into you cannot be broken. You are bonded now. It is your skin. You will master it, as I have mastered you.'

The words echo and fade, and then there is only his screaming, and the daemon's screaming.

*And the fire and the pain.*

A THIN AND cold drizzle had come in with the veil of night, and all across the star-port, the rain hissed off the cracked, battle-damaged runways and landing pads in a constant rush of sound. Water streamed off the folded wingtips of the *Ultio's* forward module, down through the broken roof of the hangar, spattering against the patch of dry ferrocrete beneath the vessel where it crouched low to the ground. It resembled an avian predator, ready to throw itself into the sky; but for now the ship's systems were running in dark mode, with nothing to betray its operable state to the infrequent patrols that passed by.

The star-port had remained largely abandoned since the start of the insurrection. It was still a long way down the clanner government's long list of important infrastructure repairs. Rebel strikes against power stations and communications towers made sure of that, although Capra had been careful that lines of supply were kept open so that the native populace would not starve. He was winning hearts and minds, for all the good that would do him in the long run.

Kell stood at the foot of the *Ultio's* landing ramp and peered into the rain through the eye band of his spy mask, letting the built-in sensors do their work, considering the freedom fighters once more. How

would they react when they found the members of
Kell's team gone? Would they think they had been
betrayed? Perhaps so. After all, they *had* been, in a
way. And when the mission reached its endpoint,
Capra would know full well who had been behind it.

'Any sign?' Tariel's voice filtered down from above
him. 'The pilot-brain reports that the passive sensors
registered a blip a short time ago, but since then,
nothing.'

Kell didn't look up at him. 'Status?'

Tariel gave a sigh. 'The Garantine has sharpened his
knives so much he could slice the raindrops in two. I
am monitoring the public and military vox-nets, and
I have prepared and loaded all my data phages and
blackouts. Koyne is in the process of mimicking the
form of the troop commander we captured. I take it
the Culexus and the Venenum have still yet to arrive?'

'Your powers of perception are as sharp as ever.'

'How long can we afford to wait?' he replied. 'We're
very close to the deployment time as it is.'

'They'll be here,' Kell said, just as something shimmered in the downpour beyond the open hangar
doors.

'I am,' said Iota, emerging from the grey rain. Her
voice had a strange, echoing timbre inside her skull-
helmet. She removed the weapon helm as she stepped
into cover, and shook loose the thin threads of her
braided hair. 'I was delayed.'

'By what?' Tariel demanded. 'There's nobody out
there.'

'Nobody out there *now*,' Iota gently corrected.

'Where's the Venenum?' said Kell, his jaw stiffening.

Iota glanced at him. 'Your sister isn't coming.'

Kell's eyes flashed with shock and annoyance. 'How–?'

Tariel held up his hands in a gesture of self-protection. 'Don't look at me. I said nothing!'

The Vindicare grimaced. 'Never mind. That's not important. Explain yourself. What do you mean, she's not coming?'

'Jenniker has taken on a mission of greater personal importance than this one,' the Culexus told him.

'I gave her an order!' he barked, his ire rising by the second.

'Yes, you did. And she disobeyed it.'

Kell grabbed the other assassin by the collar and glared at her. He felt the black shadow of the pariah's soul-shrivelling aura rise off her in a wave, but he was too furious to care. 'You saw her go, didn't you? You saw her go and you did nothing to stop it!'

A flicker of emotion crossed Iota's face, but it was difficult to know what it was. Her dark eyes became solid orbs of void. 'You will not touch me.'

Kell's skin tingled and his hand went ice-cold, as if it had been plunged into freezing water. Reflexively he let the Culexus go and his fingers contracted in pain. 'What were you thinking, girl?' he demanded.

'You don't own her,' Iota said, in a low voice. 'You gave up your part in her life.'

The comment came out of nowhere, and Kell was actually startled by it. 'I… This is about the mission,' he went on, recovering swiftly. 'Not about her.'

'You tell yourself that and you pretend to believe it.' Iota straightened up and stepped around him.

He turned; at the top of the ramp Tariel had been joined by the Garantine, the Eversor rocking back and forth, his massive hands clenching and unclenching with barely-restrained energy. A middle-aged man in PDF-issue rain slicker stood nearby, toying with a poison knife. The expression of the face that Koyne had borrowed was wrong, ill-fitting in some way that Kell could not express.

'How much longer?' snarled the Eversor. 'I want to kill an Astartes. I want to see how it feels.' His jittery fingers played with the straps of his skull-mask, and the pupils of his bloodshot eyes were black pinpricks.

Kell made a decision and stepped after the Culexus. 'Iota. Do you know where she went?'

'I have an inkling,' came the reply.

'Find Soalm. Bring her back.'

'Now?' said Tariel, his face falling. 'Now, of all times?'

'Do it!' Kell insisted. 'If she has been compromised, then our entire mission is blown.'

'That's not the reason why,' said Iota. 'But we can tell her it is, if you wish.'

The Vindicare pointed back out into the rains, which had begun to grow worse. 'Just go.' He looked away. There was something in his chest, something there he had thought long since vanished. An emptiness. A regret. He smothered it before it could take hold, turning it to anger. Damn her for bringing these feelings back to the surface! She was part of a past he had left behind, and he wanted it to remain that way. And yet...

Iota gave him a nod and her helmet rose to cover her face. Without looking back, she broke into a run and was quickly swallowed up by the deluge.

The Garantine came stomping down the ramp, seething. 'What are you doing, sniper?' He spat the words at him. 'That gutless poisoner flees the field and you make things worse by sending the witch away as well? Are you mad?'

'Is the notorious Garantine actually admitting he needs the help of women?' said Koyne, in the troop commander's voice. 'Wonders never cease.'

The Eversor rage-killer loomed over the Vindicare. 'You're not fit to lead this unit, you never were. You're weak! And now your lack of leadership is compromising us all!'

'You understand nothing,' Kell snarled back.

A steel-taloned finger pressed on his chest. 'You know what's wrong with your clade, Kell? You're afraid to get the blood on you. You're scared of the stink of it, you want things all neat and clean, dealt with at arm's length.' The Garantine jerked a thumb at Koyne. 'Even that sexless freak is better than you!'

'Charming,' muttered the Callidus.

The Eversor went on, hissing out each word in pops of spittle through bared teeth. 'Valdor must have been making sport when he put you in charge of this mission! Do you think we're all blind to the way you look at that Venenum bitch?'

In an instant, Kell's Exitus pistol was in his hands and then the muzzle of it was buried in the exposed flesh of the Garantine's throat, pressing into the stressed muscles and taut veins.

'Kell!' Tariel called out a warning. 'Don't!'

The Eversor laughed. 'Go on, sniper. Do it. Up close and personal, for the first time in your life.' His clawed hands came up and he rammed the gun into the thick flesh beneath his jaw. 'Prove you have some backbone! *Do it!*'

For a second Kell's finger tightened on the trigger; but to murder an Eversor rage-killer at point-blank range would be suicidal. The gene-modifications deep inside the Garantine's flesh contained within them a critical failsafe system that would, should the assassin's heart ever stop, create a combustive bio-meltdown powerful enough to destroy everything close at hand.

Instead, Kell put all his effort into a vicious shove that propelled the Garantine away. 'If I didn't need you,' he growled, 'I'd blow a hole in your spine and leave you crippled and bleeding out.'

The Eversor sniggered. 'You just made my argument for me.'

'This is pointless,' snapped Koyne, striding down the ramp. 'No mission plan ever works as it should. Every one of us knows that. We can complete the assignment without the women. The primary target is still within our reach.'

'The Callidus is correct,' added Tariel, working his cogitator. 'I'm reconfiguring the protocols now. There are overlapping attack vectors. We can still operate with two losses.'

'As long as no one else walks off,' said the Garantine. 'As long as nothing else changes.'

Kell's face twisted in a grimace. 'We're wasting time,' he said, turning away. 'Secure the *Ultio* and move out to your kill-points.'

THE MAN'S NAME was Tros, and he didn't talk much. He led Soalm out of the caverns through a vaulted hall of rock that had once held fuel rods for Dagonet's long-dead atmosphere converters, and to a waiting GEV skimmer.

Once they were on their way out into the wilds, the noise of the hovercraft's engines made conversation problematic at best. The assassin decided to sit back behind the rebel and let him drive.

The skimmer was fast. They wound through the canyons of the Bladecut at breakneck speed, and then suddenly the wall of rock dropped away around them, falling into the ochre desert. As storm clouds rolled in above them from the west, they went deeper and deeper into the wilderness. From time to time, Soalm saw what might have been the remains of abandoned settlements; they dated back to the early colonist decades, back to when this desert had been fertile arable land. That had been in Dagonet's green phase, before the human-altered atmosphere had changed again, shifting the good climate northwards. The population had moved with it, leaving only the shells of their former homes lying like broken, scattered tombstones.

Finally the GEV's engine note downshifted and they began to slow. Tros pointed to something in the near distance, and Soalm glimpsed the shapes of tents flapping in the winds, low pergolas and yurts arranged around the stubs of another forsaken township. As the skimmer closed in and settled to the sand in a cloud of falling dust, what caught her eye first was the mural of an Imperial aquila along one long pale wall. It looked old, weather-beaten; but at the same time it shone in the fading daylight as if it had been polished to a fine sheen by decades of swirling sand.

There had only been a handful of people in the makeshift chapel hidden in the rebel base, and Soalm had been slightly disappointed to see how few followers of the God-Emperor were counted among the freedom fighters. But she realised now that small group had only been a fraction of the real number.

The followers of the *Lectitio Divinitatus* were here.

She stepped from the skimmer and walked slowly into the collection of improvised habitats and reclaimed half-buildings. Even at first glance, Soalm could see that there were hundreds of people. Adults and children, young and old, men and women from all walks of life across Dagonet's society. Most of them wore makeshift sandcloaks or hoods to keep the ochre dust from their mouths and noses. She saw some who carried weapons, but they did so without the twitchy nervousness of Capra's rebels; one man with a lasgun eyed her as she passed him, and Soalm saw he was wearing the remnants of a PDF uniform, tattered and ripped in the places where the insignia had been stripped off – all except the aquila, which he wore proudly.

These people, the refugees, were in the process of gathering themselves together for the coming night, tying down ropes and securing sheets. Out here, the winds moved swiftly over the open desert and the particles of dark dust would get into everything. The first curls of the breeze pulled at the hems of her robes as she walked on.

Tros matched her pace and pointed to a strangely proportioned building with a slanted wall and a forest of skeletal antennae protruding from where its roof should have been. 'Over there.'

'These are Lady Sinope's followers?' she asked.

The man gave a snort of amusement. 'Don't say that to her face. She'd think it disrespectful.' Tros shook his head. 'We don't follow her. We follow Him. Milady just helps us on the path.'

'You knew her before the insurrection?'

'I knew of her,' he corrected. 'My da met her once, when she was a younger woman. Heard her speak to a secret meet at Dusker Point. Never thought I'd have the chance myself, though... Milady has done much for us over the years.'

'Your family have always been a part of the Imperial Cult, then?'

Tros nodded. 'But that's not a name we use here. We call ourselves the Theoge.'

They approached the building and at once Soalm realised that it was no such thing. The construction was actually a small ship, a good measure of its keel buried in the cracked, ruddy earth. Beyond it she saw the rusted frames of dock wharfs, extending into the air. Once this place had been a wide river canal.

There were tents arranged along the side of the old vessel, each lit from within by lamplight. 'The people here are all from Dagonet?'

'And other worlds on the axis,' said the man. 'Some of them were here on pilgrimages in secret. Got trapped when the clanner nobles tipped everything up.'

'Pilgrimage?' she repeated. 'For what reason?'

Tros just nodded again. 'You'll see.' He opened a heavy steel hatch for her and she went inside.

THE OLD SHIP had once been a freighter, perhaps a civic transport belonging to some branch of the colonial Administratum; now all that stood was the gutted shell, the sandblasted hull and the corroded metal frames of the decks. Inside, the skeleton of the vessel had been repurposed with new walls made of dry stone or steel from the hulls of cargo containers. The door closed with a solid thump behind Soalm and took the brunt of the wind with it. Only a tendril of chill air reached through to paw at the small drifts of sand in the entryway.

'Child.' Sinope approached, and she had tears in her eyes. 'Oh, child, you came. Throne bless you.'

'I… owed it,' said the Venenum. 'I had to.'

Sinope smiled briefly. 'I never doubted you would. And I know I have asked a lot from you to do this. I have put you at risk.'

'I was on a mission I did not believe in,' she replied. 'You asked me to take up another, for something I *do* believe in. It was no choice at all.'

The noblewoman took her hand. 'Your comrades will not see it the same way. They may disown you.'

'Likely,' Soalm replied. 'But I lost what I thought of as my family a long time ago. Since then, the only kinship I have had has been with others who know the God-Emperor as we do.'

'We are your family now,' said Sinope. 'All of us.'

Soalm nodded at the rightness of the old woman's words, and she felt lifted. 'Yes, you are.' But then the moment of brightness faded as her thoughts returned to the content of the voclocket message. She retrieved the device and pressed it back into Sinope's thin, wrinkled hands. 'How can I help you?'

'Come.' She was beckoned deeper into the shadowed wreck. 'Things will become clearer.'

The beached ship, like the camp beyond it, was filled with people, and Soalm saw the same expression in all of them; a peculiar mingling of fear and hope. With slow alarm, she began to understand that it was directed towards her.

'Tros said you have refugees from all over Dagonet here. And from other worlds as well.'

Sinope nodded as she walked. 'I hope… I *pray* that there are other gatherings hiding in the wilds. It would be so sad to admit that we are all that is left.'

'But there must be hundreds of people here alone.'

Another nod. 'Four hundred sixteen, at last count. Mostly Dagoneti, but a handful of visitors from other worlds in the Taebian Stars.' She sighed. 'They came so far and sacrificed so much… And now they will never return home.'

'Help is coming.' Soalm had said the lie so many times over the past few weeks that it had become automatic.

The noblewoman stopped and gave her a look that cut right through the falsehood. 'We both know that is not true. The God-Emperor is embattled and His continued existence is far more important than any one of us.' She gestured around. 'If we must perish so that He may save the galaxy, that is a price we will gladly pay. We will meet again at His right hand.'

Sinope's quiet zeal washed over her. Soalm took a second to find her voice again. 'How long has the… the Theoge been here?'

'Before I was born, generations before,' said the old woman, continuing on. 'Before the age of the Great Crusade, even. It is said that when the God-Emperor walked the turbulent Earth, even then there were those who secretly worshipped Him. When He came to the stars, that belief came with Him. And then there was the *Lectitio Divinitatus*, the book that gave form to those beliefs. The holy *word*.'

'Is it true that it was written by one of the God-Emperor's own sons?'

'I do not know, child. All we can be sure of is that it is the Imperial truth.' She smiled again. 'I grew up with that knowledge. For a long time, we and others like us lived isolated lives, ignored at best, decried at worst. We who believed were thought to be deluded fools.'

Soalm looked around. 'These people don't look like fools to me.'

'Indeed. Our numbers have started to swell, and not just here. Groups of believers all across the galaxy are coming together. Our faith knows no boundaries, from the lowliest hiver child to men who walk the palaces of Terra itself.' She paused, thinking. 'The darkness sown by the Warmaster has brought many to our fold. In the wake of his insurrection there have been horrors and miracles alike. This is our time of testing, of that I have no doubt. Our creed is in the ascendant, dear child. The day will come when all the stars bend their knee to Holy Terra and the God-Emperor's glory.'

'But not yet,' she said, an edge of bitterness in her voice. 'Not today.'

Sinope touched her arm. 'Have faith. We are part of something larger than ourselves. As long as our belief survives, then we do also.'

'The people from the other worlds,' Soalm pressed. 'Tros said they were here on a pilgrimage. I don't understand that.'

Sinope did not reply. They followed a patched metal staircase into the lower levels of the old ship, treading with care to avoid broken spars and fallen stanchions. Down here the stink of rust and dry earth was heavy and cloying. After a few metres, they came to a thickly walled compartment, armoured with layers of steel and ceramite. Four men, each armed with heavy-calibre weapons, were crowded around the only hatchway that led inside. They had hard eyes and the solid, dense builds of humans from heavy-gravity worlds. The assassin knew immediately that they were, to a man, career soldiers of long and lethal experience.

Each of them gave a respectful bow as Sinope came into the light cast from the lumes overhead, doffing their caps to the old woman. Soalm watched her go to each in turn and talk with them as if they were old friends. She seemed tiny and fragile next to the soldiers, and yet it was clear that they hung on her every word and gesture, like a troupe of devoted sons. Her smiles became theirs.

Sinope gestured to her. 'Gentlemen, this is Jenniker.'

'She's the one?' said the tallest of the four, a heavy stubber at rest in his hands.

Sinope nodded. 'You have all served the Theoge so selflessly,' she told them. 'and your duty is almost done. Jenniker will take this great burden from you.'

The tall man gave a regretful nod and then snapped his fingers at another of the four. The second soldier worked the thick wheel in the centre of the hatch, and with a squeal of rusted metal, he opened the door to the cargo compartment.

Sinope advanced inside and Soalm followed warily behind her. It was gloomy and warm, and there was a peculiar stillness in the air that prickled her bare skin. The hatch closed with a crunch.

'Dagonet is going to fall,' said the noblewoman, soft and sorrowful. 'Death is close at hand. The God-Emperor's love will preserve our souls but the ending of our flesh has already been written. He cannot save us.'

Soalm wanted to say something, to give out a denial, but nothing would come.

'He knows this. That is why, in His infinite wisdom, the Master of Mankind had you brought to us in His stead, Jenniker Soalm.'

'No,' she managed, her heart racing. 'I am here in service to a lie! To perish for a meaningless cause! I have not even been spared the grace to have a truth to die for!'

Sinope came to her and embraced the assassin. 'Oh, dear child. You are mistaken. He sent you to us because you are the only one who can do what we cannot. The God-Emperor turned your destiny to cross my path. You are here to protect something most precious.'

'What do you mean?'

The noblewoman stepped away and moved to a small metal chest. She worked a control pad on the surface – a combination of bio-sensor bloodlocks and security layers – and Soalm stepped closer to get a better look. She knew the design; the chest was of advanced Martian manufacture, a highly secure transport capsule fitted with its own internal support fields, capable of long-term survival in a vacuum, even atmospheric re-entry. It was very much out of place here.

The chest opened in a gust of gas, and inside Soalm saw the shimmer of a stasis envelope. Within the ephemeral sphere of slowed time was a book of the most ornate, fantastic design, and it seemed to radiate the very power of history from its open pages.

'See,' said Sinope, bowing deeply to the tome. 'Look, child, and see the touch of His hand.'

Soalm's gaze misted as tears pricked her eyes. Before her, gold and silver and purple illuminated a stark page of vellum. On it, the portrait of the angelic might of the God-Emperor standing over a kneeling man in the finery of a rogue trader. In the trader's hands this book; and falling from his Master's palm, the shimmering droplet of crimson vitae that rested on the recto page. The scarlet liquid glittered like a flawless ruby, frozen in that distant past, as bright and as new as it had been the second it fell.

*'Emperor's blood...'* she whispered.

Jenniker Soalm sank to her knees in unrestrained awe, bowing her head to the Warrant of Trade of the Clan Eurotas.

# FOURTEEN

### Arrival
### Let Me See You
### Kill Shot

THE DAWN WAS close as the Dove-class shuttle dropped from the cold, black sky on its extended aerofoils. The craft made an elongated S-turn and came in from over the wastelands to make a running touchdown on the only runway that was still intact. The landing wheels kicked up spurts of rock dust and sparks as the *Yelene*'s auxiliary slowed to a shuddering halt, the wings angling to catch the air and bleed off its momentum.

The shuttle was the only source of illumination out among the shadows of Dagonet's star-port, the running lights casting a pool of white across the cracked, ash-smeared ferrocrete. The surroundings had a slick sheen to them; the rains had only ceased a few hours ago.

No one came out from the dark, lightless buildings to examine the new arrivals; if anyone was still in there, then they were staying silent, hoping that the world would ignore them.

In the cockpit, the pilot and co-pilot exchanged glances. Following the operative's orders, they had made no attempt to contact Dagonet port control on their way down, but both men had expected to be challenged by the local PDF at least once for entering their airspace unannounced.

There had been nothing. When the *Yelene* slipped into orbit, no voices had been raised to them. The skies over Dagonet were choked with debris and the remnants of recent conflict. It had tested the skills of the cutter's bridge crew to keep the vessel from colliding with some of the larger fragments, the husks of gutted space stations or the hulls of dead system cruisers still burning with plasma fires. What craft they had spotted that were intact, the operative ordered them to give a wide berth.

*Yelene* came as close as she dared to Dagonet and then released the shuttle. On the way down the flight crew saw the devastation. Places where the map-logs said there should have been cities were smoke-wreathed craters glowing with the aftershock of nuclear detonations; other settlements had simply been abandoned. Even here, just over the ridge from the capital itself, the planet was silent, as if it were holding its breath.

'You saw the destruction,' said the pilot, watching his colleague skim across the vox channels. 'All that dust and ash in the atmosphere could attenuate signal traffic. Either that or they've shut down all broadcast communications planetwide.'

The other man nodded absently. 'Wired comm is more secure. They could be using telegraphics instead.'

Before the pilot could answer, the hatch behind them opened and the man called Hyssos filled the doorway. 'Douse the lights,' he ordered. 'Don't draw more attention than we need to.'

'Aye, sir.' The co-pilot did as he was told, and the illumination outside died.

The pilot studied the operative. He had heard the stories about Hyssos. They had said he was a hard man, hard but fair, not a martinet like some commanders the pilot had served with. He found it difficult to square that description with his passenger, though. All through the voyage from the Eurotas flotilla to the planet, Hyssos had been withdrawn and frosty, terse and unforgiving when he did take the time to bother speaking to someone. 'How do you wish to proceed, operative?'

'Drop the cargo lift,' came the reply.

Again, the co-pilot did this with a nod. The elevator-hatch in the belly of the shuttle extended down to the runway; cradled on it was a swift jetbike, fuelled and ready to fly.

'A question,' said Hyssos, as he turned this way and that, studying the interior of the shuttle cockpit. 'This craft has a cogitator core aboard. Is it capable of taking us to orbit on its own?'

'Aye,' said the pilot, uncertain of where the question was leading. 'It's not recommended, but it can be done in an emergency.'

'What sort of emergency?'

'Well,' began the co-pilot, looking up, 'if the crew are incapacitated, or–'

'Dead?'

Hyssos's hands shot out, the fingers coming together to form points, each one piercing the soft flesh of the men's necks. Neither had the chance to scream; instead they made awkward gasping gurgles as their throats were penetrated.

Blood ran in thick streams from their wounds, and Hyssos grimaced, turning their heads away so the fluid would not mark his tunic. Both men died watching their own vitae spurt across the control panels and the inside of the canopy windows.

SPEAR STOOD FOR a while with his hands inside the meat of the men's throats, feeling the tingle of the tiny mouths formed at the ends of his fingertips by the daemonskin, as they lapped at the rich bounty of blood. The proxy flesh absorbed the liquid, the rest of it dribbling out across the grating of the deck plates beneath the crew chairs.

Then, convinced that the daemonskin was in quietus once more, Spear moved to a fresher cubicle to clean himself off before venturing down to the open cargo bay. He decided not to bother with a breather mask or goggles, and eased himself into the jetbike's saddle. The small flyer was a thickset, heavy block of machined steel, spiked with winglets and stabilators that jutted out at every angle. It responded to his weight by triggering the drive turbine, running it up to idle.

Spear leaned forward, glancing down at a cowled display pane that showed a map of the local zone. A string of waypoint indicators led from the star-port out into the wastelands, following the line of what was once a shipping canal but now a dry bed of dusty earth. The secret destination the Void Baron had given him blinked blue at the end of the line; an old waystation dock abandoned after the last round of climate shifts. The Warrant was there, held in trust.

The murderer laughed at the pulse of anticipation in his limbs, and grasped the throttle bar, sending the turbine howling.

HE HAD TO give credit to the infocyte; the location that Tariel had selected for the hide was a good one, high up inside an empty water tower on the roof of a tenement block a kilometre and a half from the plaza. It was for this very reason that Kell rejected it and sought out another. Not because he did not trust the Vanus, but because two men knowing where he would fire from was a geometrically larger risk than one man knowing. If Tariel was captured and interrogated, he could not reveal what he had not been told.

And then there was the matter of professional pride. The water tower was too obvious a locale to make the hide. It was too… *easy*; and if Kell thought so, then any officer of the PDF down in the plaza might think the same, make a judgement and have counter-snipers put in place.

The dawn was coming up as the Vindicare found his spot. Another tenement block, but this one was removed half the distance again from the marble mall outside the Governor's halls. From what Kell could determine, it seemed as if the building had been struck two-thirds of the way up by a plummeting aerofighter. The upper floors of the narrow tower were blackened from the fires that had broken out in the wake of the impact, and on the way up, Kell had to navigate past blockades of fallen masonry mixed with wing sections and ragged chunks of fuselage. He came across the tail of the aircraft embedded in an elevator shaft, like the feathers of a thrown dart buried in a target.

Where it had impacted, a chunk of walls and floors was missing, as if something had taken a bite out of the building. Kell skirted the yawning gap that opened out to a drop of some fifty or more storeys and continued his climb. The fire-damaged levels stank of seared plastic and burned flesh, but the thick, sticky ash that coated every surface was dull and non-reflective – an ideal backdrop to deaden Kell's sensor profile still further. He found the best spot in a room that had once been a communal laundry, and arranged his cameoline cloak between the heat-distorted frames of two chairs. Combined with the deadening qualities of his synskin stealthsuit, the marksman would be virtually invisible.

He tapped a pad on the palm of his glove with his thumb. An encrypted burst transmitter in his gear vest sent a signal lasting less than a picosecond. After a moment, he got a similar message in return that high-lighted the first of a series of icons on his visor. Tariel was reporting in, standing by at his kill-point some-where out in the towers of the western business district. This was followed by a ready-sign from Koyne, and then another from the Garantine.

The two remaining icons stayed dark. Without Iota, they had to do without telepathic cover; if the Sons of Horus decided to deploy a psyker, they would have no warning of it… but then the Warmaster's Legion had never relied on such things before and the Assassino-rum had no intelligence they would do so today. It was a risk Kell was willing to take.

And Soalm... *Jenniker*. The purpose of a Venenum poisoner was as part of the original exit strategy for the Execution Force. The detonation of several short-duration hypertoxin charges would sow confusion among the human populace of the city and clog the highways with panicking civilians, restricting the movements of the Astartes. But now they would do without that – and Kell felt conflicted about it. He was almost pleased she was not here to be a part of this, that she would not be at risk if something went wrong.

The echo of that thought rang hard in his chest, and the press of the sudden emotion surprised him. He remembered the look in her eyes when she had entered the room in the Venenum manse – the cold-ness and the loathing. It was identical to the expression she had worn all those years ago, on the day he had told her he was accepting the mission to find mother and father's killer. Only then, there had also been pity there as well. Perhaps she had lost the capacity to know compassion, over time.

He had hoped, foolishly, he now realised, that she might have come to understand why he had made his choice. The killing of their parents had been an aching, burning brand in his thoughts; the need for raw vengeance, although at the time he had no words to describe it. A deed that could not be undone, and one that could not go unanswered.

And when the kill was finished, after all the deaths it took to reach it... Mother and father were still dead, but he had avenged them, and the cost had only been the love of the last person who cared about him. Kell always believed that if he had the chance to change that moment, to make the choice again, he would have done nothing differently. But after looking his sister in the eye, he found that certainty crumbling.

It had been easy to be angry with her at first, to deny her and hate her back for turning her face from him, eschewing her family's name. But as time passed, the anger cooled and became something else. Only now was he beginning to understand it had crystallised into regret.

A slight breeze pulled at him and Kell frowned at his own thoughts, dismissing them as best he could. He returned to the mission, made his hide, gathering his gear and assembling what he would need for the duration in easy reach. Backtracking, he rigged the stairwells and corridors leading to the laundry room with pairs of trip-mines to cover his rear aspect, before placing his pistol where he could get to it at a moment's notice.

Then, and only then, did he unlimber the Exitus longrifle. One of the Directors Tertius at the clade had told him of the Nihon, a nation of fierce warriors on ancient Terra, who it was said could not return their swords to their scabbards after drawing them unless the weapons first tasted blood. Something of that ideal appealed to Kell; it would not be right to cloak such a magnificent weapon as this without first taking a life with it.

He settled into a prone position, running through meditation routines to relax himself and prepare his body, but he found it difficult. Matters beyond the mission – or truthfully, matters enmeshed with it – preyed on him. He frowned and went to work on the rifle, dialling in the imager scope, flicking through the sighting modes. Kell had zeroed the weapon during their time with Capra's rebels, and now it was like an extension of himself, the actions rote and smooth.

Microscopic sensor pits on the muzzle of the rifle fed information directly to his spy mask, offering tolerance changes and detailing windage measurements. He flicked down the bipod, settling the weapon. Kell let his training find the range for him, compensating for bullet drop over distance, coriolis effect, attenuation for the moisture of the late rains still in the air, these and a dozen other variables. With care, he activated a link between his burst transmitter and the Lance. A new icon appeared a second later; the Lance was ready.

He leaned into the scope. The display became clearer, and solidified. His aiming line crossed from the habitat tower, over the stub of a nearby monument, through the corridor of a blast-gutted adminstratum office, down and down to the open square the locals called Liberation Plaza. It was there that Horus Lupercal had killed the crooked priest-king that had ruled Dagonet's darkest years, early in the Great Crusade. There, he had expended only one shot and struck such fear into the tyrant's men that they laid down their guns and surrendered at the sight of him.

A figure swam into view, blurred slightly by the motion of air across the kilometres of distance between them. A middle-aged man in the uniform of a PDF troop commander. As he looked in Kell's direction, his mouth moved and automatically a lip-reading subroutine built into the scope's integral auspex translated the words into text.

*He's coming, Kell,* read the display. *Very soon now.*

The Vindicare gave the slightest of nods and used Koyne's torso to estimate his final range settings. Then the disguised Callidus moved out of view and Kell found himself looking at an empty patch of milk-white marble.

The sandstorm hid her better than any camouflage. Iota moved through it, enjoying the push and pull of the wind on her body, the hiss and rattle of the particles as they scoured her metal skull-helm, plucking at the splines of the animus speculum.

The Culexus watched the world through the sapphire eye of the psionic weapon, feeling the pulse and throb of it on the periphery of her thoughts like a coldness in her brain. Humans moved through the arc of fire and she tracked them. Each of them would register her attention without really knowing it; they would shiver involuntarily and draw their sandcloaks tighter, quickening their step to reach warmth and light and safety a little faster. They sensed her without sensing her, the ominous, ever-present shadow of null she cast falling on them. Children, when she turned her hard, glittering gaze in their direction, would begin to cry and not know the reason. When she passed close to tents full of sleeping figures, she could hear them mutter and moan under their breath; she passed over their dreams like a windborne storm cloud, darkening the skies of their subconscious for a moment before sliding beyond the horizon.

Iota's pariah soul – or lack thereof – made people turn away from her, made them avert their eyes from the shadowed corners where she moved. It was a boon for her stealth, and with it she entered the sanctuary encampment without raising an alarm. She scrambled up a disused crane gantry, across the empty cab and along the rusted jib. Old cables whined in atonal chorus as the winds plucked at them.

From here she had a fine view of the beached ship at the centre of the settlement. What pathways there were radiated out from here, and she had already spotted the parked skimmer peeking out from beneath a tethered tarpaulin; the last time she had seen that vehicle, it had been in Capra's hideaway. She settled in and waited.

Eventually, a hatch opened, spilling yellow light into the dusty air, and Iota shifted down along the length of the crane jib, watching.

A quartet of armed men exited, two carrying a small metal chest between them. Following on behind was the Venenum and the old noblewoman who had spoken in such strange ways about the Emperor. Auspex sensors in Iota's helmet isolated their conversation so she could listen.

Soalm was reaching a hand out to brush it over the surface of the chest, and although she wore her hood up, Iota believed she could see a glitter of high emotion in her eyes. 'We have a small ship,' she was saying. 'I can get the Warrant aboard... But after that–' She turned her head and a gust of wind snatched the end of the sentence away.

The old woman, Sinope, was nodding. 'The Emperor protects. You must find Baron Eurotas, return it to him.' She sighed. 'Admittedly, he is not the most devoted of us, but he has the means and method to escape the Taebian Sector. Others will come in time to take stewardship of the relic.'

'I will protect it until that day.' Soalm looked at the chest again, and Iota wondered what they were discussing; the contents of the coffer had some value that belied the scuffed, weather-beaten appearance of the container. Soalm's words were almost reverent.

Sinope touched the other woman's hand. 'And your comrades?'

'Their mission is no longer mine.'

Iota frowned at that behind her helm's grinning silver skull. The Culexus would be the first to admit that her grasp of the mores of human behaviour was somewhat stunted, but she knew the sound of disloyalty when she heard it. With a flex of her legs, she leapt off the rusting crane, the jib creaking loudly as she described a back-flip that put her down right in front of the four soldiers. They were bringing up their guns but Iota already had her needler levelled at Sinope's head; she guessed correctly that the old woman was the highest value target in the group.

Soalm called out to the others to hold their fire, and stepped forward. 'You followed me.'

'Again,' said Iota, with a nod. 'You are on the verge of irreversibly compromising our mission on Dagonet. That cannot be allowed.' From the corner of her eye, the Culexus saw Sinope go pale as she dared to give the protiphage her full attention.

'Go back to Eristede,' said the poisoner. 'Tell him I am gone. Or dead. It doesn't matter to me.'

Iota cocked her head. 'He is your brother.' She ignored the widening of Soalm's eyes. 'It matters to him.'

'I'm taking the *Ultio*,' insisted the other woman. 'You can stay here and take part in this organised suicide if you wish, but I have a greater calling.' Her eyes flicked towards the chest and back again.

'Horus comes,' said Iota, drawing gasps from some of the soldiers. 'And we are needed. The chance to strike against the Warmaster may never come again. What can you carry in some iron box that has more value than that?'

'I don't expect you to understand,' Soalm replied. 'You are a pariah; you were born without a soul. You have no faith to give.'

'No soul...' Sinope echoed the words, coming closer. 'Is that possible?'

'In this chest is a piece of the Emperor's divinity, made manifest,' Soalm went on, her eyes shining with zeal. 'I am going to protect it with my life from the ruinous powers intent on its destruction! I believe this with my heart and spirit, Iota! I swear it in the name of the living God-Emperor of Mankind!'

'Your beliefs are meaningless,' Iota retorted, becoming irked by the woman's irrationality. 'Only what is real matters. Your words and relics are ephemeral.'

'You think so?' Sinope stepped fearlessly towards the Culexus, reaching out a hand. 'Have you never encountered something greater than yourself? Never wondered about the meaning of your existence?' She dared to touch the metal face of the skull. 'Look me in the eye and tell me that. I ask, child. Let me see you.'

Somewhere in the distance, Iota thought she heard a ripple of jet noise, but she ignored it. Instead, uncertain where the impulse came from, she reached up a hand and thumbed the release that let the skull-helmet fold open and retreat back over her shoulders. Her face naked to the winds and sand, she turned her gaze on the old woman and held it. 'Here I am.' She felt a question stir in her. 'Is Soalm right? Can you tell? Am I soulless?'

Sinope's hand went to her lips. 'I... I don't know. But in His wisdom, I have faith that the God-Emperor will know the answer.'

Iota's eyes narrowed. 'No amount of faith will stop you from dying.'

THE SHIP CAME out of the void shrouded in silence and menace.

Rising over the far side of Dagonet's largest moon like a dragon taking wing, the Astartes battleship came on, prow first, knifing through the vacuum towards the combat-cluttered skies. Wreckage and corpses desiccated by the punishing kiss of space rebounded off the sheer sides of its bow as serried ranks of weapons batteries turned in their sockets to bear on the turning world beneath them. Hatches opened, great irises of thick space-hardened brass and steel yawning to give readiness to launch bays where Stormbird drop-ships and Raven interceptors nestled in their deployment cradles. Bow doors hiding the mouths of missile tubes retreated.

What few vessels there were close to the planet did not dare to share the same orbit, and fled as fast as their motors would allow them. As they retreated, they transmitted fawning, obeisant messages that were almost begging in tone, insisting on their loyalties and imploring the invader ship's commander to spare their lives. Only one vessel did not show the proper level of grovelling fear – a fast cutter in a rogue trader's livery, whose crew broke for open space in a frenzy of panic. As a man might stretch a limb to ready it before a day of exercise, the battleship discharged a desultory barrage of beam fire from one of its secondary batteries, obliterating the cutter. This was done almost as an afterthought.

The massive craft passed in front of the sun, throwing a partial occlusion of black shadow across the landscape far below. It sank into a geostationary orbit, stately and intimidating, hanging in place over the capital city as the dawn turned all eyes below to the sky.

Every weapon in the battleship's arsenal was prepared and oriented down at the surface – torpedo arrays filled with warshots that could atomise whole continents in a single strike, energy cannons capable of boiling off oceans, kinetic killers that could behead mountains through the brute force of their impact. This was only the power of the ship itself; then there was the minor fleet of auxiliary craft aboard it, wings of fighters and bombers that could come screaming down into Dagonet's atmosphere on plumes of white fire. Swift death bringers that could raze cities, burn nations.

And finally, there was the army. Massed brigades of genetically-enhanced warrior kindred, hundreds of Adeptus Astartes clad in ceramite power armour, loaded down with boltguns and chainswords, power blades and flamers, man-portable missile launchers and autocannons. Hosts of these warlords gathered on the mustering decks, ready to embark at their dropship stations if called upon, while others – a smaller number, but no less dangerous for it – assembled behind their liege lord high commander in the battleship's teleportarium.

The vessel had brought a military force of such deadly intent and utter lethality that the planet and its people had never known the like, in all their recorded history. And it was only the first. Other ships were following close behind.

This was the visitation granted to Dagonet by the Sons of Horus, the tip of a sword blade forged from shock and awe.

Far below, across the white marble of Liberation Plaza, a respectful hush fell over the throng of people who had gathered since the previous day's dusk, daring at last to venture out into the streets. The silence radiated outward in a wave, crossing beyond the edges of the vast city square, into the highways filled with halted groundcars and standing figures. It bled out through the displays on patched streetscreens at every intersection, relayed by camera ballutes drifting over the Governor's hall; it fell from the crackling mutter of vox-speakers connected to the national watch-wire.

The quiet came down hard as the planet looked to the sky and awaited the arrival of their redeemer, the owner of their new allegiance. Their war-god.

Soalm's hands were trembling, but she wasn't sure what emotion was driving her. The righteous passion erupting from laying eyes on the Warrant rolled and churned around her as if she were being buffeted by more than just the gritty winds – but there was something else there. Iota's hard words about Eristede had come from out of nowhere, and they pulled her thoughts in directions she did not wish them to go. She shook her head; now of all times was not the moment to lose her way. The ties that had once existed between Jenniker and her brother had been severed long ago, and dwelling on that would serve no purpose. Her hands slipped towards the concealed pockets in the surplice beneath her travelling robe, feeling for the toxin cordes concealed there. She wondered if the Culexus would fight her if she refused to carry out the Assassinorum's orders. Soalm knew the God-Emperor would forgive her; but her brother never would.

The tension of the moment was broken as two figures approached out of the haze of the sandstorm, from the direction of the dry canal bed. She recognised Tros, his steady, rolling gait. At his side was a dark-skinned man whose threads of grey hair were pulled out behind him by the wind, where they danced like errant serpents. The new arrival had no dust mask or eye-shield, and he gave no sign that the scouring sands troubled him.

Sinope stepped towards him, and from the corner of her eye Soalm saw the noblewoman's men tense. They were unsure where to aim their guns.

Iota made an odd noise in the back of her throat and her hand went to her face. Soalm thought she saw a flash of pain there.

'Who is this?' Sinope was asking.

'He came in from out of the storm,' Tros replied, speaking loudly so they all could hear him. Nearby, people had been drawn by the sound of raised voices and they stood at slatted windows or in doorways, watching. 'This is Hyssos. The Void Baron sent him.'

The dark man bowed deeply. 'You must be the Lady Astrid Sinope.' His voice was resonant and firm. 'My lord will be pleased to hear you are still alive. When we heard about Dagonet we feared the worst.'

'Eurotas... sent you?' Sinope seemed surprised.

'For the Warrant,' said Hyssos. He opened his hand and there was a thickset ring made of gold and emerald in his palm – a signet. 'He gave me this so you would know I carry his authority.'

Tros took the ring and passed it to Sinope, who pressed it to a similar gold band on her own finger. Soalm saw a blink of light as the sensing devices built into the signets briefly communed. 'This is valid,' said the noble, as if she could not quite believe it.

Iota moved away, and she stumbled a step. Soalm glanced after her. The waif gasped and made a retching noise. The Venenum felt an odd, greasy tingle in the air, like static, only somehow *colder*.

Hyssos extended his hands. 'If you please? I have a transport standing by, and time is of the essence.'

'What sort of transport?' said Tros. 'We have children here. You could take them–'

'Tros,' Sinope warned. 'We can't–'

'Of course,' Hyssos said smoothly. 'But quickly. The Warrant is more important than any of us.'

Something was wrong. 'And you are here *now*?' Soalm asked the question even as it formed in her thoughts. 'Why did you not come a day ago, or a week? Your timing is very opportune, sir.'

Hyssos smiled, but it did not reach his eyes. 'Who can fathom the God-Emperor's ways? I am here now because He wishes it.' His gaze cooled. 'And who are you?' Hyssos's expression turned stony as he looked past Soalm to where Iota was standing, her whole body quivering. 'Who are you?' he repeated, and this time it was a demand.

Iota turned and she let out a shriek that was so raw and monstrous it turned Soalm's blood to ice. The Culexus girl's face was streaked with liquid where lines of crimson fell from the corners of her eyes. Weeping blood, she brought up the needler-weapon fixed to her forearm, aiming at Hyssos; with her other hand she reached up and tore away the necklet device that regulated her psionic aura.

Against the close, gritty heat of the predawn, a wave of polar cold erupted from out of nowhere, with the psyker at its epicentre. Everyone felt the impact of it, everyone staggered off their balance – everyone but Hyssos.

'You pariah whore,' The man's expression twisted in odious fury. 'We'll do this the hard way, then.'

Soalm saw his face open up like a mechanism made of meat and blood, as ice formed on the sand at her feet. Inside him there were only his glaring black eyes and a forest of fangs about a lamprey mouth.

RAGE FLARED LIKE a supernova and Spear let it fill him. Anger and frustration boiled over; nothing about this bloody mission had gone to plan. It seemed as if at every stage he was being tested, or worse, *mocked* by the uncaring universe around him as it threw obstacle after obstacle into his path.

First the interruption of the purge and his inability to rid himself of the last vestiges of Sabrat's sickening

morality; then the discovery of the fake Warrant of
Trade, and the ridiculous little secret of Eurotas's
shameful idolatry; and now, after an interminable
voyage to find it, more of these pious fools clogging
the way to his prize. He knew it was there, he could
sense the presence of the true Warrant hidden inside
that nondescript armoured box, but still they tried to
stop him from taking it.

Spear had wanted to do this cleanly. Get in, take
what he needed, leave again with a minimum of
bloodshed and time wasted. It seemed the fates had
other ideas, and the whining, pleading daemonskin
was bored. The kills on the shuttle had been cursory
things. It wanted to *play*.

In any event, his hand had been forced, and if he
were honest with himself, he was not so troubled by
this turn of events. Spear had been so set on the recov-
ery of the Warrant and what it contained that he had
hardly been aware of the gloomy presence at the edges
of his thoughts until he turned his full attention
towards it. Who could have known that something as
rare and as disgusting as a psychic pariah would be
found here on Dagonet? Was it there as some manner
of defence for the book? It didn't matter; he would kill
it.

Unseen by the mortals around them, for a brief second the psyker bitch's aura of icy negation had
clipped the raw, mad flux of the daemonskin and the
ephemeral bond that connected it – and Spear, as its
merge-mate – to the psionic turmoil of the warp.

He knew then that this encounter was no chance
event. The girl was an engineered thing, something
vat-grown and modified to be a hole in space-time, a

telepathic void given human form. A pariah. *An assassin.*

The girl's null-aura washed over him and the daemonskin did not like the touch of it. It rippled and needled him inside, making its host share in the cold agony of the pariah's mental caress. It refused to hold the pattern of Hyssos, reacting, shivering, clamouring for release. Spear's near-flawless assumption of the Eurotas operative fractured and broke, and finally, as the rage grew high, he decided to allow it to happen.

The skin-matter masquerading as human flesh puckered and shifted into red-raw, bulbous fists of muscle and quivering, mucus-slicked meat. The uniform tunic across his shoulders and back split as it was pulled past the tolerances of the cloth. Lines of curved spines erupted from his shoulders, while bone blades slick as scimitars emerged from along his forearms. Talons burst through the soles of his boots, digging into drifts of sand, and wet jaws yawned.

He heard the screaming and the wails of those all around him, the sounds of guns and knives being drawn. Oh, he knew that music very well.

Spear let the patina of the Hyssos identity disintegrate and matched the will of the daemonskin's living weapons to his own; the warpflesh loved him for that.

The first kill he made here was a soldier, a man with a stubber gun that Spear's extruded bone blades cut in two across the stomach, severing his spine in a welter of blood and stinking stomach matter.

His vision fogged red; somewhere the pariah was crying out in strident chorus with the other women, but he didn't care. He would get to her in a moment.

* * *

THE SUN ROSE off to his right, and Kell was aware of it casting a cool glow over the plaza. He changed the visual field of the scope to a lower magnification and watched the line of shadows retreat across the marble flagstones.

The morning light had a peculiarly crystalline quality to it, an effect brought on by particles in the air buoyed across the wastelands on the leading edges of a distant sandstorm. Ambient moisture levels began to drop and the Exitus rifle's internals automatically compensated, warming the firing chamber by fractions of degrees to ensure the single loaded bullet in the breech remained at an optimal pre-fire state.

The sounds of the crowd reached him, even high up in his vantage point. The noise was low and steady, and it reminded him of the calm seas on Thaxted as they lapped at the shores of black mud and dark rock. He grimaced behind his spy mask and pushed the thought to the back of his mind; now was not the time to be distracted by trivia from his past.

Delicately, so the action would not upset the positioning of the weapon by so much as a millimetre, he thumbed the action selector switch from the safe position to the armed setting. Indicator runes running vertically down the scope's display informed him that the weapon was now ready to commit to a kill. All that Kell required now was his target.

He resisted the urge to look up into the sky. His quarry would be here soon enough.

A KILOMETRE TO the west, Tariel licked dry lips and tapped his hand over the curved keypad on his forearm, acutely aware of how sweaty his palms were. His breathing was ragged, and he had to work to calm himself to the point where he was no longer twitching with unspent adrenaline.

He took a long, slow breath, tasting dust and ozone. In the corridors of the office tower, drifts of paper spilled from files discarded in panic lay everywhere, among lines and lines of abandoned cubicle work-spaces left empty after the first shots of rebellion had been fired. No one had come up here since the nobles had forced the Governor to renounce the rule of Terra; the men and women who had toiled in this place had either gone to ground, embraced the new order or been executed. At first, the dead, empty halls had seemed to echo with the sound of them, but eventually Tariel had accepted that the tower was just as much an empty vessel as so many other Imperial installations on Dagonet. Gutted and forsaken in the rush to eschew the Emperor and embrace his errant son.

The Vanus crouched by the side of the Lance, and laid a finger on the side of its cylindrical cowling. The device was almost as long as the footprint of the tower, and it had been difficult to reassemble it in secret. But eventually the components from *Ultio's* cargo bay had done as their designers in the Mechanicum promised. Now it was ready, and through the cowling Tariel could feel the subtle vibration of the power core cycling through its ready sequence. Content that the device was in good health, Tariel dropped into a low crouch and made his way to the far windows, which looked down into the valley of the capital and Liberation Plaza. The infocyte was careful to be certain that he would not be seen by patrol drones or ground-based PDF spotters.

He took a moment to check the tolerances and positioning of the hyperdense sentainium-armourglass
mirrors for the tenth time in as many minutes. It was
difficult for him to leave the mechanism alone; now
that he had set a nest of alarm beams and sonic
screamers on the lower levels to deal with any inter-
lopers, he had little to do but watch the Lance and
make sure it performed as it should. In an emergency,
he could take direct control of it, but he hoped it
would not come to that. It was a responsibility he
wasn't sure he wanted to shoulder.

Each time he checked the mirrors, he became convinced that in the action of checking them he had put
them out of true, and so he would check them again,
step away, retreat… and then the cycle of doubt would
start once more. Tariel tightened his hands into fists
and chewed on his lower lip; his behaviour was verg-
ing on obsessive-compulsive.

Forcing himself, he turned his back on the Lance's
tip and retreated into the dusty gloom of the building,
finding the place he had chosen for himself as his
shelter for when the moment came. He sat and
brought up his cogitator gauntlet, glaring into the
hololithic display. It told Tariel that the device was
ready to perform its function. All was well.

A minute later he was back at the mirrors, cursing
himself as he ran through the checks once again.

Koyne strode across the edge of the marble square,
as near as was safe to the lines of metal crowd barriers.
The shade scanned the faces of the Dagoneti on the
other side of them, the adults and the children, the
youthful and the old, all seeing past and through the

figure in the PDF uniform as they fixed their eyes on the same place; the centre of Liberation Plaza, where the mosaic of an opened eye spread out rays of colour to every point of the compass. The design was in echo of the personal sigil of the Warmaster, and the Callidus wondered if it was meant to signify that he was always watching.

Such notions were dangerously close to idolatry, beyond the level of veneration that a primarch of the Adeptus Astartes should expect. One only had to count the statues and artworks of the Warmaster that appeared throughout the city; the Emperor had more of them, that much was certain, but not *many* more. And now all the towering sculptures of the Master of Mankind were torn down. Koyne had heard from one of the other PDF officers that squads of clanner troops trained in demolitions had been scouring the city during the night, with orders to make sure nothing celebrating the Emperor's name still stood unscathed. The assassin grimaced; there was something almost… *heretical* about such behaviour.

Even here, off towards the edges of the plaza, there was a pile of grey rubble that had once been a statue of Koyne's liege lord, shoved unceremoniously aside by a sapper crew's dozer-track. Koyne had gone to look at it; at the top of the wreckage, part of the statue's face was still intact, staring sightlessly at the sky. What would it see today?

The Callidus turned away, passing a measuring gaze over the nervous lines of PDF soldiers and the robed nobles standing back on the gleaming, sunlit steps of the great hall. Governor Nicran was there among them, waiting with every other Dagoneti for the storm that was about to break. Between them and the barriers, the faint glitter of a force wall was visible with the naked eye, the pane of energy rising high in a cordon around the point of arrival. Nicran's orders had been to place field generators all around the entrance to the hall, in case resistance fighters tried to take his life or that of one of the turncoat nobles.

Koyne sneered at that. The thought that those fools believed themselves to be high value targets was preposterous. On the scale of the galactic insurrection, they ranked as minor irritants, at best. Posturing fools and narrow-sighted idiots who willingly gave a foothold to dangerous rebels. Moving on, the Callidus found the location that Tariel had chosen – in the lee of a tall ornamental column – and prepared. From here, the view across the plaza was unobstructed. When the kill happened, Koyne would confirm it first-hand.

Suddenly, there was a blast of fanfare from the trumpets of a military band, and Governor Nicran was stepping forward. When he spoke, a vox-bead at his throat amplified his voice.

'Glory to the Liberator!' he cried. 'Glory to the Warmaster! Glory to Horus!'

The assembled crowd raised their voices in a thundering echo.

THE GARANTINE RIPPED off the hatch on the roof of the security minaret as the shouting began, the sound masking the squeal of breaking hinges. He dropped into the open gallery, where uniformed officers pored over sensor screens and glared out through smoked windows overlooking the plaza. Their auspexes ranged all over the city, networking with aerial patrol mechanicals, ground troops, law enforcement units, even traffic monitors. They were looking for threats, trying to pinpoint bombers or snipers or anyone that might upset the Governor's plans for this day. If anyone so much as fired a shot within the city limits, they would know about it.

They did not expect to find an assassin so close at hand. Firstly the Garantine let loose with his Executor combi-pistol, taking care to use only the needler; bolt fire would raise the alarm too soon. Still, it was enough. Two-thirds of them were dead or dying before the first man's gun cleared its holster. They simply could not compete with the amplified, drug-enhanced reflexes of the rage-killer. All of them were moving in slow-motion compared to him, not a one could hope to match him. The Eversor killed with break-neck punches and brutal, bullet-fast stabbing. He wrenched throats into wreckage, stove in ribs and crushed spines; and for the one PDF officer who actually dared to shoot a round in his direction, he left his gift to the last. That man, he murdered by putting the fingers of his neuro-gauntlet through his eyes and breaking his skull.

With a rough chuckle, the Garantine let his kill drop and licked his lips. The room was silent, but outside the crowd cried for the Sons of Horus.

AND THEN THEY came.

A knot of coruscating blue-white energy emerged from the air and grew in an instant to a glowing sphere of lightning. Tortured air molecules screamed as the teleporter effect briefly twisted the laws of physics to breaking point; in the next second, the blaze of light and noise evaporated and in its place there were five angels of death.

*Adeptus Astartes.* Most of the people in the plaza had never seen one before, only knowing them from the statues they had seen and the picts in history books and museums. The real thing was, if anything, far more impressive than the legends had ever said.

The cries of adulation were silenced with a shocked gasp from a thousand throats; when Horus had come to liberate Dagonet all those years ago, he had come with his Luna Wolves, the XVI Legiones Astartes. They had stood resplendent in their flawless moon-white armour, trimmed with ebony, and it was this image that was embedded in the collective mind of the Dagoneti people.

But the Astartes standing here, now, were clad in menacing steel-grey from helmet to boot, armour trimmed in bright shining silver. They were gigantic shadows, menacing all who looked upon them. Their heavy armour, the planes of the pauldrons and chest plates, the fierce visages of the red-eyed helms, all of it was as awesome as it was terrifying. And there, clear as the sun in the sky, on their shoulders was the symbol of the great open eye – the mark of Horus Lupercal.

The tallest of the warriors, his battle gear decked with more finery than the others, stepped forward. He was covered with honour-chains and combat laurels, and about his shoulders he wore a metal dolman made from metals mined in the depths of Cthon; the Mantle of the Warmaster, forged by Horus's captains as a symbol of his might and unbreakable will.

He drew a gold-chased bolt pistol, raising it up high above his head; and then he fired a single shot into the air, the round crashing like thunder. The same sound that rang about Dagonet on the day they were liberated. Before the empty shell casing could strike the marble at his feet, the crowd were shouting their fealty.

*Glory to Horus.*

The towering warrior holstered his gun and unsealed his helmet, drawing it up so the world might see his face.

THERE COULD BE no hesitation. No margin for error. Such a chance would never come again.

Kell's crosshairs rested on the centre of the scowling grille of the Astartes helmet. The shimmering interference of distance seemed to melt away; now there was only the weapon and the target. He was a part of the weapon, the trigger. The final piece of the mechanism.

Time slowed. Through the scope, Kell saw armoured hands clasp the sides of the helmet, flexing to lift it up from the neck ring. In a moment more, flesh would be exposed, a neck bared. A clear target.

And if he did this, what then? What ripples would spread from the assassination of Horus Lupercal? How would the future shift in this moment? What lives would be saved? What lives would be lost? Kell could almost hear the sound of the gears of history turning about him.

He fired.

THE HAMMER FALLS. The single shot in the chamber is a .75 calibre bullet manufactured on the Shenlong forge world to the exacting tolerances of the Clade Vindicare. The percussion cap is impacted, the propellant inside combusts. Exhaust gases funnel into the pressure centre of a boat-tail round, projecting it down the nitrogen-cooled barrel at supersonic velocities. The sound of the discharge is swallowed by suppression systems that reduce the aural footprint of the weapon to a hollow cough.

As the round leaves the barrel, the Exitus longrifle sends a signal to the Lance; the two weapons are in perfect synchrony. The Lance marshals its energy to expend it for the first and only time. It will burn itself out after one shot.

The round crosses the distance in seconds, dropping in exactly the expected arc towards the figure in the plaza. Windage is nominal, and does not alter its course. Then, with a flash, the bullet strikes the force wall. Any conventional ballistic round would disintegrate at this moment; but the Exitus has fired a Shield-Breaker.

Energised fragments imbued with anti-spinward quantum particles fracture the force wall's structure, and collapse it; but the barrier is on a cycling circuit and will reactivate in less than two-tenths of a second.

It is not enough. The energy of the Lance follows the Shield-Breaker in as the force wall falls; the Lance is a single-use X-ray laser, slaved to Kell's rifle, to shoot where he shoots. The stream of radiation converges on the exact same point, with nothing to stop it. The shot strikes the target in the throat, reducing flesh to atoms, superheating fluids into steam, boiling skin, vaporising bone.

The only sound is the fall of the headless corpse as it crashes to the ground, blood jetting across the white marble and the Warmaster's shining mantle.

# FIFTEEN

**Rapture**
**Aftershock**
**Retribution**

THERE WAS SOMETHING exhilarating about taking kills in this fashion.

The many murders that lay at Spear's feet were usually silent, intimate affairs. Just the killer and the victim, together in a dance that connected them both in a way far more real, far more honest than any other relationship. No one was really naked until the moment of their death.

But this; Spear had never killed more than three people at once because the need had never arisen. Now he was giddy with the blood-rush, wondering why he had never done this before. The joy of the frenzy was all-consuming and it was glorious.

Throwing off all pretence at stealth and subterfuge was liberating in its own way. He was being truthful, baring himself for everyone to see; and they ran screaming when they witnessed it.

Through the low howl of the sandstorm, the refugees were crying out and scattering. He sprinted after them, hooting with laughter.

He had never been so *open*. Even as a child, he had hidden himself away, afraid of what he was. And then when the women in gold and silver came for him aboard their Black Ship, he concealed himself still deeper. Even the men with eyes of metal and glass who had cut upon him, plumbing the depths of his anomalous, deviant mind, even they had not seen this face of him.

Spear was a whirling torrent of claws and talons, teeth and horns, the daemonskin blurring as it shifted and reformed itself to end the life of each victim in a new and brutal way. Gasping mouths opened up all over him where vitae spattered his bare flesh, drinking it in.

The last of the soldiers was shooting at him, and he felt bursts of burning pain as thick, high-calibre shots impacted his back and legs. The daemonskin screeched as it shunted away the majority of the impact force, preventing the rounds from ever penetrating Spear's actual flesh. He spun on his heel, pivoting like a dancer, flipping over though the air. The other soldiers were lying in pools of their own fluids, the sand drinking in their last where heads had been torn open, hearts crushed. Spear skipped over the soldier's comrades and ignored the burn of a shot that caressed his face. He came close and angled on one leg, bringing his other foot up in a speeding black arc. Talons flicked out and the impact point was the man's nasal cavity. Bone splintered with a wet crunch, jagged fragments entering his brain like daggers.

How many dead was that? In the race and chase of it, the murderer had lost count.

Then he saw the witch hiding her face behind a steel skull and he didn't care about that any more. The thin, wiry female shot a fan of needles at him and he dodged most of them, a handful biting into the daemonflesh before the skin puckered and vomited them back out into the dust. This was just a delaying tactic, though. He felt the tremor moving through the warp, the alien monster sheathing his body shivering and reacting in disgust at the proximity of her.

Ill light gathered around the assassin's aura, sucked into the void within her through the fabric of her stealthsuit. The wind seemed to die off around the waif, as if she were generating a globe of nothingness that sound itself could not enter. The construct of lenses and spines emerging from the side of the grinning steel skull-helm crackled with power, and the perturbed air bowed like water ripples.

A black stream of negative energy cascaded from the weapon and seared Spear as he threw up his hands to block it. The impact was immense, and he screamed with a pain unlike any he had ever felt before. The daemonskin was actually burning in places, weeping yellowish rivulets of pus where it blistered.

All his amusement perished in that second; this was no game. The psyker girl was more deadly than he had given her credit for. More than just a pariah, she was… She was in a small way *like him*. But where Spear's abilities were inherent to the twisted, warp-changed structure of his soul, the girl was only a pale copy, a half-measure. She needed the augmentation of the helmet-weapon just to come close to his perfection.

Spear felt affronted by the idea that something could approach the power of his murdergift through mechanical means. He would kill the girl for her pretence.

The daemonskin wanted him to fall back, to retreat and take vital moments to heal; he ignored the moaning of it and did the opposite. Spear launched himself at the psyker, even as he fell into the nimbus of soul-shrivelling cold all about her. He immediately felt his own power being dragged out of him, the pain so bright and shining it was as if she were tearing the arteries from his flesh.

For a brief moment, Spear realised he was experiencing some degree of what it was like for a psyker to die at his hand; this must have been what Perrig had felt as she transformed into ashes.

He lashed out before the undertow could pull him in. Claws like razors split the air in a shimmering arc and sliced across the armoured fabric and the flesh of the waif girl's throat. It was not enough to immediately kill her, but it was enough to open a vein.

She clapped a hand to the wound to staunch it, but not quick enough to stop an arc of liquid red jetting into the air. Spear opened his mouth and caught it in the face, laughing again as she stumbled away, choking.

INSIDE IOTA'S HELMET, blood was pooling around her mouth and neck, issuing in streams from her ears, her nostrils. Her vision was swimming in crimson as tiny capillaries burst open inside her eyes, and she wept red.

The animus speculum worked to recharge itself for a second blast of power. Iota had made a mistake and fired the first discharge too soon, without letting it build to maximum lethality. Her error had been to underestimate the potentiality of this… *thing*.

She had no frame of reference for what she was facing. At first thought she had imagined he was another assassin, sent against her in some power play to undo the works of the Execution Force. She could not see the logic in such a thing, but then the clades had often pursued strange vendettas against one another to assuage trivial slights and insults; these things happened as long as there was no evidence of them and more importantly, no ill-effects to the greater mission of the Officio Assassinorum.

But this killer was something beyond her experience. That much was certain. At the very least, the glancing hit from the animus's beam should have crippled him. Iota turned the readings of her aura-sensor across him and what she saw there was shocking.

Impossibly, his psionic signature was changing, transforming. The sinuous nimbus of ghost colours spilled from the peculiar flesh-matter shrouding his body, and with a sudden leap of understanding, Iota realised she was seeing into a hazy mirror of the warp itself; this being was not one life but two, and between them gossamer threads of telepathic energy sewed them both into the inchoate power of the immaterium. Suddenly, she understood how he had been able to resist the animus blast. The energy, so lethal in the real world, was no more than a drop of water in a vast ocean within the realms of warp space. This killer was connected to the ethereal in a way that she could never be, bleeding out the impact of the blast into the warp where it could dissipate harmlessly.

The shifting aura darkened and became ink black. This Iota had seen before; it was the shape of her own psychic imprint. He was mirroring her, and even as she watched it happen, Iota felt the gravitational drag on her own power as it was drawn inexorably towards the shifting, changing murderer.

He was like her, and unlike as well. Where the clever mechanisms of the animus speculum sucked in psionic potentiality and returned it as lethal discharge, this man... this freakish aberration... he could do the same *alone*.

It was the blood that let him do it. Her blood, ingested, subsumed, absorbed.

Iota screamed; for the first time in her life, she really, *truly* screamed, knowing the blackest depths of terror. The fires in her mind churned, and she released them. He laughed as they rolled off him and reverberated back across space-time.

Iota's mouth filled with ash, and her cries were silenced.

THE MOMENT SEEMED to stretch on into infinity; there was no noise across Liberation Plaza, not even the sound of an indrawn breath. It was as if a sudden vacuum had drawn all energy and emotion from the space. It was the sheer unwillingness to believe what had just occurred that made all of Dagonet pause.

In the next second, the brittle instant shattered like glass and the crowds were in turmoil, the twin floodheads of sorrow and fury breaking open at once. Chaos exploded as the people at the front of the crowd barriers surged forwards and collapsed the metal panels, moving in a slow wave towards the ragged line of shocked clanner soldiers. Some of the troops had their guns drawn; others let themselves be swallowed up by the oncoming swell, deadened by the trauma of what they had witnessed.

On an impulse the Callidus could not quantify, Koyne leapt from the base of the pillar and ran behind the line of crackling force-wall emitters. No one blocked the way. The shock was palpable here, thick in the air like smoke.

The hulking Astartes were in a combat wheel around the corpse of their commander, weapons panning right and left, looking for a target. Their discipline was admirable, Koyne thought. Lesser beings, ordinary men, would have given in to the anger they had to be feeling without pause – but the Callidus did not doubt that would soon come.

One of them shoved another of his number out of the way, tearing off his helmet with a twist of his hand. For a fraction of a second Koyne saw real emotion in the warrior's flinty aspect, pain and anguish so deep that it could only come from a brother, a kinsman. The Astartes had a scarred face, and this close to him, the assassin could see he bore the rank insignia of a brother-sergeant of the 13th Company.

That seemed wrong; according to intelligence on the Sons of Horus, their primarch always travelled with an honour guard of officers, a group known as the Mournival.

'Dead,' said one of the other Astartes, his voice tense and distant. 'Killed by cowards...'

Koyne came as close as the Callidus dared, standing near a pair of worried-looking PDF majors who couldn't decide if they should go to the side of Nicran and the other nobles, or wait for the Astartes to give them orders.

The sergeant bent down over the corpse and did something Koyne could not see. When he stood up once more, he was holding a gauntlet in his hand; but not a gauntlet, no. It was a master-crafted augmetic, a machine replacement for a forearm lost in battle. He had removed it from the corpse, claiming it as a relic.

*But Horus does not–*

'My captain,' rumbled the sergeant, hefting his bolt-gun with a sorrowful nod. 'My captain...'

Koyne's heart turned to a cold stone in his chest, and movement caught his eye as Governor Nicran pushed away from the rest of the nobles and started down the stairs towards the Astartes. The noise of the crowd was getting louder, and the Callidus had to strain to hear as the sergeant spoke into the vox pickup in the neck ring of his breast plate.

'This is Korda,' he snarled, his ire building. 'Location is not, repeat *not* secure. We have been fired upon. Brother-Captain Sedirae... has been killed.'

*Sedirae.* The Callidus knew the name, the commander of the 13th Company. But that was impossible. The warrior Kell had shot wore the mantle, the unique robe belonging to the primarch himself...

'Horus?' Nicran was calling, tears running down his face as he came closer. 'Oh, for the Stars, no! Not the Warmaster, please!'

'Orders?' said Korda, ignoring the babbling noble-man. Koyne could not hear the reply transmitted to the sergeant's ear-bead, but the shift in set of the Space Marine's jaw told the tale of exactly what had been said. With a jolt of fear, the Callidus turned and broke away, sprinting down the steps towards the crowds.

Koyne heard the peal of Nicran's voice over the rush of the mob and turned in mid-run. The Governor was shaking his hands, wracked with sobs in front of the impassive, grey-armoured Astartes. His words were lost, but he was doubtless begging or pleading to Korda, vainly making justifications.

With a small movement, the warrior raised the barrel of his bolter and shot the Governor at point-blank range, blasting his body apart. As one, Korda's men followed his example, turning their guns towards the nobles and executing them.

Over the bass chatter of bolt-fire, the Astartes roared out an order, and it cut through the bedlam like a knife.

'Burn this city!' he shouted.


SOALM STUMBLED THROUGH the butchery clutching the bact-gun and dragging the chest behind her. Sinope was with her, trying to support the other end of the container as best she could. The noblewoman's men were all gone.

The dust-filled air was heavy with the sound of weapons-fire and pain, and there seemed nowhere they could turn that took them away from it.

Soalm stumbled against a shack just as a wave of ephemeral terror radiated out and caught her in its wake. The air turned thick and greasy with the spoor of psionic discharge – and then she heard Iota's echoing screams, amplified through the vocoder of the Culexus's helmet.

'Holy Terra…' whispered the old woman,

It could only have been Iota's death-cry; no other voice could carry such dreadful emotion in it.

Soalm turned towards the sound and saw the ending of her happen. Particles of sickly energy were liberated from Iota's twitching body in a rush of light and noise, and then her stealthsuit collapsed, the silver-steel helmet falling away. Clogged puffs of grey cinders spilled from the black uniform as it crumpled into a heap, the body that had filled it disintegrated in a heartbeat. The skull-faced helmet rolled to a halt, spilling more dark ash into the churning winds.

'Jenniker!' Sinope cried out her name as a shape blurred towards them. The Venenum felt a massive impact against her and she was thrown aside, losing her grip on the chest. She managed to fire two quick bursts from the bact-gun as she tumbled, rewarded with the pop and hiss of acids striking flesh.

Iota's killer loomed out of the buzzing sands, back-lit by the harsh light of the sunrise. She was reaching for a toxin corde as he punched her savagely, disarming her with the force of the blow. The bact-gun tumbled away and was lost. Soalm felt a jagged slash of pain in her chest as her ribs snapped. Falling to the ground, she tried to retch, and found herself in a damp patch of earth, mud formed from sand and spilled arterial blood. A clawed foot swept in and struck her where she had fallen, and another bone snapped. Soalm looked up, hearing laughter.

The writhing shadow loomed, bending towards her; then a length of iron pipe came from nowhere and slammed into the killer's spine, drawing an explosive hiss of fury. Soalm moved, agony racing through her, trying desperately to retreat.

Sinope, her face lit with righteous fury, drew back her improvised weapon and hit him again, the old woman putting every moment of force she could muster into the blow. 'For the God-Emperor!' she bellowed.

The killer did not allow her a third strike, however. He arrested the fall of the iron pipe and held it in place, his other hand snapping out to grasp Sinope's thin, bird-like neck and pull her off her feet. With a vicious shove, he twisted his grip on the pipe and used it to run the noblewoman through; then he discarded her and strode away.

He came upon the chest where it had fallen, and Soalm gave a weak cry as the murderer's inky, liquid flesh streamed into the locking mechanism and broke it open from within. The ancient book fell into the sand, and Soalm saw the stasis shell around it sputter out and die.

'No,' she croaked. 'You cannot... You cannot take it...'

The killer crouched and picked up the Warrant, flipping through the aged pages with careless speed, the paper fracturing and tearing. 'No?' he said, without turning to her. 'Who is going to stop me?'

He reached the last page and released a booming, hateful laugh. Soalm felt a lash of sympathetic pain as he ripped the leaf from the binding of the priceless Eurotas relic and cupped the yellowed vellum in his hand. For a moment, she thought she saw the shimmer of liquid on the page, catching the rays of the sunlight.

Then, as if it were some delicacy he was sampling at a banquet, the killer tipped back his head and opened his mouth, his forked jaws opening like an obscene blossom. A dozen more tiny fanged maws opened across his cheeks and neck as he tipped up the paper and swallowed the blood of the God-Emperor.

He began to scream and howl, and the riot of malformation in his flesh became a storm of writhing fronds, tenticular forms, gnashing mouths. His body lost control over itself, the red-black skin warping and distending into shapes that were nauseating and vile.

Weeping in her agony and her failure, Soalm dragged herself away towards Tros's skimmer, desperate to flee before the killer's rapture came to its end.

KELL WAS ALREADY on his way out even as the echo of his gunshot died around him. He drew up the cameoline cloak across his shoulders, pulling the Exitus longrifle over one arm. He set the timers on the emplaced explosives to ignite once he was clear. The Vindicare paused to add an extra krak charge to a support pillar in the middle of the laundry room; when it detonated, it would collapse the ceiling above and with luck, obliterate what remained intact of the habtower's gutted upper levels. He had left no trace behind him, but it paid to be thorough.

Kell heard the sounds rising up from the streets as he dropped down to the tier below, moving towards his exit point. Disorder would spread like wildfire in the wake of the assassination; the Execution Force had to get beyond the city perimeter before the pandemonium caught up to them.

He went to the edge of the shattered flooring and looked out. He could see people beneath him, the tiny dots of figures running in the avenues. Kell kicked aside a piece of fallen masonry and recovered his descent gear.

The vox link in his spy mask crackled as the seldom-used general channel was keyed.

Kell froze. Only the members of the team knew the frequency, and all of them knew that the channel was a mechanism of last resort. Even though it was heavily encrypted, it lacked the untraceable facility of the burst transmitters; the fact that one of the team was using it now meant something had gone very, very wrong.

The next sound he heard was the voice of the Callidus. Every word said was being simultaneously transmitted to Tariel and the Garantine. *'Mission fail,'* said Koyne, panting with the exertion of running. He could hear bolter shots and screaming in the background. *'Confirming mission fail.'*

Kell was shaking his head. That could not be true; the last thing he had seen through the Exitus's scope was the flash of radiation as the Lance ended the target's life. Horus Lupercal was dead...

*'Broken Mirror,'* said Koyne. *'I repeat, Broken Mirror.'*

The code phrase hit Kell like a physical blow and he sagged against the crumbling wall. The words had only one meaning – a surrogate, a sacrificial proxy had replaced their target.

A storm of questions rushed through his thoughts; how could Horus have known they would be waiting for them? Had the mission been compromised from the very start? Had they been betrayed?

The warrior Kell had placed between his crosshairs could only have been the Warmaster! Only Horus, the liberator of Dagonet clad in his mantle, would have made his grand gesture of the single shot into the sky… It could not be true! *It could not be…*

The moment of doubt and uncertainty flared bright, and then faded. Now was not the time to dwell on this turn of events. The first, most important directive was to exfiltrate the strike zone and regroup. To re-evaluate. Kell nodded to himself. He would do that, he decided. He would extract his team from this mess and then determine a new course of action. As long as a single Officio Assassinorum operative was still alive, the mission could still be completed.

And if along the way, a traitor came to light… He shrugged off the thought. First things first. The Vindicare keyed the general channel. 'Acknowledged,' he said. 'Extraction sites are now to be considered compromised. Proceed to city perimeter and await contact.'

Kell secured the longrifle and fixed his descent pack to his back. 'Go dark,' he ordered, ending the final command with the tap of a switch that deactivated his vox gear.

An explosion made his head snap up and his spy mask's optics located the thermal bloom in the corner of his vision, surrounding it with indicator icons. A vehicle had apparently been blown up by an exchange of gunfire. He wondered who would be foolish enough to shoot back at an Astartes just as a roar of engine noise swept over his head. Kell shrank into the cover of a partly-collapsed wall as a heavy, slate-coloured aircraft thundered around the habitat tower on bright rods of thruster flame – a Stormbird in the livery of the Sons of Horus.

For a moment, he feared the Astartes had detected his firing hide; but the Stormbird swept on and down into the city, passing him by unnoticed. Kell looked up into the early morning sky and saw more raptor-shapes falling from the high clouds, trailing streamers of vapour from atmospheric re-entry. Whoever it was that Kell's kill-shot had executed, the Warmaster's warriors were coming in force to avenge him.

When he was sure the Stormbird was gone, Kell backed off and then ran at the hole in the wall. He threw himself into the air and felt the rush of the wind as gravity claimed his body. For agonising seconds, the streets below rose up towards him; then there was a sharp jerk across his shoulders as the sensors in the descent pack triggered the release of the parafoil across his back. The iridescent curve of ballistic cloth billowed open and his fall slowed.

Kell dropped into the sounds of terror and violence, searching for an escape.

EVERY DECK OF the *Vengeful Spirit* shook with barely-restrained violence as drop-ship after drop-ship rocketed off the launch decks. They streamed away from the battleship in a long, unbroken chain, lethal carrion birds wheeling and turning in towards the surface of Dagonet, carrying fury with them.

Nearby, system boats in service to the PDF's space division were either turning to flee from the ships of the Warmaster's fleet, or else they were already sinking into their home world's gravity well as flames crawled down the length of them. The *Vengeful Spirit*'s gunnery crews had been sparing with the use of their megalaser batteries, striking the ships hard enough to cripple them but not enough to obliterate them. Now the PDF cruisers would burn up in the atmosphere, and the fires of their deaths would be seen the whole planet over. It was a most effective way to begin a punishment.

The *Vengeful Spirit* and the rest of her flotilla encroached slowly on Dagonet's orbital space, approaching the staging point where Luc Sedirae's vessel, the *Thanato*, was waiting for them. Most of the *Thanato*'s complement of drop-ships had already been deployed, the men of the 13th Company falling onto the capital city in a tide of unfettered rage. The handsome and ruthless master of the 13th was beloved of his warriors; and they would avenge him with nothing less than rivers of blood.

The tall viewing windows of the Lupercal's Court looked out over the bow of the *Vengeful Spirit*, the curve of Dagonet and the lone *Thanato* laid out before it. Maloghurst left the Warmaster where he stood at the windows and crossed the strategium towards the corridor outside. As he walked, he spoke in low tones to the troupe of chapter serfs who followed him everywhere he went. The equerry parsed Horus's commands to his underlings and they in turn moved away to carry those orders about the fleet.

Beyond the doorway there was a shadow. 'Equerry,' it said.

'First Chaplain,' Maloghurst replied. His disfigured face turned its perpetual scowl at the Word Bearer, dismissing the rest of the serfs with a flick of his clawed hand. 'Do you wish to speak with me, Erebus? I had been told you were engaged in your… meditations.'

Erebus did not appear to notice the mocking tone Maloghurst placed on his question. 'I was disturbed.'

'By what?'

The Word Bearer's face split in a thin smile. 'A voice in the darkness.' Before Maloghurst could demand a less obtuse answer, Erebus nodded towards the far end of the chamber, where Horus stood observing the motions of his fleet.

The lord of the Legion was magnificent in his full battle gear, his armour striped with shining gold and dark brass, hides of great beasts lying off his shoulder in a half-cloak. His face was hidden in the gloom, highlights made barely visible by the cold glow of the data consoles before him.

'I would ask a question of the Warmaster,' said the other Astartes.

Maloghurst did not move. 'You may ask me.'

'As you wish.' Erebus's lip curled slightly. 'We are suddenly at battle alert status. It was my understanding we were coming to this world to show the flag in passing, and little more.'

'You haven't heard?' Maloghurst feigned surprise, amused that for a change he knew something the Word Bearer did not. 'Brother-Captain Sedirae was given the honour of standing as the Warmaster's proxy on Dagonet. But there was an… incident. A trap, I believe. Sedirae was killed.'

Erebus's typically insouciant expression shaded dark for a moment. 'How did this happen?'

'That will be determined, in due time. For the moment, it is clear that the assurances claiming Dagonet City as a secure location were false. Through either subterfuge or inadequacy on the part of Dagonet's ruling cadres, a Son of Horus lost his life down there.' Maloghurst inclined his head towards the Warmaster. 'Horus has demanded reciprocity.'

'The nobles will die, then?'

The equerry nodded. 'To begin with.'

Erebus was silent for a few seconds. 'Why was Sedi-rae sent?'

'Are you questioning the orders of the Warmaster?'

'I only seek to understand—' Erebus trailed off as Maloghurst took a step towards the Word Bearer, moving through the doorway and into the corridor.

'You would do well, Chaplain, to remember that an honoured battle-brother was just murdered in cold blood. A decorated Astartes of great esteem whose loss will be keenly felt, not just by the 13th Company but by the entire Legion.'

Erebus's eyes narrowed, showing his doubts at the description of Sedirae's great esteem. While it was true the man was a fine warrior, many considered him an outspoken braggart, the Word Bearer among them. But as ever, the equerry kept his own opinions to himself.

Maloghurst continued. 'It would be best for the Warmaster to deal with this matter without the involvement of those from outside the Legion.' He nodded to a servitor in the lee of the doors, and the helot began to slide the towering panels closed. 'I'm sure you appreciate that.'

There was a moment when the Word Bearer seemed as if he were about to protest; but then he nodded. 'Of course,' said Erebus. 'I bow to your wisdom, equerry. Who knows the Warmaster's moods better than you?' He threw a nod and walked away, back into the shadows of the corridor.

They were killing everything that moved.

The Sons of Horus began by firing on the crowds in Liberation Plaza, routing the civilians and turning the mob into a screaming tide of bodies that trampled each other in a desperate attempt to flee back down the roads and away from the great halls.

Koyne fought through the mass, catching sight of some of the killings along the way. Kell's emergency command echoed through the vox-bead hidden in the Callidus's ear.

The Astartes walked, slow and steady, across the plaza with their bolters at their hips, firing single shot after single shot into the people. The missile-like bolt shells could not fail to find targets, and for each person they hit and instantly killed, others fell dead or near to it from the shared force of impact. The blasts rippled out through flesh and bone, the crowds were so closely packed together. And although Koyne never saw it, the assassin heard the hiss and crackle of a flamer being used. The smell of burned flesh was familiar.

The panic was as much a weapon as the guns of the Astartes. People running and pushing, drowning in animal fear; they trampled one another blindly as they tried to escape along the radial streets leading from the plaza. Some transformed their fear into violence, brandishing weapons of their own in vain attempts to cut a path through the madness.

Koyne rode the terrified mob as one might have floated on a turbulent sea, not fighting it, letting the frenzied currents of push and pull shove a body here and there. As the roads opened up into wider boulevards, the crush lessened and people broke into an open run; some of them were met by strafing fire from the first of the Stormbirds that swooped in low between the buildings.

The Callidus was carried to the edge of the street and found passage through a storefront damaged in the early days of the insurrection. Hidden for a moment from the screaming throng outside, Koyne dared to consult a small holo-map of the city; any one of the avenues would take the assassin straight out of the metropolis to the city perimeter, but down each street the Astartes were advancing in small groups, coldly pacing their kills into those who ran and those who surrendered alike.

After a moment, Koyne peered over the lip of a shattered window and saw that the leading edge of the crowds had passed by. Stragglers were still running past, heading southwards. Behind them, walking as if it were nothing more than a morning stroll, the Callidus spotted a single Astartes in grey ceramite, moving with a bolter at his shoulder. Sighting down the weapon as he went, he was picking targets at random and ending them.

This was not a military exercise; this was a castigation.

'This is your fault!' The voice was full of terror and fury.

Koyne spun and found a man, his clothes freshly torn and a new cut staining his forehead with blood. He stood across the rubble-strewn shop floor, glaring at the Callidus, pointing a shaky finger.

It was the uniform he was indicating. The dun-coloured tunic of the Dagonet Planetary Defence Force, in disarray now, but still a part of the false identity Koyne was operating under.

The man shambled through the glass, kicking it aside without a care for the noise he was making. 'You

brought them here!' He stabbed a finger at the street.
'That's not Horus! I don't know what those things are!
Why did you let them come to kill us?'

Koyne realised that the man had no idea what had
happened; perhaps he hadn't seen the Shield-Breaker
and the Lance. All he saw was a monstrous killing
machine in armour the colour of storms.

'Stop talking,' said Koyne, pulling open the PDF
tunic and feeling for a fleshpocket holster. With a
gasp, the Callidus tabbed the seam. Koyne's weapon
was in there, but the assassin's muscles were tight with
tension and it was proving difficult to relax and ease
the skin-matter open. 'Just be silent.'

There was movement outside. Someone on a higher
floor in the building across the street, probably some
bold member of Capra's rebellion or just a Dagoneti sick
of being a victim, tossed a makeshift firebomb that shattered wetly over the warrior's helmet and right shoulder.
The Son of Horus halted and swiped at the flames where
they licked over the ceramite, patting them out with the
flat of his gauntlet. As Koyne watched, the Astartes was
still dotted with little patches of orange flame as he pivoted on his heel and aimed upward.

A heavy thunderclap shot rang out, and the bolter
blew a divot of brick from the third floor. A body,
trailing threads of blood, came spiralling out with it,
killed instantly by the proximity of the impact.

'They... they want you!' snarled the man in the
shop, oblivious to what was taking place outside.
'Maybe they should have you!'

'No,' Koyne said, fingers at last touching the butt of
the pistol nestling inside the false-flesh gut over the
Callidus's stomach. 'I told you to–'

Stone crunched into powder and suddenly the warrior was there in the doorway of the gutted shop, too big to fit through the wood-lined threshold. The emotionless eyes of the fearsome helmet scanned them both and then the figure advanced, its bolter dropping onto a sling. Koyne stumbled backwards as the Son of Horus tore through the splintering remains of the doorway, drawing his combat blade as he came. The knife was the size of a short sword, and the fractal edge gave off a dull gleam.

Before the Callidus could react the Astartes struck out with the pommel and hit the assassin in the chest. Koyne felt bones snap and spun away, landing hard. In a perverse way, the assassin was pleased; Koyne's cover was clearly still intact. If the Astartes had known what he was facing, the kill would have come immediately.

The man was pointing and shouting; the Son of Horus, having decided to preserve his ammunition for the moment, advanced on the survivor, the top of his helmet knocking light fittings down from the patterned ceiling. A sweep of the combat blade silenced the man by taking his head from his shoulders; the body gave a peculiar little dance as nerves misfired, and fell in a heap.

Koyne had the gun but the twitching of the muscles and the flesh-pocket would not let it go; pain from the impact injury robbed the Callidus of the usual concentration and control needed at a moment like this.

The Son of Horus changed his grip on the knife, holding it by the blade, ready to throw it; in the next second a crash of bolter fire echoed and impact points appeared in a line of silver blooms across the chest plate and left shoulder pauldron of the Astartes.

Through blurry vision, Koyne saw a man-shape moving faster than anything human should have; and a face, a mask, a fanged skull made of discoloured gunmetal.

Scrambling backwards, the assassin watched as the Garantine sprinted around the Astartes in a tight arc, rolling over fallen counters and leaping from pillar to wall. As he moved, his Executor pistol was snarling, spitting out low-gauge bolt shells that clattered and sparked off the towering warrior's armour.

The Astartes let the combat blade drop and brought up his bolter; the weapon was of a far larger calibre than the Executor. A single direct hit at the ranges these close quarters forced upon the combatants would mean death for the Eversor; but to kill him, first the Astartes had to hit him.

Koyne moaned in pain as the gun slowly eased out of the stress-tensed flesh pocket, watching as the two combatants tried to end each other. In the confined space of the destroyed store the bray of bolt shells was deafening, and the air filled with the stench of cordite and the heavy, choking dust from atomised flakboard. A support pillar exploded, raining plaster and wood from the broken flooring above. The Callidus could hear the animalistic panting of the Eversor as he moved like lightning back and forth across the Space Marine's line of sight, goading the Astartes into firing after him. Stimm-glands chugged and injectors hissed as the Garantine's bloodstream was flooded with bio-chemicals and cocktails of drugs that pushed him beyond the speed of even an Astartes's enhanced reflexes.

Koyne's gun, slick with mucus and fluids, finally vomited itself out of the assassin's stomach and on to the floor. The Callidus clutched at it and released a shot in the direction of the grey-armoured hulk. The neural shredder projected a spreading plume of sickly energetic discharge around the Son of Horus and the warrior staggered with the hit, one hand coming up to clutch at his helmet.

The Garantine roared past, sprinting over Koyne where the Callidus lay propped up against a wall. 'My kill!' he was shouting, the words repeating and coming so fast they became a single stream of noise. 'My killmykillmykillmykill–'

He was a blur of claws and gun, too fast for the eye to process the images. Sparks flew as the Eversor assassin collided bodily with the Astartes and knocked him down, the Garantine firing his Executor into the impact holes in the warrior's chest at point-blank range, clawing wildly at his helmet with the spiked talon of his neuro-gauntlet. Koyne could hear the Astartes snarling, angrily fighting back, but the Eversor was like mercury, slipping through his clumsy armoured fingers.

Then dark, arterial blood spurted as the armour was cracked and the Garantine dug into the meat he found inside. His bolter dry, the Astartes punched and bludgeoned the Eversor, but if any pain impulses reached the Garantine's mind, the brew of rage-enhancers and sense-inhibitors swimming through his bloodstream deadened them to nothing.

With a croaking, wet rattle, the Astartes sank back and collapsed. Chattering with coarse laughter, the Garantine swept up the fallen combat blade and pressed all his weight behind it. The weapon sank through sparking power cables and myomer muscles until it pierced flesh and cut bone.

After a minute or so, the Eversor dropped to the floor, still shaking with the aftershock of his chemical frenzy. 'Ss-so...' he began, struggling to speak clearly, forcing himself to slow down with each panting gulp of breath. 'Th-this is how it feels to k-kill one of them...' He grinned widely behind the fanged mask. 'I like it.'

The Callidus stood up. 'We need to move, before more of his brethren arrive.'

'Aren't you... aren't you going to th-thank me for saving your life, s-shape-changer?'

Without warning, the Astartes suddenly lurched forwards, gauntlets snapping open, savage anger fuelling a final surge of killing fury. Koyne's neural shredder was at hand and the assassin fired a full-power discharge into the skull of the Son of Horus; the blast disintegrated tissue in an instant wave of brain-death.

The warrior lurched and fell again. Koyne gave the Garantine a sideways look. 'Thank you.'

# SIXTEEN

**Collision**
**The Choice**
**Forgiveness**

A BOMBARDMENT HAD begun, and the people of Dagonet's capital feared it was the end of the world.

They knew so little of the reality of things, however. High above in orbit, it was only the warship *Thanato* that fired on the city, and even then it was not with the vessel's most powerful cannons. The people did not know that a fleet of craft were poised in silence around their sister ship, watchful and waiting. Had all the vessels of the Warmaster's flotilla unleashed their killpower, then indeed those fears would have come true; the planet's crust cracked, the continents sliced open. Perhaps those things would happen, soon enough – but for now it was sufficient for the *Thanato* to hurl inert kinetic kill-rods down through the atmosphere, the sky-splitting shriek of their passage climaxed by a lowing thunder as the warshots obliterated power stations, military compounds and the vast mansion-houses of the noble clans. From the ground it seemed like wanton destruction; from orbit, it was a shrewd and surgical pattern of attack.

KOYNE AND THE Garantine stayed off the main avenues and boulevards, avoiding the roadways where processions of frightened citizens streamed towards the city limits. Hours had passed now since the killing in the plaza, and the people had lost the will to run, numbed by their own terror. Now they stumbled, silently for the most part, some pushing carts piled high with whatever they could loot or carry, others clinging to overloaded ground vehicles. When people did speak, they did so in whispers, as if they were afraid the Adeptus Astartes would hear the sound of a voice at normal pitch from across the city.

Listening from the shadows of an alleyway across from a shuttered monorail halt, the Callidus heard people talking about the Sons of Horus. Some said they had set up a staging point in Liberation Plaza, that there were hordes of Stormbirds parked there disgorging more Astartes with each passing moment. Others mentioned seeing armoured vehicles in the streets, even Battle Titans and monstrous war creatures.

The only truth Koyne could determine from what he gleaned was that the Sons of Horus were intent on fulfilling the orders of Devram Korda to the fullest; Dagonet City would be little more than a smouldering funeral pyre by nightfall.

The assassin looked up to where a massive streetscreen hung at a canted angle from the front of the station building. The display was cracked and fizzing with patchy static; text declaring that the metropolitan rail network was temporarily suspended was

still visible, the pixels frozen in place. Koyne eyed the
device warily. The public screens all had arrays of vid-
picters arranged around them, connected to the
municipal monitoring network. The Callidus had a
spy's healthy disdain for being caught on camera.

As if it had sensed the shade's train of thought,
Koyne saw very clearly as one of the picters jerked on
its gimbal, stuttering around to face the line of
refugees. The assassin retreated back into the shadows,
unsure if the monitor had caught sight.

A few metres down the alley, the Garantine was sitting atop a waste container, shivering with the
come-down from his reflex-boosters, working with a
field kit to close up the various wounds the Son of
Horus had inflicted on him during the earlier melee.
Koyne grimaced at the chewing sound of a dermal sta-
pler as it knitted flesh back to flesh.

The Garantine looked up; his mask was off, and one
of his eyes was torn and damaged, weeping clear fluids. He grinned, showing bloodstained teeth. 'Be with
you in a trice, freak.'

Koyne ignored the insult, shrugging off the ragged
remains of the PDF troop commander tunic and
replacing it with a brocade jacket stolen from a fallen
shop-window dummy. 'May not have that long.'

The Callidus shrank back against the wall and let the
face of the portly PDF officer slip away. It was painful to
make a change like this, without proper meditation
and time spent, but the circumstances demanded it.
Koyne's aspect flowed to resemble that of a young man,
a boyish face under the same unruly mop of thin hair.

'Do you remember what you used to look like?' said
the Eversor, disgust thick in his tone.

Koyne gave the other assassin a sideways look, making a point of gazing at the topography of scarification and the countless implants both atop and beneath his epidermis. 'Do *you*?'

The Garantine chuckled. 'We're both so pretty in our own ways.' He went back to his wounds. 'Any sign of more Astartes?'

The Callidus made a negative noise. 'But they'll be coming. I've seen this kind of thing before. They march through a city, putting the torch to everything they pass, daring anyone to stop them.'

'Let them come,' he grunted, tying the last field dressing around his thick thigh.

'There will be more than one next time.'

'Don't doubt it.' The Eversor's hands were still twitching. 'The poisoner girl was right. We're all going to die here.'

That drew a harsh look from the Callidus. 'I have no intention of ending my life on this backwater world.'

He chuckled. 'Act like you have a choice.' The Garantine made a metronome motion with his fingers. 'Ticky-tocky. Odds are against us. Someone must've talked.'

That made the other assassin fall silent. Koyne had not wanted to dwell on the possibility, but the Garantine was right to suspect that their mission had been compromised. It seemed a logical deduction, given what had happened in the plaza.

The sharp cry of an animal drew Koyne's attention away from such troubling thoughts and the assassin looked up to see a raptor bird flutter past the end of the alleyway, pivoting on a wing to glide in their direction.

There was a flurry of movement and the Eversor had his Executor aimed upward, the sensor mast of his

Sentinel gear drawing a bead; the combi-weapon's needler made a snapping sound and the bird died in mid-turn, falling to the ground like a stone.

Koyne went to the animal's body; there had been something odd about it, a flicker of sunlight off metal…

'Hungry, are you?' The Garantine lurched along behind, limping slightly.

'Idiot.' Koyne held up the bird's corpse; a single needle-dart bisected its bloody torso. The raptor had numerous augmetic implants in its skull and pinions. 'This is a psyber eagle. It belongs to the infocyte. He's looking for us.' Koyne glanced up at the streetscreen once more, and the imagers beneath it.

'Maybe it was him who talked,' muttered the Eversor. 'Maybe *you*.'

The image on the streetscreen flickered and changed; now it was an aerial view of the street, then shots of the alleyway, then a confused tumble of motion. Koyne suddenly understood the display was showing a replay of the visual feed from the eagle's auto-senses.

Some of the refugee stragglers saw the same thing and stopped to watch the loop of footage. Koyne tossed the dead bird aside and stepped out into the street. Immediately, all the imagers along the bottom of the streetscreen whirred, moving to capture a look at the Callidus.

For a moment nothing happened; if Koyne was right, if it was Tariel watching through those lenses, the Vanus would be confused. Koyne's face was different from the last one the infocyte had seen. But then the Garantine shuffled out into the open and all doubt was removed.

The refugees saw the hulking rage-killer and backed away in fear, as if suddenly becoming aware of a wild animal in their midst. In that, Koyne reflected, they were almost correct. The Garantine leered at them, showing his teeth.

A hooter sounded from the monorail halt, and in juddering fits and starts, the heavy metal gate closing off the station from the street began to draw open on automated mechanisms. The screen above flickered again, and this time the text displayed there announced that the rail system was now in operation.

Koyne smiled slightly. 'I think we have some transport.' The Callidus took a step, but a clawed hand grabbed the assassin's arm.

'Could be a trap,' hissed the Garantine.

In the distance, another orbital strike screamed into the earth and sent a tremor through the ground beneath their feet. 'Only one way to find out.'

ON THE ELEVATED platform above the street level a single train was active. The web of monorail lines had been inert ever since the start of the insurrection against Terra, first shut down by the clanner troops as a way of imposing order by restricting the movement of the commoners through the city, and later forced to stay idle because of the mass breakout at the Terminus. But some lines were still connected to what remained of the capital's rapidly-dying power grid, and the autonomic control systems that governed the operation of the trains and lines and points were simplistic devices; they were no match for someone with the skills of a Vanus.

Another psyber eagle roosted on the prow of the train and it called out a strident caw as Koyne and the

Garantine sprinted on to the platform. The Callidus threw a glance down the wide stairwell; some of the bolder refugees were venturing inside the station after them.

'Quickly,' Koyne found an open carriage door and climbed inside. The train was a cargo carrier, partitioned off inside by pens suitable for livestock. The air within was thick with the stink of animal sweat and faeces.

As the Garantine climbed in, the eagle took wing and the train shunted forwards with a grinding clatter, sending sparks flying from the drive wheels gripping the rail. Ozone crackled and the carriages lurched away from the station, picking up momentum.

The train rattled along, a dull impact resonating off the metalwork as it shouldered a piece of fallen masonry off the rails. Koyne drew the neural shredder and moved back through the cargo wagon, kicking open the hatch to the next carriage, and then the two more beyond that. In the rear car the shade found the corpses of groxes, the bovines lying where they had fallen on the gridded metal flooring. They were still tethered to anchoring rings on the walls, doubtless forgotten and left to starve in this reeking metal box after the fighting had begun.

Satisfied they were alone, the Callidus walked back the length of the train to find the Garantine in the stubby engine car, watching the chattering cogitator-driver. Through the broken glass of the engine compartment canopy, the elevated track was visible ahead, dropping away down to the level of one of the main boulevards, paralleling the radial highway's course.

'If we're lucky, we can ride this heap all the way out of the city,' said Koyne, absently examining the charge glyph on the neural weapon.

The Eversor had his fang-mask back on, and he was growling softly with each breath, peering into the distance like a predator smelling the wind. 'We're not lucky,' he retorted. 'Do you see?' The Garantine pointed a metal-taloned finger ahead of the train.

Koyne pulled a pair of compact magnoculars from a belt clip and peered through them. A fuzzy image swam into focus; grey blobs became the distinct shapes of Adeptus Astartes in Maximus-pattern armour, moving to block the path of the monorail. As the Callidus watched, they dragged the husks of burned-out vehicles across the line, assembling a makeshift barricade.

'I told you this was a trap,' rumbled the Garantine. 'The Vanus is delivering us to the Astartes!'

Koyne gave a shake of the head. 'If that was so, then why aren't we slowing down?' If anything, the train's velocity was increasing, and warning indicators began to blink on the cogitator panel as the carriages exceeded their safety limits.

The wheels screeched as the train raced down the incline from the elevated rails to the ground level crossing, and metal flashed off metal as the Sons of Horus began to open fire on the leading carriage, pacing bolt shells into the hull from the cover of their obstruction.

The Garantine blind-fired a burst of full-auto fire through the broken window and then followed Koyne back through the wagons at a sprint. Shots punched through the walls of the cargo cars, rods of sunlight stabbing through the impact holes into the musty interior. The decking rocked beneath their feet and it was hard to stay upright as the train continued to gather speed.

They made it to the rearmost wagon as the engine car slammed into the barricade and crashed through it. The husks of a groundcar and a flatbed GEV spun away across the boulevard, throwing two Astartes aside with the force of the collision. Metal fractured, red-hot and stressed beyond its limits, and the guide wheels broke away from the axle. Instantly freed from the monorail, the train lurched up and twisted over on to its side. The carriages crashed down to the black-top and scored a gouge down the length of the street, spitting cascades of asphalt and gravel.

In the rear car, the assassins were thrown into the grox carcasses, the impact absorbed by the foetid meat of the dead animals. Screeching and vomiting clouds of bright orange sparks, the derailed cargo train finally slowed to a shuddering halt.

Koyne lost awareness for what seemed like long, long minutes. Then the Callidus was aware of being dragged upwards and then propelled through a tear in what had once been the wagon's roof. The shade took several shaky steps out on to the roadway, smelling hot tar and the tang of burned metal. Koyne blinked in the sunlight, feeling for the neural shredder. The weapon was still there, mercifully.

The Garantine lurched past, reloading his Executor. 'I think we upset them,' he shouted, pointing past Koyne's shoulder.

Turning, the assassin saw armoured giants running down the road towards them, firing from the hip.

Bolt-rounds cracked into the ground and the shattered train with heavy blares of concussion. Koyne drew the neural weapon and hesitated; the pistol had a finite range and was better suited to a close-in kill. Instead, the Callidus retreated behind part of the cargo wagon. Perhaps a lucky shot might take down one of the Sons of Horus, even hobble two of them... but that was a tactical squad back there, bearing down on the pair of them.

'We're not lucky,' the assassin muttered, considering the possibility that this backwater would indeed be the place that claimed the life of Koyne of the Callidus. A ricochet careened off the roadway and the Garantine staggered back into cover. Koyne smelled the thick, resinous odour of bio-fluids; there was a deep purple-black gouge in the Eversor's back. 'You're wounded.'

'Am I? Oh.' The other assassin seemed distracted, clearing a fouled cartridge from the breech of his gun. A metal canister rattled off the wagon and landed near their feet; without hesitation, the Garantine scooped up the krak grenade and threw it back in the direction it had come. Koyne could see that his every movement was an effort, as more thick, chemical-laced blood seeped from the injury.

The Eversor let out a low, ululating gasp as injectors discharged, nullifying his pain. He glared back at Koyne and his pupils were pinpricks. 'Something's coming. Hear it?'

Koyne was about to speak, but a sudden roar of jet wash smothered every other noise. From between the towers lining one of the side streets came a blunt-prowed flyer, the boxy fuselage suspended between two sets of wings that ended in vertical thruster pods; it was painted in bright stripes of white and green, the livery of the city's firefighting brigade. There was a man in a black stealthsuit at an open hatch, a longrifle in his grip. A shot snapped from the gun muzzle and further down the road a car exploded.

Koyne pulled at the Garantine's arm as the aircraft dropped towards the street. 'Time to go,' the Callidus shouted.

The Eversor's muscles were bunched hard like bales of steel cable, and he was vibrating with wild energy. 'He said he killed one of them, before.' The Garantine was glaring at the oncoming Astartes. 'That's two now, if he's to be believed.'

The flyer was spinning about, trying to find a place to settle as the Sons of Horus split their fire between the assassins and the aircraft. 'Garantine,' said Koyne. 'We have to move.'

The rage-killer twitched and a palsy came over him. 'I don't like you,' he said, slurring the words. 'You realise that?'

'The feeling is mutual.' Koyne had to yell to be heard over the noise of the thrusters. The flyer was hovering less than a metre from the roadway. Tariel was at the canopy, beckoning frantically.

'Good. I don't want you to confuse my motives.' And then the Eversor surged into a loping run, his legs blurring as he hurtled out of cover and straight into the lines of the Astartes. Shell casings cascaded out behind him in a stream of brass, falling from the ejection port of his combi-weapon.

The Callidus swore and sprinted in the opposite direction towards the flyer. Kell was in half-cover by the open hatch, the Exitus rifle bucking in his grip as he fired Turbo-Penetrator rounds into the enemy squad. Koyne leapt up and scrambled into the crew compartment of the aircraft.

Tariel was cowering behind a panel, pale and sweaty. He appeared to be puppeting the aircraft's pilot-servitor through the interface of his cogitator gauntlet. The infocyte looked up. 'Where's the Garantine?' he yelled.

'He's made his choice,' said Koyne, slumping to the deck.

THE EVERSOR RAN screaming into the cluster of rebel Astartes, blasting the first he found off his feet with a screeching salvo of rounds from the Executor. He collided with the next and the two of them went down in a crash of ceramite and metal. The Garantine felt the boiling churn of energy racing through his veins, his mech-enhanced heart beating at such incredible speed the sound it made in his ears was one long continuous roar. The stimm-pods in the cavities of his abdomen broke their regulator settings and flooded him with doses of Psychon and Barrage pumped directly into his organs, while atomiser grilles in the frame of his fang-mask puffed raw, undiluted anger-inducers and neuro-triggers into his nostrils.

He rode on a wave of frenzy, of black and mad hate that sent him howling with uncontrollable laughter, each choking snarl rattling like gunshots. He was so fast; so lethal; so *satisfied* like this.

The Garantine had been awake now for the longest period of his life since before they had found him in the colony, the gnawed bones of his neighbours in his little child's hand, the tips sharpened to make a kill with. He missed the dreamy no-mind bliss of the stasis cowls. He felt lost without the whispering voices of the hypnogoges. This kind of living, the hour-to-hour, day-by-day existence that the rest of them found so easy… it was a hell of stultifying torpor for the Garantine. He hated the idea of this interminable *yesterday* and *today* and *tomorrow*. He craved the *now*.

Every second he was awake, he felt as if the pure rage that fuelled him was being siphoned away, making him weak and soft. He needed his sleep. Needed it like air.

But he needed his kills even more. Better than the hardest hit of combat philtre, more potent than the jags of pleasure-analogue that issued from the lobochips in his grey matter – the kills were the best high of them all.

He was pounding on the Space Marine's helmet, smashing in the eye-lenses, beating his clawed hands bloody. The Executor was a club he used to bludgeon and swipe.

Impacts registered on him, blasts of infernal heat throwing him off his victim, driving him hard into the road. Heavy, drug-tainted vitae frothed at his mouth and bubbled through the maw of the fang-mask. He felt no pain. There was only a white ball of warmth in the middle of him, and it was growing. It expanded to fill the Garantine with a rush the like of which he had never felt before. The implants in him stuttered and died, shattered by glancing bolter hits and knife stabs. He had nothing but rags below the right knee.

Every muscle in his body shuddered as the death-sign triggered a dormant artificial gland beneath his

sternum. The engorged, orb-shaped organ spent its
venom load, bursting as the end came close. The Terminus gland poured a compound into the Garantine
that made the blood in his veins boil, turning it to
acid. Every drug and chemical mixed uncontrollably,
becoming potent, toxic, *explosive*.

The soft tissues of the Eversor's eyes cooked in their
orbits, and so he was blind to the final flash of
exothermic release, as his body was consumed in an
inferno of spontaneous combustion.

THEY HUGGED THE contours of the city streets, moving
fast and as low as they dared, but out on the edge of
the capital the Sons of Horus had little presence.
Instead, the rebel Astartes had allowed their orbital
contingent to hammer at the walled estates and park-
lands belonging to the noble clans. The city was now
ringed with a dirty chain of massive impact craters.
The blackened bowls of churned earth were fused into
glassy puddles in some places, where the force of the
kinetic strikes had melted the ground into distended
fulgurite plates.

The lines of refugees crossed the craters beneath
them, streamers of people moving like ants across the
footprint of an uncaring giant. The thick, smoke-
soiled air over the destruction veiled the passage of the
flyer. Tariel told them they were fortunate that the
Adeptus Astartes had not deployed air cover; in this
wallowing, keening civilian aircraft they would have
been no match for a Raven interceptor.

On Kell's orders the infocyte directed the flyer out
over the wastelands beyond the city walls and into the
dusty churn of the deserts. With each passing second

they were putting more and more distance between them and the star-port hangar where the *Ultio* had been concealed.

Nothing followed them; at one point the sensors registered something small and fast – a jetbike perhaps – but it was far off their vector and did not appear to be aware of them.

Finally, Koyne broke the silence. 'Where in the name of Hades are we going?'

'To find the others,' said the Vindicare.

'The women?' Koyne was still hiding behind a young man's face and the expression the Callidus put on it was too old and too callous for such a youthful visage. 'What makes you think they're any less dead than the Eversor?'

Kell held up a data-slate. 'You don't really think I'd let the Culexus out of my sight without knowing exactly where she was, do you?'

'A tracking device?' Koyne immediately glared at Tariel, who shrank back behind the hologram of the flyer's autopilot control. 'One of your little toys?'

The infocyte gave a brisk nod. 'A harmless radiation frequency tag, nothing more. I provided enough for all of us.'

Koyne turned the glare back on Kell. 'Did you plant one on me as well?' The boy's eyes narrowed. 'Where is it?'

Kell smiled coldly. 'Those rations aboard the *Ultio* were tasty, weren't they?' Before the Callidus could react, he went on. 'Don't be so difficult, Koyne. If I hadn't factored in a contingency, we never would have found you. You'd still be in the city, marking time until Horus's warriors cut you down.'

'You thought of everything,' said the shade. 'Except the possibility that our target would know we were coming!'

Tariel began to speak. 'The target in the plaza–'

'*Was not the Warmaster*!' snarled Koyne. 'I am an assassin palatine of more kills than I care to mention, and I have survived every sanction and prosecuted each kill because I had no secrets. No one to confide in. No chance for a breach in operational security. And yet here we are, with this grand and foolish scheme to murder a primarch crashing down around us, and for what? Who spoke, Kell?' The Callidus crossed the flyer's small cabin and prodded the marksman in the chest. 'Who is to blame?'

'I don't have an answer for you,' said Kell, in a moment of candour. 'But if any of us were traitors to the Emperor, we've had opportunities aplenty to stop this endeavour before it even left the Sol system.'

'Then how did Horus foresee the attack?' asked Koyne. 'He let one of his own commanders perish in his stead. He must have known! Are we to believe he's some kind of sorcerer?'

A chime sounded from Kell's data-slate, and he left the question unanswered. 'A return. Two kilometres to the west.'

Tariel opened another pane of ghostly hololithic images and nodded. 'I have it. A static location. The flyer's auspex is detecting a metallic mass... conflicting thermal reads.'

'Set us down.'

Below them, dust clouds whirled past, reducing visibility to almost nothing. 'The sandstorm and the contaminants from the orbital bombing...' The Vanus looked up and his argument died on his lips as he saw Kell's rigid expression. He sighed. 'As you wish.'

TWO OF TARIEL'S eyerats found her, slumped over the yoke of a GEV skimmer half-buried under a storm-blown dune. From what the infocyte could determine, she had been injured before getting into the vehicle, and at some point as she tried to escape into the deep desert, her wounds had overcome her and the skimmer controls had slipped from her grip.

Kell, an expression of stony fury on his face, shoved Tariel out of the way and gathered up Soalm where she lay. Her face was discoloured with bruising, and to the infocyte's amazement, she still lived.

Koyne drew something from the back seat of the GEV: a sculpted silver helmet in the shape of a skull, crested with lenses and antennae of arcane design. When the Callidus held it up to look it in the eye, black ash fell from the neck and was carried away on the moaning winds. 'Iota...'

'Dead,' Soalm stirred at the mention of the psyker's name. 'It killed her.' Her voice was slight, thick with pain.

'*It?*' echoed Tariel; but Kell was already carrying the Venenum back towards the flyer.

Koyne was the last inside, and the Callidus drew the hatch shut with a slam. The shade brought Iota's helmet back, and sat it on the deck of the cabin. It fixed them all with its mute, accusatory gaze. Outside, the winds threw rattling curls of sand across the canopy, plucking at the wings of the aircraft.

Across the compartment, Kell tore open a medicae pack and emptied the contents across the metal floor.

He worked to load an injector with a pan-spectrum anti-infective.

'Ask her what happened,' said Koyne.

'Shut up,' Kell snapped. 'I'm going to save her life, not interrogate her!'

'If she was drawn away on purpose,' continued the Callidus. 'If it was deliberate that Soalm was attacked and Iota killed...'

'What could have killed *her*?' Tariel blurted out. 'I witnessed what she was capable of in the Red Lanes.'

Koyne scrambled across the cabin towards the sniper. 'For the Throne's sake, man, *ask her*! Whatever she is to you, we have to know!'

Kell hesitated; and then with deliberate care, he replaced the anti-infective agent with a stimulant. 'You're right.'

'That could kill her,' Tariel warned. 'She's very weak.'

'No,' Kell replied, placing the nozzle of the injector at her pale neck, 'she's not.' He pressed the stud and the drug load discharged.

Soalm reacted with a hollow gasp, her back arching, eyes opening wide with shock. In the next moment, she fell back against the deck, wheezing. 'You...' she managed, her gaze finding Kell where he stood over her.

'Listen to me,' said the Vindicare, that curious unquantifiable expression on his face once again. 'The Garantine is dead. The mission was a failure. Horus sent a proxy in his place. Now his Astartes are punishing the city for what we have done.'

Soalm's eyes lost focus for a moment as she took this in. 'A killer...' she whispered. 'An assassin... hiding behind the identity of a rogue trader's agent.' She looked up. 'I saw what it did to Iota. The others it just murdered, but her... And then the blood...' The woman started to weep. 'Oh, God-Emperor, the blood...'

'What did she just say?' Koyne asked. 'Idolatry is outlawed! Of all the–'

'Be quiet!' Tariel snapped. The infocyte leaned forward. 'Soalm. There is another assassin here? It killed Iota, yes?'

She gave a shaky nod. 'Tried to end me... Murdered Sinope and the others in the sanctuary. And then the book...' She sobbed.

Kell extended a hand and laid it on her shoulder as she wept.

'I can show it,' said Tariel. Koyne turned to see the Vanus grasping Iota's helmet in his hands. 'What happened, I mean. There's a memory coil built into the mechanism of the animus speculum. A mission recorder.'

'Do it,' said Kell, without looking up.

In short order, Tariel used his mechadendrites to prise open panels along the back of the metal skull, and connected cords of bright brass and copper between the hidden ports on the device and the hololith projector built into his cogitator.

Images flickered and jumped. Fractured moments of conversation blurred and sputtered in the air as the infocyte plumbed the depths of the memory unit, cutting though layers of encryption; and then it began.

Soalm looked away; she did not want to witness it a second time.

\* \* \*

TARIEL WATCHED IOTA die through her own eyes.

He saw the man in the Eurotas uniform transform into the thing that called itself 'Spear'; he saw the perplexing readouts on the aura scans that matched nothing the psyker had encountered before; and he saw the horrific act of the taking of her blood.

'It tasted her...' Soalm muttered. 'Do you see? In the moment before the kill.'

'Why?' Koyne was sickened.

'A genetic lock,' Tariel said, nodding to himself. 'Powerful psionic rituals require the use of an organic component as an initiator.'

'A blood rite?' Koyne shot him a look. 'That's primitive superstition.'

'It might appear so to a certain point of view.'

Iota died again, the audio replay catching the raw terror in her death-scream, and Tariel looked away, his gorge rising. The peculiar waif-like psyker had not deserved to perish in so monstrous a way as this.

No one spoke for a long time after the playback ended. They sat in silence, the images of the daemonic abomination embedded in their thoughts, the revolting spectacle of the girl's murder echoing in the howling winds outside.

'Sorcery,' said Kell, at length. His voice was cold and hard. 'The rumours about Horus's sinister plans are true. He is in league with allies from beyond the pale.'

'The ruinous powers...' muttered Soalm.

'It is not magick,' Tariel insisted. 'Call it what it is. Science, but the darkest science. Like Iota herself, a creation of intellects unfettered by morals or boundaries.'

'What are you saying, that this witchling Spear is like her?' Koyne's eyes narrowed. 'The girl was something bred in a laboratory, deliberately tainted by the touch of the warp.'

'I know what it... what *he* is,' said Tariel, yanking out the cables from the gauntlet and dousing the hologram's deathly images. 'I have heard the name of this creature.'

'Explain,' demanded Kell.

'This must never be repeated.' The infocyte sighed. 'The Vanus watch all. Our stacks are filled with information on all the clades. It is how we maintain our position.'

Koyne nodded. 'You blackmail everyone.'

'Indeed. We know that the Culexus seek to improve upon their psychic abilities through experimentation. They gather subjects from the care of the Silent Sisterhood. Those they do not induct into their ranks, they spirit away for... other reasons.'

'This Spear was one of ours?' Koyne was incredulous.

'It is possible,' Tariel went on. 'There was a project... it was declared null by Sire Culexus himself... they called it the Black Pariah. A living weapon capable of turning a target's psionic force back upon it, without the aid of an animus device. The ultimate counter-psyker.'

'What became of it?' said Kell.

'That data is not available. The starship the Culexus used as their base of operations was to be piloted into a sun. So the orders said. I know this because my mentor was tasked with gathering this intelligence.'

'And this Spear is the Black Pariah?' Kell frowned. 'Not dead, but in service to the Warmaster.' He shook his head. 'What have we been thrown into?'

'But why is it here, on Dagonet?' insisted Koyne. 'To destroy Iota? To disrupt our plan against Horus?'

Soalm gave a shuddering breath. 'Iota was just in the way. Like all the pilgrims and the refugees. Collateral damage. Spear wanted the book. *The blood.*'

'What are you talking about?' Kell took her arm and pulled her around. 'Jenniker, what do you mean?'

She told them; and as he understood, Tariel went weak and slumped against the side of the hull, shaking his head. His mouth silently formed the words *no, no, no,* over and over again.


KOYNE SNORTED. 'THE Emperor's blood? That cannot be! This is madness... Horus's assassin tears a page from some ancient tome and with that he can strike at the most powerful human being who ever lived? The very idea is ridiculous!'

'He has what he wants now,' Soalm went on. 'Synchrony with the God-Emperor's gene-marker. Spear is like a primed bomb, ready to detonate.' She blinked back tears. 'We have to stop him before he leaves the planet!'

'You saw what Spear did to Iota,' Kell looked towards the Callidus. 'If this thing is a mirror for psychic might, can you imagine what would happen if he got through to Terra? If he came close enough to turn that power on the Emperor?'

'A cataclysm...' husked Tariel. 'The same thing that happened to Iota, but multiplied a million times over. A collision of the most lethal psychic forces conceivable.' The infocyte swallowed hard. 'Throne's sake... He might even... *kill him*.'

Koyne gave a sarcastic snort. 'The Emperor of Mankind wounded by something so fantastic, so ephemeral? I can't believe it is possible. Spear will be swatted away like an insect. This woman's reason cannot be trusted! Her kind are governed by archaic spiritual fanaticism, not facts!'

'The God-Emperor alone guides me...' she insisted.

The Callidus stabbed a finger at the poisoner. 'You see? She admits it! She's part of a cult forbidden by the Council of Terra!' Before anyone else could respond, the shade went on. 'We have a mission *here*! A target! Horus may have sent this Captain Sedirae to his death by design, or we may have tipped our hands by moving too soon, but it does not matter! The end result remains the same. Our mission is not yet ended.'

'He will come down to Dagonet,' said Tariel. 'The Warmaster has no choice now. The punishment of this world must be seen to come from his hand.'

'Exactly,' insisted Koyne. 'We have another chance to kill him. The only chance. A moment like this will never come again.'

Soalm painfully pushed herself to her feet. 'You understand nothing about me, shapechanger, or what I believe!' she snarled. 'His divinity is absolute, and you delude yourself by your denial of it. Only He can save humanity from the darkness that gathers around us. We cannot fail Him!' She lurched and fell against Kell, who caught her before she could stumble to the deck. '*I* cannot fail Him... Not again.'

Tariel spoke up. 'If Soalm is right, if this is the Black Pariah and he has ingested a measure of Imperial blood… Spear will seek to flee this world and make space to Terra as quickly as possible. And if he has a ship that can get him to the warp, or worse, if Horus's fleet is waiting for the assassin to come to them, there will be no way to stop him. Spear must be killed before he leaves Dagonet.'

'Or we can trust in the Emperor and follow our orders,' Koyne broke in. 'You think him divine, Soalm? I may not agree, but I do believe he is strong enough to shrug off any attack. I believe that he will see this Spear coming and strike him from the sky.' The Callidus's boy-face twisted. 'But Horus? The Warmaster is a serpent, rising for just one moment from his hiding place. We kill him here on this world and we end the threat he represents forever.'

'Will it be that simple?' Soalm snapped back. 'A city full of people is being put to the sword out there because we killed a single Astartes. Do you think if the Warmaster dies, every rebel will fall to his knees and be crippled by grief? It will be anarchy! Destruction and chaos!'

'I am mission commander,' Kell's voice cut through the air. 'I have authority here.' He glared at Soalm. 'I will not be disobeyed again. The decision is mine alone.'

'We can't kill them both,' said Tariel.

'Get us airborne,' said the Vindicare, reaching for his rifle.

There was a ragged group of men on the perimeter wall of the star-port, some of them soldiers, some of them not, all with looted firearms and the aura of hot fear about them. They saw the jetbike hurtling in from across the desert and they fired on it without hesitation. Everything had been trying to kill them since the shock of the dawn broke, and they did not wait to find out if this vehicle was friend or foe. Insanity and terror ruled Dagonet now, as men turned on men in their panic to flee the doomed city.

The stubby aerodyne had a single, medium-wattage lascannon mounted along the line of the fuselage, and Spear aimed it with twists of the jetbike's steering handles, lashing along the battlement of the wall with lances of yellow fire. Bodies exploded in blasts of superheated blood-steam as shots meant to knock down aircraft eradicated men with each hit. Those who didn't die in the initial volley were killed as they ran when Spear came around in a tight loop to strafe them off the line of the wall.

Threads of sinew and knots of transformed tissue flared out behind the killer's head in a fan. Fronds from the daemonskin fluttered, sucking the mist of blood from the air as the bike passed over the wall and skimmed the runway towards the parked shuttle.

The Eurotas ship was untouched, although Spear noted two corpses off by the prow. The autonomic guns in the shuttle's chin barbette had locked onto the pair of opportunists, who had clearly thought they could claim the craft to escape. The little turret turned to track the jetbike as Spear came in but it did not fire; the sensors saw nothing when they looked at him, only a jumble of conflicting readings the primitive machine-brain could not decipher.

He abandoned the flyer and sprinted towards the shuttle. Spear was electric; his every neuron sang with bubbling power and giddy anticipation. The tiny droplet of blood he had consumed was like the sweetest nectar. It bubbled through his consciousness like potent, heady wine; he had a flash of Yosef Sabrat's memory, a sense-taste of drinking an elderly vintage with Daig Segan, savouring the perfection of it. This was a far greater experience. He had dared to sip from the cup of a being more powerful than any other, and even that slightest of tastes made him feel like the king of all creation. If this were an echo of it, he thought, what glory the Emperor must feel to simply *be*.

Spear released a deep, booming laugh to the clouded skies. He was a loaded gun, now. Infinitely lethal. Ready to commit the greatest murder in history.

He just needed to be *close*...

Under the starboard wing, he glimpsed a small drum-shaped vehicle on fat tyres; it was a mechanised fuel bowser, governed by simple automata. The device was one of many such systems in the star-port, machines that could do the jobs of men by loading, unloading or servicing the ships that passed through the facility; but like so many things on Dagonet, in the disorder that had engulfed the planet no one had thought to stand down the robots, and so they went on at their programmed tasks, ignorant of the fact that buildings had collapsed around them, unaware that their human masters were most likely dead in the rubble.

The automaton had dutifully done its job, and refuelled the shuttle with fresh promethium. Spear hesitated on the cockpit ladder and his ebullient mood wavered.

Overhead, red light and thunder rolled in across the runway from the burning city, and Spear's fanged

mouth twisted in something like a scowl. In truth, he
had not expected the Sons of Horus to be so close
behind him to Dagonet. He had hoped he might have
a day, perhaps two – but the tides of the warp were
capricious. He wondered if some intelligence had
been at work to bring all these players to the same
place at the same time. To what end, though?

Spear shook the thought away. He was so set on
leaving this place behind he had not stopped to think
that his means of escape might no longer be in place.
It was likely that if the Warmaster's fleet was here, then
the cutter *Yelene* was either in their possession or
smashed to fragments.

'I must get to Terra…' He said the words aloud, the
need burning in him; and then he sensed a distant
taint upon his perception. A powerful, sinister presence. Unbidden, Spear looked up again, into the
storm.

*Yes*. The master was up there, looking down on
Dagonet, searching for him. The killer could see the
dark, piercing gaze of Erebus in the patterns of the
clouds. The master was waiting for him. Watching to
see what he would do next, like a patient teacher with
a prized student.

Spear dropped off the ladder and moved back to the
front of the shuttle. It was all falling into place. With
the blood taken, he needed only to ride to his target
and perform his kill. Erebus was here to help him; the
master would give him the ship he needed. It would
be his final act as a mentor.

The killer took one of the bodies on the runway and
dragged it into the lee of the wing, under cover from the
thick gobbets of black rain that were falling. Spear

remembered the rituals of communication that Erebus had seared into his memory. It would only take a moment to arrange. He dipped his fingers into a deep wound on the man's torso and cupped a handful of thickening blood; then, quickly, Spear used it to draw glyphs of statement on the cracked ferrocrete surface. He made the circles and crosses, building the shape of an eightfold star line by line. Once complete, it would be visible to Erebus like a flare on a moonless night. The master would see it and know. He would understand.

The wind changed direction for an instant, blowing the smell of the corpse and the tang of promethium across the sensing pits in Spear's fanged maw; and, too, it brought him the skirl of humming turbines.

His head snapped up, catching sight of a white-and-green shape dropping down through the mist. Something flashed in the open hatch and Spear jerked away on reflex.

A bullet creased the surface of his daemonflesh face like a razor blade, opening a ragged gouge that spat out a fan of ebon fluid; the tainted blood spattered over the half-drawn glyphs, ruining the pattern. Spear stumbled. A fraction of a second slower and the bullet would have struck him between the fathomless black pits of his eyes.

Tightening the muscles in his arms, Spear put up his palms with a snap of the wrist, and the daemonflesh grew new orifices. Long spars of sharp bone clattered into the air in a puff of pinkish discharge.

'WATCH OUT!' TARIEL called, stabbing at controls to throw the flyer into a half-roll that showed the belly of the aircraft to their target.

Kell staggered, losing his balance for a second as he clung on to his rifle. Koyne, surprisingly strong for wearing a body that seemed insubstantial, grabbed him and held him up. Nearby, Soalm hung on for dear life, shivering in the cold draught billowing through the open hatch.

Bone shards peppered the hull of the flyer and punched through the metal fuselage. Kell flinched as several impacted his chest and buried themselves in the armour there. Koyne cried out and as the aircraft righted itself, the Callidus fell backwards, a circle of bright crimson blossoming through the material across the shade's thigh.

Kell swept a hand over his chest, flicking the shards away. As they fell to the deck they denatured, becoming soft and pliant. To the Vindicare's disgust, the shards began to writhe like blind worms. He stamped them into patches of white pus and brought the Exitus up to his shoulder. 'Tariel! Bring us around!'

The flyer had come in upwind, their approach masked by the clouds and the thunder from the shelling of the capital. Now they were circling the parked shuttle, the livery of the Eurotas Consortium clear as day across the hull. What Kell saw through his targeting scope was disturbing; he had faced humans of every stripe, mutant creatures, even xenos. Spear was unlike any of them. Even from this distance, it exuded a tainted menace that sickened him to look at.

'It's making for the cockpit,' Tariel called out. '*Kell!*'

The marksman saw the blur of the assassin-creature as it ran; the thing hazed the air around it like waves of heat rising from a searing desert, making it hard to draw a bead. His finger tensed on the trigger. There was a high-velocity Splinter round in the chamber – on impact with an organic target it would fracture into millions of tiny hair-like fragments, each a charged piece of molly-wire. The wires would expand in a sphere and rip through flesh and bone like a tornado of blades.

It would do this, if he hit his target. But Kell had missed with the first shot. Even from a moving platform, through rain, against a partly-occluded target, he should have found the mark.

The Vindicare made a snap decision and worked the slide of the rifle, ejecting the unspent Splinter bullet, in one swift motion thumbing a red-tipped round from a pocket on his arm into the open chamber.

'What are you waiting for?' Koyne shouted. 'Kill it!'

The breech of the Exitus closed on the Ignis bullet and Kell swung the longrifle away from the target. He ignored Koyne's cries and his scope filled with the shape of the fuel bowser.

The incendiary compound in his next shot hit the main promethium tank and combusted. A fist of orange fire flipped the shuttle over and engulfed it in flames. Shockwaves of damp air struck the flyer and the aircraft was forced down hard, the impact of the landing snapping off the undercarriage.

Kell got up as bits of hull metal clattered out of the sky, bouncing off the runway. For a moment, all he saw was the jumping, twisting shapes of the flames; but then something red and smoking tore itself out of the wreckage and began to run for the star-port terminal building.

The Vindicare snarled and raised the rifle, but the weight of the gun told him the magazine was empty. He swore, slamming a new clip into place, knowing as he did that it would not matter. When he peered back through the scope, Spear had vanished. 'He's gone for cover,' he began, turning. 'We need to–'

'Eristede?' His sister's voice stopped him dead. She lay on the deck, and her face was waxy and dull. There was blood on her lips, and when she moved her hands he saw a jagged length of bone protruding from her chest.

He let the rifle fall and ran to her, dropping into a crouch. Old emotions, strong and long-buried, erupted inside him. 'Jenniker, no…'

'Did you kill it?'

He felt the colour drain from him. 'Not yet.'

'You must. But not out of fury, do you understand?'

The cold, familiar rage that had always sustained him welled up in Kell's thoughts. It was the same burning, icy power that had spurred him on ever since that day in the schola, since the moment the woman in the Vindicare robes had told him they knew the name of the man who had killed his parents. It was his undying fuel, the bottomless wellspring of dark emotion that made him such a superlative killer.

His sister's fingertips touched his cheek. 'No,' she said, her eyes brimming with tears. 'Please don't show me that face again. Not the revenge. There is no end to that, Eristede. It goes on and on and on and it will consume you. There will be nothing left.'

Kell felt hollow inside, an empty vessel. 'There's nothing now,' he said. 'You took it all when you broke away. The last connection I had.' He looked down at his hands. 'This is all I have left.'

Jenniker shook her head. 'You're wrong. And so was I. I let you go that night. I should have made you stay. We could have lived another life. Instead we doomed ourselves.'

She was fading now, and he could see it. A surge of raw panic washed over him. His sister was going to die and there was nothing he could do to stop it.

'Listen to me,' she said. 'He is watching. The God-Emperor waits for me.'

'I don't—'

'Hush.' She put a finger on his lips, trembling with her agony. 'One day.' Jenniker pressed something into his palm and closed his fingers over it. 'Save His life, Eristede. He will draw me to His right hand, to be with mother and father. I'll wait for you there. We will wait for you.'

'Jenniker...' He tried to find the right words to say to her. To ask her to forgive him. To understand; but her eyes were all the answer he needed. He saw such certainty there, such absence of doubt.

With difficulty she pulled a slim toxin corde from her pocket. 'Do this, my brother,' she told him, her pain rising. 'But not for revenge. For the God-Emperor.'

Before he could stop her, she touched the tip of the needle-like weapon to her palm and pierced the flesh. Kell cried out as her eyes fluttered closed, and she became slack in his hands.

The rains drummed on the canopy and the flames hissed; then he became aware of a presence at his side. Koyne stood there, holding his longrifle. 'Vindicare,' said the shade. 'What are your orders?'

Kell opened his fingers and saw a gold aquila there, stained with dots of red.

'In the Emperor's name,' he said, rising to his feet and taking the weapon, 'follow me.'

# SEVENTEEN

**Confrontation**
**Duel**
**Termination**

KELL LOOKED UP as Koyne emerged from the hangar where the *Ultio* was hidden and his expression stiffened. The boyish face, the pretence at the shape of a human aspect, these were all gone now. Instead, the Callidus had stripped down to what existed in the core of the shade's persona. An androgynous figure in the matt black overall of a stealthsuit similar to that worn by Kell and Tariel, but with a hood that clung to every contour of the other assassin's face. The only expression, if it could be said to be such a thing, was from the emerald ovals that were the eyes of the mask. Cold focus glittered there, and little else. Kell was reminded of an artist's wooden manikin, something without emotion or animation from within.

Koyne's head cocked. 'There's still time to reconsider this.' The voice, like the figure, was neutral and colourless. Without someone else's face to speak from, the Callidus seemed to lose all effect.

He ignored the statement, rechecking the fresh clips of ammunition he had taken from the ship for the paired Exitus longrifle and pistol. 'Remember the plan,' said the Vindicare. 'We've all seen what it can do. There's just the three of us now.'

'You saw it,' Tariel said, in a small voice. 'We all saw it. On the memory coil, and out there... It's not human.'

Koyne gave a reluctant nod. 'And not xenos. Not *alien* in that way.'

'It's a target, that's all that matters,' Kell retorted.

The Callidus scowled. 'When you have been where I have been and seen what I have seen, you come to understand that there are living things out there that go beyond such easy categorisation. Things that defy reason... even sanity. Have you ever peered into the warp, Vindicare? What lives there–'

'This is not the warp!' grated Kell. 'This is the real world! And what lives here, we can end with a bullet!'

'But what if we can't kill the fiend?' said Tariel, a long ballistic coat pulled tight over him. Congregating under the shadows near his boots, Kell saw rodent-like forms sheltering from the rain.

'I wounded it,' said the Vindicare. 'So we *will* kill it.'

Tariel gave a slow nod. Overhead, a crackling roar crossed the sky as something burning crimson-purple passed above them, obscured by the low, dirty clouds. Seconds later, impact tremors made the runway quiver all around them, and the winds brought the long, drawn-out rumble of buildings collapsing. The city was entering its death-throes, and when it was finally smothered, Kell doubted the fury of the Sons of Horus would be sated.

Tariel looked up. 'Vox communications will be sporadic, if they even work at all,' he said. 'The radioactives and ionisation in the atmosphere are blanketing the whole area.'

Kell nodded as he walked away. 'If one of us finds the target, we'll all know quickly enough.'

THE PAIN ACROSS his back was a forest of needles.

Spear ran on, skirting around the rings of broken ferrocrete that had been sections of the control tower, now fallen in a line across the landing pads and maintenance pits. He could feel the daemonskin working against the myriad fragments of metal that were embedded in him, deposited there by the explosion of the shuttle. One by one, the pieces of shrapnel were being expunged from his torso, the living flesh puckering to spit them out in puffs of black blood.

The burn from the blast was torture, and with every footfall jags of sharp agony raced up Spear's changed limbs and tightened around his chest. When the fuel bowser had detonated, the concussion had caught him first and thrown him clear. The shuttle took the brunt of the explosion, and it was lost to him now. He would need to find another way off Dagonet. Another way to signal the master.

He slowed, clambering over a pile of rubble sloughed from the front of the terminal building, dragging himself up on spars of twisted rebar over drifts of shattered blue glass.

At the apex he dared to pause and throw a glance back through the filthy downpour. The shuttle wreckage was still burning, bright orange flames shimmering where the wet runway reflected them like a dark mirror. Spear's segmented jaws parted in a low growl. He had allowed himself to become distracted; he was so enraptured by his own success at taking the Warrant he had not stopped to consider the meaning of the witch-girl's company with the cultists of the Theoge.

Her appearance there had not been happenstance. At first he thought she was merely some defender, a palace guard put in place as a last line of defence by Eurotas's fanatic cohorts; now it was becoming clearer. He was facing assassins, killers of his own stripe with their own weapons of murder.

He considered what their presence meant, and then discarded the concern. If his purpose on Dagonet had been known, if the forces of the arrogant Emperor had really, truly understood the threat Spear posed to their precious liege lord, this world would have been melted into radioactive glass the moment he set foot on it.

Spear chuckled. Perhaps they expected him to feel fear at his pursuit, but he did not. If anything, he became more certain of his own victory. The only thing that could have faced him on his own terms was the witch-girl, and he had boiled her in the crucible of her own powers. He had little fear of gun or blade after that.

The killer dropped through the yawning space of a tall broken window and landed in a cat-fall on the tiled floor of the terminal. Dust and death hung in the air. Sweeping his gaze around, he saw the remnants of a massive display screen where it had been blown from its mounts by the concussion of an impact several miles away. Across the debris-strewn floor there were a handful of corpses, ragged and gory where carrion-fowl had come to prey on them. The jackal birds glared at Spear from the gloomy corners of the chamber, sitting in their roosts and sniffing at the air. They smelled his blood and they were afraid of its stench.

The daemonskin rippled over him and Spear let out a gasp. It could sense the others coming, it could feel the proximity of bloodletting, of new murder.

He sprinted away into the shadows to prepare; he would not deny the needs of his flesh.

TARIEL EXPECTED TO feel a crippling terror when the others vanished into the shadows of the building, but he did not. He was never really alone, not if he were to be honest with himself. The infocyte found the makings of a good hide in a blown-out administra-tum room on the mezzanine level of the main terminal, a processing chamber where new arrivals to Dagonet would have been brought for interview by planetary officials before being given formal entry. The eyerats scrambled around him, sniffing at the cor-ners and patrolling the places where there were holes in the walls or missing doorways; his two remaining psyber eagles were watching the main spaces of the atrium and occasionally snapping at the native car-rion scavengers when they became too curious.

In a corner formed by two fallen walls, Tariel dropped into a lotus settle and used the cogitator gauntlet to bring up a schematic of the building. It was among the millions of coils worth of files he had copied from the stacks of the Dagonet governmental librariums over the past few weeks, the data siphoned into his personal mnemonic stores. It was habitual of him to do such a thing; if he saw information untended, he took it for himself. It wasn't theft, for nothing was stolen; but on some level Tariel regarded data left unsecured – or at least data that had not been secured well – as fundamentally belonging to him. If it was there, he had to have it. And it always had its uses, as this moment proved.

Working quickly, he allowed the new scans filtering in from the rats and the eagles to update the maps, blocking out the zones where civil war, rebel attack and careless Astartes bombardments had damaged the building. But the data took too many picoseconds to update; the vox interference was strong enough to be causing problems with his data bursts as well. If matters became worse, he might be forced to resort to deploying actual physical connections.

And there was more disappointment to come. The swarm of netflys he had released on entering the building were reporting in sporadically. The infrastructure of the star-port was so badly damaged that all its internal scrying systems and vid-picters were inert. Tariel would be forced to rely on secondary sensing.

He held his breath, listening to the susurrus of the contaminated rainfall on the broken glass skylights overhead, and the spatter of the runoff on the broken stonework; and then, very distinctly, Tariel heard the sound of a piece of rubble falling, disturbed by a misplaced footstep.

Immediately, a datum-feed from one of the eyerats out in the corridor ceased and the other rodents scrambled for cover, their adrenaline reads peaking.

The infocyte was on his feet before he could stop himself. The lost rat had reported its position as only a few hundred metres from where he now stood.

*I will make sure that nothing ever gets close enough to kill me.* Tariel's skin went clammy as his words to Kell returned to him, damning the Vanus with his foolish arrogance. He moved as quickly as he dared, abandoning his makeshift hide and ducking out through a rent in the fallen wall. He heard the psyber eagles take wing above as he moved.

Tariel flinched as he passed through a stream of stale-smelling water dripping down from above, dropping from ledge to ledge until he was in the atrium. He glanced around quickly; the chamber was modelled on a courtyard design. There were galleries and balconies, some ornamental, some not. Through the eyes of one of the birds, he saw a spot that had strong walls to the back and three distinct lines of approach and escape. Pulling his coat tighter, he moved towards it in the shadows, quick and swift, as he had been taught.

As he ran he tabbed the start-up sequence for the pulse generator and sent dozens of test signals to his implanted vox bead; only static answered him. Now, for the first time, he felt alone, even as the feeds from the implanted micropicters in the skulls of his animals followed him in his run. The tiny images clustered around his forearm, hovering in the hololithic miasma.

He was almost across the span of the courtyard when Spear fell silently out of the dimness above him and landed in a crouch on top of an overturned stone bench. The face of red flesh, silver fangs and black eyes looked up and found him.

Tariel was so shocked he jumped back a step, every muscle in his body shaking with surprise.

'What is this?' muttered the killer. Those blank, sightless eyes cut into him. The voice was almost human, though, and it had a quizzical edge, as if the monstrosity didn't know what to make of the trembling, thin man in front of him.

And now the fear came, heavy and leaden, threatening to drag Tariel down; and with it there was an understanding that lanced through the infocyte like a bullet. He had fatally exposed himself, not through the deception of a superior enemy, but because he had made a beginner's mistake. The falling stone, the lost signal – those had been nothing. Happenstance. Coincidence. But the infocyte had still run. He had committed the cardinal sin that no Vanus could ever be absolved of; he had misinterpreted the data.

Why? Because he had allowed himself to think that he could do this. The past days spent in the company of the Vindicare, the Callidus and Culexus, the Eversor and Venenum, they had convinced him that he could operate in the field as well as he had from his clade's secret sanctums. But all Fon Tariel had done was to delude himself. He was the most intelligent person in the Execution Force, so why had he been so monumentally foolish? Tariel's mind railed at him. What could have possibly made him think he was ready for a mission like this? How could his mentors and directors have abandoned him to this fate, spent his precious skills so cheaply?

He had revealed himself. Shown his weakness before the battle had begun. Spear made a noise in its throat – a growl, perhaps – and took a step forward.

The eyerats leapt from the rubble all around the red-skinned freak, claws and fangs bared, and from above in a flutter of metal-trimmed wings, the two psyber eagles dived on the killer with talons out. The slave-animals had picked up on the fear signals bleeding down Tariel's mechadendrites and reacted in kind.

Spear's arms went up to bat away the prey birds and he stamped one of the rodents to death with a clawed foot. The other rats clawed their way up the killer's obscene, fleshy torso; another of them was devoured as a mouth opened in Spear's stomach and bit it in half. The last was crushed in a balled fist.

The psyber eagles lasted a little longer, spinning about the killer's horned head, fluttering and slashing with claws and titanium-reinforced beaks. They scored several bloody scratches, but could not escape the fronds of sinewy matter that issued out of Spear's hands to entrap and strangle them.

Curiosity gave way to anger as the killer dashed the corpses of the birds to the ground; but for his part, Tariel had used the distraction well.

Dragging it from an inner pocket, the infocyte threw a stubby cylinder at Spear and hurled himself away in the opposite direction, falling clumsily over a collapsed table. Lightning fast, the freakish murderer snatched up the object; a grenade. When they had paused to rearm at the *Ultio*, Tariel had returned to the case of munitions he had presented to Iota during their voyage to Dagonet.

Spear sniffed at the thing and recoiled with a sputtering gasp. It was thick with the stench of dying stars. He hurled it away in disgust; but not quickly enough.

The device exploded with a flat bang of concussion and suddenly the courtyard was filled with a shimmering silver mist of metal snow.

The killer stumbled to his knees and began to scream.

His psyche was being flensed; the layers of his conscious mind were peeling away under an impossibly sharp blade, bleeding out raw-red thought. The agony was a twin to the pain the master had inflicted on Spear all those times he had dared to disobey, to question, to fail.

It was the particles in the air; they were hurting him in ways that the killer thought impossible, frequencies of psionic radiation blasting from every single damned speck of the glittering powder, bathing him in razors. Spear's mouthparts gaped open and the sound he released from his chest was a gurgling cry of pain. His nerves were alight with phantom fires unseen to the naked eye. In the invisible realms of the immaterium, the shockwave was sawing at the myriad of threads connecting the killer to his etheric shadow. The daemonskin was battering itself bloody, tearing at his subsumed true-flesh as it tried to rip away and flee into the void.

Spear collapsed, shuddering, and mercifully the effect began to lessen; but slowly, far too slowly. He saw the human, the pasty wastrel that had come stumbling into his kill zone. The gangly figure peered out from behind his cover.

Spear wanted to eat him raw. The killer was filled with the need to strike back at the one who had hurt him. He wanted to tear and tear and tear until there was nothing left of this fool but rags of meat–

*no*

The word came like the tolling of a distant bell, drifting across the churning surface of Spear's pain-laced thoughts. Quiet at first, then with each moment, louder and closer, more insistent than before.

*no no No No NO NO NO*

'Get out!' Spear screamed the words as loud as he could, the amalgam of his once-human flesh thrashing turbulently against the embedded sheath of the dae-monskin symbiont that cloaked him. Skin and skin flexed, tearing and shredding. Black fluids bubbled from new, self-inflicted wounds, staining the broken stonework. He swung his head down and battered it against the rubble, hearing bone snap wetly. Real, physical agony was like a tonic after the impossible, enveloping pain from the cloud-weapon. It shook the grip of the ghost-voices before they could form.

*NO NO NO*

'NNNNNnnnnnoooo!' Spear bellowed, so wracked with his suffering he could do nothing but ride it out to the bitter end.

The pale-skinned man was coming closer. He had what could have been a weapon.

TARIEL OPENED HIS hand and the emitter cone for the pulse generator grew out of the gauntlet's palm, tiny blue sparks clustering around the nib of the device. He was shaking, and the infocyte grabbed his wrist with his other hand to hold it steady, trying to aim at the writhing, horrible mass that lay on the stones, scream-ing and bleeding.

The psy-disruptor grenades had only been an experiment. He hadn't really expected them to work;

at best, Tariel thought he might be able to flee under the cover of the discharge, that it might blind Horus's monstrous assassin long enough for him to escape.

Instead, the thing was howling like a soul being dragged into the abyss. It tore at itself in anguish, ripping out divots of its own flesh. Tariel hesitated, grotesquely fascinated by it; he could not look away from the twitching spectacle.

Faces grew out of the creature's torso and abdomen. The quivering red skin bowed outwards and became the distinct shape of a male aspect, repeated over and over. It was silently mouthing something to him, but the words were corrupted and blurred. The expression was clear, however. The faces were begging him, imploring him.

The fizzing wash of static issuing from his vox broke for a moment and Tariel heard Koyne's flat, emotionless drone in his ear. 'Do not engage it, Vanus,' said the static-riddled voice. 'We're coming to you–'

Then the signal was swallowed up again by interference as somewhere off in the distant city, a new slew of warheads were detonated.

The killer's spasms of pain were calming, and Tariel came as close as he dared. He hesitated, the question spinning in his thoughts, the pulse generator humming and ready. Attack or flee? Flee or attack?

The faces faded, melting back into the crimson-hued flesh, and suddenly those black, abyssal eyes were staring into him, clear as nightfall.

Tariel triggered the blast of focussed electromagnetic force, but it was too late. Spear moved at the speed of hate, diving into him with his hands aimed forwards in a fan of unfolding claws, knocking his arms away. Wicked talons punctured the Vanus's torso and tore through dermal flex-armour and meat, down into bone and organs; then the hands split apart and ripped Tariel's ribcage open, emptying him on to the wet stones.

THE SLAUGHTERHOUSE STINK of Fon Tariel's bloody demise reached Koyne as the shade bolted from the broken-ended skywalk spanning the main terminal atrium. The Callidus skidded to a halt and spat in annoyance as what was left of the infocyte was shrugged off his killer's claws and pooled at the feet of the red-fleshed thing.

Koyne saw the shoals of mouths emerging all over the surface of the monstrosity, as they licked and lapped at the steaming remains of the Vanus. A furious surge of censure ran through the assassin's mind; Tariel had been a poor choice for this mission from the start. If Koyne had been given command of the operation, as would have been the more sensible choice, then the Callidus would have made sure the Vanus never left the *Ultio*. Tariel's kind were simply incapable of the instincts needed to operate in the field. There was a reason the Officio Assassinorum kept them at their scrying stations, and now this wasteful death had proven it. This was all the Vindicare's fault; the entire mission was breaking apart, collapsing all around them.

But it was too late to abort now. The killer, the Spear-creature, was looking up, sensing the Callidus's presence – and now Koyne's options had fallen to one.

With a flexion of the wrist, the haft of a memory sword fell into Koyne's right hand and the Callidus leapt from the suspended walkway; in the left the shade had the neural shredder, and the assassin pulled the trigger, sending an expanding wave of exotic energy cascading towards Spear.

The red-skinned freak skirted the luminal edge of the neural blast and dodged backwards, performing balletic flips that sent Spear spinning through pools of dark shadow and shafts of grey, watery sunlight.

Koyne pivoted to touch down on altered legs, shifting the muscle mass to better absorb the shock of the landing. The koans of the change-teachers learned in the dojos of the clade came easily to mind, and the Callidus used strength of will to forcibly alter the secretions of polymorphine from a series of implanted drug glands. The chemical let bone and flesh flow like tallow, and Koyne was a master at manipulating it from moment to moment. The assassin allowed the compound to thicken muscle bunches and bone density, and then attacked.

Spear grew great cleavers made of tooth-like enamel from orifices along the bottom of his forearms, and these blades whistled as they slashed through the air around Koyne's head. A downward slash from the memory sword briefly opened a gouge on Spear's shoulder, but it was knitting shut again almost as soon as it was cut. Another neural blast went wide. Koyne was too close to deploy the pistol properly, and feinted backwards, resisting the temptation to engage the enemy killer in close combat.

Spear opened his mouth and shouted awls of black cartilage into the air. Glancing hits peppered Koyne's green-eyed hood and the darts denatured, dissolving into tiny crawling spiders that ate into the ballistic cloth with their sharp mandibles. Before they could chew through the emerald lenses to the soft tissues of Koyne's eyes, the Callidus gave a snort of frustration and tore the hood away, discarding it.

The assassin saw a glimpse of a familiar face-that-was-no-face, reflected in a sheet of fallen glass. It was not as blank a canvas as it should have been; Koyne's aspect trembled, moving of its own accord. The Callidus's anger deepened, and so in turn the face became more defined. There was a slight resemblance there that veered towards the scarred visage of the Garantine.

Koyne didn't like the thought of that, and turned away as Spear attacked again. The tooth-blades were continuing to grow, lengthening and becoming brownish-grey along the edges. Before the killer could close the range, Koyne aimed the neural shredder and depressed the trigger pad. Energy throbbed from the focussing crystal in a widening stream that swept over Spear and knocked him backwards.

The Callidus had claimed many victims with the weapon. It was a singular horror in its own way; not content with the cessation of a life, instead the pistol behaved as an intellivore, disintegrating the connections between the neurons of an organic brain, killing only memory and mind with the brutality of a hurricane sweeping through a forest.

On any other target, it might have worked. But this was an amalgam of uncontrolled human mutation, merged with a predatory form from a dimension made of madness. What it had that could be called

mentality was a lattice of instinct and obedience suspended somewhere beyond the reach of anything in
the physical plane.

Spear shrugged off the flickers of energy, folds of
skin and fronds of flesh-matter crisping and peeling
away from its head like a tattered layer of ablative
armour. The grinning, fang-lined mouth underneath
was wet with fluids and pus. The killer's cutting blades
swept in and the barrel of the neural shredder was severed cleanly.

The gun screamed and spat watery orange fluids in
jerking sputters, twitching so hard that it jolted itself
from Koyne's grasp and tumbled away, falling into the
shadows beneath collapsed sheets of flakboard. The
Callidus shrank back, grasping for the twin to the
memory sword already at point and ready.

The killer and the assassin fell into a blade fight, fat
yellow sparks flying as the molecule-thin edges of
Koyne's rapiers cut into the organic swords and broke
off brittle, sharp fragments with every hit. Spear's
blades flawed without blunting, as the Callidus
learned at cost, the wet lines of them cutting deeply
into the stealthsuit. Where blood was drawn, it was
slow to clot. The tooth-matter exuded some kind of
oily venom that kept the wounds from scabbing over.

Spear changed the balance of the combat, powerful
muscles bunching beneath his red flesh, forcing
Koyne back and back towards the fractured walls of
the courtyard.

The animated contours of the Callidus's face altered
as each blow landed or was deflected. A whirlwind of
parries flew from Koyne's arms, but Spear was gaining
ground, pushing the assassin deeper into a defensive

stance with each passing moment. Koyne's inconstant aspect showed a carousel of old faces and new faces, all of them in fury and frustration.

Spear laughed, threads of drool stringing from the split between the halves of his shovel-faced jaw, and in that second Koyne managed a downward slash of both blades. Spear barely parried the move – it was overly aggressive and unexpected, and the tips of the memory swords carved a cross over the killer's scalp that penetrated to the blackened bone. Wire-thin worms poured from the wound, exposing a milky eye beneath the injury that wept ichor. Spear's laugh turned to a howl of agony.

There was something fundamentally *wrong* with this creature. The assassin was not touched by witch-mark like Iota and her Culexus kindred, but still Koyne could sense on a marrow-deep level that Spear was not meant to exist in this world. The creature, whatever amorphous amalgamation of warp-spawn and human it was, flaunted reason by the mere fact of its existence. It was a splinter in the skin of the universe.

Koyne did the trick with the koans once again, marshalling the density of bone and lining of musculature for a leap into the air that defied human potential. The Callidus jumped upwards and pivoted in midflight, falling out of Spear's line of sight over a buckled wall.

The killer came rushing over the hillock of rubble and followed his foe into the atrium proper. The wide, high chamber ran almost the entire length of the terminal, the litter of the dead and the wreckage of the port building lying ankle deep and swimming in stagnant falls of rainwater.

Koyne was rising back into a fighting stance, slower than the Callidus would have liked, but the stress of muscle reformation on the run took its toll. All the no-mind focussing mantras in the pages of the clade's *Liber Subditus* were worth nothing against a blade in the hand of an enemy like this one.

When Spear spoke, Koyne knew that the moment was near. The fury in the killer's hissing, sibilant voice was the sound of a serpent uncoiling, hood fanning open before the bite. 'I murder and murder, and there is no end to you,' he spat. 'You are not challenges to me, you are only steps on the road. Markers for my path.'

'What monstrosity gave birth to you?' Koyne asked the question, thinking aloud, the changing face shifting anew. 'You're just a collision of freakish chance, an animal. A weapon.'

'Like you?' Spear's mucus-slicked blades flicked back and forth, gleaming dully. 'Like the wretch back there and the dark-skinned one I killed with my mind? But what have you done of worth, faceless?' He threw an inelegant, bored attack at Koyne that the Callidus avoided, splashing back through a puddle into the shadows. 'Nothing you have murdered has any weight. But what I destroy will tip the balance of a galaxy.'

'You'll be stopped!' Koyne shouted the words with sudden, vicious energy, boiling up from a place of naked hatred.

'You will never know.' Spear gave a flick of his hand and shot a fan of bone shards at the assassin. Instead of dodging, Koyne rocked forwards, into the path of the darts, and parried them away with a web of mnemonic steel. Blades flashing, the Callidus pushed into the attack, aiming for the single vulnerable point in the killer's stance.

Spear had left just such an opening to entice the shade, and seized the moment with vicious delight. New blades of fang-like matter burst from the surface of his churning skin and caught Koyne's twinned strike, blocking the blow even as it fell.

Koyne's changing face darkened with fright and then agony. Spear crossed his sword-arms like a falling guillotine and both of the Callidus's slender, delicate hands were severed at the wrists.

Fountains of blood jetted across Spear's torso as Koyne fell backwards with the force of the pain-shock, and the killer caught his victim before the assassin could tumble into the sloshing, grimy waters. 'We're alike,' he told the Callidus. 'Beneath the skin. Both the same.'

Koyne was a moment from death, and so Spear reached up and drove needle-sharp nails into the trembling skin of the assassin's face; then with a single, horrific tearing, he ripped the flesh away to show the red meat underneath. Koyne's body bucked with the sheer violence of the act, and Spear gave it a brutal shove.

The Callidus spun away and landed on a fallen spire of masonry, a pinnacle of marble bursting through the stealthsuit fabric. Pinned there, the body bled out and twitched, denied a quick death.

'You see?' Spear asked the question to the rag of skin in his hand. 'The same, in our ways.'

The killer tipped back his head and ate his prize morsel. Now this matter was done with, now the

Emperor's ineffectual foot soldiers had been disposed of, Spear could return to the matter of the signalling. He looked around, searching for a wide, flat space where he might begin again on the drawing of the runes.

*no*

'Be silent,' he hissed.

The daemonskin muttered. Something was touching its surface. A breath of faint energy, a pinprick of ultraviolet light. Spear turned, senses altering to follow–

The bullet entered the killer's head through the hollow black pit of his right eye, the impact transferring such kinetic force it blew Spear off his feet and into a spinning tumble, down into the debris and floodwater. The shot fractured into thousands of tiny, lethal shards that expanded to ricochet around inside the walls of his skull, shredding the meat of his brain into ribbons.

The faceless had given up life in order to draw him into the atrium, into a space under a sniper's gun.

In those fractions of seconds as the blackness engulfed him, there was understanding. There had been another. In his arrogance, he had failed to account for a third attacker; or perhaps it been Sabrat's final victory, clouding his mind at the crucial moment.

The killer was killed.

KELL LOWERED THE longrifle and allowed the cameoline cloak to fall open. The echo of the gunshot, hardly louder than a woman's gasp, still echoed around the rafters of the atrium. Carrion birds roosting nearby flashed into the air on black wings, circling and snarling at each other in their raucous voices.

The Vindicare slung the rifle over his shoulder and felt a tremor in his hands. He looked down at the gloved fingers; they seemed foreign to him, as if they belonged to someone else. They were so steeped in blood; so many lay dead at their touch. The single, tiny pressure of his finger on a trigger plate, such a small amount of expended force – and yet magnified into such great destructive power.

He willed himself to stay away from that secret place in his heart, the stygian well of remorse and wrath that had claimed him on the day he killed the murderer of his parents. He willed it, and failed. Instead, Kell succumbed.

It HAD BEEN *his first field kill.*

The man, in transit via aeronef through the valleys of Thaxted Dosas, the dirigible floating beneath the hilltops, skimming the sides of the low peaks. Eristede Kell had made his hide eight days before, in the long grasses. The long grasses like those he and Jenniker played in as children, their games of fetch-find and hunt-the-grue. He waited under the suns and the moons, the former his father's glory, the latter his mother's smile.

And when the 'nef came around the hill, he fired the shot and did not make the kill. Not at first. The cabin window was refracted, disrupting his aim. He should have known, adjusted the sights. A lesson learned.

Instead of cold and steely determination, he unchained his anger. Kell unloaded the full magazine of ammunition into the cabin, killing everything that lived within it. He executed all who saw that moment of error, target and collaterals all. Men and women and children.

*And he had his revenge.*

ONCE MORE, HE was in that place. Life taken to balance life taken from him, from his family – and once more, there was no sweetness in the act. Nothing but bitter, bitter ash and the rage that would not abate.

With an angry flourish, he grabbed the cable rig on his belt and used the fast-fall to drop quickly from his hide to the waterlogged floor below. The cloak billowing out behind him like the wings of the prey birds overhead, he strode towards the body of the Spear-thing, one hand snaking down to the clasp on the holster at his hip. He did not spare Koyne's brutalised corpse more than a second glance; despite every tiny challenge to Kell's authority, in the end the Callidus had obeyed and died in the line of duty. As with Iota, Tariel and the others, he would ensure their clades learned of their sacrifices. There would be new teardrops etched upon the face of the Weeping Queen in the Oubliette of the Fallen.

The monstrous killer lay cruciform, floating on the surface of the floodwater. Rust-coloured billows of blood surrounded the body, a halo of red among the dull shades of the rubble and wreckage.

Kell gave the corpse a clinical glare, barely able to stop himself from drawing a knife and stabbing the crimson flesh in mad anger. The skull, already malformed and inhuman in its proportions, had been burst from within by the lethal concussion of the

Shatter bullet. Cracked skin and bone were visible in lines webbing the face; it looked like a grotesque terracotta mask, broken and then inexpertly mended.

Putting the longrifle aside, he drew the Exitus pistol, sliding his hand over the skull sigil on the breech and cocking the heavy handgun. He would leave no trace of this creature.

Kell's boot disturbed the blood-laced floods and the misted water parted. Motion drew his eye to it; the rusty stain was no longer growing, but shrinking.

The wounds across the body of the killer were drinking it in.

He spun, finger on the trigger.

Spear's leg made an unnatural cracking sound and bent at the wrong angle, hitting Kell in the chest with the force of a hammer blow. The Vindicare stumbled as the red-skinned creature dragged itself out of the water and threw itself at him. Spear no longer moved with the same unnatural stealth and grace he had seen down the sights of the longrifle, but it made up for what it lacked in speed and aggression. Spear battered at him, knocking the pistol from Kell's grip, breaking bones with every impact of his jagged fists.

The skin of the killer moved in ways that made the Vindicare's gut tighten with disgust; it was almost as if Spear's flesh were somehow dragging about the bones and organs within, animating them with wild, freakish energy. Brain matter and thick fluids dribbled from the impact wound in the killer's eye, and it coughed globules of necrotic tissues from its yawning mouth and ragged nostrils. The marksman took another hit as he tried to block a blow, and Kell's shoulder dislocated from its socket, making him bellow in agony.

Stumbling, he fell against the crimson-stained spire where Koyne lay impaled. Spear advanced, with each footfall his body bloating and thickening as it drew in more and more of the blood-laced fluids sloshing about their feet.

There was a face in the bubbling skin of its torso. Then another, and another, biting and chewing at the thin membrane that suffocated them, trying to break free. Spear twitched and halted. It turned its clawed fingers on itself, slashing at the protrusions in its flesh, making scratches that oozed thin liquid.

The faces cried out silently to Kell. *Stop him*, they screamed.

THE DAEMONSKIN HAD saved Spear's life, if this could be considered life. It was so ingrained in the matter of his being that even the obliteration of his cerebellum was not enough to end him. The proxy-flesh of his warp-parasite contained the force of the bullet detonation – or as much as it was capable of, forcing the broken pieces of Spear back together into some semblance of their undamaged form.

But the daemonskin was a primitive creature, unsophisticated. It missed out petty things like control and intellect, holding tight to instinct and animal fury. The killer was self-aware enough to know that he had been murdered and returned from it, but his mind was damaged beyond repair and what barriers of self-control it had once had were in tatters.

Without them, his cages of captured memory broke open.

The formless force of a fragmented persona-imprint came crashing into Spear's wounded psyche with the impact of a falling comet, and he was spun and twisted beneath the force of it.

Suddenly, the killer's thoughts were flooded by an overload of sensation, a bombardment of pieces of emotion, shards of self.

*–Ivak and the other boys with a ball and the hoops–*

*–the smell of matured estufagemi wine was everywhere. The warm, comforting scent seemed cloying and overly strong–*

*–Renia says yes to his earnest offer of a marriage contract, and he basks in her smile–*

*–shiny lumps of organ meat that caught the light, and other things pasty-white and streaked with fluid–*

*–I hate you!–*

*–the shot that kills the Blue Towers Rapist comes from his gun, finally–*

*–I've heard rumours. Stories from people who know people on other worlds, in other systems–*

*–No–*

*–a flicker of guilt–*

*–I've been absent a lot recently–*

This was all that there was of Yosef Sabrat's psyche, an incomplete jigsaw puzzle of a self, driven by the single trait that marbled all the man had been, and all that Spear had destroyed.

He had been waiting. Patient, clever Yosef. Buried deep in the dungeons of Spear's dark soul, struggling not to fade away. Waiting for a moment like this, for the chance to strike at his murderer.

The phantom-taint of the dead lawman wanted justice. It wanted revenge for every victim in the killer's bloody annals.

Every soul of those that Spear had slaughtered and looted, every ghost he had pillaged to assume them,

to corrupt them into his disguises, each had tasted like
a special kind of fear. A fear of loss of self, worse than
death.

Now that fear was in him, as Spear clawed at the
ragged edge of his own mind, dangling over the brink
of a psychic abyss.

And when he spoke, he heard Yosef Sabrat's voice.

'STOP HIM!'

The face was not the thing of fangs and horns and
dark voids any more. It belonged to a man, just a man
in pain and sorrow, peering out at him as if through
the bars of the deepest prison in all creation.

Kell's breath was struck from him by the grief in
those all-too-human eyes. He had seen it enough
times, witnessed at a distance in the moment when
death claimed a life. The sudden, final understanding
in the eyes of a target. The pain and the truth.

He raced forward, ignoring the spirals of hot agony
from the broken, grinding edges of his ribcage, stabbing slim throwing knives from his wrist-guard into
the torso of the Spear-thing.

It cried out and he pushed past it, falling, slipping
on the wet-slick tiles beneath his feet. Kell rolled,
clutching for the fallen pistol, fingers grasping the
grip.

The killer was coming for him, festoons of claws
and talons exploding from every surface on its lurching body, the human face disappearing as it was
swallowed by the fangs and spines. It thundered
across the debris, crashing through the water.

Kell's gun came up and he fired. The weapon
bucked with a scream of torn air and the heavy-calibre

Ignis bullet crossed the short distance between gun-man and target.

The round slammed into the meat of Spear's shoul-der and erupted in a blare of brilliant white fire; the hollow tip of the bullet was filled with a pressurised mixture of phosphoron-thermic compound. On impact, it ignited with a fierce million-degree heat that would burn even in the absence of oxygen.

Spear was shrieking, his body shuddering as if it were trying to rip itself apart. Kell took aim again and fired a second shot, then a third, a fourth. At this range he could not miss. The rounds blew Spear back, the combustion of hot air boiling the water pooled around him into steam. The white flames gathered across the killer's body, eating into the surface of his inhuman flesh.

Kell did not stop. He emptied the Exitus pistol into the target, firing until the slide locked back. He watched his enemy transform from a howling torch into a seething, roiling mass of burned matter. Spear wavered, the screams from its sagging, molten jaws climbing the octaves; and then there was a concussion of unnatural sound that resonated from the creature. Kell saw the ghost of something blood-coloured and ephemeral ripping itself from the killer's dying meat, and heard a monstrous, furious howl. It faded even as he tried to perceive it, and then the smoking remains fell. A sudden wash of sulphur stink wafted over him and he gagged, coughing up blood and thin bile. The ghost-image had fled.

Nursing his pain, Kell watched as Spear's blackened, crumbling skeleton hissed and crackled like fat on a griddle.

To his surprise, he saw something floating on the surface of the murky floodwaters; tiny dots of bright colour, like flecks of gold leaf. They issued out from the corpse of the killer, liberated by Spear's death. When he reached for them they disintegrated, flickering in the wan light and then gone.

'Not for revenge,' he said aloud, 'For the Emperor.'

The Vindicare sat there for a long time, listening to the drumming of the rains and the distant crashes of destruction across the distance to the capital. The explosions and the tremors were coming closer together now, married to the gouts of harsh light falling from the sky above. The city and everything in it was collapsing under the rage of the Sons of Horus; soon they would turn their weapons to the port, to the wastelands, to every place on Dagonet where life still sheltered from their thunder.

The Warmaster's rebels and traitors would not stop on this world, or the next, or the next. They would cut a burning path across space that would only end at Terra.

That could not come to pass. Kell's war – *his mission* – was not over.

Using the Exitus rifle to support his weight, he gathered what he needed and then the Vindicare marksman left the ruins of the terminal behind, beginning a slow walk across the cracked runways under darkening skies.

In the distance, he saw the *Ultio*'s running lights snap on as the ship sensed his approach.

# EIGHTEEN

### I Am The Weapon
### Into The Light
### Nemesis

THE GUNCUTTER CLIMBED the layers of cloud, punching through pockets of turbulent air thrown into the atmosphere by storm cells, the new-born thunderheads spawning in the wake of orbit-fall munitions.

Somewhere behind it, down on Dagonet's surface, the landscape was being dissected as lance fire swept back and forth. The killing rains of energy and ballistic warheads had broken the boundaries of the capital city limits; now they were escaping to spread across the trembling ground, cutting earth like a keen skinning knife crossing soft flesh.

The burning sky cradled the arrow-prowed ship, which spun and turned as it wove a path through the cascades of plasma. No human pilot could have managed such a feat, but the *Ultio*'s helmsman was less a man and more the ship itself. He flew the vessel through the tides of boiling air as a bird would ride a thermal, his hands the stabilators across the bow, his legs the blazing nozzles of the thrusters, fuel-blood pumping through his rumbling engine-heart.

*Ultio*'s lone passenger was strapped into an acceleration couch at the very point of the ship's cramped bridge, watching waves of heat ripple across the invisible bubble of void shields from behind a ring-framed cockpit canopy.

Kell muttered into the mastoid vox pickup affixed to his jawbone, subvocalising his words into the humming reader in the arm of the couch. As the words spilled out of him, he breathed hard and worked on attending to his injuries. The pilot had reconfigured the gravity field in the cockpit to off-set the g-force effects of their headlong flight, but Kell could still feel the pressure upon him. But he was thankful for small mercies – had he not been so protected, the lift-off acceleration from the port would have crushed him into a blackout, perhaps even punctured a lung with one of his cracked ribs.

It remained an effort to speak, though, but he did it because he knew he was duty bound to give his report. Even now, the *Ultio*'s clever subordinate machine-brains were uploading and encoding the contents of the memory spool from Iota's skull-helm, and the pages of overly analytical logs Tariel had kept in his cogitator gauntlet. When they were done, that compiled nugget of dense data would be transmitted via burst-signal to the ship's drive unit, still hiding in orbit, within the wreckage of a dead space station.

But not without his voice to join them, Kell decided. He was mission commander. At the end, the lay of the choices were his responsibility and he would not shirk that.

Finally, he ran out of words and bowed his head. Tapping the controls of the reader, he pressed the playback switch to ensure his final entry had been embedded.

'*My name is Eristede Kell,*' he heard himself saying. '*Assassin-at-Marque of the Clade Vindicare, Epsilon-dan. And I have defied my orders.*'

Nodding, he silenced himself, discarding the mastoid patch. Kell's voice seemed strange and distant to him; it was less a report he had made and more of a confession.

*Confession.* The loaded connotations of that word made him glance down, to where he had secured Jenniker's golden aquila about the wrist of his glove. He searched himself, trying to find a meaning, a definition for the emotion clouding his thoughts. But there was nothing he could grasp.

Kell pressed another switch and sent the vox recording to join the rest of the data packet. Outside, the glowing sky had darkened through blue to purple to black, taking the rush of air with it. *Ultio* was beyond the atmosphere now, and still climbing.

Each breath he took felt tainted and metallic. Thick fluids congested at his throat and he swallowed them back with a grimace. The smell in his nostrils was no one's blood but his own, and while the painkillers he had injected into his neck had gone some way towards keeping him upright, they were wearing thinner by the moment.

An indicator rune on the control console flared green; *Ultio* had been sent a line-of-sight signal from the drive unit. Out there in the wreckage-strewn orbits, the drive module was awakening, stealthily turning power to its

warp engine and sublight drives. In moments, the
astropath and Navigator on board would be roused from
their sense-dep slumber. The *Ultio*'s descent module
needed only to cross the space to the other section of the
ship and dock; then, reunited, the vessel could run for
the void and the escape of the immaterium.

Kell leaned forwards to stare out of the canopy. The
only flaw in that otherwise simple plan was the gathering of warships between the guncutter and the drive
module.

An armada barred his way. Starships the size of a
metropolis crested with great knife-shaped bows,
blocks of hideously beweaponed metal like the heads
of god-hammers, each one detailed in shining steel
and gold. Each with the device of an opened, baleful
eye about them, glaring ready hate into the dark.

At the centre of the fleet, a behemoth. Kell recognised the lines of a uniquely lethal vessel. A
battle-barge of magnificent, gargantuan proportions
haloed by clouds of fighter escorts; the *Vengeful Spirit*,
flagship of the Warmaster Horus Lupercal.

'Pilot,' he said, his voice husky with the pain, 'put us
on an intercept heading with the command ship. Put
all available power to the aura cloak.'

The cyborg helmsman clicked and whirred.
'Increased aura cloak use will result in loss of void
shield potentiality.'

He glared at the visible parts of the pilot's near-
human face, peering from the command podium. 'If
they can't see us, they can't hit us.'

'They will hit us,' it replied flatly. 'Intercept vector
places *Ultio* in high-threat quadrant. Multiple enemy
weapon arcs.'

'Just do as I say!' Kell shouted, and he winced at the jag of pain it caused him. 'And open a link to the Navigator.'

'Complying.' The Vindicare thought he heard a note of grievance in the reply as the guncutter turned, putting its bow on the *Vengeful Spirit*. The sensors were showing the first curious returns from the picket ships in Horus's fleet. They were sweeping the area for a trace, uncertain if their scry-sensors had seen something; but the *Ultio*'s aura cloak was generations ahead of common Naval technology. They would be inside the fleet's inner perimeter before anyone on the picket vessels could properly interpret what they had seen.

Another rune on the console glowed; a vox channel was open between the forward module and the drive section. Kell spoke quickly, fearful that the transmission would undo all the work of the cloak if left active a second too long. 'This is Kell. Stand by to receive encoded burst transmission. Release only on Omnis Octal authority.' He took a shaky breath. 'New orders supersede all prior commands. Protocol Perditus. Expedite immediate. Repeat, go to Protocol Perditus.'

It seemed like long, long seconds before the Navigator's whispering, papery voice returned through the speaker grille. '*This will be difficult,*' it said, '*but the attempt will be made.*' Kell reached for the panel to cut the channel just as the Navigator spoke again. '*Good luck, assassin.*'

The rune went dark, and Kell's hand dropped.

Beyond the canopy, laser fire probed the sky around the ship, and ahead the battle-barge grew to blot out the darkness.

* * *

CLOSE-RANGE LASCANNONS ON the hull of the drive
module blew apart the paper-thin sheath of metals
hiding the aft section of the ship, and the Ultio's drive
section blasted free of the station wreck in a pulse of
detonation. Fusion motors unleashed the tiny suns at
their cores and pushed the craft away, climbing the
acceleration curve in a glitter of void shields and dis-
placed energy. In moments, the vessel was rising
towards one-quarter lightspeed.

Picket ships on the far side of the Warmaster's fleet,
ex-Imperial Navy frigates and destroyers crewed only
by human officers, saw it running and opened fire.
Most of the ships belonging to the Dagoneti had been
obliterated over the past few hours, and the stragglers
had either been forced down to the surface or cut in
two by their beam lances.

Targeting solutions on the odd craft that had suddenly appeared on their holoscopes behaved
unexpectedly, however. Weapon locks drifted off it,
unable to find a true. Scans gave conflicting readings; the ship was monstrously over-powered for
something of its tonnage; it seemed unmanned,
and then it seemed not. And strangest of all, the
glimmer of a building warp signature built up
around its flanks the further it strayed away from
the gravity shadow of the planet, racing for the
jump point.

Warships dropped out of formation and powered
after it, following the unidentified craft up and out of
the plane of the Dagonet system's ecliptic. They would
never catch it.

Alone now on their headless beast of a vessel, the
Ultio's Navigator and astropath communed with one

another in a manner most uncommon for their respective kinds; with words.

And what they shared was an understanding of mutual purpose. *Protocol Perditus*. A coded command string known to them both, to which there was only one response. They were to leave their area of operation on immediate receipt of such an order and follow a pre-set series of warp space translations. They would not stop until they lay under the light of Sol. The mission was over, abandoned.

Weapons fire haloed the space around the ship as it plunged towards the onset of critical momentum, the first vestiges of a warp gate forming in the void ahead.

THE BLOOD CONTINUED to stream from Erebus's nostrils as he shoved his way out of the elevator car and through the cluster of helots waiting on the command deck. The fluid matted his beard and he grimaced, drawing a rough hand across his face. The psychic shock was fading, mercifully, but for a brief while it had felt as if it would cut him open.

There, in his chambers aboard the flagship, meditating in the gloom over his spodomancy and mambila divination, he attempted to find an answer. The eightfold paths were confused, and he could not see their endpoints. Almost from the moment they had arrived in the Dagonet system, Erebus had been certain that something was awry.

His careful plans, the works he had conceived under the guidance of the Great Ones, normally so clear to him, were fouled by a shadow he could not source. It perturbed him, and to a degree undeserving of such emotion. This was only a small eddy in the long scheme, after all. This planet, this action, a minor diversion from the pre-ordained works of the great theatre.

And yet Horus Lupercal was doing such a thing more and more. Oh, he followed where Erebus led, that was certain, but he did it less quickly than he had at first. The Warmaster's head was being turned and he was wilful with it. At times, the Word Bearer allowed himself to wonder; was the master of the rebels listening to other voices than he?

Not to dwell, though. This was to be expected. Horus was a primarch. One could no more hope to shackle one down and command him than a person might saddle an ephemeral animus. The First Chaplain reminded himself of this.

*Horus must be allowed to be Horus,* he told himself. *And when the time is upon him… He will be ready.*

Still; the voyage to Dagonet, the fogging of the lines. That did not disperse. If anything, it grew worse. In his meditations Erebus had searched the egosphere of the planet turning below them, but the screaming and the fear drowned out every subtle tell. All he could divine was a trace of the familiar.

*The pariah-thing.* His Spear. Perhaps no longer on this world, perhaps just the spoor of its passing, but certainly something. For a while he was content to accept this as the truth, but with the passing of the hours Erebus could not leave the matter be. He worried at it, picked at the psy-mark like a fresh scab.

Why had Spear come to Dagonet? What possible reason could there be for the killer to venture off the path Erebus had laid out for him? And, more to the troubling point of it, why had Horus chosen to show the flag here? The Word Bearer believed that coincidence was something that existed only in the minds of men too feeble-brained to see the true spider web of the universe's cruel truth.

It vexed him that the answer was there below on the planet, if only he could reach out for it.

And so he was utterly unprepared for what came next. The rising of the black shriek of a sudden psionic implosion. In the chamber, sensing the edges of it, turning his thoughts to the dark places within and allowing the void to speak to him.

A mistake. The death-energy of his assassin-proxy, hurtling up from the planet's surface, the escaping daemon beast brushing him as it fled back to the safety of the immaterium. It hit him hard, and he was not ready for it.

He felt Spear die, and with him died the weapon-power. The phantom gun at the head of the unknowing Emperor, shattered before it could even be fired.

Erebus's fury drove him from his chambers, through the corridors of the ship. His plan, this thread of the pathway, had been broken, and for Hades's sake he would know why. He would go down to Dagonet and sift the ashes of it through his fingers. *He would know why.*

Composing himself, the Word Bearer entered the Lupercal's Court without waiting to be granted entry, but even as Maloghurst moved to block his path, the Warmaster turned from the great window and beckoned Erebus closer. He became aware of alert sirens hooting and beyond the armourglass, fashioned in the oval of an open eye, he saw rods of laser fire sweeping the void ahead of the flagship's prow.

Horus nodded to him, the hellish light of the weapons discharges casting his hard-edged face like blunt stone. He was, as ever, resplendent in his battle gear. In his haste, Erebus had come to the Court still in his dark robes, and for a moment the Word Bearer felt every bit of his inferiority to the Warmaster, as Horus seemed to loom over him.

None of this he showed, however. He bottled it away, his aspect never changing. Erebus was a prince of lies, and well-practised with it. 'My lord,' he began. 'If it pleases the Warmaster, I have a request to make. A matter to address–'

'On the surface?' Horus looked away. 'We'll visit Dagonet soon enough, my friend. For the work to be done.'

Erebus maintained his outwardly neutral aspect, but within it took an effort to restrain his tension. 'Of course. But perhaps, if I might have leave to venture down before the rites proper, I could… smooth the path, as it were.'

'Soon enough,' Horus repeated, his tone light; but the chaplain knew then that was the end to it.

Maloghurst hobbled closer, bearing a data-slate. He shot the Word Bearer a look as he stepped in front of him. 'Message from the pickets,' he said. 'The other target is too fast. They scored hits but it will make space before they catch it.'

The Warmaster's lips thinned. 'Let it go. What of the other, our ghost?' He gestured at the inferno raging outside.

'Indeterminate,' the equerry sniffed. 'Gun crews on the perimeter ships report phantom signals, multiple echoes. They're carving up dead sky, and finding nothing.' Erebus saw his scarred face's perpetual frown deepening. 'I've drawn back the fighter screen as you ordered, lord.'

Horus nodded. 'If he dares come so close to me, I want to look him in the eyes.'

The Word Bearer followed the Warmaster's gaze out through the windows.

The slate in Maloghurst's gnarled fingers emitted a melodic chime, at odds with the urgency of its new message. 'Sensors read… *something*,' said the equerry. 'Closing fast. A collision course! But weapons can't find it…'

'An aura cloak,' said Erebus, peering into the stormy dark. 'But such a device is beyond the Dagoneti.'

'Yes.' Horus smiled, unconcerned. 'Do you see him?' The Warmaster stepped to the window and pressed his hands to the grey glass.

Out among the maelstrom of energy, as javelins of fire crossed and recrossed one another, scouring the sky for the hidden attacker, for one instant the Chaplain saw something like oil moving over water. Just the suggestion of a raptor-like object lensing the light of the distant stars behind it. 'There!' He pointed.

Maloghurst snapped out a command over his vox. 'Target located. Engage and destroy!'

The gun crews converged their fire. The craft was close, closer than the illusory ghost image had suggested. Unbidden, Erebus backed away a step from the viewing portal.

Horus's smile grew wider and the Word Bearer heard the words he whispered, a faint rumble in the deepest register. 'Kill me,' said the Warmaster, 'if you dare.'

* * *

Ultio burned around him.

The pilot was already dead in the loosest sense, the cyborg's higher mental functions boiled in the short-circuit surge from a hit on the starboard wing; but his core brain was intact, and through that the ship dodged and spun as the sky itself seemed to turn upon them.

The ship trailed pieces of fuselage in a comet tail of wreckage and burning plasma. The deck trembled and smoke filled the bridge compartment. A vista of red warning runes met Kell's eyes wherever he looked. Autonomic systems had triggered the last-chance protocols, opening an iris hatch in the floor to a tiny saviour pod mounted beneath the cockpit. Blue light spilling from the hatch beckoned the Vindicare for a moment. He had his Exitus pistol at his hip and he was still alive. He would only need to take a step…

But to where? Even if he survived the next ten seconds, where could he escape to? What reason did he have to live? His mission… The mission was all Erist-ede Kell had left in his echoing, empty existence.

The command tower of the *Vengeful Spirit* rose through the forward canopy, acres of old steel and black iron, backlit by volleys of energy and the red threads of lasers. Set atop it was a single unblinking eye of grey and amber glass, lined in shining gold.

And within the eye, a figure. Kell was sure of it, an immense outline, a demigod daring him to come closer. His hand found the manual throttle bar and he pressed it all the way to the redline, as the killing fires found his range.

He looked up once again, and the first sighting-mantra he had ever been taught pressed itself to the front of his thoughts. Four words, a simple koan whose truth had never been more real than it was in this moment.

Kell said it aloud as he fell towards his target.

'*I am the weapon.*'


ACROSS THE MOUNTAINOUS towers of the Imperial Palace, the sun was rising into the dusky sky, but its light had yet to reach all the wards and precincts of the great fortress-city. Many districts were still dormant, their populace on the verge of waking for the new day; others had been kept from their slumber by matters that did not rest.

In the ornate corridors of power, there was quiet and solemnity, but in the Shrouds, any pretence at decorum had been thrown aside.

Sire Eversor's fist came down hard on the surface of the rosewood table with an impact that set the cut-glass water goblets atop it rattling. His anger was unchained, his eyes glaring out through his bone mask. 'Failure!' he spat, the word laden with venom. 'I warned you all when this idiotic plan was proposed, I warned you that it would not work!'

'And now we have burned our only chance to kill the Warmaster,' muttered Sire Vanus, his synth-altered voice flat and toneless like that of a machine.

The master of Clade Eversor, unable to remain seated in his chair, arose in a rush and rounded the octagonal table. The other Sires and Siresses of the Officio Assassinorum watched him stalk towards the powerful, hooded figure standing off to one side, in the glow of a lume-globe. 'We never should have listened to you,' he growled. 'All you did was cost us more men, Custodian!'

At the head of the table, the Master of Assassins looked up sharply, his silver mask reflecting the light. Behind him there was nothing but darkness, and the man appeared to be cradled in a dark, depthless void.

'Yes,' spat Sire Eversor. 'I know who he is. It could be no other than Constantin Valdor!'

At this, the hooded man let his robes fall open and the Captain-General was fully revealed. 'As you wish,' he said. 'I have nothing to fear from you knowing my face.'

'I suspected so,' ventured Siress Venenum, her face of green and gold porcelain tilting quizzically. 'Only the Custodian Guard would be so compelled towards ensuring the deaths of others before their own.'

Valdor shot her a look and smiled coldly. 'If that is so, then in that way we are alike, milady.'

'Eversor,' said the Master, his voice level. 'Take your seat and show some restraint, if that is at all possible.' The featureless silver mask reflected a twisted mirror of the snarling bone face.

'Restraint?' said Sire Vindicare, his aspect hidden behind a marksman's spy mask. 'With all due respect, my lord, I think we can all agree that the Eversor's anger is fully justified.'

'Horus sent one of his men to die in his stead,' Sire Eversor sat once more, his tone bitter. 'He must have been warned. Or else he has a daemon's luck.'

'That, or something else…' Siress Venenum said darkly.

'Missions fail,' interrupted the silk-faced mistress of the Callidus. 'It has ever been thus. We knew from the start that this was a target like no other.'

Across from her, the watchful steel skull concealing Sire Culexus bent forward. 'And that is answer enough?' His whispering tones carried across the room. 'Six more of our best are missing, presumed dead, and for what? So that we may sit back and be assured that we have learnt some small lesson from the wasting of their lives?' The skull's expression did not change, but the shadows gathered around it appeared to lengthen. 'Operative Iota was important to my clade. She was a rarity, a significant investment of time and energy. Her loss does not go without mark.'

'There's always a cost,' said Valdor.

'Just not to *you*,' Venenum's retort was acid. 'Our best agents and our finest weapons squandered, and still Horus Lupercal draws breath.'

'Perhaps he cannot be killed,' Sire Eversor snapped.

Before the commander of the Custodians could reply, the Master of Assassins raised his hand to forestall the conversation. 'Sire Vanus,' he began, 'shall we dispense with this hearsay and instead discuss what we know to be true of the fallout from our operation?'

Vanus nodded, his flickering, glassy mask shifting colour and hue. 'Of course.' He pushed at a section of the pinkish-red wood and the table silently presented him with a panel of brass buttons. With a few keystrokes, the hololithic projector hidden below came to life, sketching windows of flickering blue light above their heads. Displays showing tactical starmaps, fragments of scout reports and feeds from long-range observatories shimmered into clarity. 'News from the Taebian Sector is, at best, inconclusive. However, it appears that most, if not all, of the prime worlds along the length of the Taebian Stars trade spine are now beyond the influence of Imperial governance.'

On the map display, globular clusters of planets winked from blue to red in rapid order, consumed by revolt. 'The entire zone has fallen into anarchy. We have confirmation that the worlds of Thallat, Bowman, Dagonet, Taebia Prime and Iesta Veracrux have all broken their ties with the lawful leadership of Terra and declared loyalty to the Warmaster and his rebels.'

Sire Culexus made a soft hissing sound. 'They fall as much from their fears as from the gun.'

'The Warmaster stands over them and demands they kneel,' said Valdor. 'Few men would have the courage to refuse.'

'We can be certain of only two factors,' the Vanus went on. 'One; Captain Luc Sedirae of the 13th Company of the Sons of Horus, a senior general in the turncoat forces, has been terminated. Apparently by the action of a sniper.' He glanced at Sire Vindicare, who said nothing. 'Two; Horus Lupercal is alive.'

'Sedirae's death is an important success,' said the Master, 'but it is no substitute for the Warmaster.'

'My clade has already engaged with the information emerging from the Taebian Sector,' said Sire Vanus. 'My infocytes are in the process of performing adjustments in the overt and covert media to best reflect the Imperium's position in this situation.'

'Papering over the cracks with quick lies, don't you mean?' said Siress Callidus.

The colours of the Vanus's shimmer-mask blue-shifted. 'We must salvage what we can, milady. I'm sure–'

'Sure?' The silk mask tightened. 'What are you sure of? We have no specifics, no solutions! We've done nothing but tip our hand to the traitors!'

The mood of the room shifted, and once again the anger and frustration simmering unchecked threatened to erupt. The Master of Assassins raised his hand once more, but before he could speak a warning bell sounded through the room.

'What is that?' demanded Sire Vindicare. 'What does it mean?'

'The Shrouds...' The Master was coming to his feet. 'They've been compromised...' His silvered face suddenly turned towards one of the mahogany-panelled walls, as if he could see right through it.

With a bullet-sharp crack, ancient wood and rigid metals gave way, and a hidden door slammed open. Beyond it, in the ever-shifting puzzle of the changing corridors, three figures filled the space. Two wore amber-gold armour chased with white and black accents, their faces set and grim. They were veteran Space Marines of the VII Legiones Astartes in full combat plate; but eclipsing their presence was a warrior of stone cast and cold, steady gaze standing a head higher than both of them.

Rogal Dorn stepped into the Shrouds, his battle gear glittering in the light of the lume-globes. He cast his gaze around the room with an expression that might have been disgust, dwelling on Valdor, then the Master, and finally the deep shadows engulfing the farthest side of the chamber.

It was Siress Venenum who dared to shatter the shocked silence that came in the wake of Dorn's intrusion. 'Lord Astartes,' she began, desperately trying to rein in her fear. 'This is a sanctum of–'

The Imperial Fist did not even grace her with a look. He advanced towards the rosewood table and folded his arms across his titanic chest. 'Here you are,' he said, addressing his comments towards Valdor. 'I told you our conversation was not ended, Custodian.'

'You should not be here, Lord Dorn,' he replied.

'Neither should you,' snapped the primarch, his voice like breaking stones. 'But you brought both of us to it. To this... place of subterfuge.' He said the last word as if it revolted him.

'This place is not within your authority, Astartes.' The voice of the Master of Assassins was altered and shifted, but still the edge of challenge was clear for all to hear.

'At this moment, it is...' Dorn turned his cold glare on the mirrored face staring up at him. 'My Lord Malcador.'

A thrill of surprise threaded across the room, as every one of the Sires and Siresses turned to stare at the Master.

'I knew it...' hissed Culexus. 'I always knew you were the Sigillite!'

'This is a day of revelations,' muttered Sire Vanus.

'I have just begun,' Dorn rumbled.

With a sigh, Malcador reached up and removed the silver mask, setting it down on the table. He frowned, and an eddy of restrained telepathic annoyance rippled through the air. 'Well done, my friend. You've broken open an enigma.'

'Not really,' Dorn replied. 'I made an educated guess. You confirmed it.'

The Sigillite's frown became a brief, intent grimace. 'A victory for the Imperial Fists, then. Still, I have many more secrets.'

The warrior-king turned. 'But no more here today.' He glared at the other members of the Officio. 'Masks off,' he demanded. 'All of you! I will not speak with those of such low character who hide their faces. Your voices carry no import unless you have the courage to place your name to them. Show yourselves.' The threat beneath his words did not need to break the surface.

There was a moment of hush; then movement. Sire Vindicare was first, pulling the spy mask from his face as if he were glad to be rid of it. Then Sire Eversor, who angrily tossed his fang-and-bone disguise on to the table. Siress Callidus slipped the silk from her dainty face, and Vanus and Venenum followed suit. Sire Culexus was last, opening up his gleaming skull mask like an elaborate metal flower.

The assassins looked upon their naked identities for the first time and there was a mixture of potent emotions: anger, recognition, amusement.

'Better,' said Dorn.

'Now you have stripped us of our greatest weapon, Astartes,' said Siress Callidus, a fall of rust-red hair lying unkempt over a pale face. 'Are you satisfied?'

The primarch glanced over his shoulder. 'Brother-Captain Efried?'

One of the Imperial Fists at the door stepped forwards and handed a device to his commander, and in turn Dorn placed it on the table and slid it towards Sire Vanus.

'It's a data-slate,' he said.

'My warriors intercepted a starship beyond the edge of the Oort Cloud, attempting to vector into the Sol system,' Dorn told them. 'It identified itself as a common freighter, the *Hallis Faye*. A name I imagine some of you might recognise.'

'The crew…?' began Sire Eversor.

'None to speak of,' offered Captain Efried.

Dorn pointed at the slate. 'That contains a datum capsule recovered from the vessel's mnemonic core. Mission logs. Vox recordings and vid-picts.' He glanced at Malcador and the Custodian. 'What is spoken of there is troubling.'

The Sigillite nodded towards Sire Vanus. 'Show us.'

Vanus used a hair-fine connector to plug the slate into the open panel before him, and immediately the images in the ghostly hololith flickered and changed to a new configuration of data-panes.

At the fore was a vox thread, and it began to unspool as a man's voice, thick with pain, filled the air. '*My name is Eristede Kell. Assassin-at-Marque of the Clade Vindicare, Epsilon-dan... And I have defied my orders.*'

Valdor listened in silence along with the rest of them, first to Kell's words, and then to fragments of the infocyte Tariel's interim logs. When Sire Vanus opened the kernel of data containing the vid-records from Iota's final moments, he watched in mute disgust at the abomination that was the Black Pariah. As this horror unfolded before them, Sire Culexus bent forwards and quietly wept.

They listened to it all; the discovery of military situation on Dagonet and the plan to reignite the dying embers of the planet's civil war; Jenniker Soalm's rejection of the mission in favour of her own; the assassination of Sedirae in Horus's stead and the brutal retribution it engendered; and at last, the existence of and lethal potential within the creature that called itself Spear, and the choice that the Execution Force had been forced to make.

When they had heard as much as was necessary, the Sigillite shouted at Sire Vanus to cease the playback. Valdor surveyed the faces of the clade directors. Each in their own way struggled to process what they had been brought by the Imperial Fists.

Sire Eversor, confusion in his gaze, turned on the Culexus. 'That freakish monstrosity... you created that? For Terra's sake, cousin, tell me this is not so!'

'I gave the orders myself!' insisted the psyker. 'It was destroyed!'

'Apparently not,' Dorn replied, his jaw tightening.

'But it *is* dead now, yes?' said Sire Vanus. 'It must be...'

Dorn's dark eyes flashed with anger. 'A narrow view. That is all your kind ever possess. Do you not understand what you have done? Your so-called attempts at a surgical assault against Horus have become nothing of the kind!' His voice rose, like the sound of storm-tossed waves battering a shoreline. 'Sedirae's death has cost the lives of an entire planet's population! The Sons of Horus have taken revenge on a world because of what your assassins did there!' He shook his head. 'If the counter-rebellion on Dagonet had been allowed to fade, if their war had not been deliberately and callously exacerbated, Horus would have passed them by. After my brothers and I have broken his betrayal, the Imperium would have retaken control of Dagonet. But now its devastation leads to the collapse of keystone worlds all across that sector! Now the traitors take a strong foothold there, and it will be my battle-brothers and those of my kindred who must bleed to oust them!' He pointed at them all in turn. 'This is what you leave behind you. This is what your kind *always* leave behind.'

Valdor could remain silent no longer and he stepped forward. 'The suffering on Dagonet is a tragedy, none will deny that,' he said, 'and yes, Horus has escaped our retribution once more. But a greater cause has been served, Lord Dorn. Kell and his force chose to preserve your father in exchange for letting your errant brother live. This assassin-creature Spear is dead, and a great threat to the Emperor's life has been neutralised. I would consider that a victory.'

'Would you?' Dorn's fury was palpable, crackling in the air around him. 'I'm sure my father is capable of defending himself! And tell me, Captain-General, what kind of victory exists in a war like the one you would have us fight?' He gestured at the room around them. 'A war fought from hidden places under cover of falsehood? Innocent lives wasted in the name of dubious tactics? Underhanded, clandestine conflicts, fuelled by secrets and lies?'

For a moment, Valdor half-expected the Imperial Fist to rip up the table between them just so he could strike at the Custodian; but then, like a tidal wave drawing back into the ocean, Dorn's anger seemed to subside. Valdor knew better, though – the primarch was the master of his own fury, turning it inward, turning it to stony, unbreakable purpose.

'This war,' Dorn went on, sparing Malcador a glance, 'is a fight not just for the material, for worlds and for the hearts of men. We are in battle for *ideals*. At stake are the very best of the Imperium's ultimate principles. Values of pride, nobility, honour and fealty. How can a veiled killer understand the meaning of such words?'

Valdor felt Malcador's eyes on him, and the tension in him seemed to dissipate. At once, he felt a cold sense of conviction rise in his thoughts, and he matched the Imperial Fist's gaze, answering his challenge. 'No one in this room has known war as intimately as you have, my lord,' he began, 'and so surely it is you who must understand better than any one of us that this war cannot be a clean and gallant one. We fight a battle like no other in human history. We fight for the future! Can you imagine what might have come to pass if Kell and the rest of the Execution Force had not been present on Dagonet? If this creature Spear had been reunited with the rebel forces?'

'He would have attempted to complete his mission,' said Sire Culexus. 'Come to Terra, to enter the sphere of the Emperor's power and engage his... murdergift.'

'He would never have got that far!' insisted Sire Vanus. 'He would have been found and killed, surely. The Sigillite or the Emperor himself would have sensed such an abomination and crushed it!'

'Are you certain?' Valdor pressed. 'Horus has many allies, some of them closer than we wish to admit. If this Spear could have reached Terra, made his attack... Even a failure to make the kill, a wounding even...' He trailed off, suddenly appalled by the grim possibility he was describing. 'Such a psychic attack would have caused incredible destruction.'

Dorn said nothing; for a moment, it seemed as if the primarch was sharing the same terrible nightmare that danced in the Custodian's thoughts; of his liege lord mortally wounded by a lethal enemy, clinging to fading life while the Imperial Palace was a raging inferno all around him.

Valdor found his voice once more. 'Your brother will beat us, Lord Dorn. He will win this war unless we match him blow-for-blow. We cannot, we must not be afraid to make the difficult choices, the hardest decisions! Horus Lupercal will not hesitate–'

'I am not Horus!' Dorn snarled, the words striking the Custodian like a physical blow. 'And I will–'

'*Enough.*'

THE SINGLE UTTERANCE was a lightning bolt captured in crystal, shattering everything around it, silencing them all with an unstoppable, immeasurable force of will.

Rogal Dorn turned to the sound of that voice as every man, woman and Astartes in the chamber sank to their knees, each of them instinctively knowing who had uttered it. The Sigillite was the last to do so, shooting a final, unreadable look at the primarch of the Imperial Fists before he too took to a show of obeisance.

The question escaped Dorn's lips. 'Father?'

The darkness, the great curtain of shadows that had filled the furthest corner of the chamber now became lighter, the walls and floor growing more distinct by the moment as the unnatural gloom faded. He blinked; strange how he had looked directly into that place and seen it, but without really seeing it at all. It had been in plain sight for everyone in the room, even he, and yet none of them had registered the strangeness of it.

Now from the black came light. A figure stood there, effortlessly dominating the space, his patrician features marred by a mixture of turbulent emotions that gave even the mighty Imperial Fist a second's pause.

The Emperor of Mankind wore no armour, no finery or dress uniform, only a simple surplice of grey cloth threaded with subtle lines of purple and gold silk; and yet he was still magnificent to behold.

Perhaps he had been listening to them all along. Yet, it seemed to be a defiance of the laws of nature, that a being so majestic, so lit with power, could stand in a room among men, Astartes and the greatest mortal psyker who ever lived, and be as a ghost.

But then he was the Emperor; and to all questions, that was sufficient answer.

His father came towards him, and Rogal Dorn bowed deeply, at length joining the others at bended knee before the Master of the Imperium.

The Emperor did not speak. Instead, he strode across the Shrouds to the tall windows where the sail-cloth drapes hung like frozen cataracts of shadow. With a flick of his great hands, Dorn's father took a fist of the cloth and snatched it away. The hangings tore free and tumbled to the floor. He walked the perimeter of the room, ripping away every last cover until the chamber was flooded with the bright honey-yellow luminosity of the Himalayan dawn.

Dorn dared to glance up and saw the golden radiance striking his father. It gathered its brightness to him, as if it were an embrace. For an instant, the sunlight was like a sheath of glowing armour about him; then the primarch blinked and the moment passed.

'No more shadows,' said the Emperor. His words were gentle, summoning, and all the faces in the room turned to look upon him. He placed a hand on Dorn's shoulder as he passed him by, and then repeated the gesture with Valdor. 'No more veils.'

He beckoned them all to stand and as one they obeyed, and yet in his presence each of them felt as if they were still at his feet. His aura towered over them, filling the emotions of the room.

Dorn received a nod, as did Valdor. 'My noble son. My loyal guardian. I hear both your words and I know that there is right in each of you. We cannot lose sight of what we are and what we aspire to be; but we cannot forget that we face the greatest enemy and the darkest challenge.' In the depths of his father's eyes, Dorn saw something no one else could have perceived, so transient and fleeting it barely registered. He saw sorrow, deep and unending, and his heart ached with an empathy only a son could know.

The Emperor reached out a hand and gestured towards the dawn, as it rose to fill the room around them. 'It is time to bring you into the light. The Officio Assassinorum have been my quiet blade for too long, an open secret none dared to speak of. But no longer. Such a weapon cannot exist forever in the shadows, answerable to no one. It must be seen to be governed. There must be no doubt of the integrity behind every deed, every blow landed, every choice made... or else we count for naught.' His gaze turned to Dorn and he nodded slowly to his son. 'Because of this I am certain; in the war to come, every weapon in the arsenal of the Imperium will be called to bear.'

'In your name, father.' The primarch returned the nod. 'In your name.'

DAGONET WAS ALL but dead now, her surface a mosaic of burning cities, churned oceans and glassed wastelands. And yet this was a show of restraint from the

Sons of Horus; had they wished it, the world could have suffered the fate of many that had defied the Warmaster, cracked open by cyclonic torpedo barrages shot into key tectonic target sites, remade into a sphere of molten earth.

Instead Dagonet was being prepared. It would be of use to the Warmaster and his march to victory.

Erebus stood atop the ridgeline and looked down into the crater that was all that remained of the capital. The far side of the vast bowl of dirty glass and melted rock was lost to him through a mist of poisonous vapour, but he saw enough of it to know the scope of the whole. Transports were coming in from all over the planet, bringing those found still alive to this place. He watched as a Stormbird swooped low over the crater and opened its ventral cargo doors, dropping civilians like discarded trash amid the masses that had already been herded into the broken landscape. The people were arranged in lines that cut back and forth across one another, crosses laid over crosses. Astartes stood at equidistant points around the kilometres of the crater's edge, their presence alone forbidding any survivor from making an attempt to climb out and flee. Those that had at the beginning were blasted back into the throng, bifurcated by bolt shells. The same fate befell those who dared to move out of the eightfold lines carved in the dust.

The supplicants – for they did not deserve to be known as prisoners – gave off moans and whispers of terror that washed back and forth over the Word Bearer Chaplain like gentle waves. It was tempting to remain where he stood and lose himself in the sweet sense of the dark emotions brimming across the great hollow; but there were other matters to attend to.

He heard bootsteps climbing the wreckage-strewn side of the crater, and moved to face the Astartes approaching him. All about them, thin wisps of steam rose into the air from the heat of the bombardment still escaping from the shattered earth.

'First Chaplain.' Devram Korda gave him a wary salute. 'You wished me to report to you regarding your... operative? We located the remains you were looking for.'

'Spear?' He frowned.

Korda nodded, and tossed something towards him. Erebus caught the object; at first glance it seemed to be a blackened, heat-distorted skull, but on closer examination the cleft, scything jawbone and distended shape were clearly the work of forces other than lethal heat and flame. He held it up and looked into the black pits of its eyes. The ghost of energies clung to it, and Erebus had a sudden impression of tiny flecks of gold leaf on the wind, fading into nothingness.

'The rest of the corpse was retrieved along with that.' Korda pointed. 'I found other bodies in the same area, among the ruins of the star-port terminal. Agents of the Emperor, it would appear.'

Erebus was unconcerned about collateral damages. His irritation churned and he brushed Korda's explanation away with a wave of his hand. 'Leave it to rot. Failures have no use to me.' He dropped the skull into the dust.

'What was it, Word Bearer?' Korda came closer, his tone becoming more insistent. 'That thing? Did you unleash something on this backwater world, is that why they killed my commander?'

'I am not to blame for that,' Erebus retorted. 'Look elsewhere for your reasons.' The words had barely left his lips before the Chaplain felt a stiffening in his chest as a buried question began to rise in him. He pushed it away before it formed and narrowed his eyes at Korda. 'Spear was a weapon. A gambit played and lost, nothing more.'

'It stank of witchcraft,' said the Astartes.

Erebus smiled thinly. 'Don't concern yourself with such issues, brother-sergeant. This was but one of many other arrows in my quiver.'

'I grow weary of your games and your riddles,' said Korda. He swept his hand around. 'What purpose does any of this serve?'

The warrior's question struck a chord in the Word Bearer, but he did not acknowledge it. 'It is the game, Korda. The greatest game. We take steps, we build our power, gain strength for the journey to Terra. Soon…' He looked up. 'The stars will be right.'

'Forgive him, brother-sergeant,' said a new voice, an armoured form moving out of the mist below them. 'My brother Lorgar's kinsmen enjoy their verbiage more than they should.'

Korda bowed and Erebus did the same as Horus crossed the broken earth, his heavy ceramite boots crunching on the blasted fragments of rock. Beyond him, Erebus saw two of the Warmaster's Mournival in quiet conversation, both with eyes averted from their master.

'You are dismissed, brother-sergeant,' Horus told his warrior. 'I require the First Chaplain's attention on a matter.'

Korda gave another salute, this one crisp and heartfelt, his fist clanking off the front of his breastplate. Erebus fancied he saw a scrap of apprehension in the warrior's eyes; more than just the usual respect for his primarch. A fear, perhaps, of consequences that would come if he was seen to disobey, even in the slightest degree.

As Korda hurried away, Erebus felt the Warmaster's steady, piercing gaze upon him. 'What do you wish of me?' he asked, his tone without weight.

Horus's hooded gaze dropped to the blackened skull in the dust. 'You will not use such tactics again in the prosecution of this conflict.'

The Word Bearer's first impulse was to feign ignorance; but he clamped down on that before he opened his mouth. Suddenly, he was thinking of Luc Sedirae. Outspoken Sedirae, whose challenges to the Warmaster's orders, while trivial, had grown to become constant after the progression from Isstvan. Some had said he was in line to fill the vacant place in the Mournival, that his contentious manner was of need to one as powerful as Horus. After all, what other reason could there have been for the Warmaster to grant Sedirae the honour of wearing his mantle?

A rare chill ran through him, and Erebus nodded. 'As you command, my lord.'

*Was it possible?* The Word Bearer's thoughts were racing. Perhaps Horus Lupercal had known from the beginning that the Emperor's secret killers were drawing close to murder him. But for that he would need eyes and ears on Terra... Erebus had no doubt the Warmaster's allies reached to the heart of his father's domain, but into the Imperial Palace itself? That was a question he dearly wished to answer.

Horus turned and began to walk back down the ridge. Erebus took a breath and spoke again. 'May I ask the reasoning behind that order?'

The Warmaster paused, and then glanced over his shoulder. His reply was firm and assured, and brooked no argument. 'Assassins are a tool of the weak, Erebus. The fearful. They are not a means to end conflicts, only to prolong them.' He paused, his gaze briefly turning inward. 'This war will end only when I look my father in the eyes. When he sees the truth I will make clear to him, he will know I am right. He will join me in that understanding.'

Erebus felt a thrill of dark power. 'And if the Emperor does not?'

Horus's gaze became cold. 'Then I – *and I alone* – will kill him.'

The primarch walked on, throwing a nod to his officers. On his command, the lines of melta-bombs buried beneath the hundreds of thousands of survivors detonated at once, and Erebus listened to the chorus of screams as they perished in a marker of sacrifice and offering.

## ACKNOWLEDGMENTS

ONCE MORE, TIPS of the helm to Dan Abnett and Graham McNeill for that moment when the core concept for *Nemesis* emerged from our shared creative flux; to Nick Kyme and Lindsey Priestley for sterling editorial guidance, and once again, to the great Neil Roberts for crafting another stunning cover.

## ABOUT THE AUTHOR

James Swallow's stories from the dark worlds of Warhammer 40,000 include the Horus Heresy novel *The Flight of the Eisenstein*, the Blood Angels books *Deus Encarmine*, *Deus Sanguinius* and *Red Fury*, the Sisters of Battle novel *Faith & Fire*, as well as a multiplicity of short fiction. Among his other works are *Jade Dragon*, *The Butterfly Effect*, the *Sundowners* series of 'steampunk' Westerns and fiction in the worlds of Star Trek, Doctor Who, Stargate and 2000AD, as well as a number of anthologies.

His non-fiction features *Dark Eye: The Films of David Fincher* and books on scriptwriting and genre television. Swallow's other credits include writing for Star Trek Voyager, scripts for videogames and audio dramas. He lives in London.

# WARHAMMER 40,000

## A SPACE MARINE BATTLES NOVEL

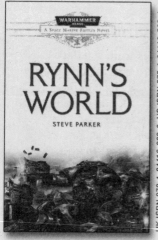

# RYNN'S WORLD

### STEVE PARKER

# HELSREACH

### AARON DEMBSKI-BOWDEN

# HUNT FOR VOLDORIUS

### ANDY HOARE